THE DEATH OF THE SUN

THE BLESSED OF THE DRAGON

Book Four

Patrik Martinet

CONTENTS

ACKNOWLEDGMENTS 7

MAPS OF DRADONIA 8

BEFORE...13

CHAPTER 1...16

AFTER 367

DRAKE FAMILY TREE 375

ABOUT THE AUTHOR...377

To mom and dad

ACKNOWLEDGMENTS

I would like to thank my wife, Carrie, for supporting me as I have pursued my various hobbies. Thank you also for your keen literary eye. Most importantly, thank you for cultivating the love of reading in our children.

Thank you, Elayne Morgan, for your amazing editing skills. Thank you, Jake, of J Caleb Design, for once again making an amazing cover. And thank you, Zach Bodenner, for bringing Dradonia to life with your wonderful maps.

A list of acknowledgements wouldn't be complete without also thanking all those who have helped me one way or another along the way. To each of you, I say thank you.

MAPS OF DRADONIA

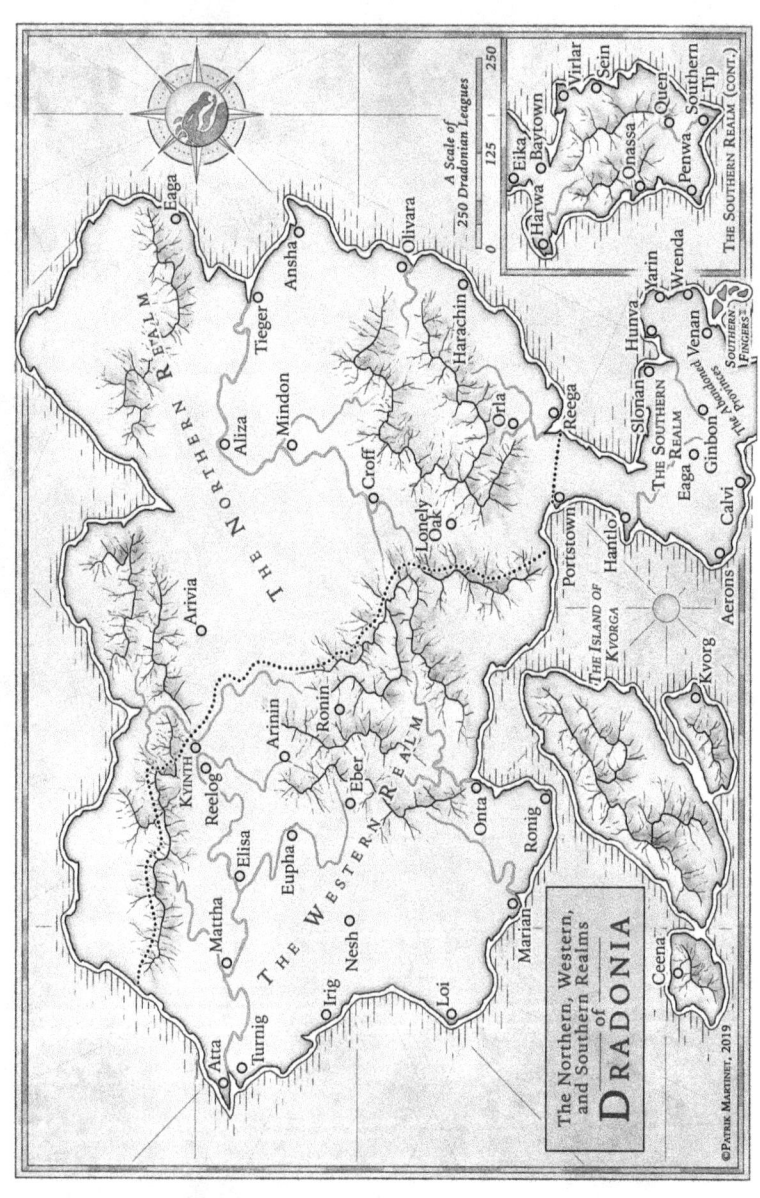

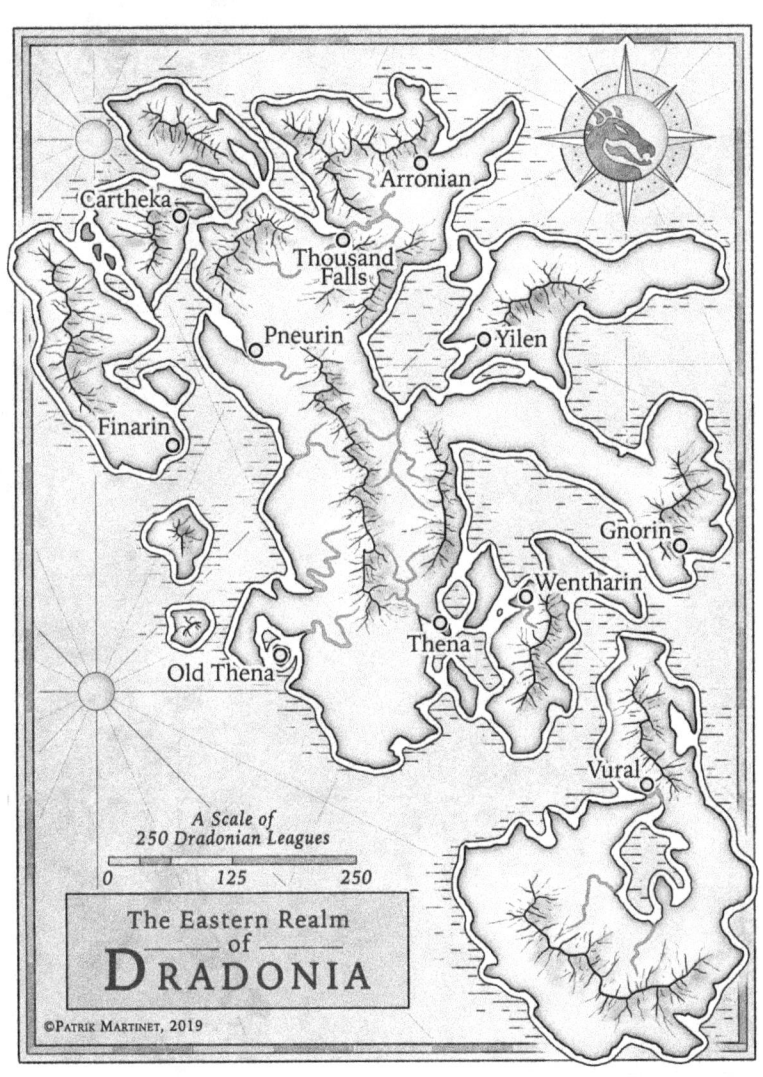

Cartheka

Arronian

Thousand
Falls

Pneurin

Yilen

Finarin

Gnorin

Wentharin

Thena

Old Thena

Vural

A Scale of
250 Dradonian Leagues

0   125   250

The Eastern Realm
— of —
DRADONIA

THE DEATH OF THE SUN

BEFORE

Previous Era

Marcin lay on his back in the tall blood-soaked grass, staring up at the sky. A lifetime of service to his king, and this was how it ended. A part of him had always known that sooner or later his life would end the same way he'd ended so many others.

Death was imminent. There was nothing to do but wait. Thankfully, no one was left to drag him back to Crenalin because the healers wouldn't be able to save him. All they'd do was prolong his death, which meant more pain. He'd witnessed it happen too many times. It was a horrible way to die. Death on the battlefield was the best that a knight could hope for. And that was what he'd been granted. He was thankful Aliza wouldn't have to watch him die.

While Marcin waited, he tried to focus on the peacefulness above instead of the pain. A sort of calmness existed in the clouds floating slowly by, occasionally shading him from the sun. He tried to remember what the sun felt like shining on him on a crisp spring morning, but all he felt was pain.

A dragon soared into view. It glided serenely in and out of the clouds, high in the sky, barely discernible. Spotting a dragon wasn't unusual; they were often seen soaring about. What *was* unusual was talking to one. As far as he knew, no human had ever interacted with a dragon. They avoided humans like deer avoided wolves. As the beast soared overhead, Marcin reflected on the recent conversation he'd had with a dragon. *That* he could remember. Who could forget talking with a dragon?

His horse had almost thrown him when they'd rounded a bend and found the dragon blocking his path. It was just lying there, waiting. It was the closest he'd ever been to one. He'd spun his horse to flee, but the dragon spoke. It *asked* him to stop. So he did. Its deep, sonorous voice was calming. It wanted to know why he killed—why humans killed. The strangest part—stranger than a dragon talking to him; stranger even than the dragon knowing Marcin's language—was that it admitted to watching Marcin. But what it never said was *why*. And then it left, leaving Marcin wondering what had just happened.

In the weeks since, Marcin had reflected on that strange meeting. What was the purpose of it? And why him? He was nobody. He'd never told Faran about it, and he never kept secrets from his king—he would never have become First Knight if he had. It didn't matter now, though. If Faran wasn't dead yet, he likely would be soon.

And Aliza… poor Aliza. He hoped she was safe. She didn't deserve to die. He hated that he had brought her into the middle of a war, but their marriage had been vital to a treaty with her father. And it had worked: Varias had sent his knights to help defend Crenalin. But in the end, the treaty had come too late. Barely a week had expired, and Marcin was about to make her a widow. She should be back in her home, safe in her father's castle. Instead, she was far from anyone she knew or loved, alone in an unfamiliar kingdom. When the enemy sacked Crenalin, she would be killed… or worse. And he wouldn't be there to stop it, to protect her like he'd promised he would.

The dragon still circled. Strangely, instead of gliding out of his view, it remained overhead. The clouds changed as they drifted by, but the dragon remained stationary, high above. As Marcin watched the dragon, darkness slowly enveloped him. It started at the edges of his vision and moved inward. He'd lost consciousness before, so he knew what was happening—only this time, he wouldn't wake. The end had come.

Before long, all Marcin could see was a small circle of sky at the end of a long, dark tunnel. Then, in the little window of blue that remained at the far end, the dragon tucked its wings and dove like a hawk diving for prey. The dragon grew in the tunnel until it was all Marcin could see.

He never imagined a dragon would be the last thing he saw when death took him.

But instead of death, he felt warmth—the warmth of the sun. It wasn't the warmth of a crisp spring morning; this warmth permeated him throughout. It dulled—no, *stopped* the pain. Marcin's vision returned. He felt as hale as he ever had. He would have stood and run to Crenalin, to Aliza, were it not for the dragon's muzzle looming uncomfortably close, its breath incredibly hot.

"In exchange for life eternal," the dragon boomed, "you will end the wars."

Pain exploded in Marcin's chest before he could ask the dragon what it meant.

CHAPTER 1

410 United Era

The sun rose over the towering mountains that had once been home to dragons—a peaceful species wiped from Dradonia by greed and hate. The mountains now stood over the ruins of forgotten kingdoms. They stood over fields that, time and time again, drank the blood of the dying. They stood over a realm lost to the empire nearly a century ago.

The sun rose over a troubled sea. As it passed overhead it added Energy to the never-ending stream of cyclones. Then it passed over calmer waters and began to illuminate the skies in the easternmost reaches of the Northern Realm. It woke the city of Tieger and glinted off the Mindon where the river curved around Aliza, the city named after Draeko's innocent bride.

When the sun's light reached Kyinth, the capital of the United Realms, its towering buildings shimmered. Yolken squinted, but kept his eyes focused on the orb slowly creeping higher. He stood atop the tallest building in the empire—a place he didn't want to be—pondering a problem he didn't know how to solve.

The sun was dying.

Nobody knew how long Dradonia had left, but Yolken now

knew it was up to him to save the troubled world.

When his eyes began to hurt from looking at the sun, Yolken closed them. He felt a twitch in the corner of each eye, then opened them again. Colorful streams of Energy flowed toward him. He looked left and right, watching the streams flow by. Deth had told him he had to restore balance to the sun by replacing the Energy taken during Drakonias' war.

It hadn't taken long for Yolken to figure out why Drakonias had issued the edict banning the use of Machines: Machines required Energy to operate. Drakonias must have realized that post-war Machines were no different than those used during the war, and that they were draining Energy from the sun too quickly. It was too late for Drakonias to stop what was happening, and he must have thought banning Machines would slow the process, which it did. But in recent days, Yolken wondered if Drakonias went far enough. He should have banned Synthesizing altogether. Dragons, Yolken had learned, *created* Energy, so they didn't take from the sun more than it naturally provided. And his lessons with Jax had taught him that plants Synthesized passively, only absorbing what the sun gave. The same wasn't true of humans. Every time someone Synthesized— as he had started doing even this morning to stave off the chill— they took more from the sun than it gave. The sun somehow compensated, providing more Energy than was natural, but every bit of extra Energy the sun provided when anyone Synthesized moved it further out of balance.

Yolken forced himself to stop Synthesizing, to feel the cold.

Back on the Island of Kvorga, he'd learned that the Great Dragon—Draego—had blessed Dimras, the first dragon, and Dimras, along with his mate, gave birth to the Assembly. The Assembly, with their combined strength, ignited the ability to create Energy in each and every hatchling. It was a rite of passage: When hatchlings were big enough, they traveled to the Great Mountain and received Draego's Fire from the Assembly. But there was no Assembly now, and Yolken didn't have

Draego's Fire. He couldn't create Energy. He was a leech, just like everyone else.

Yolken felt arms slip around him from behind and hug him tightly.

"Good morning, husband," Kaylan said.

Yolken closed his eyes again and felt them return to normal. When he opened them, the colorful streams of Energy were once again invisible. He turned around and kissed Kaylan on the top of the head as she nuzzled in close to him. It had been an agonizing two weeks for her; she wanted to properly mourn her mother, but his advisors—the former members of the Council—wanted to be present for Deborah's funeral. The Order of the Dragon had worked for four hundred years to overturn the illegitimate rule of Drakonias, and Deborah's death was the last required to achieve that goal. So Kaylan had agreed to wait. But when she was reunited with Yolken after they'd been separated in Onta, she refused to wait another day to marry him.

"The empire will expect a ceremony befitting the Emperor of the United Realms," Tabora said when he and Kaylan declared their intention to marry immediately.

"But that's not us," Kaylan had objected.

"It is now," Jax said.

"Jax is right," Deanna said. "Being a ruler requires you to do things you don't want to."

"Fine," Yolken said. "But not now. We have bigger things to worry about right now than a wedding ceremony."

"But I don't want to wait," Kaylan protested.

"Neither do I," Yolken said, looking Kaylan in the eyes. "I've wanted to marry you for as long as I can remember."

"I'm marrying you *today*."

Yolken wanted the exact same thing. He'd thought about marrying her almost nonstop since that day in Croff when Jax and Deborah had suggested it. Back then, the idea had been to provide a cover for their travels to the Island of Kvorga, but he and Kaylan had decided to wait until they rescued Javen. They'd both wanted Javen present when they became man and wife. It was important to them to have him there, to have his blessing. And now he *was* there.

Yolken looked at Jax and the others, hoping for a compromise. "I'm the emperor, aren't I?"

"Yes," Jax said.

"Which means I get to do what I want…"

"To an extent, I suppose."

"Well, I want to marry Kaylan."

"What about a compromise," Javen said. When everyone looked at him, he said, "What if you get married now and have the big ceremony later?"

"I suppose—" Jax started.

"Yes!" Kaylan exclaimed.

"Yes, a small ceremony," Yolken agreed. Gesturing toward those in the room—Javen, Jax, Deanna, and Tabora—he added, "Just us."

"Yes," Kaylan said.

Yolken turned to Kaylan. "Are you sure? I mean… your mother…"

"I agreed to wait to mourn her. And when it's time, I will. But right now… right now it's me and you."

"You're sure?" Yolken said.

Kaylan nodded.

"Then it's agreed." Yolken turned to Jax. "At sundown, in my quarters."

"Yes, Your Highness," Jax said with a bow.

That evening Yolken realized the greatest desire of his life by wedding Kaylan at the top of the tallest building in the empire. And even though it wasn't how he'd pictured it happening, it couldn't have been more perfect.

He closed his eyes and breathed deeply, drawing in the scent of Kaylan's hair.

"You're so warm," she said. "Feels nice out in this air." She looked up at Yolken and kissed him. When he turned back to face the rising sun, she said, "Drakonias did this, you know."

"What?"

"Came out here every morning at sunrise."

"He did?"

"Mmm-hmm."

"How do you know that?"

"Sahri told me."

Sahri had been Drakonias' servant. "Did she?"

"Said he never missed a day."

"Did she say why?" Yolken said.

"I asked her, but she didn't know," Kaylan said. "What about you?"

"What?"

"You've come out here every morning we've been wed."

"Sorry, I thought I was being quiet enough to not wake you."

"You don't have to be sorry. And I can't help but notice when my husband gets out of bed. So?"

"It's just… I have no idea what I'm supposed to do. I didn't come here to overthrow Drakonias."

"What happened wasn't your fault," Kaylan said.

He certainly hadn't intended to kill Drakonias. Jax had spoken about how sometimes the need arose to take another's life. He'd been referring to his duty with the Order of the Dragon, but Yolken was never sure he wanted to join the Order. And no one had told him to kill Drakonias. But as he watched Drakonias try to flee from Deth, as Drenan and Devin had, Yolken had acted without really thinking about it. Now he tried not to think about how, for the second time, he was directly responsible for taking someone else's life.

"It was my idea to come here. But all I wanted was a truce between the Order and the Regency so we could come together and figure out how to restore balance to the sun. I didn't want to replace him."

"He's the one who attacked Deanna and Reago. You were defending them."

"I know. But now Drenan is out there plotting Draego knows what and I have no idea what I'm doing. I don't want to be the emperor—or Dragon King—or whatever it is I'm supposed to be."

"But you *are* the emperor, Yolken." Kaylan squeezed him tightly. "And the fact that you don't want to be will make you a great one."

"Even if that was true, it won't matter if I can't figure out how to restore balance to the sun—replace what was taken, Deth says. I mean, just saying it aloud it sounds ludicrous. Replace what was taken? How am I supposed to restore centuries' worth of Energy to the sun? Deth says I can create Energy like dragons could, but I can't."

"Maybe it's not your job. Not any of ours."

"Deth said—"

"Well, Deth isn't doing anything to help!" Kaylan exclaimed.

"Because he can't," Yolken said.

"So you're somehow supposed to be able to do what Deth is unable to?"

"We've been over this."

"Because you're the *Blessed* of the Dragon. Maybe Deth's wrong."

"He's not."

"How do you know?"

"Because I'm different. I can do things nobody has been able to do before. It's like..."

"What?" Kaylan said when Yolken paused and didn't continue.

"I can do things only dragons could do—I can store Energy in my bones, and I can *see* Energy. But the one thing they do that I can't is create Energy."

"So that's what we need to figure out," Kaylan said.

"That's what I've been trying to do."

"And you have help from the others."

"They don't know. Even Deanna's at a loss, and she's been around since the Previous Era."

"We'll figure it out, Yolken. Come on," Kaylan said, taking

him by the arm. "We still have a little time before we need to get ready and I want to walk with you a little."

"I'm sorry," Yolken said, realizing he'd been so focused on himself that he'd completely forgotten today was the day Kaylan was going to be saying goodbye to her mother.

"You don't have to be sorry, Yolken."

They walked around the perimeter of the balcony and marveled at the amazing view. The buildings shimmered as the sun's light reflected off them. He stopped when they reached the northern side and looked out beyond the city walls at the towering snow-covered mountains.

"They're beautiful, aren't they?" Kaylan said.

"Very," Yolken said. "I always enjoyed looking out the window of my room and seeing the Mindon Mountains, but this… I never imagined there could be something more beautiful than the Mindons."

Despite the beauty stretching as far as he could see to the east and west, Yolken thought about the North River flowing through the mountains. Here it wasn't perceptible, but local advisors had told him of vast flooding in the northern river plains from unprecedented snow melt-off. Even though it was now fall, the flooding had yet to abate. The Kyinth River, which found its headwaters in the Ontalis south of Arinin, was also still causing flooding. Both were evidence that the northern reaches of Dradonia were also feeling the effects of the sun's march toward death. He'd noticed it back in Lonely Oak when the Little Mindon hadn't experienced its annual run-off. At the time he'd simply written it off as a poor winter's snowpack, which wasn't unheard of.

Yolken pushed his worries aside as they continued around the balcony in the cool morning air. They took in the view from every angle, until Sahri approached. With a bow, she said, "It's time, Your Highness."

Yolken looked down at Kaylan, his wife. Her eyes were glistening. "You ready?"

Kaylan blinked, making the tears in her eyes run down her cheeks, and nodded.

CHAPTER 2

Yolken followed three caskets being carried by the Dragon Guard down the Hall of Relics. Their white armor contrasted with the black armor he was wearing. Under Drakonias' rule, black had been the color of judgment, but one of his first acts as emperor was to disband the Synod and Black Sodality. No longer would members of the Order of the Dragon—or any citizen of Dradonia—be assassinated by the Black.

Kaylan walked next to him, holding his hand, wearing black as well. Apart from Drakonias' Regency, black was the color of mourning. It was the traditional color of funeral garb in Lonely Oak, whether services were conducted at the Dragon Shrine for the pious or elsewhere for those who didn't worship the Great Dragon.

As the procession passed the empty display where the Dragon King's armor and crown had once sat, Yolken glanced over at it and tried not to fiddle with the dragon-shaped gold crown on his head. It wasn't exactly comfortable. The front was a dragon's head turned upward, with flames spewing from its mouth. The dragon's long neck curved down and around, its body wrapping around in a circle to form the crown. The legs and claws were situated so that they extended down over his ears, and the tail continued around to join the dragon's upturned neck, finishing off the body of the crown. Intricately carved scales covered the dragon's body, individual teeth were visible in its mouth, and the razor-sharp claws had pricked his ears the first time he'd put it on. Honestly, he felt silly wearing it. But Jax and Deanna had succeeded in convincing him that doing so would show any regents who might be rethinking their loyalty that he was indeed who he said he was. What his advisors walking in line behind him didn't know, however, was that after the funeral, he planned on putting the armor back. The edict he was planning to issue was going to make them all very upset.

Guards at the end of the long hallway pulled the gilded doors to the throne room open as the procession approached. One by one, the wooden caskets entered the throne room. As he and Kaylan approached the entrance, Yolken glanced at the large tapestries on either side of the doors, depicting dragons soaring among the clouds.

After passing through a small alcove with stairs leading up to the balconies on the left, they entered the throne room. The metal ceiling covers had all been retracted, letting light fill the room. At the front of the room, where Deth had crashed through the ceiling, a few bent covers were jammed in place, casting long shadows on the floor. Yolken blinked, shifting the lenses in his eyes, and saw the colorful streams of Energy. With those lenses in place, everything turned various shades of gray— everything except Energy. The sun's Energy flowed to the ground as a river of color. Every color imaginable.

The marble floor and balcony were packed with black-clad mourners. Yolken permitted those regents who wanted to attend to do so; however, he had forbidden them from wearing dragon armor. He wasn't particularly worried about an attack, but he wanted them to be just as vulnerable as everyone else should one occur. As it was, those who had taken him up on his offer were indistinguishable from the other mourners. If any of them chose to Synthesize, he would see it—as would the dragon curled up behind the throne.

The procession made its way through the crowd to the front. As they approached, Deth lifted his head. Yolken felt as though Deth's eyes were locked on him, condemning him for wearing armor made from the scales of the only black dragon that had ever existed. The black dragon had been one of the original six hatchlings of Dimras and Devrith, the first of the dragons, yellow and red. Together with Dimras and Devrith, the hatchlings—blue, violet, orange, green, white, black—made up the Assembly. Yolken felt dirty, knowing he was literally wearing the remains of Deth's ancestors. He looked up at Deth and thought, *I know. I'm sorry. Soon.*

At the foot of the dais, the Dragon Guard spread out and set the caskets in front of three pyres. Reago's casket was on the left, Deborah's in the center, and Corin's on the right. Drakonias had killed Reago when he and Deanna had attempted to convince Drakonias to join Yolken in saving Dradonia. Drakonias tried to kill Deanna as well, but she survived; Deborah and Corin had died in the ensuing fight. Yolken tried not to remember his desperate attempt to keep Deborah from being pulled into the inferno swirling around them. He'd strengthened his grip with Synthesis until he'd crushed her hand trying to save her. It wasn't enough.

Yolken led Kaylan by the hand up to the center casket and wrapped his arm around her when she touched the smooth wood and started to cry. Javen and Jax joined them, each placing a hand on Kaylan.

"I still... can't believe... she's gone," Kaylan said between heaving sobs.

"She was as much a mother to me and Javen as Selena was," Yolken said. He hugged Kaylan from the side, knowing that nothing he said could comfort Kaylan in this moment of grief.

Movement in the corner of his eye caused Yolken to look over at Reago's casket. Deanna had placed a hand on it and was wiping away tears. When she looked over at Yolken, he nodded.

The sun's rays started bending toward Deanna. Energy shot out all around her and then reversed direction, proceeding back to her. Yolken felt air move in her direction. After a moment, Reago's casket lifted into the air and came to rest on top of the pyre.

Led by Enif, Yolken's advisors filed past Corin's and Deborah's caskets. A few of them offered words of condolence to Kaylan as they passed. After the last of them was gone, Jax worked to position Corin's casket on a pyre. It took longer than it had taken Deanna, but Corin's casket eventually lifted into the air and settled on the pyre prepared for him.

"Take as much time as you need," Yolken said, looking back at Kaylan.

She stepped back from her mother's casket and said, "I'm ready."

Yolken drew in the sun's Energy. Gathering air around Deborah's casket, he easily lifted it off the ground. With care, he guided it over the pyre and slowly decreased the pressure of the air under it, gently setting it down on the rectangular pile of wood.

Yolken turned to Kaylan, hugged her, then led her back to join the others.

A bell started chiming in the back of the room and heads turned. Another procession entered through the gilded doors, led by the high priest, head of Draego's Servants, proctors of the Dragon Shrine. He wore a light-blue robe with a round yellow patch representing the sun in the center of it. Straight yellow strips of cloth—rays—left the sun and circled around the priest's body. He carried before him a long staff, keeping it perfectly vertical. A large flame burned at the top of it. Yolken eyed the staff as the high priest passed by, noticing the dragons carved into it.

Two dozen acolytes, wearing plain orange robes, followed behind the high priest in two rows. Each of them carried a golden candle lighter, curved at the end with a little flame. The high priest stopped before the center pyre, and the acolytes walked around him to the left and the right. Behind the pyres, they started up the dais. Candelabras were positioned along the edges of the steps, and at each one, one of the acolytes stopped. Finally, when they were all in position before the candelabras, the acolytes simultaneously lit the candles, then snuffed out their candle lighters and made their way back down the steps. They retraced their steps around the pyres, past the high priest, and back toward the rear of the throne room.

The high priest held the staff high before the pyre upon which Deborah's casket rested and, in a booming voice, spoke words Yolken didn't recognize. It was part of the reason he had never been very pious growing up—whenever he did attend the shrine, he couldn't understand what the priest said. The high priest moved to his right and repeated the process before Corin's pyre, then moved over to Reago's casket and repeated the incantation a third time. When he finished, he walked around the pyre and climbed the steps of the dais, stopping before a temporary mount positioned at the center of the dais, between the uppermost sets of candelabras. He slid the staff into the mount and turned to face the crowd.

"Please kneel," the high priest said. The rustling sound of people lowering themselves to their knees filled the chamber. When the noise died down, the priest gestured to the coffin on his right and said, "We have gathered today to send Reago Draeko Yarin Drake, Deborah Browning, and Corin Foler"— he gestured at each casket as he named the dead—"back to the Great Dragon. The Energy that once burned within them, which burns within each of us, becomes one again with Draego."

The high priest's speech transitioned back to the language Yolken didn't understand. As the man droned on, Yolken's mind wandered. Given that he was listening to the priest talk, Yolken wondered how his assuming the Dragon Throne would affect those who worshiped Draego. For centuries, the story that propagated throughout Dradonia was that Drakonias and the Regency were the Blessed of the Dragon, Draego's chosen rulers, and therefore entities deserving of worship. He worried that Drakonias' death would send negative ripples throughout the empire. What would people do when they learned the truth—that the Blessed were never truly blessed?

Even though he had never been very pious, many citizens of the empire—Kaylan included—believed what the Regency taught. The revelation that the Blessed weren't blessed wouldn't directly affect the rituals conducted in the Dragon Shrines by the priests, but only because those rituals focused on the Great Dragon and not his Blessed. However, many of the pious saw the Blessed as vassals of the Great Dragon's power and looked to them for the everyday, tangible displays of Draego's blessings—such as how Kristana had looked to Dorlan to heal Issa. It had only been a couple of weeks and people were already looking at him the same way. It made Yolken extremely uncomfortable. He knew he had a gift for healing, and he had fond memories of helping Issa, the beggars in Onta, and, most recently, Javen and Deanna, but being worshiped was the last thing he wanted.

But then, he didn't want any of what had happened.

And he wasn't here to wallow in self-pity. He was here to mourn a loved one.

He didn't know Reago or Corin, so what he felt for them was different than what he felt for Deborah. The little he knew about Reago he'd learned from Deanna. In the early decades of the Dragon King Era, he'd been a loyal ruler. Deanna remembered being surprised by Reago's decision when the family finally split between those loyal to their father and those who went with Drakonias. Reago somehow knew the truth about what was happening to Dradonia, despite the emperor trying to hide it. After Devin confronted Yolken in Onta, Javen told him, Reago had decided to travel to Kyinth in a Train to confront Drakonias. After all he'd done, he'd decided to sacrifice everything he had to do the right thing. He died helping Yolken.

When Yolken had asked for the Order's help in finding Javen, Corin voted against it, but then volunteered to accompany Yolken to Kyinth. They got to know each other better during their travels. Corin had been one of the many early members of the Order Yolken's father recruited, and listening to tales of missions they'd done together had been a welcome distraction from the monotony of traveling to Kyinth. It also helped keep his mind off of his impending meeting with the emperor.

Kaylan sniffled as the high priest continued speaking. Yolken wrapped his arm around her and pulled her tightly to him. Of the three they were gathered to mourn, Deborah was the only one he knew. He didn't remember the day his parents had died, but he knew she was the one who'd kept him and Javen safe from the Black Sodality—safe from Drenan. Deborah had been a loving, motherly presence in their lives. He fondly remembered the sweet cakes she sometimes added, free of charge, to Selena's daily order. There had been a few times when their aunt had to travel—he presumed now to go meet with the Council in Croff—and he and Javen stayed with the Brownings. Even though Deborah and Selena weren't technically family, they were the closest thing to family he and Javen had.

Now that he thought about it, Selena had never had a proper funeral.

Yolken didn't really remember his last moments with Selena. It had been right after he healed Issa—she'd sent him to the Mindons with Jax and stayed behind to find Javen. After Drenan murdered her and took Javen captive, Deborah fled to the Mindons with Kaylan. He vividly remembered Deborah recounting finding Selena in the tavern cellar. But what happened to her body? Had Deborah been able to attend to her, or was she left for someone else to find? Maybe old Relan found her. He hoped so. He tried not to think of the alternative. Not knowing and still carrying guilt for his role in her death, he imagined her up on the pyre with Deborah.

The high priest droned on for a few more minutes then switched back to the common language. "The Great Dragon, who eternally floats through the ribbons of Ether, breathed fire into the sun. The sun, in turn, breathes life into Dradonia. To the Energy by which we exist, we are destined to return."

The priest turned and lifted the staff from the pedestal. Turning to face the audience again, he said, "For four hundred years, Draego's Fire has burned on the great altar of the Dragon Shrine, lit by Emperor Drakonias at the advent of his rule. That fire was extinguished and lit anew by His Blessed Highness, Yolken Danavin Dairion Drake, consecrating his rule, ordained by Draego himself. This fire," he said, holding the staff high, "is that fire."

Participating in what he knew was a made-up ritual— Drakonias had invented it to establish his rule after his war— was one of the most embarrassing moments of Yolken's life. The Priesthood of the Dragon had existed long before Draeko or Drakonias came into their power, and Drakonias claiming to be Draego's chosen ruler was not new. Deanna told about visiting shrines during the Previous Era and how many of the rulers back then also made the same claim. They fought wars over their competing claims. Her marriage to the former king of Thorea had taken place before the altar in Kyinth's Dragon Shrine in the first year of the Dragon King Era, she said, and Draego's Fire burned then, too.

The high priest stepped off the dais and walked around the pyres to stand before the crowd. "Let those who would light the pyres come forward."

Deanna and Enif stepped forward. With his hand on the small of her back, Yolken guided Kaylan forward as well. She wiped tears from her eyes as they went. Three acolytes approached and handed Deanna, Enif, and Kaylan a candle lighter, then scurried away.

"There is no better way to return to the Great Dragon than

by Draego's Fire," the high priest said.

That was exactly how his parents had gone, Yolken thought. And even though he wasn't especially pious, the thought comforted him.

The high priest tipped his staff, lowering the flame to eye level.

The three mourners lit their candle lighters with the fire. Deanna moved over to the pyre upon which Reago rested, and Enif over to Corin's. When the high priest moved out of the way, Kaylan, joined by Yolken, began lighting several spots of tinder at the base of her mother's pyre. Deanna and Enif lit their pyres as well.

The flames spread quickly, inching from the kindling to progressively larger pieces of wood. Within minutes, the pyres were blazing infernos.

Sun rays began bending to Yolken's left. He watched as Deanna used Energy to start a cyclone of air moving around Reago's blazing pyre. She guided the flames and smoke up through the broken ceiling, something they had agreed to do in advance. He followed her lead, starting a cyclone above Deborah's pyre, and Enif did likewise.

Enif's cyclone was nowhere as powerful, or effective, as Yolken's. He resisted the urge to help, but when smoke began drifting away from the cyclone, he siphoned some of the Energy he was directing toward his own cyclone and added strength to Enif's.

The high priest began speaking in the foreign language again, giving what Yolken assumed was some sort of a benediction, then started walking toward the rear of the throne room. The acolytes gracefully stepped up onto the dais behind the three swirling infernos, lit their candle lighters, then snuffed out the candles before following the high priest out.

After that, the crowd began dispersing. Before long, the only people remaining in the throne room were Yolken and Kaylan, Javen, Jax, Deanna, and Yolken's advisors.

"Now that that is over," Enif said, "let us discuss this edict you're thinking of issuing."

Yolken glared at Enif, keeping the cyclones active.

"As one of your advisors, I have to say—"

"No," Yolken said. "We're not discussing that here."

"But Your High—"

"I said no!" Yolken said, and Enif flinched. "The funeral may be over, but we're not finished yet. We'll talk later."

"Yes, Your Highness," Enif said with a bow. He stepped back from Yolken and Kaylan.

They stayed and chatted, offering up remembrances of Deborah and Corin. Yolken listened, but he also reflected on the decisions he had to make before tomorrow's court. He looked past the tunnels of smoke swirling up through the broken roof to the dragon lying at the top of the dais. His head was resting on the ground and his eyes were closed. Yolken knew the decisions he needed to make wouldn't be popular—he imagined that at one time or another, every ruler, no matter what level they were at, even the mayor of Lonely Oak, had to make them—but he knew they needed to be made.

Drakonias' edict to ban the wide-spread use of dragon bones and Machines hadn't been popular. It had thrown Dradonia back centuries in terms of technology. But Yolken now knew that Drakonias had made the right decision.

He also knew that Drakonias hadn't gone far enough.

CHAPTER 3

Javen peered over the edge of the balcony and looked down at the hole in the ceiling of the throne room. It had been two weeks since what happened between Yolken and Drakonias, but he could still hardly believe there was a dragon in there.

"Why so morose?" a woman's voice said.

Javen looked up to find Melina standing next to him on the balcony, holding out a glass. She'd changed from her black mourning clothing to a violet dress, a color appropriate for the Regent of Arinin. He accepted it from her and took a sip. When the burning of the whiskey subsided, he said, "The funeral."

"That woman... you knew her well?"

Javen nodded. "Missus Browning. And yeah. She was Kaylan's mother. She had a bakery we used to get bread from every day for our tavern."

Melina took a drink of her own whiskey, then said, "I'm sorry for your loss."

"What about you? You're not sad about Reago?"

"Not particularly."

He looked over at Melina. "He was your uncle, though, right?"

"Yes, but any affection I might have felt toward him was lost centuries ago. He was the Chancellor of the Western Realm, which meant I reported to him, but I hadn't dealt directly with him for ages. He was so reclusive—and now I know it was because he'd been planning to betray the emperor the whole time."

"But now we know he did the right thing," Javen said. He took another sip of whiskey and tried not to make a face as it went down.

"Do we?"

"My brother said—"

"What exactly *did* your brother say? Besides the cryptic words he and Deanna exchanged with the emperor, he hasn't said anything. All we've seen or heard from your brother since he assumed the throne was when we were all paraded before him to swear our allegiance. None of us know what's going on—except for you. You're the only regent who has access to Yolken."

"He's my brother."

"Not anymore. I mean, he is, but he's also the emperor now, which means you're on the same footing as the rest of us."

"I can't help it if he lets me be around him."

"No," Melina said, upending her glass and downing the remainder of her whiskey in one gulp, "I suppose you can't. But what you *can* do is tell us what—"

"Javen!" a jovial voice said.

Both he and Melina turned and saw Jax approaching, ale sloshing out of the glass he carried.

"Hello, Jorgan," Javen said.

Jax clapped him on the back and said, "Jax, lad, Jax. We don't have to hide who we are any longer."

"Sorry. Habit, I guess."

"Don't be sorry, lad. You're a regent now—congratulations, by the way. Someone such as yourself doesn't have to be sorry."

Congratulations? It wasn't like this was the first time he'd seen Jorg—*Jax* since Yolken had become emperor. He'd seen them every day. Maybe he'd had too much to drink.

"Melina," Jax said, looking over at her. He bowed slightly and held out his hand, but she ignored it, snorting instead.

"I'll see you later?" Melina said, directing her attention to Javen.

Javen gave Jax a quick look, then nodded. Melina touched him on the arm and walked away. With everything that had happened over the last couple of weeks, everything that had changed, he was glad his nights with Melina and Lannary hadn't.

Jax ran his hand through his greying beard. "With that fine ale your brother makes, I never would have taken you for a whiskey drinker."

"I'm not, really."

"Let me get you a real drink, then." Jax looked around and, finding the nearest waiter, flagged him down.

The man approached, holding an empty tray. He bowed toward Javen and said, "Your Majesty," then, "Master Jax. What can I get you?"

"An ale for the lad," Jax said. He held up his half-empty glass and added, "And another for me."

The waiter nodded his head and walked off.

"She never did like me," Jax said.

"Who?"

Jax took a drink of ale. "Melina."

"Why?" Javen looked around the balcony, but she was already out of sight. Through the open doors, he could see Yolken and Kaylan standing in the center of the room with the semicircular couch. A few individuals he recognized from the West Tower—the official Kyinth residence of the Chancellor of the Western Realm—were talking with him. "Because you were a member of the Order?"

"That. And a certain… setback… at several of her distilleries."

Melina had never mentioned any setbacks to Javen when they were in Arinin. "What happened?"

"You're going to see her later; ask her yourself."

Javen felt his face redden. "Uh... I..."

"What? You don't owe me an explanation. You're the Regent of Onta, she's the Regent of Arinin—you probably have business to discuss. Ah. Here we go," Jax said, turning toward the approaching waiter. The waiter handed Javen a glass first, then handed one to Jax. After the waiter bowed his head and walked off, Jax held up his first glass and said, "To Deborah."

"To Missus Browning," Javen said. They clinked glasses and Javen took a drink. The truth of who she was and what she had done for him and Yolken was still new to him. He could still hardly believe it. He had grown up believing what everyone else did about the rebels—that their mission was to overthrow the Regency—so finding out that the people he knew and loved were rebels had caused him great strife. He'd been forced to choose between family loyalty and imperial loyalty—and he knew what happened to those who rebelled against the Regency. "It's still hard to believe she's gone. Selena, too."

Jax grunted and finished his first glass.

"Truth is, I feel horrible," Javen said.

"Why?"

"Because I never got to mourn Selena. And because I barely felt bad that she'd died. She was a rebel, so part of me thought she got what she deserved." He lifted his glass and took a sip.

"It wasn't your fault, lad. People's emotions are often limited by what information they have at the time," Jax said.

"I thought she betrayed me and Yolken by lying to us, but now I feel like I betrayed her."

"You didn't."

"I chose to ignore the lifetime of love she showed us because I liked how Dorlan was treating me."

"What do you mean?" Jax said.

"I mean... I love my brother, but most of the time I felt like I was nothing but his errand boy. Selena's too. After what happened that night, Dorlan made me feel important."

"Trust me, lad, you're being too hard on yourself."

"Maybe. But Hadie tried warning me about the Regency and I ignored her too."

"You think I don't know what it feels like to betray someone?" Jax set his glass roughly on the balcony ledge, sloshing ale out of it. "I left your father to die. When he needed me most, I left! And he *died!*" Jax's sudden shouting made Javen take a step back. "Worse... it was all my fault."

Javen and Jax had spent a lot of time talking while they waited for Yolken's advisors to arrive from Croff, and one of the things Javen had learned was what really happened to his parents. He'd grown up thinking they died in an accident, but during his one lesson with Drenan he'd learned that Drenan had actually murdered them. But what Javen didn't learn until he talked with Jax was the circumstances leading up to the Black Sodality finding his father—the meeting in Lonely Oak with members of the Council to witness the destruction of the planet Detron.

Javen looked sheepishly out over the city, then realized what Jax was trying to tell him. "You did what you could with the information you had at the time," he said.

"Exactly," Jax agreed. They stood in silence for a while, drinking their ale, then Jax said, "Speaking of Hadie, what do you think Yolken's gonna do?"

When Drakonias started asking questions about Hadie, Javen had honestly thought his life was in danger. She'd killed all the regents? *And* Dorlan? Even after all this time, he still hardly believed it. No one knew how she did it, but the rumors abounded. And as many rumors as there were about how she managed to best the entire southern Regency, there were almost as many about how Yolken was going to respond. With the east long since lost and the south currently controlled by Hadie—the Queen of the South—the United Realms was now half what it once was.

"I have no idea," Javen finally responded. "Drakonias was

planning to send me and Drenan to Hantlo to take the realm back from her."

"Drenan..." Jax said.

Javen shuddered. Every time he thought of Drenan—of what he had done to Astora—his stomach roiled. He'd witnessed Drenan's deep-seated hatred for him and Yolken multiple times. And then to find out that Drenan was responsible for coercing Nera—the head of the Synod and thus the Black Sodality—into ordering his assassination at Drakonias' meeting with Yolken... They still didn't understand how that had been foiled—only that someone had warned him by calling his name. And someone had killed the assassin.

Javen felt the scar at his throat. "They haven't located him yet, have they?"

"No. Devin either."

Not wanting to discuss Drenan further, Javen changed the subject. "So you don't know what Yolken's planning either?"

"I don't."

"Don't you specialize in gathering information or something?" Jax looked at him askance. "What do your sources say?"

"My sources can't say anything if there's nothing to be said." Jax turned from the balcony and looked into the palace, where Yolken was now talking with a few of his advisors. "Tomorrow's going to be interesting, regardless of what he decides."

"Do you think he'll still send me?" Javen said. The thought of traveling to Hantlo with Drenan had given Javen nightmares about Hadie. But now the thought of going to Hantlo *without* Drenan quickened his pulse.

"Why? Do you want to go?"

Javen felt his face redden.

Jax snickered and leaned against the balcony.

"What?" Javen said.

"Nothing, lad. Nothing."

"It doesn't matter what I want anyway." Javen turned back

around and rested his elbows on the smooth stone.

"What is it?" Jax said, looking over at him.

Javen stared silently out over the city. Even though everything he'd learned about the Regency had turned out to be a lie, he was still glad he'd been given the opportunity to be someone other than Yolken's errand boy. And as thankful as he was that he now knew the truth of Drakonias' war and that Yolken was trying to right the wrongs Drakonias inflicted with his rebellion, he was at the same time a little annoyed that, once again, he found himself under Yolken's authority. It was ironic, really.

"You're mad he was chosen, aren't you?"

"What?" Javen said, turning to look at Jax, who had a smug look on his face. "No," he lied.

"Maybe he'll name you chancellor."

"I hope not."

"Why? You'd be in charge of the entire Western Realm."

"Because I don't even know how to be a regent yet."

"You think he knows how to be emperor? He's having to learn as much about how to rule as you."

"Maybe."

Jax sipped his ale, then said, "Ask him."

"To make me Chancellor?"

"To send you to Hantlo."

"No."

"Admit it, you want to go."

Jax was right; he did.

"I know you're enjoying the, uh… attention… you've been getting here, but that's not love."

Javen looked over at Jax.

"I knew it!"

"What?"

"You love her."

Javen looked away.

"Admit it."

"I don't know what I feel." But what he did know was that he missed Hadie. Something about her had captivated him from the very moment he first met her. He'd tried to find her ever since they had been separated in Portstown, but without success. He was convinced now that Devin had deliberately ignored his request for help—probably at Karina's behest.

"Want me to ask him for you?"

"No," Javen said.

Jax shoved off the balcony with a foot and stepped away. "I think I just might."

Javen instinctively responded, letting Energy from the sun flow into his Core. He reached out with a thread of it and wrapped it around Jax's stomach, freezing him in place. "I said *no.*"

Jax laughed. "Just messing, lad."

Javen let go of Jax and drained the remainder of the Energy in his Core into the marble. The rock grew warm to the touch.

Jax flagged down a waiter and ordered them another round of ale, and they spent the next hour bantering and drinking. Jax didn't mention Hadie again, but she lurked in the back of Javen's mind.

He glanced inside at his brother and Kaylan, the line of people seeking to give their condolences to Kaylan never-ending. He had loved her, but she didn't return his affections, which he had come to terms with. She loved Yolken, and they were now married. Even though he still loved her—and likely always would—he shook his head at the idea of trying to win her away from his brother. *I'd end up memorialized in Lovers,* he thought. The regent who stole the heart of the emperor's wife…

While Jax rambled about the time he had tricked him and Yolken into thinking Brall had dragon eggs in his cellar, Javen thought about what he really wanted. He was certainly enjoying himself with Melina and Lannary, but they weren't it. He had always been flirtatious with the lasses in Lonely Oak and those who passed through town on their way north, but he always told himself it was only until he had won Kaylan's heart. And now she wasn't an option, his feelings for Hadie began to resurface.

Jax was right, even if he didn't want to admit it to him. Now that he wouldn't be going to Hantlo with Drenan—which he knew would have ended with Hadie's death—he'd often wondered if Yolken would still send him. He looked in at his brother again. Yolken wasn't like Drakonias, but he was the emperor now. Was he then obligated to take the south back? What if Hadie wouldn't renounce her title? He didn't want to go to the south only to have to do something he didn't want to do. The question was, did he have a choice? He hoped Yolken wouldn't put him in that position.

CHAPTER 4

Yolken entered the throne room from the side door that led directly to the emperor's private Lift. He was surrounded by the Dragon Guard, now comprising Reago's former guards wearing their white armor. He wore the yellow armor of the Dragon King and carried the Dragon Scepter, which was still deformed from when he'd used it to kill Drakonias. The ornate dragon that had once adorned it was now a disfigured lump of gold. It was heavy enough that he had to Synthesize in order to carry it comfortably. The Harachin sword—his father's sword— hung on his left hip.

Neither the scepter nor the sword held any Energy in them.

He climbed the steps of the dais and the Dragon Guard parted at the top step to let him through. He paused and looked at the dragon, who still lay unmoving behind the throne. Deth lifted his head, considering Yolken, but his expression was unreadable. Yolken felt guilty about wearing the dragon armor and carrying two weapons made from dragon bones, even though he had Deth's permission. He'd considered not wearing the armor or carrying either bone but had decided that what he was going to do would have more of an effect if he did. Reflecting on what the entire dragon species had gone through, he knew he was making the right decision.

Yolken proceeded to the front of the dais, and everyone in the balcony and on the marble floor sank to their knees and bowed.

Jax, whom he had named First Advisor, stood halfway up the dais; projecting his voice, he said, "The court of His Blessed Highness, Yolken Danavin Dairion Drake, is now in session."

Yolken sat on the throne, then the gathered crowd rose to their feet. He looked up at the balcony as its occupants sat and caught Kaylan's eye. She gave him a reassuring smile.

Jax climbed the remaining steps and, trying his best to ignore the dragon lying behind Yolken, said in a quiet voice, "You ready for your first official day as emperor?"

Yolken nodded.

An acolyte stepped forward and handed Jax the first scroll. He broke the wax seal and unrolled it. Yolken was not looking forward to what Jax was about to read. He'd been very reluctant to undertake most of the decisions he'd had to make—and he imagined many of his decisions in the future would be similar.

Jax began reading, using Synthesis to amplify his voice. "On this first day of the second month of autumn in the year 410, Yolken Danavin Dairion Drake hereby claims to be the one and only true Blessed of the Dragon and chosen ruler of Dradonia." At first, Yolken didn't understand what officially made him emperor: Had it been because he killed Drakonias? Or when he lit Draego's Fire in the Dragon Shrine? Then he realized it wasn't either. It was when he'd turned to the regents in the throne room after killing Drakonias and declared himself the chosen ruler of Dradonia. When they'd knelt, *that* was when it had been official. This declaration was just so it'll be recorded in the official annals of the empire. "His Blessed Highness thereby avers Drakonias Arvarin Draeko Drake to be both a tyrant and an illegitimate ruler. His Blessed Highness accuses Drakonias of committing treason against Draeko Dairion Drake in the year 1019 of the Dragon King Era. He is also accused of murdering tens of millions of citizens of Dradonia, as well as the annihilation of an entire species, the dragons."

Jax paused as a murmur washed over the crowd. "Therefore," he continued, "His Blessed Highness declares this first day of the second month of autumn to be the beginning of a new era." Yolken gripped the scepter tightly, fighting the urge to groan. "The Blessed Era."

Cheers erupted in the throne room.

Yolken resisted the urge to run. Instead, he rose to his feet, which made the cheering grow louder. He'd fought against this particular declaration, and only reluctantly agreed to it because his advisors were correct: He needed to make it known that the rule of Drakonias was over. Calling it the Blessed Era asserted that he was indeed the chosen Blessed ruler of Dradonia, unlike the rule of Draeko or Drakonias.

He hadn't even had time to figure out what it meant to him that he now sat on the Dragon Throne, or what kind of empire he wanted to sit atop. *The Blessed Era...* This was not what he wanted. What he wanted—desperately—was just to be back in Lonely Oak, running his tavern with Kaylan at his side.

Yolken sat back down on the throne and the cheering slowly died down. When the chamber was largely quiet, Jax handed the scroll back to the acolyte, who then handed him another. While Yolken waited for Jax to begin reading, he thought about what Jax was about to read. Every fiber of him wanted to avoid it, but he knew that, having claimed he was the true ruler of Dradonia, it couldn't be avoided. Not if he wanted to be a just ruler.

"As the Great Dragon's chosen ruler," Jax continued, "His Blessed Highness demands that Devin Drakonias Metra Drake and Drenan Drakonias Loid Drake be brought before the Dragon Throne to stand trial for the many crimes of which they are accused."

Yolken didn't know how he was going to do that. No one had seen Devin or Drenan since they'd fled from the throne room, and he wondered if the loyalty the regents had pledged to him was deep enough that they would turn the two men over if they were found. Realistically, he was left with the resources of the Order—which pretty much added up to Jax's networks—and they had yet to turn anything up. So far, their only lead was that after word of the emperor's death spread throughout the city, a stableman named Henald had pulled a wagon up to the front steps of the palace with armor in it. A guard demanded to know where he got the armor so Henald explained that the Blessed had entered his stable and exchanged their armor for his son's clothes.

So Devin and Drenan had fled the capital. But where they'd gone was anyone's guess.

Yolken tried to pay attention as Jax read one edict after another, largely administrative in nature, but was thinking about the scroll selected to be read last. It was an edict that he knew would make his advisors and everyone in the Regency angry. Even though it wasn't customary for the emperor to read the edicts himself, he'd decided to announce this one personally—he didn't want it to seem as though he was hiding behind his decision. Even though his advisors would be furious, the presence of the dragon behind him reassured him that he had made the right decision.

Drakonias had banned the use of Machines when the astronomer's study revealed what his war had done to the sun. Yolken had recently learned of the unrest when Drakonias issued the edict—both amongst the Regency and the people of Dradonia—because the ban undid centuries of technological advancement. After Drakonias' war, Machines of war gave way to Machines that vastly improved the quality of everyone's lives. The people had largely forgotten of their existence due to the Sodality killing anyone who spoke of them.

"With regard to the event that transpired nineteen days ago in the Southern Realm…"

Hearing Jax mention the south brought Yolken's attention back to the present. His decision on what to do with the south was the last edict Jax would read today. He deliberately did not refer to what had happened as a rebellion. It would anger the Regency, he knew, but his plan for the south would anger them more. He shifted on the throne. He never liked doing or saying something that he knew would anger someone else. He had always hated confronting Javen about his dereliction of duties in the tavern.

"It is the intention of His Blessed Highness to send an emissary to Hantlo to meet with the Queen of the South."

The Order's position was that the Regency was an illegitimate ruling authority, a position with which Yolken agreed, so he didn't consider what had happened there a rebellion. More importantly, what the south needed was not more bloodshed to bring it back into the empire, but help.

Dorlan, the Chancellor of the Southern Realm, had been petitioning Drakonias for help for quite some time, but Drakonias refused to publicly admit that there was a problem. In fact, he'd kept the Regency in the dark about what was happening. Communication with the east had been lost because of the continuous battery of storms plaguing the East Sea, and worsening weather conditions forced regents to abandon much of the Southern Realm. But nobody knew why. Drakonias had murdered his own son, Drashon, to keep the secret close.

Now that Yolken found himself in power, he could understand why Drakonias hadn't told anyone what was happening: The news would likely have created pandemonium across what was left of the empire. He agreed with his advisors not to reveal it to the general public, but at the same time he wasn't going to force the south to rejoin the empire against their will.

"It is no secret that environmental conditions have been deteriorating in the south for some time," Jax continued, "so the primary mission of said emissary will be to ascertain what aid the south requires. The emissary's secondary mission is to negotiate the terms under which the south would be willing to rejoin the

United Realms."

A din rose in the throne room as the audience talked amongst themselves about the edict. Yolken knew there would be much private discussion—and that there would be those who would try to change his mind.

Jax rolled up the scroll and handed it to the acolyte, who then handed Jax the final scroll. When Yolken stood and Jax handed it over to him, the throne room fell silent. Yolken looked over his shoulder at Deth. His lizard-like eyes looked directly at him. Yolken turned back to face the crowd below. He tilted the scepter toward Jax and Jax took it from him. He took a step forward and broke the seal.

The last two weeks had been a mix of supporting Kaylan, his new wife, as she grieved the loss of her mother, and trying to figure out how to restore balance to the sun. Part of this involved not just making things right with the sun but making things right with the dragons—with Deth. He'd visited Deth several times over the last two weeks and realized there were no easy solutions. The way the Regency used the remains of the once-peaceful species was grotesque, but it had always been understood that banning the use of armor and dragon bones would handicap the Regency, putting them at a disadvantage. The question now was: Against whom?

If the Regency was no longer fighting the Order, there wasn't really a threat anymore. There were still regents—including the Chancellor of the Northern Realm—who were traveling to Kyinth and had not yet pledged their allegiance to Yolken, but it wasn't likely any would refuse. That left Devin and Drenan as the only remaining threats. He had to determine, then, whether the threat they posed was worth the continued use of dragon remains for protection.

Yolken unrolled the scroll and started to read. "Just like everyone else, I grew up thinking dragons were a myth. Under Drakonias' authority, the Regency hid the truth from those they ruled. But the truth is, as evidenced by the dragon behind me, dragons once inhabited Dradonia. Unlike ourselves, they were a species that lived in peace. Their history was not written in blood as was ours.

"During Drakonias' war, Drakonias subjected the dragons to great injustice. He initiated an assault on the dragons which resulted in the complete annihilation of the species, save for one.

"Therefore, on this first day of the Blessed Era, I, Yolken Danavin Dairion Drake, Blessed and chosen ruler of Dradonia, do hereby declare the use of armor made from the scales of dragons to be unlawful." Gasps exploded around the throne room. "I also declare," he said, amplifying his voice so he would be heard over the din, "the use of dragon bones to be unlawful. All those in possession of said armor and bones are hereby ordered to immediately turn them over to such persons as designated by myself. The armor and bones will be collected and disposed of as Dethoicrinth sees fit."

The throne room erupted in an uproar.

Yolken retrieved the scepter from Jax and stepped to the front of the dais. He held the scepter up in front of him. He had to push more Energy into his arm to have the strength to hold it steady, but he turned his wrist until the heavy gilded bone was level with the ground, and set it down. Next, he unsheathed the Harachin sword. He held it in both hands, looking down at it and remembering the first time he'd held the sword. Actually, it hadn't been the first time—he didn't remember that, much to Jax's amusement. But he clearly remembered sitting at the table in an unfamiliar cabin up in the Mindon Mountains. He'd just found out that his aunt was dead and the Regency had taken Javen prisoner. All because of something *he* had done. All his life he'd been hard on Javen, complaining that Javen's behavior was affecting the day-to-day operation of their tavern. He'd thought for sure Javen would one day do something really stupid and disrupt all of their lives—but in the end, it had been *him*. Jax and Deborah had hidden the real extent of who he was, so it was at that moment he'd learned he was not just a simple brewer, a commoner hoping never to catch the attention of the Regency. He'd picked the sword up from the table and held it just as he was doing now.

Yolken bent over and set the Harachin sword down next to the Dragon Scepter.

Jax stepped up behind Yolken and placed his hand on Yolken's shoulder. Yolken turned his head and nodded. Jax began unclasping the straps on Yolken's yellow dragon armor. When he finished, he helped Yolken take it off. Underneath, he wore a thin yellow shirt. Lastly, Yolken stepped out of the armor leggings.

Yolken felt awkward standing in what amounted to his smallclothes in front of hundreds of people, but he knew the effect would be worth it. The blank stares that met him as he scanned the throne room told him that his gesture had the effect he'd hoped for. No one had to agree with him, but they *would* adhere to his decision.

Now that he lacked the dragon armor's protection against Energy attacks, Yolken blinked and shifted his eyes to those of a dragon. There were no unnatural bends in the Energy flowing into the room from the hole in the ceiling. At least for now, it seemed they would comply.

CHAPTER 5

Javen loitered on the marble floor of the throne room with Yolken's advisors—members of the former Order of the Dragon Council—as the throne room slowly cleared out. When Yolken had declared himself to be the Dragon King after returning to Croff from his trip to the Island of Kvorga, he'd disbanded the Council but retained its members as advisors. Most of them seemed content in their new roles, but by the way the former High Councilman, Enif Maldon, had reacted to each edict read today, Javen knew he was not pleased with how Yolken had chosen to begin his rule.

Yolken had instructed his advisors to wait for him in the throne room after court adjourned, and they were all wondering why. Traditionally the emperor met with his advisors in his personal chambers, not in the throne room. As they waited for Yolken to reemerge from the anteroom, which the Dragon Guard wouldn't allow until the main room emptied out, the advisors drifted into two groups and began talking quietly with each other. Enif, Dannl Kand, Aleena Harrin, and Onig Frell made up one group; Tabora Alon, Rheena Drew, Jerle Sage, Sherya Mernn, and Deanna were in the second. Even though he felt more comfortable with Tabora and Deanna, Javen chose to stand with the first—he was interested in what Enif had to say.

"This decision cannot be permitted to stand!" Enif said tersely.

"It was his decision to make," Aleena said.

"But we are his advisors. Advisors *he* chose. He is supposed to listen to our advice."

"We had our say," Onig said.

"But he obviously didn't listen," Enif said.

"Listening to our advice does not mean he has to follow it," Aleena said. "And you know it. How many times over the years did you ignore the advice of the Council?"

"That is not the same!"

"Why not?"

"Because the Order has just gained access to valuable resources, and he single-handedly castrated us!"

"There is no Order any longer, Enif," Jax said, joining the group. "It would be wise to remember that if you wish to remain an advisor."

"As if that meant something to His Highness."

"What's that supposed to mean?"

"It means that he has advisors for a reason," Enif said.

"I'm sure His Highness had his reasons," Jax said. "You're free to ask him if you wish, but you must also respect the decision he made, whether you agree with it or not."

"Respect is something to be earned."

"Then you must give him time to earn it."

Javen hung back as the two groups waited and continued talking amongst themselves. He needed to get back to the West Tower to begin implementing the edicts relevant to the Onta Province, as all the other regents were doing. As much as he wanted to visit with his brother, the duties of his newfound position and responsibilities called to him—and made him antsy as well. He pulled Jax aside and asked, "Do you know what Yolken wants?"

"I don't," Jax said. "He just asked me—instructed me,

rather—to tell you to wait."

"They don't seem to be too pleased with his decisions," Javen said in a hushed voice.

With Javen at his side, Jax edged farther away from the group congregating with Enif, and said, "Enif has been in charge for a very long time. It'll take him a while to get used to being the one *taking* orders rather than giving them."

"He seems so vocal against Yolken, though."

"He knows his place. Yolken wouldn't have allowed him to stay an advisor if he didn't, believe me."

The two men headed for the other group. Tabora and Deanna smiled as they approached.

"How's our young regent?" Tabora said.

Javen shrugged his shoulders. Her green eyes reminded Javen of Kaylan. In fact, the way she braided her hair reminded him of Kaylan as well.

"That bad?"

"No. It's just a lot to get used to. I've never been in charge of anything before. People look at me like I know what I'm doing and most of the time I have no idea what to tell them."

"I think I understand how you're feeling," Deanna said.

"Really?" Javen said. He still had a hard time believing she was the fabled Anivera. She certainly wasn't the woman doubled over with age with white hair and a knobby nose. She was rather beautiful, he thought. The way her black hair shimmered was almost unnatural. It made her look... radiant.

"Things haven't always been as they are. The people here in the capital, and those who work for the regents and chancellors throughout the empire, have always worked for people who've been in power for centuries. They've never encountered someone new to a position of authority. But it wasn't always like that."

"What do you mean?"

"The world was a different place during the Previous Era," Deanna said. "Before my father was given the gift of Synthesis and taught the art of Regeneration, rulers lived just as long as everyone else. Nobles were groomed from childhood, but even so, their transitions into power were often messy. But what I found," Deanna continued, "is that those who adapted best were those who didn't have the opportunity to prepare in advance."

"Really?" Javen said. He wasn't sure if he believed her or not. How could someone unprepared, such as himself, do better than someone who at least had some idea of what they were doing?

"Really. I know you're going to be busy for a while, but when you get the chance, remind me to tell you the story of how my father started off. He spent his whole life being someone else's servant—not unlike you." Javen smiled uneasily, still unsure. "You'll do fine, Javen. Much better, I imagine, than any the empire has seen in a long time."

The two groups continued chatting amongst themselves for several minutes after the throne room was empty of all spectators. Finally the side door—where the emperor had direct and secure passage from the throne room to his personal Lift—opened and Yolken entered. He was now wearing a multi-toned yellow suit. Javen still wore his blue armor—the color used by male regents from the Western Realm—which suddenly made him feel awkward.

Enif broke away from his group and strolled determinedly toward Yolken. He stopped abruptly a few feet away and spoke, his displeasure evident in his tone. "Your Highness—"

"Yes?" Yolken said, unbuttoning his suit coat.

Javen followed the rest of the advisors as they joined Yolken and Enif at the foot of the dais.

"Please don't misconstrue my question as impertinent," Enif said, "but I must inquire as to why you chose to ignore our advice on a matter of such importance."

"Which matter is that?" Yolken said, working at loosening his tie. After making a little room, he undid the top button of his shirt. Javen understood what Yolken was feeling. The new positions they were both in came with dress codes that were unfamiliar and uncomfortable.

Enif hesitated a moment, looking a little taken aback. "The matter which I believe has put us all in great peril."

Yolken looked annoyed. "Enif, just say what you have to say."

"Why would you ban the use of dragon bones and armor? The Order has struggled for centuries to maintain an adequate supply of bones and has always pined for the protection afforded to those possessing dragon armor—not to mention Glasses! And now, after we finally have access to these assets, you take them away. Why?"

"First of all, we don't need them anymore. And second—"

"Don't *need* them?"

Yolken clenched his jaw. He kept it clenched just long enough for Javen to start feeling uncomfortable, then said, "Please don't interrupt me."

"I'm terribly sorry, Your Highness," Enif said with a curt bow, "but this matter is very serious. I don't understand how you can think we no longer need the protection these items provide."

"I understand the seriousness of the matter perfectly," Yolken said. "We don't need the protection because there is no longer a threat."

"But how can you say that? The Chancellor of the Northern Realm is still on his way to Kyinth, as are many of the regents. You haven't received their pledges yet. As we've previously discussed, it's premature to assume they'll all pledge their loyalty to you. Several of us agree on this."

"My decision is final, Enif," Yolken said. "Whatever threat may be posed by those who have yet to pledge their loyalty is nothing compared to the harm inflicted upon Deth by the continued use of the artifacts."

"The dragon," Enif said. "*That's* what this is about?"

"What we did to the dragons was a level of wrongness I can't even begin to fathom."

"*We* didn't do anything to the dragons."

"And I owe my life to Deth. If it weren't for him, I would have died back in Onta, and I won't repay him by wearing his king as armor or using the bones of his relatives as weapons. My decision stands."

"As much as I—we—" Enif said, gesturing to the group of advisors he was conversing with, "—understand the intricacies of our situation..." He glanced up at the dragon, partially visible at the top of the dais, then continued, "your decision will grind the efficient operation of the city to a stop. The Lift, for instance, operates on Energy stored in dra— it operates on stored Energy, Your Highness."

"I understand that," Yolken said.

"Even the servants use the Lift to get up to Drakonias'... I mean, your quarters. Using the stairs to climb up would be—"

"Arduous," Yolken interjected.

"Yes. And how are the servants supposed to accomplish their tasks? You can't possibly expect them to use the pulley system. Has anyone even tested it to see if it still works?"

"No, Enif, I would never expect the servants to do something I wasn't willing to do."

Javen couldn't be sure, but he thought Yolken looked like he was enjoying making Enif squirm.

"What, then?"

"I can operate the Lift easily enough myself."

Enif stared at Yolken, his face blank. "How? How can you possibly operate the Lift from... inside of it?"

"I'm the Blessed of the Dragon, remember?"

Enif let out a sigh. "Er, yes. Well, what about your daily council? Where will you hold that?"

"The quarters above are Kaylan's and my *personal* quarters. I've already selected what I think is a reasonable location to hold council in," Yolken said.

"Reasonable, Your Highness?" Aleena said.

"Yes. In fact, I instructed my staff to make the arrangements during court."

"And what are these... arrangements?" Enif said.

"There are some empty rooms on the tenth floor that I think will be more than sufficient."

"The *tenth* floor?" Enif exclaimed. It was obvious to Javen that, even though they were all on level footing in Yolken's eyes, Enif still thought of himself as being in charge of the advisors, since he was doing most of the talking. "Isn't there something more convenient than the tenth floor? Surely one of the back rooms here would suffice."

"Perhaps. But my mind is made up."

Enif let out another sigh.

"And," Yolken said, "I was going to put you in charge of implementing this particular edict, but your questioning of my decision has led me to reconsider."

"I-I didn't mean to—"

"Deanna," Yolken said, turning from Enif to her, "would you be willing to see my wishes fulfilled?"

"I'd be honored," Deanna said with a bow. "I still remember being mortified when I heard what Drakonias was doing to the dragons, and I fought my father's decision to follow suit, even though I understood why he had to."

Javen watched as Enif stared icily at Deanna.

"Then we'll talk later," Yolken said, "about what I want done with the armor and bones when they're collected."

"Yes, Your Highness," Deanna said.

"Now, regarding my decision concerning the south..."

Javen could tell by the look on Enif's face that he wasn't pleased with Yolken's decision about the Southern Realm either.

"I know it's not what some of you recommended, but forcefully taking back the south is not in anyone's best interest, and you all know it. I think what happened in the south happened because Drakonias refused to do anything about their growing problems. Attacking them would accomplish nothing but more bloodshed. If I'm to rule over the south successfully, I must show that I care more about them than Drakonias did.

"As I said, the emissary I'm sending will have two missions: to see what aid they require, and under what terms they might be willing to rejoin the empire. And the reason I asked Javen to stay is because I want to extend an official invitation to him to lead this mission."

Javen's eye's locked on his brother. "Me?"

Yolken nodded.

"I-I don't know if I would be..." Javen began, then looked down as he trailed off.

"Excuse us for moment," Yolken said, then gestured to Javen and said, "Come here."

Javen followed Yolken around the side of the dais. When they were out of earshot of the others, Yolken stopped and turned toward him.

"Yolken—"

"I thought—"

"I haven't even learned how to be a regent yet. How could you think I'd be a good emissary? I don't know the first thing about petitioning to... to a queen. I haven't been back to Onta yet since all of this. I can't possibly..."

"You're exactly who I need to do this," Yolken said.

"Why?"

"Well, for one, you're one of the few I can trust with such a sensitive assignment. And two, I understand you know the... queen."

The truth was that since the moment he'd learned about what had happened in the south, Javen couldn't stop thinking about Hadie. He hadn't seen her since... since the day Drenan murdered Astora but, even though he'd been distracted by Synthesis lessons with Devin and by the stream of women Karina sent him, he'd thought about her often. And despite his earlier reservations, when Jax had read the edict that Yolken was sending an emissary to the south, he'd hoped Yolken would send him—even if he didn't know the first thing about being an emissary.

"I know her," he admitted. "But Yolken, this is all so new, and I don't want to screw it up."

"You don't have to worry about that, Javen, because I'm sending Jax with you. Turns out his spy in Hantlo—Dorlan's personal servant—is helping the queen. Plus, it'll be the perfect opportunity for you to talk more with him, to learn more of the stuff I had the opportunity to learn. He was close to our parents and I want to you to have the same opportunity I've had to get to know them."

"He's talked about them already," Javen said.

He wanted to go, but he was afraid—of both the task and the prospect of seeing Hadie again—so he was looking for any excuse to get out of it. But at the same time he would be lying if he said he didn't want to see Hadie. Melina and Lannary would be annoyed, but did he really care? He had never felt the same way toward them as he did about Hadie.

"I'll do it," he said, before he had time to think of another excuse.

"Excellent," Yolken said. "Now let's go make Enif really mad."

CHAPTER 6

Loosely holding his horse's reins in one hand, Drenan absentmindedly flexed his other hand into a fist. The feeling of stretching from the scars on the back of his hand was gone. He'd borne those scars, and the ones on the rest of his body, as a reminder of loose ends yet to be taken care of. He didn't want them to be just tied off, though—he wanted them to be cauterized like the ends of a rope. He hated loose ends, and despised those who caused them. Over the years, the scars had turned him into a legend—the scarred man—but the time for frightening simpletons like the stable lad back in Kyinth was past. Now was the time to remain unnoticed.

He closed his eyes and remembered the heat that had burned in him while Devin finished what the healers in Hantlo had been unable to do. Any number of times he could have had his father or Devin remove the scars he'd carried for nearly two decades, but he'd needed to remember—not that he could have forgotten. The memory of the fire that nearly took his life was never far from mind.

With his eyes closed, the rhythm of the horse beneath him lulled him into a sort of trance. Through Glasses, he watched as the elder of Danavin's get proceeded toward the dais upon which Drakonias sat. He wore dirty traveling clothes—certainly not the attire of the *Dragon King*. The younger of Danavin's get, now a *regent*—the Regent of Onta, no less—stood along the wall on the far side. He'd feigned outrage when he'd learned Javen would be among those chosen to guard the emperor during that ridiculous meeting with the so-called Dragon King, but the truth was he'd wanted him there—*needed* him there.

The moment pained Drenan. It had been all he could do not to attack Deanna the instant he saw her. The last time he'd seen her had been the final parlay between Drakonias and Drakonias' father. She was the only one of Draeko's children who'd eluded Drenan while he was an Overseer in the Black Sodality. She was a loose end—one that he thought would never be cauterized. The sight of Reago hadn't bothered him like he thought it would. He should have been dead. He was a loose end as well, but not Drenan's concern. His desire to strike had grown to feverish levels when he recognized the man walking with them, wearing a tattered leather coat—Jax. Hanging at his hip was the very sword he had stolen from Drenan—the Harachin sword. He distinctly remembered the pull of his scars as he'd tightened his grip on the dragon bone he'd held. As badly as he'd wanted to strike, the emperor would have been furious if he had.

Drenan's thoughts turned to the emperor's conversation with the elder of Danavin's get—the so-called Dragon King. Yolken had claimed that the Great Dragon had named him Dragon King, and Drakonias called him mad. Drenan didn't know why Drakonias hadn't killed them all right then, rather than engaging them in a pointless conversation—especially since his plan was to kill them anyway. But then Yolken had said something that caught Drenan's attention: He'd claimed that none of them were the Blessed of the Dragon... that only *he* was.

Drenan snorted when he remembered the Dragon King asking the emperor for a truce—more like begging him for one. But then the conversation had turned confusing. The get spoke of restoring balance lost during the war and trying to prevent the same fate as Detron. Drenan didn't even know who Detron was; nor did Devin. Then Deanna had spoken of confronting the evil the war had unleashed, and that it was as clear as the sun. What in Draego's Fire had she been talking about? He'd added his voice to the growing murmur in the room, shouting that Deanna was mad. And Reago made his treason even clearer when he accused Drakonias of killing Drashon, Drenan and Devin's brother.

He'd been glad when the charade ended and Drakonias shot a stream of Energy down to Deanna. Watching her fall to her knees as her eyes went wide had made him feel almost giddy. Drakonias attacked Reago as well—then Danavin's foolish get Synthesized, giving Drenan the opportunity he'd been waiting for. Draego's Fire erupted from his hands. But instead of consuming Deanna, Jax, and Danavin's get, the firestorm swirled around them. But he'd expected that. They had dragon bones, and the ensuing struggle was an oft-repeated dance. Others added to his inferno. All they had to do was wait out their Energy supply.

He remembered glancing across the throne room at the younger of Danavin's get. He'd stood, frightened and unmoving, not adding to the inferno. Drenan had smiled, knowing the get's time was short. Drenan's persuasions had finally goaded Nera into action. Another loose end soon to be cauterized.

As Devin dragged one of the rebels into the fire with a tendril of Energy, Drenan had reached out for Jax. He'd almost felt Jax's impending death, and reveled at the thought of finally cauterizing another loose end. But his tendril dissolved when it touched Jax.

Drenan reflexively squeezed the pommel of the saddle, hoping to feel the scars he knew were no longer there.

Jax must have had dragon scales woven into his coat.

Drenan had shifted to another rebel—a woman—whom another regent was trying to pull into the fire. The elder of

Danavin's get was preventing it. He sent a tendril out and grabbed the woman by her other leg, and their combined force was enough to slowly pull her into the fire. The Dragon King had continued to struggle against them, but eventually lost his grip on the woman. Her screams as she died had fueled his own internal fire.

The pure joy he felt had spiked when someone yelled Javen's name. He'd looked over just in time to see a steel dagger pierce Javen's throat. But then a thunderous clap and the sound of breaking marble had diverted Drenan's attention—and immediately killed his joy.

At the back of the throne room crouched a bearded man, surrounded by shattered marble.

Drenan remembered the tickle of familiarity he'd felt.

He drew Energy into his Core and squeezed the pommel, crushing it.

Impossible, he'd thought.

Danavin was alive. After all this time… somehow, he was alive.

Therese.

Cara.

Thoughts of his dead wife and daughter flooded his mind—Danavin was responsible for their deaths. And Drenan had sworn to make his get pay.

A cauterized loose end unraveled in his mind.

Drenan remembered directing Draego's Fire toward Danavin. Others joined him, but he didn't want their help. He wanted Danavin to himself. But he'd barely taken a step toward Danavin when the ceiling crashed down around them. He'd somehow deflected the falling debris. The deafening roar still echoed in his head.

A cold autumn wind blowing across the Mindon River sent a chill down Drenan's spine, yanking his mind back to the present.

Devin was turned in his saddle, looking back at him.

"What?" Drenan said.

"What was that all about?"

Drenan looked down at the crushed pommel and said, "Nothing." He pulled the ratty cloak he wore tighter around himself, and flipped the hood up over his head. He refused the temptation of drawing further Energy from the sun to warm himself. He looked down at the crushed pommel again, cursing himself for Synthesizing.

As Drenan and Devin had headed east, toward Tieger, they'd passed Sheal's caravan heading west. It was then that he realized the Regency could no longer be trusted. If Sheal was going to Kyinth, it meant only one thing: He had decided to pledge fealty to the so-called Dragon King. And when they'd arrived in Aliza, they learned that Dane, the provincial regent, was among the traitors who had gone to Kyinth.

At first, Devin wanted to return as well. He argued that with Drakonias dead and with Sheal and so many regents going to Kyinth, it was not worth resisting the Dragon King; doing so would only result in more death—especially since Danavin's get had a dragon on his side. But Drenan had successfully dissuaded Devin—who, he suspected, only wanted to return for Karina.

As the horse swayed beneath him, Drenan realized that he'd failed in every regard. That Queen of the South had somehow managed to kill Loid and Rik. Now his only surviving child was his bastard, Crin—if he even *was* still alive. He hadn't heard from Crin since he'd discovered Danavin's get in that cursed town. He was going to burn that town to the ground. The stupid tree as well. And now, not only was Danavin's get not dead, but neither was Danavin. Somehow, he had survived.

It was impossible. *I saw his corpse...* And yet, he had seen Danavin with his own eyes.

No, Drenan was not returning to Kyinth to pledge fealty to that Dragon King. But he *would* return to Kyinth. And when he did, it would be to cauterize every single loose end. He would do whatever it took to ensure he never failed again.

CHAPTER 7

Drenan looked with great interest at the growing spires in the distance. The towering buildings and the smell of the sea heralded the approaching end of their arduous journey. He wasn't accustomed to spending so long in the saddle. Along the way he'd often pined over the days of travel before their father's infamous edict banning Machines. The Blessed were meant to live and travel in luxury, though even their carriages were nothing compared to Trains and Autos. But now, after a little over a month in a saddle, they'd finally arrived at Tieger—the capital of the Northern Realm.

Drenan scratched at his beard, part of the disguise he and Devin had taken on to further blend in with other travelers. The annoyance of the near constant itch was overshadowed only by Devin's constant whining about Karina—that, and the traitors they'd passed on the way.

How petulant must Sheal still be over not originally being given the chancellorship of the Northern Realm when Drakonias was first establishing his empire. Was his grudge for being relegated to the Regent of Hantlo so strong that he would betray Drakonias' legacy without a care? Obviously, it was—the emperor was barely a month dead. Drenan and Devin had sat on their horses on the side of the road and watched Sheal's caravan lumber by, and Drenan had wanted to attack the unsuspecting traitor with Energy and end Sheal's miserable life. Only Devin's firm grip on his arm prevented him.

Drenan understood why Torin, the Regent of Arivia, would follow in the footsteps of Sheal's capitulation—he was Sheal's son. But Dane? Dane ruled over Aliza, one of the most valued provinces in the Northern Realm. And his father, Akim, had been one of Drakonias' earliest supporters in his decision to overthrow Draeko.

The farther they moved from Kyinth, the more dire Drenan realized their situation was. He had been certain that, once they got away from the capital, they would be able to easily rally the rest of the Regency in Tieger and strike back at Danavin and his get. But after passing through first Arivia and then Aliza and finding the regents in both those cities already gone, he began to doubt. The rumors out of the west didn't help, either. Several of the Western Realm's regents were Reago's children and were already throwing their loyalties in with Danavin's. Combined with the fact that Drakonias had put the younger of Danavin's get in charge of Onta and that the boy was also bedding Melina, the west was now all but guaranteed to be securely in the Dragon King's control. Drenan was still beside himself that the Order had somehow managed to kill Dorlan and all the regents in the south, including his two remaining sons. His only hope was that Sheal maintained control over enough of the regents of the north. But that hope was shattered the day they'd watched Sheal's caravan lumber by.

Devin's horse stopped.

Drenan pulled up beside him. "What is it?"

Devin turned his horse around and started back the opposite direction.

"Where are you going?" Drenan said.

"I'm going back for Karina," Devin said. "I shouldn't have left."

"But we're nearly there!"

"Nearly where? You saw for yourself; Sheal's going to hand the north over to—"

"Stop," Drenan said. "Do *not* say his name."

"He's won."

"No. He hasn't. Not yet."

"Drenan, the south is gone. Sheal is giving him the north, and much of the west was loyal to Reago."

"*Reago* is dead."

"And you think his children will remain loyal to a dead emperor who killed their father? No. If we want to survive, we have to go back and pledge our loyalties."

"What about Thena?"

"*Thena?*"

"She doesn't know what's happened."

"It's been seventy years since anyone's heard from her. I'm sorry, Drenan, but she's long dead. And it's doubtful that whatever remains in the east bears any loyalty to our father."

"That's where you're wrong."

Devin finally reined his horse in. "Where, exactly?"

"Thena lives."

"How?"

"Think about it, Devin. When was the last time she came for Regeneration?"

"The last time she made the crossing, I imagine. But even then, she'd still be dead by now."

"Unless he taught her how to do it."

"Why would he? The last time someone shared the secret, it started a war, remember?"

Drenan urged his horse closer to Devin's. "You're dangerously close to speaking treason."

"Father's dead, Drenan. My only motivation now is getting Karina out of Kyinth. And do you honestly think that Father would have rebelled—whatever the reason—if Grandfather hadn't shared the secret? No. Because without Regeneration it would have been his death." Devin urged his horse back into motion. "I'm going back to Kyinth. I'm going to get Karina and go home, where I plan to consume all of Onta's wine."

"You need her!" Drenan called after Devin. "Without her you'll die, just like everyone else!"

Devin stopped and turned his horse back around.

Drenan trotted his horse back to Devin. "I'm sure Father didn't want to—he wouldn't have forgotten that he was only able to become emperor because he'd talked Grandfather into teaching *him*—but he had no choice. He was losing control and thought that, by teaching Thena Regeneration, he could show he wasn't abandoning her."

"Still, there's no way to know that he taught her. Or that she still lives. And even if she *is* still alive, how does that help us? The East Sea hasn't been successfully crossed in seventy years, remember?"

"There's a way."

"No. There isn't."

"That's what everyone thinks, but Father ensured there was."

Devin narrowed his eyes. "If there was a way across, then why hasn't anyone crossed?"

"Because it's not safe. But he ensured that, if absolutely necessary, there would be a way." Seeing that he had his brother's attention and hoping he could convince him, Drenan continued, "If we go to Thena, we have a chance of staying in power."

"We?"

"Yes."

"You mean Thena?"

"She would be better than *him*. Do you think you'll keep the chancellorship with him on the throne? With her, though, you get to keep your precious Onta."

Devin kept a tight grip on his reins, preventing his horse from moving. "How?"

"Father kept a guide." Drenan looked over his shoulder at the city behind him. "In Tieger."

"A guide?"

Drenan had him. "Yes. Who knows how to navigate the storms."

"A guide who can navigate the storms?" Devin said with obvious incredulity.

"You've already come this far. At least come with me the rest of the way to Tieger and see for yourself."

Devin looked back down the road toward the west, then at the city before them. He didn't say anything, but he started back toward Tieger.

Drenan smiled and urged his horse into motion. He'd succeeded in buying more time with Devin—and lucky for him, he'd been to the guide's home. But with Drakonias dead, he hoped the guide was still young enough to do what Drakonias had kept him alive all these years for.

* * *

Devin glanced over at the ruins perched atop a hill to the north. The domed structure was all that bore witness to Astronomy, the discipline Drakonias had banned in 245. It was as curious a mystery as his decision to ban the use of Machines. But one knew better than to question the emperor. His word was as good as divine.

The road started getting crowded as they drew closer to Tieger's thick walls. Instead of riding around the carts and wagons traveling through the tunnel entrance to the city, they fell in line and followed along.

Devin tried to hide his surprise when he saw that the guards inspecting the wagons wore gray uniforms instead of armor. He looked up to the balconies, halfway up the walls on each side of the tunnel, where Watchers normally stood. There were armor-less guards standing on each balcony, but none of them wore Glasses. *That's odd,* he thought.

His puzzlement about the guards' lack of armor or Glasses

was soon replaced with curiosity about where Drenan was taking them. The horses' hooves clopped on the stone roadway and echoed off the buildings, which grew taller as they neared the center of the city. When they entered the roundabout at the center of the city, Drenan moved with the flow of traffic around the island and glanced up at the bronze statue of his now-dead father. The palace was visible behind the statue to the north, atop a hill. Drenan led Devin halfway around the roundabout and exited to the east.

The road ended at the harbor. No ship had crossed the East Sea in nearly seventy years, but the harbor still bustled with activity. Except during the cyclone season, which spanned the summer and fall months, ships still moved up and down the coast with regularity, though this was only made possible by the breakers that had been installed up and down the coast. Even in the calmer winter and spring months, waves from the storms at sea had reached the shore, making traveling up and down the coast difficult. The breakers had taken nearly a decade of work by regents, but slowly marine traffic was restored. And given that they were now at the tail end of the worst of the cyclone season, travel had resumed.

Drenan turned left down the harbor road, which was lined on the right by docked ships and on the left with two- and three-story buildings covered in well-seasoned wood shingles. The house he stopped in front of was in disrepair: Several of the shingles were missing from the wall and the paint on the railings leading up to the door was peeling.

Drenan proceeded up the creaky wooden steps without a second thought for his horse. Devin quickly slid out of the saddle, wrapped the reins of both horses around the banister, then followed Drenan up.

Drenan opened the door and entered without knocking.

The building was one large room with a worn couch, two equally tattered chairs, and an iron stove and sink at the back. There were also steep iron stairs in the back corner next to the stove.

"Erigin!" Drenan shouted. When there was no reply, he shouted again. "Erigin!"

"Erigin?" Devin said. "The fleet commander?"

Drenan moved toward the stairs.

Devin followed, asking, "He's still alive? How's that possible?" His question was rhetorical; he knew exactly how. What he didn't know, though, was why.

The stench of urine and feces in the room at the top of the stairs overwhelmed Devin. He plugged his nose as he stepped closer to the bed. A wan face and sunken eyes greeted him. From the neck down Erigin was covered in a filthy blanket.

Drenan pulled the blanket back, revealing Erigin's nakedness. Both he and the mattress were covered in his feces. "Get some soap and water," Drenan said.

Devin didn't ask why; he only obeyed—though he didn't know why it was *him* taking the subservient role. He found a pail in the kitchen, but there wasn't any soap. Before going in search of some, he tested the sink to ensure it still worked. When water started flowing after pumping the handle, he went outside.

He knocked on three doors before someone answered.

"What is it?" a sun-darkened man said. He looked like he hadn't shaved in a week.

"I need soap," Devin said.

"Soap? Wha for?"

"Why else would I need soap?"

"Buzz off."

The man moved to shut the door, but Devin drew Energy into his Core and, reaching out with a tendril of it, he grabbed the man by the throat. The man gasped and struggled for air.

Devin squeezed tighter and said, "Do you have any soap?"

The man nodded, unable to speak. Devin let go of him and the man croaked, "Jus a moment."

Devin waited at the door; the man disappeared inside and returned a moment later with a bar of soap. Devin took it from the man's trembling hand and returned to Erigin's home. He filled the pail with water and took a deep breath before climbing the iron stairs.

Drenan was sitting next to the bed, seemingly undisturbed by the smell. Their very presence in such stench was demeaning. Regents shouldn't be subjected to this. Devin handed Drenan the pail and soap.

"Prepare food," Drenan said as he started washing Erigin.

Devin sighed, but obeyed. There wasn't any food to be found in the house. He contemplated making the man who'd given him the soap do it, but elected to go in search of a market instead.

At the first one he found, rumors abounded about what had happened in Kyinth. They weren't much different than what he'd heard on the way to Tieger. The most fantastical of them was that a man had swooped down out of the sky on the back of a dragon. The emperor had been on his balcony on the top of his palace, and the dragon had snatched him up in its mouth and swallowed him in one gulp. Though largely untrue, the tales were disturbing because they all shared the same basic message: The emperor was no longer in power.

He returned an hour later with warm bread, soup, and skewered chicken. Running errands was one thing, but he certainly wasn't going to be relegated to cooking. When he returned to Erigin's home, the windows were open. Drenan and Erigin were sitting at the small round table in the kitchen. Erigin was clean, but still looked like death.

Devin set the food on the table. With a frail arm and aged fingers, Erigin took up a skewer and ravenously tore into it with his rotten teeth. Hungry himself from not having eaten all day, Devin grabbed a skewer and stepped back. He leaned against the cold oven and chewed the seasoned meat, watching Erigin eat like it was his first meal in a month.

When the chicken was gone, Erigin moved to the soup. He tried to remove the lid, but his trembling hand couldn't manage it so Drenan removed it for him. Erigin tore the bread and dipped it in the soup. When the bread and soup were gone, Erigin leaned back with a deep sigh.

"What happened to Gan?" Drenan said.

"He died a month ago," the old man said in a raspy voice. "Was fixing to die myself."

"Not before you take us across the sea."

Erigin shook his head. "Can't."

"I know, the storms. But I need you to try."

Erigin shook his head again.

"You'll have our help."

Erigin shook his head a third time.

Drenan's brow furrowed. "You'll do as we say."

"No."

Devin could tell Drenan was holding back rage. He was infamous for not tolerating impertinence.

"Then at least tell us how to cross," Drenan said.

Erigin stared blankly.

Drenan's hands clenched into fists. His mannerisms betrayed his thoughts, and Devin knew he was moments away from killing Erigin.

"It's not impossible to cross," Erigin said.

"Then why did you recommend we stop?" Drenan said.

"Too many ships were lost. But it's not impossible."

"Tell us how."

"Follow the storms from left to right as they rotate. If they're far enough apart, you might make it. But only if they're far enough apart… and you have to keep to the edges. Chances are slim; you'll need Draego's luck."

"If passage is possible, why has no one ever come from the east?"

Erigin shrugged.

"You won't help us?" Drenan said.

Erigin's hands began trembling again. "W-where's the emperor?"

"Take us to the east and back and you'll never have to sail again. Your youth will be restored and you can claim Tieger's palace as your home."

Erigin looked up at Drenan. "Who are you to give me the chancellor's home?"

"Do *not* presume to question me, peasant." Drenan stood and clenched his hands into fists again.

Erigin feebly pushed himself to his feet as well, but leaned heavily on the table. "I've lived longer than I ever desired to."

Devin simply stared, knowing Erigin's fate was sealed.

Drenan stepped past Devin to a window with a ray of sunlight shining in.

Erigin began choking. Reflexively, he reached up with one hand to grasp his throat—but unable to support himself with just one hand, he collapsed onto the table. The weight of his body snapped one of the table's legs, causing it to tip over. Erigin fell to the ground. His struggle ended quickly.

CHAPTER 8

Drenan was walking with purpose toward the docks, and Devin had to hurry to keep up.

"I'm beginning to second-guess your plan, Drenan." There was no answer. "Maybe if Erigin had agreed to take us—though I don't know how much use he would have been. But without him it's impossible."

Without slowing or turning his head, Drenan said, "You're a seasoned sailor, aren't you? I've seen what you can do in a storm."

"Storms through the gap are nothing compared to cyclones."

Drenan turned so abruptly that Devin nearly ran into him.

"You want to get your precious Karina back or not?"

"Of course I do."

"Well, unless you're planning on going back to Kyinth and swearing fealty to... *him,* your only other option is to come with me. We'll go to Thena and return with her regents."

Devin looked around. The street was surprisingly empty. "What about Machines? Let's go to the cache, get a couple of Guns—better yet, a couple of Tanks—and take care of him ourselves."

"Do you know where the cache is?"

"No."

"Then going to Thena is our only option."

"You're confident she's alive?"

"She has to be. Father wouldn't have left the east ungoverned."

"If I'm going to risk my life trying to cross the East Sea, I don't want it to be for naught, Drenan."

"It won't be."

Devin clenched his jaw.

"I need your help, brother," Drenan said. "I don't have the sailing expertise you do."

Devin looked out at the breakers and the waves crashing over them. Karina was all he wanted. He wanted to return to Kyinth. With their father, Dorlan, and Reago dead, and Nera and Sheal both pledging fealty to Danavin's son, he was the next in line for the throne. But he didn't want to be the emperor. He was perfectly happy being the Chancellor of the Western Realm. All he wanted was to go back to Onta with his wife.

If he returned to Kyinth he had two choices: pledge fealty to Danavin's son, knowing there was no guarantee Yolken would permit him to keep his chancellorship, or lay his own claim to the throne. But if he went with Drenan—as insane as attempting to cross the East Sea was—then Thena could become empress. And with Thena, he would get what he wanted.

"Let's be about it, then," he acquiesced.

* * *

Devin spent the next day and a half preparing the *Soaring Dragon*, the flagship of the once-mighty royal fleet, for sea. It wasn't the largest vessel in the fleet; it was a ship of pleasure. Unlike his own *Vineyard*, it didn't even have the ability to defend itself. When the emperor was aboard the *Soaring Dragon* at sea, it relied on a fleet to defend it. Each ship in that fleet was heavily armed with Cannons and the requisite complement of Synthesizers. He'd argued with Drenan about taking one of those ships instead, but Drenan had insisted that they needed to arrive in the east with a display of power.

Drenan split his time between hiding in their father's cabin and pacing the quarterdeck while Devin worked. "How is it that I'm the one doing all the work?" he said when Drenan came near. He knew why—Drenan, a regent, wouldn't deign to do it himself. But, annoyed, he'd asked anyway.

"Why is this taking so long?" Drenan replied. "Tell me again why we need to carry all those rocks."

"Because there isn't any cargo."

"So…"

"For as much time as you've spent at sea, you're rather obtuse, you know."

Drenan sneered.

"It's ballast stone, Drenan, not rock," Devin said impatiently. "We need it if we want to have any hope of keeping the ship upright through the cyclones."

"Well, it's taking forever."

"You could help."

"And where's our crew?"

"We're it," Devin said.

Drenan's sneer changed to a look of surprise. "You can't be serious."

"Nobody's willing to sail with us."

"You weren't supposed to give them a choice."

"So, die here or die at sea? Those were the options I was to give them?"

Drenan scowled.

"You know, Drenan, if you're in such a rush you could help a little."

"Such menial tasks are beneath us."

"You mean beneath *you*," Devin said. "I've been working all day loading these stones and trying to find a crew willing to sail to certain death." Devin tamped down his annoyance with Drenan. His brother's ruthless nature had annoyed him for a long time—personally, he preferred to rule in such a manner that his subjects adored him rather than feared him—and he never really enjoyed being around Drenan. He just needed to put up with him long enough to put Thena on the throne and get Karina back. "Like it or not, Drenan, it's just going to be the two of us. And given your *expertise* in sailing, you're going to have to do exactly what I say."

Drenan glared at him.

"What? You thought you were going to be able to hide in Father's quarters pretending to be in charge while others risked their lives to get you across the sea? No. You're going to be standing right here beside me the entire way."

"Doing what?"

"Helping me keep this ship from being torn apart."

A glimpse of fear showed in Drenan's eyes. But only a glimpse.

* * *

They set sail the next morning at dawn. Waves crashed against the protective rock breakers, sending water cascading high into the air. Backlit by the rising sun, it looked like fire climbing into the sky. The fire transformed back into water as it fell on the rocks. The ease with which the *Soaring Dragon* glided across the still water would shortly end, Devin knew.

From a distance, the breaker looked like one continuous, uninterrupted wall, but as they drew closer, its slight curve became visible. Devin turned the helm so they sailed left of the curve.

Another wave crashed against the rocks.

Devin glanced over at Drenan, who stood next to him with his arms clasped behind his back. "You look like Father."

"What are you talking about?"

"The way you're standing there with your hands behind you."

Drenan dropped his hands to his sides, then fidgeted like he didn't know what to do with them.

"Are you ready for this?" Devin said.

Drenan looked over at him. "We don't have a choice."

"Once we pass the breakers we'll have to work without rest until we arrive in the east." He glanced over at his brother again. "Let me show you how I—"

"I already know how," Drenan said.

"Do you now?" He couldn't remember Drenan ever helping him sail a storm. Javen probably knew more than he did.

"I've watched you enough to know."

"Even if you have, you need to practice."

Drenan rolled his eyes.

"Now's not the time to be proud, Drenan. If we're going to survive this, I'm going to need your help. More importantly, I'm going to need you to know what you're doing."

Drenan rolled his eyes again, but eventually said, "Fine."

"Slip on your Glasses. It'll be easier for you to see what I'm doing than having me explain it."

"I said I know how to do it."

"Still, it's easier to see what you're doing if you can see your threads." Devin stepped back from the helm and gestured for Drenan to replace him. He pointed to the gap in the breakers and said, "Guide us through there."

Waves continued to crash over the rocks as they approached the breakers. Ships seldom ventured past them. The risk of immediately capsizing was too high. Passing through the breakers forced you to enter the sea parallel to the swells. If your timing was wrong and the ship didn't get turned into the swell fast enough, that was the end.

Drenan steered the ship into the gap, which was wide enough for two ships to pass. Devin wondered if it had ever happened. The breakers hadn't even existed until the seas became too turbulent to navigate, so he didn't imagine many ships had sailed beyond them.

The channel was about a hundred paces long. Another wave crashed against the sea-side rocks. The next swell loomed after the spray settled. It hit the breakers just before the *Soaring Dragon* reached the opening and continued past the end of the opening at about eye level, which meant it was about five paces tall.

"Draego's Fire," Devin said. He seriously doubted whether he could battle swells like that all the way across the East Sea. And it wouldn't be *just* the swells. They would eventually have to pass through the cyclones. As the ship passed the end of the breaker, he said, "Swing it left."

Drenan spun the helm, making the ship lean into the turn. Devin gripped the railing as spray crashed over the side of the ship. Out of the corner of his eye, he saw Drenan slip on the wood, but the muscles in his scarless forearms flexed and he held his grip on the helm. When the ship faced the next swell, Drenan spun the helm in the opposite direction, straightening the ship.

The sails lulled. The strong onshore breeze now blew straight at them.

"You need to—"

"I know, I know," Drenan said.

Devin slipped on his Glasses, turning the water and ship gray. He watched as the sun's colorful streams of Energy bent toward Drenan. Then Energy burst forth from Drenan and he began diverting the air that pushed against them, sending it around the ship. With a river of Energy, he pushed it forward, back into the sails. His hand was not as adept as Devin's, but the sails filled with air nonetheless and the ship lurched forward just as the swell arrived. The *Soaring Dragon* pitched upward. Devin looked up at a wall of water, and in moments the ship leveled.

His eyes widened at the lineup of swells, one after another for as far as he could see. A sense of foreboding filled him— even worse than when he'd heard the roar of the dragon over Onta. "Draego's Fire," he said again.

This was definitely worse than anything he'd ever seen in the gap.

The ship pitched forward, leaving Devin looking down at the water below. A blessed few seconds passed before the next swell hit and the ship pitched up again.

"Is it going to be like this the whole way?" Drenan said.

Devin looked over at him. Drenan was looking ahead in what looked like deep concentration. "No," he said. "It'll be much worse when we encounter our first storm. In fact," he said, realizing it was going to take continuous Synthesizing to keep the ship moving forward, "why don't you go down and get some rest."

"How am I supposed to rest when the ship keeps pitching like this?"

"I don't know, but navigating the storms is going to require our combined efforts."

"I'm not a novice, Devin. I can manage Synthesizing without needing to rest."

"When was the last time you Synthesized continuously for days on end?"

"Are you saying I'm lazy?"

"No, but I know it's been centuries since the last time I had to Synthesize for that long. We aren't in the shape we once were, brother. Now, go down and get some rest."

Drenan glared at him, but finally relinquished control of the helm to Devin. As he stepped toward the stairs the ship pitched, causing him to stumble. He reached out for the railing to catch himself, then walked more carefully, hand on the railing, to the stairs.

When Drenan was gone, Devin turned his thoughts back to the next approaching swell. The next several days, or week, or however long it was going to take to cross the East Sea—if they somehow managed—were going to be long.

Over the next few hours, he settled into the routine. He was a skilled sailor, and his task was simple: Keep the *Soaring Dragon* moving forward. As long as they kept their forward momentum, the swells posed no real threat. The storms would be another matter, however. But in the meantime, he thought about the only thing that drove him forward: Karina.

* * *

When Drenan came and relieved Devin, he went below deck with a little more confidence in Drenan's ability to sail. He settled into the bed in his father's cabin, which they had stuffed with fresh feathers. He quickly realized that Drenan had been right: resting with the ship constantly pitching up and down was going to be difficult. In fact, during his first attempt, he didn't fall asleep. Despite the time he'd spent at sea, the motion was more than he was used to. It wasn't until his third attempt that he was finally exhausted enough to fall asleep.

The next couple of days passed without issue. They alternated manning the helm, keeping the ship moving steadily forward from one swell to the next, and sleeping. But Devin woke abruptly the morning of the fourth day when the ship lurched sharply enough to roll him off the bed.

The water's changing.

He scrambled as best he could out of the cabin and up the stairs to the main deck as the ship lurched and rolled. He stepped onto the deck just as a wave broke over the bow. The water crashed onto the wooden deck and drenched him. The sun was up but the sky was dark. The wind was blowing much harder than when he had gone below, and the sails were luffing.

Devin waited until the water drained off the sides of the ship before heading for the stairs leading up to the quarterdeck. He joined Drenan, who gladly ceded the helm to him. Devin quickly surveyed the situation. Instead of a steady stream of swells all moving in the same direction, the water was now an erratic array of waves rising and falling around them at random.

Presently they were in a trough, surrounded by white-capped waves. Devin took command of the wind, which was hitting the ship at an angle, and directed it into the sails. A wave was approaching from the side, so he turned the helm to point the ship directly at it. When the wave arrived, the ship pitched up. He gripped the helm tightly; out of the corner of his eye, he saw Drenan holding the rail.

The ship crested the wave, then pitched violently down.

Devin found himself looking down at a valley of water. He'd been in more storms than he cared to remember, but he had never seen waves this big. A pang of fear surged into him, making him consider the wisdom of what they were doing.

The ship slid into the trough on the back side of the wave, sending a wall of water over the bow and onto the main deck. Devin watched the water as it ran overboard, then looked for the next threat. It wasn't far away.

Remembering what Erigin had told them about following the storms, Devin assessed the direction of the wind. As it was, the wind was blowing from the aft-left quarter of the ship; if they kept moving in that same direction, they would sail toward the center of the oncoming storm. But he also had to keep the ship pointed directly into any wave that approached them so they wouldn't capsize.

Devin guided the ship up the next wave when it arrived, then, when they crested it and started down the back side, he turned the helm to the right, causing the ship to descend the wave at an angle. He got a little zealous in his maneuver, and when they got to the bottom the ship was leaning so far to the starboard side that the railings almost went into the water. He kept the helm steady, though, and guided the ship through the next trough at an angle with the wind that would take them farther from the center of the storm.

When the next wave arrived, Devin turned the ship to face it head on, then turned back to the right in the trough. He repeated this process for the next several hours—hours which would have been mind-numbingly fatiguing were it not for the constant flow of Energy through his Core. The intensity of the waves gradually lessened, until they were back to the swells they'd been just outside the breakers.

He took this period of relative calm to check the status of the helm. The entire thing was made from dragon bone, for storing Energy to be used at night. Thus far in their journey he'd been using Energy directly from the sun, but he'd have to keep the ship sailing in the right direction after the sun set. Thankfully the bones were completely charged.

"How are the bones in the railing?" he asked Drenan.

"They're charged," Drenan said. "Is it going to be like that all the way across?"

"Worse, I imagine."

"How could it possibly be worse?"

"Well, based on the strength of that wind, I'd guess that we just clipped the edge of a storm. The closer we get to the center of one of them, the stronger the wind'll be."

Drenan shook his head. "This is ridiculous."

"Don't forget that this was *your* idea."

CHAPTER 9

Javen looked helplessly at the row of scars across Hadie's throat. Tears poured from her eyes. The moment the sun crested the horizon, Drenan opened Hadie's throat anew. The invisible bonds holding him on the couch evaporated, allowing him to move. He scrambled to his feet and yelled at the sun.

"I'm really growing bored with this, you know," Drenan said callously.

Javen didn't even bother trying to plead with him; Drenan had refused time and time again. Instead he pleaded with the sun until he inevitably fell to his knees.

"Curious," Drenan said "My father's formula has never failed me before."

Fear. Anger. Desperation. The words echoed through Javen's head with every pulse of blood spurting from Hadie's throat, repeating over and over.

"Perhaps," Drenan said, walking back toward Hadie while he idly tapped the bloody knife, "I should just let her die."

"No!" Javen screamed. "P-please… I-I-I—"

"You *what?*"

"I… I love her."

"Then *heal* her, *get,*" Drenan sneered. Spittle flew from his mouth.

Javen stood and again pleaded with the sun. He tried to draw its Energy in, but he couldn't. And as Hadie's bloody hands once again slipped from her throat, her wound knitted itself back together.

Hadie gasped for breath, startling Javen awake. He sat up in the saddle, trying to orient himself.

"Another dream?" Jax said. Against his many protestations, Yolken had sent Jax and Tabora to accompany Javen as emissaries to meet with Hadie.

Javen nodded. "I must have dozed off."

"The warmth of the sun and the lull of the horse'll do that to ya."

Javen was about to ask where they were but stopped short when they crested a hill and a valley came into view. Beyond a steady stream of southerners fleeing their homes on the road ahead, smoke rose from dozens of chimneys in the small town. An oak tree towered over the buildings making up the town square. Lonely Oak. There were dozens more encampments surrounding the town than there had been when he'd left.

For the first time since being taken prisoner, he saw his home. He'd never been gone so long before. It seemed like an eternity ago. He had grown up watching soldiers ride into town on their horses, men and beasts both clad in their curious-looking armor. The rare appearance of Dalia, the regent of the Croff province, had been cause for celebration in the small town. He had fond memories of watching caravans pass through, carrying regents and chancellors from faraway places. It was one of those very occurrences that had completely upended their lives, sending Yolken fleeing with Jax while the Regency had taken him captive. His entire life had changed since the fateful night of the festival honoring the Chancellor of the Southern Realm. He wondered if Lonely Oak really was his home anymore.

That night somehow felt like a distant memory, yet at the

same time remained as vivid as if it had happened yesterday. The anticipation of finally putting aside his flirtatious nature and letting Kaylan know how he felt. Scouring the square for her, but being unable to find her amid the crowd of people celebrating the presence of the chancellor. Nearly brushing off the captivating brunette sitting on the fence. Dancing. Food. Seeing the revered chancellor in his gleaming orange armor. More dancing. Yolken sitting under the oak tree with Kaylan. Hadie's warm embrace and soft lips. Drenan. Selena's body slamming into the hearth.

The memories were both good and bad, warm and painful.

As their horses continued down the dusty road in the cool fall air, Javen wondered if the locals would look at him as he rode into town with the same awe he used to feel when the Blessed visited. None of them wore the tell-tale sign of the Blessed—armor made from the mysterious scales that he'd always thought resembled fish scales—because Yolken had banned their continued use, but Javen and Tabora wore finely made yet comfortable riding clothes, befitting representatives of the new ruler of Dradonia. Jax had insisted on wearing his tattered leather coat.

"You know Yolken would freak out if he knew you still had that," he'd said.

"Consider it my not-so-silent protest at being sent away," Jax had replied.

Javen knew Jax hadn't wanted to come; he had wanted to stay by Yolken's side to protect him from Enif's manipulations, but Yolken sent him anyway. He'd reassured Jax that he had Deanna there to help him, but that hadn't stopped Jax from pouting.

Javen knew it wasn't just that. Jax wanted to be where Yolken was because he thought that was more important. Yolken was supposed to somehow restore balance to the sun, though he had no clue how he was supposed to do that, and Jax wanted to be there to help him figure it out. Or maybe just to be there *when* he figured it out, instead of being sent away on what he considered a meaningless errand.

Eventually Jax got over it, and warmed to one of the reasons Yolken had wanted him to accompany Javen. Javen had always remembered, and looked forward to, the stories Jax, in his role as Kaylan's uncle, told around the tavern hearth. His visits had always motivated Javen to be on his best behavior—Aunt Selena never had to remind him twice to do his chores whenever Uncle Jorgan was visiting. He'd missed getting to stay up late and listen to his stories one time, and that had been enough for him to learn. Most of the time Jorgan showed up unannounced, but on occasion Selena knew he was coming ahead of time and she never refrained from using it to keep Javen motivated.

Jax was a natural storyteller. It was, in large part, why they always enjoyed listening to his stories. Regardless of how mundane the topic might have been, he had a way of drawing people in and making them feel as though they were a part of the story. So when Jax started telling Javen stories about his mother and father, the time they spent on the road began to fly.

And now he was home.

Familiarity began returning after they passed Edis, one of Lonely Oak's two neighboring towns—or cities, as Hadie had once insisted. He remembered going there a couple of times as a lad. Returning to Edis was the first time he'd felt he was where he belonged. He remembered being excited about leaving Lonely Oak when Dorlan offered to train him in Synthesis, but the longer he was away, the more he realized he'd missed it.

Now, the sight of the small but growing town overwhelmed him with joy.

"Well, I haven't been here since—" Tabora started.

"Since the day I sent Orwyn to his death," Jax finished.

Javen looked over at Jax. Until Jax had opened up about what had happened to his parents, Javen hadn't realized Jax blamed himself for his father's death.

"Don't start with that again," Tabora said. "We all knew the risks and shared the responsibility."

"But I—"

"Yes, yes. You brought the bone and you should have charged it. And we should have respected Orwyn's decision and left him alone."

"But if I'd—"

"Let it go, Jax," Tabora said.

Jax furrowed his brow and looked away. He dug his pipe and tobacco box out of his coat and shortly had it lit, using nothing visible to light it.

Javen was still amazed at the things he'd learned—and continued to learn—they could do with their gift. It was a shame that their abilities were now severely curtailed due to Yolken's edict about dragon bones. He was surprised at how vulnerable he felt at night or indoors now. Yolken was the only one not hampered by the edict, and maybe that was by design. Javen still couldn't understand how Yolken had that ability. The idea that the Great Dragon had selected Yolken to be Blessed of the Dragon was still hard to believe, especially since neither of them had been particularly pious growing up. He couldn't help but wonder if it was really true, but Yolken's demonstrated ability proved that, at the very least, he was indeed different from other Synthesizers.

Javen tried his best to not be jealous, but he couldn't help it. His whole life had been spent in Yolken's shadow. And then to stand in the throne room and hear his brother speak to the emperor—looking back on it, it was almost comical. Of *course* it would be Yolken and not him. It hadn't taken him long to come to terms with it—he didn't want that responsibility anyway. He'd spent so much time over the years resenting Yolken, especially over the last several months after he'd been taken from Lonely Oak. He was just glad things had ended up the way they did.

Before long, Norin's Goods came into view. They'd passed three wagons bearing his insignia between Croff and Lonely Oak. Two wagons with horses attached were parked in front, and several more along the side. Norin's had been a big part of his routine at the tavern—he went regularly to order and pick up supplies. He used to hate pick-up days because it always took him so much longer to get his daily errands done.

Seeing Norin's made the lurking familiarity Javen had felt when he'd first met Norin the servant in Reago's Train return. With everything that had been happening, he hadn't thought about the man recently. But now that he was back in Lonely Oak, that feeling was back. Who was he? He'd told Javen that love couldn't be forced. And he was right. No matter how hard he tried, he couldn't make Kaylan love him. Later, as they were getting off the Train in Kyinth, Norin had told him to never forget who he was. Both times he had spoken to Javen, he'd told Javen exactly what he'd needed to hear. The question was, why? How would a mere servant know who he was? Why would he speak to him so familiarly?

Then there was what had happened in the throne room. Most of the details were blurry. He remembered hesitating once chaos broke out. He remembered Norin's words echoing in his mind. He remembered choosing family over power. He remembered the pain. And then after, he remembered people talking about the bearded man who had jumped from the balcony and disrupted the fight.

He'd never spoken to anyone about Norin or what he'd said, but upon hearing descriptions of the man, he knew it was Norin. He'd seen him in the throne room, in fact, up on the balcony, and knew then that Norin wasn't a mere servant.

The orange and red leaves of the oak tree in the center of town were visible over the roofs of the buildings lining the town square. Their beauty made Javen lose his train of thought. He focused on the tree as they carefully led their horses around other pedestrians and those leading horse-drawn wagons. They kept left of the tree when they entered the square, passing by the Oak, the largest inn in town. In the fenced-off grassy area around the tree, children rolled around in the leaves littering the ground and swung from the tree's lower branches. Javen pulled back on the reins, stopping his horse.

"Javen," Jax said through clenched teeth when Javen slid out of the saddle.

Javen handed the reins to Jax, otherwise ignoring him, and walked into the sweet shop he'd solicited almost daily. Ignoring the blank stare of the owner, he purchased a handful of sweets in a small brown bag. Leaving the store, he walked right past Jax and Tabora, who were looking at him with great annoyance, and stopped at the fence. His eyes were fixed on a particular little girl wearing a worn brown coat, her hair in two braids. She was playing in the leaves with the other children.

Javen hopped the fence and waited. One by one the children stopped playing and looked up at him. He fell to his knees when Issa looked up. It took a moment for Issa's eyes to brighten in recognition, but then she ran to him, crashing into his embrace.

"Javen!" Issa sobbed.

Javen squeezed his eyes closed, feeling the warm tears stream down his cheeks. The overwhelming joy he'd felt when he had watched Dorlan heal Issa's legs returned to him.

Issa pushed back from the hug and said, "Where'd you go?"

"I had to go away for a while."

"But you're back!" Issa embraced him with another hug.

Javen hugged her a while longer, then gently pushed her back. "I'm afraid I'm only passing through."

Issa looked at him, tears in her eyes. "I miss you."

"I miss you, too, my little lily." He stood up and handed Issa the brown bag. "I got this for you."

Issa snatched the bag, pulled a piece of candy out, and promptly shoved it into her mouth. "Will you be back?" she said in a garbled voice.

"One day," Javen said.

"When?"

"I don't know for sure. But I promise I'll return and buy you as much candy as you like, all right?"

Issa nodded.

Javen bent over and kissed her on the top of the head, then hopped back over the fence.

Jax pulled his pipe out of his mouth when Javen was back in his saddle and said, "What was that all about?"

"I used to buy candy for Issa almost every day," Javen said.

"*That* was Issa?"

Javen nodded.

"Huh."

"What?"

"I just… she was the catalyst that set everything that's happened in motion. I never knew who she was, is all." Jax chewed on his pipe for a moment, then, pulling it back out of his mouth, he said, "I wonder if she has any idea what her fall out of that tree brought about."

"I don't think so."

They exited the square and continued toward the tavern—his home—but then the Haven came into view.

Astora.

Tears filled his eyes. He didn't like thinking about Astora because the memory was very painful—she haunted his dreams just as much as Hadie did. But as painful as it was to think about her, he refused to forget what happened to her. He couldn't. And now he realized that her parents probably didn't know what had happened to her.

"We have to stop," he said.

"What?" Jax said. "Why?" They'd agreed to stop at the tavern—Javen didn't know when he'd get the chance to see his home again—but they'd also agreed not to stay the night. Jax and Tabora wanted to avoid mingling with the locals too much.

"Because Astora's parents don't know what happened to her."

"Who's Astora?" Tabora said.

"The lad's right," Jax said. "We need to stop."

Tabora nodded assent. "But who is she?"

"A lass Drenan used to goad Javen into Synthesizing."

"Oh… right."

Javen's stomach roiled. He did *not* want to face Astora's father. He hadn't even wanted to face him the morning after he'd bedded her in the hayloft, let alone about this. His mind became so wrapped around what he was going to say, he hardly noticed the faces of those who stopped and looked. He felt like he was going to vomit.

"If you're going to be an effective ruler," Jax said, "you're going to have to get used to it."

Javen looked over at him apprehensively. "Get used to what?"

"It's impossible to rule without being responsible for the inevitable shedding of innocent blood."

"It wasn't my fault."

"I understand. But it happens. I feel guilty every day for what happened to your parents. All I'm saying is that if you're going to be the Regent of Onta, it's gonna happen."

Javen didn't like the thought of that. He knew Jax was telling the truth, though. As Regent of Onta, he was responsible for the whole province of Onta. "That was the way the Regency operated under Drakonias," he said. "Maybe it'll be different with Yolken ruling."

"Undoubtedly. His heart's certainly in the right place. But even Draeko had to make tough decisions that cost lives. Granted, things were better than they were in the Previous Era, but they weren't perfect. And they won't be with Yolken ruling. So you need to get used to it."

"How?"

"That, I don't know," Jax said.

Javen pulled on the reins, bringing his horse to a stop. The others stopped with him. The Haven stood before him. Javen slid out of the saddle and hitched his horse to a post.

"You want us to come in with you?" Tabora said.

"Sure," Javen said. He could use the additional support. The memory of Astora's blood spurting from the gash in her neck was vivid in his mind. He took a deep breath, fighting back the desire to vomit.

"You go in with him, Tabora," Jax said.

"Where are you going?" Javen said.

Jax turned his horse around and said, "I imagine you're going to want an ale when you're done, no?"

"I hadn't thought—"

"Trust me, lad. I'll meet you at the tavern."

Javen nodded and Jax urged his horse into a trot. Javen took another deep breath and opened the door to the Haven.

CHAPTER 10

The hooves of Jax's horse clomped over the wooden bridge spanning the Little Mindon. This late in the year it ran almost dry. The poor snowpack of the previous winter was definitely taking its toll on the valley. The farmers of the valley relied on the waters of the Little Mindon; if this winter was a repeat of the last one, Jax figured they would be in trouble.

On the other side of the bridge, he dismounted and walked the horse to the front door of the tavern. He gave it a tug but wasn't surprised to find it locked. He led the horse by the reins around to the back, down the cart path between the creek and the stone annex. The back door was locked as well. He tied the horse to a post by the shed and tested the shed door. It was unlocked. He cracked the door open and went inside. Giving the brewing implements a once-over, he determined the shed had likely remained undisturbed for some time. Satisfied, he went back outside.

Jax rubbed the horse's nose as he drew some Energy from the sun into his Core. He stepped closer to the door and reached under it with a strand of Energy. Bending it upwards, he felt for a bolt. When he found one, he slid it back, then felt for another. After locating all three, he opened the door.

He stepped inside, keeping a pool of Energy in his Core, even though he still had the small bones in his coat. He shut the door, revealing another door hidden behind it. He opened that one and cautiously descended the steps leading to the cellar. Thankfully, he found it empty save for seven barrels sitting on a rack. Jax went back up to the kitchen and peered through the window dividing the kitchen from the tavern. The tables were neatly arranged, the chairs upside down on top of them.

He didn't see anyone through the window, so he pushed the swinging door open and entered the tavern. He inspected it more closely, first behind the bar, then around and under all the tables. He wiped sweat from his brow and went upstairs, where he checked each room. Finally, satisfied that no one was in the tavern, he touched a wall and dispelled the Energy from his Core. It wasn't enough Energy to leave any sort of mark.

He went back downstairs and walked around the back side of the bar. He picked up a mug and filled it with the bitter ale. After taking a long drink, he refilled the mug and looked around the tavern. It was a room full of memories. In the first iteration of the tavern, he'd argued with Orwyn in this room more than once. The first and last stood out.

Their first argument had come not long after Orwyn finished building the tavern. He'd wanted—*begged*—Jax to help him build it, but Jax refused. He couldn't accept that Orwyn was just giving up on everything he'd worked his entire life for. He'd refused to visit at first, but gave in when he found out Orwyn and Elen had had their first child. Their reunion went well—he was joyful in their happiness—but when Elen went upstairs to put the baby to bed the conversation had soon turned toward the inevitable. Although happy for them, Jax refused to accept Orwyn's retirement. The conversation degenerated quickly, and he ended up leaving in a fit of anger.

Their last argument had been the night Orwyn died. Jax had come to warn Orwyn that the Black Sodality was coming for him, but instead of heeding Jax's warning and fleeing, Orwyn had convinced Jax to stay and fight. But then he'd changed his mind again and insisted Jax leave. He'd objected, but eventually agreed. And Orwyn died as a result.

Jax didn't know if he could have prevented Orwyn's death—the Sodality was there in great force—but he would rather have died with his friend than leave him to die alone.

Of course, he had plenty of good memories as well. There were countless nights when he'd told Yolken, Javen, and Kaylan stories around the hearth. When they went to bed, he'd help Selena close the tavern; then it was just the two of them. They weren't romantic anymore, but there had been a handful of times their passions overcame the logical decision they'd made.

But he wasn't here to reminisce. He had come to tidy up so Javen's inevitable visit wouldn't be only about remembering what happened the day Selena died. He doubted Javen would have another opportunity to return any time soon, so Jax wanted his memory of the tavern to be as pleasant as possible.

Someone else, however, had already cleaned up after Drenan's disastrous visit.

Both doors were bolted shut and there were no lower-level windows for anyone to enter and exit through. He set his mug of ale down and went back upstairs to check the windows on the second level, but they were all locked from the inside.

Jax went back downstairs, into the kitchen, and down to the cellar again. According to Deborah, she'd found Selena at the bottom of the stairs lying in a pool of blood, as if she had stumbled and fallen to her death. But there was no blood.

He returned to the tavern again and retrieved his mug. He took a drink, looking across the bar at the table where Javen said Drenan had made him sit. Drenan had poured him a mug of ale, Javen said, but he'd left it untouched on the table. There was no mug. All the mugs were clean and neatly stacked in their proper place.

The only explanation was that someone who could Synthesize had been here and cleaned the place up. But who? And why? Deborah said she'd attended to Selena's body but hadn't cleaned the tavern. And she hadn't remembered if she'd locked the kitchen door on her way out.

He looked around the tavern for anything out of the ordinary. He checked in the kitchen as well. Surely, whoever had come here and taken the time to clean up after Drenan would have left some sort of a clue as to who they were.

Was it the Regency? The Sodality was meticulous and worked diligently to avoid leaving any evidence of their presence, but what happened here that night wasn't the Sodality. There had been no time to run anything through the Synod—the Regency had been responding to an immediate threat. Jax was certain that, after Drenan left with Javen, someone from the Regency—likely Dalia or one of her minions—had come to Lonely Oak and assured the residents that the Thornhills had been rebels in hiding and what happened to them was just and deserved. But if that was the case, why would they then clean up the tavern to make it look as though nothing happened?

It didn't make any sense.

Not finding anything in the kitchen, Jax went back into the tavern to refill his mug. He probably shouldn't be drinking this much, but it had been a long time since he'd had any of Yolken's ale.

Could it have been Relan? But he couldn't think of a way Relan could get in and out of the tavern with the doors and windows locked.

Jax filled his mug anew and turned around. A stick leaning against the hearth caught his eye. He furrowed his brow, wondering why he hadn't noticed it before. He crossed the room, weaving around the tables, and stopped in front of the hearth. It was one of Yolken's brewing paddles.

Jax hesitated, wondering how it got there, then reached out and picked it up. He turned it over and over, inspecting it. He looked over his shoulder, half-expecting to see someone in the room behind him, but then looked at the paddle again and almost dropped it. There was something carved along its edge.

Jax brought the paddle closer to his face and read, "*Weren't there two of these?*"

"Draego's Fire," he said.

CHAPTER 11

When he stepped into the Haven, Javen realized he had never been inside the inn before. How was that possible? He'd lived his entire life in Lonely Oak. Kena was kept in the stable around the back, but the stable hands handled the day-to-day operation of the stable, so keeping her there had never required him to go inside. And he certainly didn't come through the front door when he wanted to roll around in the hay with Astora. He met her either in the hay loft—which, for a coin or two, the stable hands never mentioned—or somewhere else.

The common room wasn't very busy. Only a couple of tables were occupied. Everyone turned and looked at Javen and Tabora when the bell over the door rang. Unlike his brother, being the center of attention didn't bother him, but when the heads of the few patrons in the room and the woman wearing the apron simultaneously turned toward them, he suddenly felt self-conscious. His attire told everyone in the room who he was, or at least what his status was.

The woman wearing the apron rushed over to him and bowed, saying, "Your Majesty, how might I be of service?"

At first Javen didn't know what to say. The woman was Astora's mother, but she didn't recognize him.

"*Javen?*" came a younger voice from off to the side.

Javen looked over at Astora's younger sister, Aubryn. She was only a few years younger than Astora. She'd flirted with him a couple of times, but he made it a rule to not to dally with sisters.

"*Javen?*" Astora's mother repeated, confusion evident in her voice. She recognized him now. "You're a... a regent? How? What? Your aunt—"

Javen nodded and said, "Can I have a word with you, Missus Freyalsn? You and Mr. Freyalsn?"

Missus Freyalsn looked questioningly at Javen—well, at his clothes—then said, "Sure. Sure. What's this about? I mean... I'll go get him. Uh... Your Majesty."

She turned to walk away but Javen stopped her. "Missus Freyalsn?"

"Yes?"

"I'd like to speak with the two of you in private."

"Sure. Sure." She gave quick, nervous nods of her head. "Come with me."

"I'll wait here," Tabora said.

Javen nodded and followed Astora's mother to the back of the inn, through a swinging door and into the kitchen. He realized what she must be thinking. Whereas visits from the Regency weren't entirely uncommon in Lonely Oak, having one come into your home or place of work and ask after you personally was. The Regency, although worshiped by many as the Blessed of the Dragon, had a reputation for being swift and brutal toward those they suspected of rebellion or any other form of malfeasance toward the Blessed. His visit wasn't supposed to be about fear. He shouldn't have come wearing a regent's attire.

"Hani, Terra," Missus Freyalsn said with a quaver in her voice. Two more of their daughters looked up, one from the sink and the other from the stove. "His Majesty needs a word in private." Hani and Terra, ages twelve and fifteen, looked blankly at Javen. They knew who he was. Seeing him in the suit he was wearing was an obvious shock to them. "Now!" their mother said tersely. Both girls stopped what they were doing and hurried through the swinging door into the common room. When the door closed behind them, Missus Freyalsn turned to Javen and said, "I'll get Branold."

Javen waited as Missus Freyalsn exited through the back door, which he knew led to a small alley between the inn and the stable. He'd never been on this side of the door before, but he'd waited numerous times in the alley while Astora snuck into the kitchen in search of a snack they could take up to the hayloft.

As he stood alone in the kitchen waiting, he realized he had no idea what he was going to tell Astora's parents. How much did they—or anyone in Lonely Oak—know about what had happened that day? He'd worked diligently to ensure Branold never learned he was bedding his daughter in his hayloft, but he worried Branold might have found out the morning of the festival—at least that's what Norin had told him. He never had confirmed it, since he'd avoided Astora for the rest of the day. Should he confess? Or did he only tell Astora's parents what happened to her? His stomach was not happy.

The back door opened and Astora's father entered. Astora was at his side. Blood pulsed from the gaping wound in her throat. Her shirt was drenched in it.

Javen fell to his knees and vomited.

He felt a comforting hand on his shoulder.

"Leave him, Anna," Branold said. "He's lucky bile's the only taste in his mouth right now."

"Dear," Anna said over Javen's shoulder, "I know you think he ran off with her, but now you know that isn't true."

"And why in Draego's Fire not?"

"Because if it was then she'd be here right now, with him."

"That doesn't mean he doesn't know what happened to her."

Javen stood up and accepted the towel Anna offered him. He looked over at Branold, who still stood by the door. Astora was gone. He wiped his mouth, then said, "I didn't run off with Astora, but I do know what happened to her." He wished for a glass of water, but somehow the taste of bile felt appropriate for what he was about to say.

Astora's parents looked at him expectantly. There was no tempering what he needed to say so he just said it, before he lost what little resolve he possessed. "The Regent of Hantlo murdered her."

Anna gasped and covered her mouth with both hands.

"The Regent of *Hantlo*?" Branold said.

Both of them stared at him with disbelief.

"It's a long story," Javen said. He gestured to a table against the wall and said, "I'm willing to tell you everything if you want."

Anna wiped tears from her eyes with a sleeve and Branold nodded.

Javen waited until they sat at the table, then sat with them. He started by telling them what had happened the day the Chancellor of the Southern Realm visited Lonely Oak, beginning when he'd come down from breakfast. He skipped the part where he left the hayloft at sunrise and snuck back into his room at the tavern.

"You watched him murder your aunt?" Anna said when Javen got to the confrontation between Drenan and his Aunt Selena.

Javen nodded. "At the time, I was in shock and didn't know what to believe. I mean, we were all taught the same thing as everyone else: that the Blessed were the chosen rulers of Dradonia. I knew rebels existed—at least I heard old Relan talk about them enough. But I never suspected my aunt could be one. But I witnessed her use some mysterious power to fight back against Drenan. I didn't know what to think. And then Drenan killed her and took me prisoner."

He wasn't able to convey his story with the same skill Jax showed when recounting events. But he did his best.

"What does any of this have to do with our daughter?"

Branold said.

"I didn't run off with Astora. But when I was on my way to Dorlan's carriage for my lesson I ran into her…"

"She was in the caravan?" Branold said. "Why?"

"At first I didn't know. But when I saw her, she was upset. I asked—"

"Out with it already," Branold said impatiently.

"All she told me was that she'd been 'cast off.' I didn't know what that meant, so I asked the teamsters."

Anna placed a hand on Javen's and said, "And?"

"They told me it was common for the Blessed to take a local girl to…" Javen couldn't bring himself to say it.

"To what?" Anna said.

"To warm their beds," Branold said gruffly.

"Oh…" Anna's hand left Javen's and rose to cover her mouth.

"But then he grew tired of her and got rid of her," Javen said. "I thought maybe she could find some merchants or someone to help her get back to Lonely Oak, but the teamsters I was traveling with said that would be too dangerous for her. I searched the camp for her—I was going to offer to let her stay with me in my carriage until we could find a way to get her home."

"How chivalrous of you," Branold said.

"Bran…" Anna cautioned.

"I couldn't find her, though," Javen continued. "The next day my lessons were with Drenan, the Regent of Hantlo. When I arrived at his carriage, she…" Javen stopped when Astora appeared behind her mother. She looked at him with the same pleading eyes as when her life had drained from her throat. He squeezed his eyes shut and felt the tears flow. He forced them open and stood. He stepped around Branold's chair toward Astora and said, "I'm so sorry…" He fell to his knees. "I wanted to help you, to save you, but I couldn't. I don't know how Yolken… I was supposed to do what he did, but I couldn't. I didn't know how. You have to believe me. I didn't want you to..." He reached out and tried to take her by the hand, but she disappeared.

"Javen, dear." Anna knelt beside him and took both of his hands into hers. "What happened?"

"He tried forcing me to use my gift. He... he... he was a monster!"

"Javen, please."

"He cut her throat and told me to heal her." Anna covered her mouth again. "I wanted to... just like Yolken healed Issa... but I couldn't." Anna put an arm around his shoulder. "I don't know why, but I couldn't." He looked into Anna's eyes, Astora's eyes, and said, "I watched her die. I tried to stop the bleeding, but I couldn't. Her blood... it was... he wouldn't... He just stood there, taunting me, telling me to heal her. I'm so sorry. You have to believe me. I didn't want her to... I wanted to heal her, to send her back home where she was safe."

"I believe you, Javen," Anna said. She pulled him close and hugged him tight. "It's not your fault."

Javen tried holding back the tears—he was the Regent of Onta, after all—but he couldn't. The pain and self-loathing he'd kept bottled up about Astora's fate that day all came flowing out. In Anna's arms, he cried harder than he'd ever cried before.

CHAPTER 12

The whole town was in shock when we heard your brother was the new emperor," Anna said.

"I still hardly believe it myself," Javen said.

"And you? A regent? How did all this happen?"

"It's a very long story. One that I'm afraid I don't have time to tell. At least not right now."

"Yes. I imagine you have responsibilities elsewhere."

"Unfortunately," Javen said.

"Which province are you regent of, anyway?" Branold said.

"Onta," Javen said.

"Onta? Huh."

"What?"

"Probably fits, with your—"

"Branold," Anna said with a cross look.

"Yes, well," Branold said. "I suppose I'm glad to see you making something of yourself besides... you know."

"Thanks, I think," Javen said. "Look, I want to stay, more than anything, but the others are waiting for me."

"We understand," Anna said.

"On my way back north, I'll have more time to stay. I'll tell you everything then." Javen finished the tea Anna had made after he regained his composure, then pushed his chair back and stood. "Again, I can't tell you how terribly sorry I am about Astora. I truly hope you can forgive me."

"It wasn't your fault. We're just thankful that we finally know what happened."

"He's out there somewhere," Javen said, "and I promise you: Astora will receive the justice she deserves."

Anna stood and took Javen by the hand. "Thank you," she said.

"Yes," Branold said, rising, "we're indebted to you."

"No. It's me who's indebted to you." Javen turned to leave. Before returning to the common room, he asked, "You're sure it's all right that Kena stays?"

"She may be old, but she earns her keep," Branold said.

Javen nodded. "Good. I'll see you again soon."

He made his way into the common room. Tabora set a teacup down and met him at the door.

"It's time for that ale," he said as they stepped outside.

"Jax knew you'd want to stop," Tabora said as she mounted her horse.

"I'm sorry. I didn't plan that," Javen said, settling into his own saddle, "but I needed to tell them."

"I understand," Tabora said. She urged her horse into motion. "And not just about her. Those of us who were in the Order didn't often get the chance to visit our homes. It was too dangerous, especially when we still had family that was alive."

"All of your family's gone?" Javen said.

"I was with the Order longer than was natural."

"Oh. I didn't realize the Order knew how to Regenerate."

"We didn't."

"Then how did you?"

"Your father," Tabora said. "He was the only one who knew how to do it. So his retirement put the Order in a very difficult position. We subsisted for a while, but the Order eventually decided to use you and your brother to persuade Deanna to come out of hiding. Your brother healing that little girl just forced the Order's hand a little sooner than we'd planned. I don't know what Jax might have told you," Tabora said, looking over at Javen, "but we had no choice."

"What do you mean?" Javen said.

"We were getting old. What little advantage the Order had was slowly disappearing as we got older and the Regency didn't."

"You should have been honest with him," Javen said. "Instead of sending him all the way to Kvorga under false pretenses."

"There are a lot of things the Order should have done differently."

The conversation lulled as they made their way to the tavern. Javen had only been gone for a few months, but being in Lonely Oak made him feel nostalgic. Which was odd, because he'd often dreamed of leaving Lonely Oak, to get out from under his brother's control and live life for himself. Now the sight of his former home made him pine for things to return to the way they had been before Dorlan's visit.

Jax's horse wasn't hitched in front of the tavern, so they made their way down the cart path between the annex and the creek. They found the horse tied up by Yolken's brewing shed and tied their own horses up alongside it.

"Want to do the honors?" Tabora said when they found the kitchen door locked.

"Sure." He took several backward steps so he could see the afternoon sun over the tavern, and drew some Energy into his Core. He stepped back to the door and a moment later they were carefully making their way into the kitchen.

"I'm in here!" they heard Jax shout from the tavern.

Javen pushed open the swinging door that divided the kitchen from the tavern and walked in. He looked briefly at the hearth on the far side of the room before he saw Jax, sitting at a table with a mug in hand. The room was tidied, all the chairs up on the tables except the one on which Jax sat.

"It has been entirely too long since I had any of the lad's ale," Jax said. "Just as he set to brewing some up at the cabin, Drenan's bastard flushed us out of hiding. Had I known he was alone, I might have stood our ground so Yolken could finish. Do you think he'll still have time to brew now that he's the emperor?" Jax thoughtfully rubbed his beard and said, "I suppose not."

"How many of those have you had?" Tabora said.

"You know what? I think Javen was right, we should stay here tonight."

"I never said that," Javen said.

"You didn't?" Jax took a drink. "Ah well, it's getting late."

"It's not late," Javen said.

"It's not?"

"No."

"Well, if there's one thing I've learned from all the traveling that I've done over the decades, it's that you never pass on the opportunity to sleep in a bed."

"It's not late," Tabora said.

"Well, then." Jax took another drink. He held the mug toward Javen and said, "Are you telling me you're willing to pass up the opportunity to drink as much of Yolken's ale as you want, knowing you don't have to get up with the sun to run errands for him?"

"I hadn't thought of that."

"Jax, we didn't agree to stay the night so we could drink ourselves stupid," Tabora said.

"Honestly, I think this sounds like a great idea," Javen said.

"There's nothing to eat here," Tabora said.

"We'll go out for food," Jax said.

"Yeah, there's a pub in the square I really like," Javen said.

"I suppose I could use a mug or two myself," Tabora said with a shrug. "I've never had Yolken's ale and I hear it's really good."

Javen smiled. He went behind the bar and picked up two

mugs. "What kind do you like?"

"I don't know. I'm more of a wine person, honestly."

Jax laughed.

"Mild it is," Javen said. He filled a mug and slid it across the bar to Tabora. Then he filled himself a mug of the bitter.

Tabora and Javen joined Jax at the table.

The moment they sat down Jax said, "So, who's hungry?"

* * *

When Javen woke, he rubbed his eyes and sat up, momentarily confused about where he was. When he realized he was in his own bed an odd feeling washed over him. He tried to remember whose hayloft he'd spent the night in before sneaking into his room just before dawn, but then realized he'd spent the evening reminiscing with Jax in the tavern. He fell back onto his bed and covered his eyes with an arm. His headache brought back too many memories as well. Before he knew it, he was sleeping again.

The smell of bacon pulled him from sleep a second time. For the briefest of moments, he thought he was smelling his aunt's cooking. Knowing better, he sat up and looked for his clothes in the corner where he'd tossed them hundreds of times. They weren't there. Instead, they were folded neatly over a chair. *Did I do that?* Maybe he'd matured a little since the last time he had slept in his bed.

He got dressed and went downstairs to find Jax in the kitchen. Bacon was sizzling on a skillet.

"You cook?"

"I've been known to from time to time," Jax said. "I had a great teacher, you know. Though your brother was never a fan."

"Where'd you get the supplies?"

"Went out while you were sleeping."

"Where's Tabora?" Javen said.

"Out getting other supplies," Jax said over his shoulder. He scooped eggs and bacon onto a plate and set it on the table in the middle of the kitchen. "Eat."

Javen didn't have to be told twice. He half expected a list of errands to be handed to him as he ate.

"You'll be continuing on to Hantlo without me," Jax said.

Javen looked up from his plate, nearly choking on his eggs. He swallowed and said, "*What?*"

"Something's called me away, so you'll be continuing to Hantlo with Tabora."

Javen stared at Jax, not sure what to say. Eventually he just repeated, "What?"

"What what?"

"Did you get new orders from Yolken?"

"Orders?"

"Yes. My brother specifically made you a part of this mission."

"Well, no. But—"

"But what? How can you just ignore Yolken's orders?"

"I'm not ignoring them," Jax said, "but something very important came up."

"What?"

"I can't say."

Javen furrowed his brow. "Why not?"

"Because I'm not at liberty to."

Javen let out a sigh of exasperation. "Does Tabora know?"

"Yes. And she's not pleased."

"*I'm* not pleased!" Javen shouted.

"Don't yell at me, lad," Jax said tersely.

"I'm not a lad," Javen said. "I'm the Regent of Onta. And I command you to tell me where you're going."

"You *command* me?"

"Yes."

Jax stared at Javen. Normally Javen would have looked down, but he held Jax's gaze. Even though Jax was much older than him, Javen was in a position of higher authority.

"Fine," Jax said.

"Fine, what?"

"Someone who wasn't supposed to be here was."

"What do you mean?"

"One of the reasons I came ahead of you was to look the place over before you arrived. I wanted to make sure that... you know, that things weren't as you'd left them when you were last here. Turns out someone was here."

"Who?"

"I don't know. But I'm going to find out."

"Now? Can't it wait until after we're finished in Hantlo?"

"Javen, someone who wasn't supposed to be here *was*. And I think it's important that we know who. And more importantly, why."

Javen looked intently at Jax, but finally acquiesced. "Fine. But at the first opportunity I'm sending a condor to Kyinth to tell Yolken."

Jax rolled his eyes, but said, "Agreed."

CHAPTER 13

Jax brought his horse to a stop and looked down into the ravine. With dexterous fingers, he found the black bone protruding from the frayed cuff of his coat. He listened mentally to the pulsing inside, confirming for the hundredth time that the interconnected bones woven throughout the coat were fully charged. Deep down he knew who would be waiting for him at the cabin, but he wanted to be prepared in case he was wrong.

Jax guided the horse down the trail into the ravine. The air was cool, not freezing like it should have been this time of year. Snow should be blanketing the ground by now, but each winter the effects of the changing weather were becoming more and more evident.

On the valley floor, Jax slid out of the saddle and tied the horse to a branch near the edge of the creek. Heart thumping, he then walked carefully down the trail, gripping the tiny bone firmly.

His mind raced as he made his way to the cabin. He had an excellent memory, paid great attention to detail, and he'd gone over what had happened that day more times than he could remember. *This doesn't make sense*, he thought. But who else would have even known that one of Yolken's brewing paddles was missing from the tavern, let alone known where it was?

He died.

I saw his body.

Elen's, too.

The nausea he'd felt at the smell of their burned flesh still haunted him.

And now he smelled... bread?

The cabin was located in just about as remote an area as he'd ever come across in his travels. It had originally been built as a safe house for the Order. Its location at the bottom of this ravine made it an ideal place to Synthesize—unless someone was wearing Glasses while standing on the precipice of the ravine, the bending of the Energy from Synthesizing wasn't visible. But in the end, the cabin had barely been used. He still wanted to know how Drenan's bastard found them there.

He stepped behind a bush when a corner of the cabin came into view and pulled a branch aside. The front door was open, and someone was smoking a pipe on the porch.

Who in Draego's Fire...?

It took Jax only a moment to recognize the man. The glimmer of hope he'd clung to as he ascended the mountain evaporated. He walked out from behind the bush and approached the cabin.

The man pulled the pipe from his mouth and exclaimed, "Jax!"

"What are you doing here, Relan?"

"Waiting for you, of course," Relan said.

"What? I don't... how did you know about this place? Or the paddle?"

"What paddle?"

"The paddle in the tavern," Jax said.

"I don't know anything about any—"

"Then what in Draego's Fire are you doing here?" This didn't make any sense. How did the paddle get...

"That's what I was just going to tell you."

"What?"

"I was just walking by the tavern like I done every day since Selena and the lads disappeared, wondering what happened to 'em, when the front door opened, and he walked out."

It was impossible, Jax knew, but his hope returned.

"Scared Draego's Fire out of me. I was used to seeing him when I had too much to drink, but I knew it was only the drink. Only, when he walked out the door, I hadn't had none yet."

"Relan. What are you talking about? Who did you see?"

"It's probably better if I didn't tell you."

"Why not?"

"Because you wouldn't believe me."

"Relan…"

"Better for you to see for yourself." Relan put his pipe back in his mouth and pointed off to his right. Through clenched teeth he said, "Round back, in the shed."

Jax stared at Relan, confused. As he'd made his way up to the cabin, he had thought for sure he knew who he would find there once he arrived, but when he saw Relan his hope had vanished. It was too good to be true. But now… Relan wasn't alone? He couldn't be. There was no way he could have known about this place.

Relan took the pipe out of his mouth and said, "Go."

Jax walked around the side of the cabin. The creek bubbled to his left and wind rustled the trees overhead. He smelled bread again.

He stopped at the back corner of the cabin and peered around the rough-hewn logs at the shed. The large doors were open and steam was coming out of the round metal smokestack. He saw movement inside. He watched curiously for a few minutes, rolling the bone sewn into his coat between his forefinger and thumb. If Relan was here, then whoever was in there was not here to cause him harm, so he let go of the bone. Who would lure him all the way up here and casually brew ale while he waited? His thoughts returned to his initial intuition.

But standing here, he still refused to believe it.

He's dead. I saw his corpse.

Jax stepped around the corner of the cabin and tentatively walked toward the shed. Curiously, the Harachin sword was propped against the door jamb. *What in Draego's Fire?* He stopped at the entrance and looked in. The third kettle, farthest on the right, was steaming vigorously. A bearded man was dumping a bucket of small cone-shaped green flowers into it. The man set the bucket down and picked up another. Before dumping it into the kettle he looked over at Jax and said, "Took you long enough."

Jax fell to his knees.

"Come now," the man said, "there's no need for kneeling."

"But…"

"Even if I am the lad's father, that doesn't make me the emperor. If we're going to follow that line of logic, then Deanna should be empress. No, the lad's the rightful ruler."

Jax was beside himself. He couldn't believe it. "I saw your body."

"You saw *a* body."

"*What?*" The flood of emotions Jax felt—confusion, anger, joy—prevented him from thinking clearly. The stench of burned flesh was clear in his mind. "No. I'm sure. I buried you."

The bearded man smiled. "You buried Elen—and for that I'm grateful—but the other body wasn't me."

"I don't under—"

Orwyn stepped toward Jax and offered him a hand. "Come, off the ground."

Jax accepted the hand, and Orwyn pulled him up. Orwyn retrieved the Harachin sword and walked out of the shed, past Jax. Utterly confused, Jax watched Orwyn walk toward the cabin with the sword blade propped nonchalantly on a shoulder.

Orwyn stopped and turned. "You coming?"

In complete disbelief, Jax followed Orwyn back to the cabin. Relan stood when they appeared around the corner. Jax looked up at Relan, who sported a wide grin. "*Relan* knew?" he said.

"No," Orwyn said.

"He said he saw you..."

"He's spent the better part of the last twenty years drunk," Orwyn said.

Jax pointed a finger at Relan and said, "No more ale for you."

"What? I didn't know!"

Jax shook his head and followed Orwyn through the front door. He watched as Orwyn set the sword down and retrieved three mugs. He filled them with ale from a barrel in the corner and handed one to Jax, who numbly accepted. Orwyn handed the third mug to Relan.

"I've been waiting up here for over a month, which is plenty of time to brew up a batch, in case you were wondering." Orwyn gestured toward the table and said, "Now, please sit."

Jax sat at the table, across from Relan, but set his mug down without drinking from it.

Orwyn sipped from his mug, then said, "The second body you buried wasn't mine. Obviously, it couldn't have been because here I am sitting with you."

"Who was it then?"

"One of the assassins."

Jax could hardly believe it. Every fiber of him knew he had lost his friend that night in Lonely Oak, but here he was looking at Orwyn sitting across from him, drinking ale. "I thought you were dead."

"I know," Orwyn said.

"We mourned you. Elen, too."

Orwyn nodded.

Tears itched his cheeks, but he didn't wipe them.

He'd left Lonely Oak the morning after he buried Orwyn and Elen; he didn't stick around for their funeral. He couldn't bring himself to.

"The boys... they..." Deborah had told him how hard it had been for them.

"I did what I had to, Jax," Orwyn said.

Jax wiped his eyes. For years, what happened that night in Lonely Oak had haunted him. The moment he'd learned the Synod was sending the Sodality after Orwyn, he'd raced to Lonely Oak as quickly as he could. Orwyn's decision to stay had stunned him. It was the first time the Order had advance notice of the Sodality's plans and Orwyn ignored it. Said he was tired of hiding. He'd quit the Order, started the family he'd always wanted, but for some reason he chose *that* moment to once again fight back. Jax remembered being beside himself, but he decided to stay with Orwyn, refusing to leave his friend.

But then, in the middle of the fight, Orwyn had changed his mind again and made Jax leave. And, like a coward, he'd left. He'd only agreed to it because he trusted Orwyn; still, he fought with himself the entire time he fled to their rendezvous point. But Orwyn never showed up. Jax had regretted it ever since.

He lost control of his composure and broke into a shuddering sob. Orwyn stood and stepped around the table. He wrapped his thick arms around Jax, squeezing him in a tight hug. Jax hugged his friend back, completely shocked at what was happening. Orwyn was dead—or for the last twenty years he'd thought he was. He'd mourned him more times than he could remember.

When he regained some composure, Orwyn handed him his mug and said, "Drink."

Jax accepted it and drank. It was the first time in twenty years he'd tasted ale made by his friend. It was good. Very good. Jax laughed through his tears and said, "His is better, you know."

Orwyn laughed. "And I would very much like to sit and drink with him—both of them."

Jax took another long drink, then said, "Why'd you send me away?"

"Because Yolken needed to know I was dead."

"Yolken?" Jax said, looking at Orwyn in confusion. "What do you mean?"

"Do you remember when I went to see Deanna?" Orwyn said.

"That was two hundred years before I was born."

"Well, did she tell you about my visit?"

Jax nodded.

"Did she tell you she took me to meet Dethoicrinth?"

"Not initially, but she confessed just before we arrived in Kyinth."

"Yes, well, she did what she had to, just as I did. You see, when I went to see the dragon, he told me what I would have to do. Somehow, he already knew what was going to happen. He didn't know all the details, but he told me I would one day sire a *hatchling* who would restore the balance lost during Drakonias' war. At the time, I had no idea what that meant; no one did. Drakonias wouldn't commission the astronomer for another hundred and fifty years. I thought maybe my future son would exact revenge on Drakonias for what Drakonias did to his father, but that wasn't it."

"Yeah, yeah, yeah," Jax said, wiping his cheeks again. "Get to the part about you faking your own death."

"Well, Dethoicrinth also told me that in order for my *hatchling* to accomplish what would be asked of him, I couldn't be a part of it."

"Why not?" Jax said. "Seems to me everything would have been a lot easier if you'd been around."

"I was—behind the scenes, when I was able," Orwyn said. "But he needed to believe that I wasn't."

"So, what happened that night at the tavern was planned?"

"No," Orwyn said. "I had no clue how I was going to extricate myself from his life. From the moment he was born I knew I would have to abandon him—both of them—but I couldn't bring myself to do it. I wrestled with it every single day of his life. But when the assassins killed Elen, I knew it was time. You didn't honestly believe the Sodality was a threat, did you?"

"Wait," Jax said, shaking his head. "You mean this whole

time Elen's been buried with one of those assassins?"

"No. I removed his body the first opportunity I had. Of course, I had to wait until Relan quit hanging around the grave so much."

Relan kept his face buried in his mug.

"How'd you do it?"

"Do what?"

"Convince Drenan the body was yours?"

"It wasn't that hard, really. When I attempted to open the kitchen door, they tried to overwhelm me by first ambushing me with soldiers. I'm guessing they wanted me to expend as much Energy as possible before the Overseers moved in. I played along with their plan and let the Overseers think they were getting the better of me."

"How?"

"I just pretended I was out of Energy. They used the growing inferno to attack, and I let them."

"You willingly let them burn you?" Jax said incredulously. He tried to imagine what it would have felt like, but couldn't begin to fathom it.

"I healed myself just enough to not cause any suspicion. When they thought I was dead they made the mistake of leaving me in the tavern."

"What if they hadn't?"

Orwyn shrugged and took a drink of his ale. "I suppose I would have had to adapt."

"So, while they let your supposed corpse burn in the tavern you put the assassin in your place and left?"

"They were none the wiser."

"You should have told someone."

"If I had, my plan wouldn't have worked."

"So why come out of hiding now?"

"Because there's something I need you to do."

"All right," Jax said, "but first tell me how you got the Harachin sword. Yolken banned dragon bones."

"He did."

"Then how'd you get it?"

"Deth brought it to me."

Jax just stared at Orwyn, dumbfounded. Finally, he managed to get out, "Why?"

"Because I need it."

CHAPTER 14

A screeching noise tore Drenan from sleep. The moment the last cyclone had begun to let up and the torrential rain abated, he'd sunk to the ground on the quarterdeck and collapsed into sleep, exhausted from days of helping Devin navigate the never-ending storms.

He winced in pain from the blinding sun when he opened his eyes. Shielding them, he saw a large object pass over the ship at great speed. He pushed himself to his feet, keeping the sun blocked with his hand, and watched the object move toward a towering island in the distance. "What in Draego's Fire is *that*?" he said.

"It appears Thena has ignored Father's edict," Devin said.

"A *flying* Machine?" Drenan said in complete amazement. It resembled a gliding bird with outstretched wings. He'd never imagined such a thing before. "That's incredible!"

"Indeed," Devin said.

Drenan watched the Machine as it flew away from them, growing smaller and smaller. He'd wanted to arrive in Thena unannounced, but it seemed that wasn't going to happen.

He surveyed the island of Finar and gauged that the strange Machine was heading straight toward Finarin. As soon as that thing alit—he wondered whether it took off and landed like a bird—news of a ship emerging from the storms would reach their aunt.

"Take over," Devin said. "I need to rest."

Drenan filled his Core from the sun and took the helm from his older brother. Devin tiredly walked away, holding onto the railing and banister as he descended the steps to the main deck. When Devin was out of sight, Drenan guided the ship toward the island, keeping the sails filled with air.

It had taken them twelve days to cross the East Sea. Twelve harrowing days. Devin had been right when he'd said that the wind and waves would get worse. The second storm that crossed their path came at them from the south. Devin went against Erigin's instructions and tried to pass north of it, but they lacked the strength to redirect all the wind that was blowing directly at them. Unable to turn around and attempt to get around the south end of the storm and afraid of how far north it would take them if they tried to get out of the storm's northern bands, Devin had been forced to turn directly into it. The chaos they'd experienced was not something he soon wanted to repeat. But he knew he would likely have to. They hadn't come to the east to live in exile, but to retrieve Thena and return to reclaim the Dragon Throne. How they were going to cross the East Sea with ships enough to transport an army, and arrive at the mainland intact, he did not know. That was a question for another day.

The sight of the strange flying Machine made him wonder what exactly Thena had been up to during the last seventy years. He'd never agreed with his father's edict banning the use of Machines, nor had he understood it—it had thrown the empire back centuries in terms of technological advancement—but seeing that Thena, separated from the rest of the empire, had chosen not to listen to Drakonias gave him hope. That Machine was evidence that she hadn't spent the last seventy years sitting idly by while the rest of the empire slowly fell apart.

As the hours slipped by and Drenan navigated swells

uninhibited by breakers, he thought about his own realm. Drakonias never came out and said it, but with Dorlan dead, he was sure to take over as chancellor. But a part of him wondered what the point was. That flying Machine gave him the initial impression that the east was still thriving, despite its isolation, but the same was not true for the south. No, he decided, it was time to abandon the south—or at the very least make it a part of the west or north. With Sheal kowtowing to Danavin's get, he intended to press Thena—if she indeed became empress—for the northern chancellorship.

But first he needed to deal with Danavin's get. He flexed his hands on the helm, trying to feel the scars that were no longer there. Nothing else mattered until those loose ends were cauterized. Only then would he claim his new, glorious position as Chancellor of the Northern Realm—the new realm he would make by combining the salvageable remains of the south with the north. And no longer would he have to subsist in the least desirable capital in all of Dradonia. His new home would be Tieger.

But first Danavin... and his get.

Drenan hated acknowledging their existence. But he forced himself to say their names. "Yolken Drake... Javen Drake." The names tasted like bile.

They were Drakes, whether he liked it or not. Drae's blood flowed in their veins. Blood nearly as pure as his own. And he would deal with them just as he'd dealt with the other traitors. He sneered at the thought of never being properly rewarded for helping Sheal round up the emperor's rogue siblings. "I should have been made a regent, not Sheal," he muttered. "*The Black Sodality...* I was the one who actually killed them, not Sheal. All he did was... supervise. But *he* was rewarded, and I was stuck in the Black. And he wasn't even satisfied, the selfish *scale*."

As they drew nearer to the island, Drenan was beginning to get his bearings. In centuries past, he had crossed the East Sea enough to know that there were three primary ports ships aimed for when arriving from the west: Cartheka farther to the north on the island of Carth, Finarin at the southern end of Finar, and Thena itself. He turned the helm to the right, guiding the ship until it almost paralleled the towering mountains in the distance. Although there were fishing villages peppered up and down the coast, none of them could handle a ship of such size, so he decided to shave off some time by angling as much as he could in the unsettled waters toward Finarin.

Drenan and Devin didn't talk much, but Drenan could tell with each day they sailed south that Devin was experiencing the same growing concern he was. Two things were causing it: the daily overflight of the perplexing flying Machines and the complete lack of any seafaring activity up and down the coast.

Devin was at the helm when they arrived at the southern end of the island, where its shores curved east. When he turned the helm to the left Drenan said, "Where are we going?"

"Aren't you curious why we haven't seen any ships?"

He was, but he figured their absence was not the most pressing of issues. They needed to get to Thena. Drenan looked up as another Machine approached. *They're keeping an eye on us.*

They passed through breakers similar to those protecting the Northern Realm and sailed into calmer waters. It became apparent as the coast slipped by why they hadn't seen any sea activity: The villages had been abandoned. Not just abandoned—decimated. Hardly any buildings still stood, and there was not a single intact boat to be seen.

Finarin had once been a thriving city but now it appeared to be no different than the remains of the villages they'd passed. Devin guided the ship toward the empty stone dock. Without dockworkers to put a gangplank in place, Drenan jumped down, using Synthesis to land softly on the weatherworn stone, and secured the ship in place with rope from the ship.

When the ship was secure, Devin followed him down. Together they walked up the dock toward the abandoned city. The skeletal remains of the stone buildings were all that still stood. Wooden doors and shutters were gone. In some places, there were empty spots between stone buildings where a wooden one had probably once been.

"I don't understand why they would abandon an entire city," Drenan said.

"I remember back when communication with the east was becoming sporadic that there were reports of total devastation in some places," Devin said.

"Same thing happened in the south. But we rebuilt."

"This isn't the south."

Drenan couldn't understand. As bad as things were getting in the south he would never have given up on his province and those he ruled. He'd learned long ago from his father, in the frozen mountains north of Kyinth, that death only came to those who let it. This island, this city, which had once been the provincial seat, was nothing more than a skeleton picked clean of its marrow.

"Rebeka," Drenan said, remembering the name of the provincial regent, "should not have given up."

"Perhaps it wasn't up to her," Devin said.

Devin started down a cobbled street long overgrown. Drenan stared after him. Only the emperor could make such a decision. Dorlan had made similar decisions in the south but only after the emperor told him to 'do what he deemed necessary.' Hastening to catch up to Devin, he said, "Are you suggesting that Thena ordered this?"

"No," Devin said.

"Because if she did, she's guilty of—"

"Nothing, Drenan."

"You can't be serious."

"The east hasn't been a part of the empire for nearly a century."

"What are you saying?" Drenan said.

"That I'm sure Thena made decisions she thought prudent. She couldn't very well ask Father's permission, now could she?"

Still, he wouldn't have dared make such a decision without

explicitly being told to do so by the emperor. Several provinces in the south had been all but abandoned, their regents taking up permanent residence in Hantlo, but Dorlan hadn't acted until Father gave him permission. Even still, Dorlan continued to seek advice from the emperor, sought to address the problem rather than run from it, despite the fact that Drakonias never provided answers.

"Even after we rid Dradonia of Danavin and his get, what are we going to do?" Drenan said.

Devin stopped and looked over at him. "What do you mean?"

"About the weather." Devin probably hadn't paid as much attention as he and Dorlan had, given that his realm had largely escaped the woes afflicting the south, but he'd heard Deanna. They'd known in Hantlo for a while that something wasn't right, even if Father never admitted it. *The evil we unleashed from our war is as real as is the sun that daily shines from on high.* Deanna's words had managed to pierce through the ire he was feeling at the time. He hadn't understood what she was talking about, and unfortunately the conversation had ended before she'd had a chance to explain what she'd meant. Drenan concluded that whatever the *evil* Deanna spoke of was, it had to be the cause of their problems in the south. When Devin said nothing, Drenan added, "It's changing."

"I know. What can *we* do?" Devin turned around and started walking back toward the ship.

Drenan gestured at the ruins. "So we just let the empire wither away like this?"

"We barely survived a single crossing of the East Sea, Drenan. You think we can somehow, all of a sudden, control the weather?"

"No, but we have to do *something*. Else everything we're doing is pointless."

"We can do something."

"What?"

"Adapt."

CHAPTER 15

It took another five days to sail from Finarin to Thena. If Onta was the pearl of the empire, Thena was the emerald. The island city, standing tall on an island in the middle of the Evinora Bay, was as beautiful as Thena. So much so, everyone thought, that she named it after herself. As first born to the Dragon King after his conquest of the world, she had received the city as a gift on her twentieth birthday. The island city, once called Trual, had been built by King Evin before the Dragon King's conquest. No other kingdom, as they were once called, came close to its opulence. The glass windows in the towering palace were tinged green, and when the sun glinted on them the palace resembled a fine-cut jewel.

The destruction Drenan and Devin had observed along Talon Point, the curved peninsula that formed the western side of Evinora Bay, was overwhelming. The trees that had once densely forested the peninsula were largely toppled. They all lay in rows facing away from the sea. A few branchless trunks stood in seeming defiance.

A great sense of anticipation filled Drenan when the fortifications built along the tip of the peninsula came into view. The series of towering stone structures had protected King

Evin's capital from maritime attacks for generations. Not until Draeko began his conquest of the world had they failed. Lighter-colored stone marked towers and portions of walls that had been rebuilt after they were destroyed during Drakonias' war. They were mostly useless in the United Era, largely serving as a reminder of Drakonias' Blessed rule. Only the Order of the Dragon and a few independent rebels dared resist Drakonias, but rarely was an attempt made by sea. Nevertheless, the towers remained occupied by a regent—Drenan couldn't remember the name of the distant cousin—in charge of a regiment of soldiers. Each tower had a Watcher. All told, the series of structures was home to a small city.

The dense forest had once stood as a backdrop to the sprawling towers, enshrouding them, but the trees here were toppled as well. As the now stark towers—some broken, all battered to some extent—passed slowly by, a sense of foreboding crept over Drenan. Like Finarin, the towers appeared to have been abandoned. Nary a person was seen on any of the battlements.

Disappointment rose in Drenan when they rounded the largest of the towers and the bay came into view. The typically crowded bay was empty. Thena, the island city, rose in the distance. As the *Soaring Dragon* slowly sailed closer, the city's spires became individually distinguishable. Most of the glass in the palace was shattered, and the towers lacked the thousands of flags that normally waved in the breeze.

"She can't have abandoned Thena, can she?" Drenan said. It was the capital of the Eastern Realm!

Devin stood silently at the helm.

As they drew close to the city, its disrepair became evident. Its walls looked battered. In some places, there were long gouge marks in the stone. In other spots huge chunks dug deep, and in a few places the wall was broken completely, save for rubble piled at the base. And the palace... its gleam should have beckoned to them the moment they rounded Talon Point, but it stood like a broken mirror. There was only an occasional glint of light from a stray shard.

There used to be three long docks that stretched out into the bay—one to the east, one to the south, and one to the west. The southern dock was completely gone, and although he couldn't see the eastern or western docks from their present position, he should have been able to see moored ships there. But he didn't.

Devin steered the ship around the western side of the city.

Soon enough Drenan confirmed that the western dock was gone as well.

The ship followed the curve of the island and the palace—or what was left of it. Entire towers were toppled. The tallest, home of the Chancellor of the Eastern Realm, stood precariously. Drenan wondered how it hadn't fallen. He hadn't seen such destruction since Drakonias' war.

"What in Draego's Fire happened here?" he said.

Devin swung the helm left and the ship turned away from the city. He steered them north, farther out into the empty bay.

Hours later, as they approached the innermost portion of the bay, Drenan stared in disbelief. The large stone structure that had once hosted nearly half the empire's fleet came into view and, as they drew close, they saw that it looked just as battered as Thena did. Where there had once been a vast network of docks was now hardly anything. All that remained were portions of the stone structure jutting out into the water.

Devin turned the ship and followed the curve of the land around the bay. The remains of villages that had once lined the waterfront were barely discernible. The occasional remains of a brick building were all that stood to testify to what had once been. The forests that surrounded the villages matched the forest that had once stood on Talon Point.

After a few more hours they arrived at the mouth of the Thena River, which emptied into the bay. It was one of dozens of rivers that flowed from the mountains known as Draego's Spine. Jnora, the small city that had once risen above its waters, had been reduced to broken foundations along the river's banks. There used to be fifteen bridges spanning the river, Drenan remembered, but now only a few stone pylons remained.

Devin turned the ship away from Jnora and back toward Thena while Drenan contemplated the implications of what was unfolding. They'd risked crossing the East Sea to rally Thena and return to Kyinth with her army and expel Danavin's get. But if Thena was gone, then what?

Devin guided the ship around the eastern side of the island city, confirming that the docks on that side were gone as well. Drenan stared up at the battered walls in disbelief as Devin turned the ship toward the inlet.

"We're not going to stop?" Drenan said.

"To what end?" Devin said. "Thena is obviously not here."

He had a point, Drenan knew. "Where to, then?"

"She has to be somewhere."

"Unless she's dead," Drenan said, even though he didn't believe that was true. At least, he didn't want it to be. Where was she, then? And what could possibly have done this kind of damage to the city? Certainly not the Order of the Dragon. They were a mere remnant of what they'd once been. Not even in their strongest days could they have inflicted such damage on one of the most defensible port cities in all of Dradonia. More importantly, if the capital of the Eastern Realm no longer stood, what did that mean for their hope of reclaiming Kyinth?

They left Evinora Bay and kept close to the shore, searching for signs of inhabitance. For three days, not a single village—or what was left of them—showed signs of anyone still living in the area. The only sign that humans were still somewhere nearby was the occasional flying Machine passing overhead.

On the fourth day, after rounding the bottom tip of the continent, they saw their first sign of human habitation, a small fishing vessel, and followed it to shore. The boat moored at a small dock at what looked like a typical poor fishing village.

Devin stopped the flow of Energy that kept the sails full of wind, then used it to lower the sails instead. The anchor dropped into the water, and he said, "Shall we?"

Drenan gestured toward the dinghy secured to the main deck and said, "By all means."

"I'm not here to run errands for you, Drenan. If anyone should be running errands, it should be you, as the younger brother."

Drenan ignored Devin. He'd spent his childhood being bossed around by his older siblings. They'd thought that, since he couldn't Synthesize, they were superior to him. He'd hated every moment of it, but their father couldn't be bothered with their childish games. Now, instead of lashing out at his brother, he redirected the annoyance that crept up in him toward Danavin and his get, adding to his burning desire to return to the mainland and reclaim his rightful place of authority.

"We go together," he said.

Devin nodded and even took the lead, using Synthesis to untie the ropes securing the dinghy and get it positioned into the pulleys. Once they were both in, he again Synthesized to operate the mechanism that lowered them to the water.

Drenan still thought this whole exercise of sailing a ship themselves was below them, but at least with their gift they didn't have to do actual labor—though sailing across the sea was more labor than he'd done in a very long time. He took the lead once they were in the water and propelled the dinghy toward the shore.

Villagers working near the dock stopped and watched as they approached. More and more people gathered along the sandy shore. One of the grimy men standing on the dock tossed a rope down when the dinghy pulled close. Devin secured the rope, then they climbed out.

The dock workers just stared at them when they reached the top. He ignored their complete lack of respect, deciding to pass along to the province's regent—whoever that was—that they were in need of discipline, and strode up the dock toward the stone buildings lining the waterfront. Drenan stopped at the end of the dock, where the wood met a stone walkway, and Devin nearly bumped into him. He turned and surveyed the crowd. The people looked at them with curiosity, not the fear that he was accustomed to.

"Where's Thena?" Drenan said.

"The empress?" one of them said.

"*Empress?*" Drenan said, looking at the man who spoke. He wore odd-looking pants that only came to the middle of his thighs, and an unbuttoned white shirt. In fact, looking around, most of the people wore similar clothing—it was a style he'd never seen before.

"New Thena." The man spoke as though the answer was obvious.

"New Thena?"

"Yes... sir."

"Sir?" *What an odd way to address a regent.* "Where's that? And what happened to the *old* Thena?"

"Pardon, but, who *are* you?"

Drenan had little patience for these people who showed them no respect, and now it ran out. He drew Energy into his Core and simultaneously reached out with a thread of Energy, wrapping it around the man's neck. He lifted the man a few inches off the ground, just enough that the man's neck supported his weight and walked up close to him. "It doesn't matter who I—"

Something behind the man caught Drenan's eye.

He let go of the man's throat and walked around him toward the building immediately behind him. He stepped under the overhang, which stretched the length of the building, and stopped in front of a lidded grey rectangular box, a pace tall and two long.

It hummed quietly.

Drenan lifted the lid and looked in. The box was filled with fish. He reached in and touched one. It was cold. He closed the lid and turned around to face the crowd. Devin was still standing where he had been, seemingly in shock. Pointing back at the box, he said, "What is this?"

The crowd just stared at him with blank faces.

Devin, regaining control of his faculties, strode up to Drenan, lifted the lid, and looked inside. "It appears to be an Icebox."

"It's a Fridge, sir," a woman said.

"A *what?*" Drenan said.

"A …Fridge?" The tone of the woman's voice echoed the man's. They seemed perplexed that Drenan and Devin wouldn't know about something so commonplace.

"That's a curious name for an Icebox," Devin said.

Drenan stepped away from the Icebox and into the middle of the walkway, the crowd backing up to give him room, and looked down the row of buildings in both directions. Several of the buildings had Iceboxes outside of them. *What are they doing using Machines?* He pushed the door open and stepped into the windowless building. Soft light greeted him. Not the flickering light of candles or oil lamps, but steady light—the kind only made possible with Energy. It was a convenience that had been lost when the edict of 295 was issued. The flying Machines were one thing, but this made it clear that Thena was completely ignoring the edict.

Going back outside, Drenan located the man he'd previously been talking to, used Energy to grab him by the neck again, and said, "Where's *New* Thena?"

"Is this really necessary?" Devin said.

Drenan swallowed the desire to lash out at his brother again. The man choked, unable to speak, but pointed to the east.

Drenan let him go and said, "Where?"

"Revald," the man said.

"What about it?"

"That's New Thena."

That was all he needed to know. He turned to leave, but then his curiosity got the better of him. "What happened to *old* Thena?"

"The storms. They got to be so bad the empress was having a hard time keeping up repairs. The story is the city was slowly being destroyed, so she decided to move."

"The story?"

"Yeah. Alls I know is that it happened before any of us here was born."

"I see." Drenan turned to go. He'd gotten what he came for, and had nothing else to discuss with these people. But before he got more than a few paces down the dock the man he'd been talking to called after him.

"Sir!"

Drenan stopped and turned around, and once again Devin almost bumped into him.

"Who are you? I mean, you have their power…"

"The Regent of Hantlo."

"What's that?"

"You've never heard of…?" Drenan took a step toward the man but stopped when he heard one of those flying Machines fly overhead. Both he and Devin looked up. Drenan fought down the urge to strangle the man to instill proper fear and respect into him, and pointed up. "What are those things?"

"Sir?"

"What is that thing?"

"It's an Aeroplane, sir."

"Aeroplane," Drenan said. "And what's it doing?"

"Patrols, sir."

"I see." Drenan turned once again to leave.

He stepped into the dinghy and used Synthesis to untie the rope. He barely allowed Devin time to get back in before he used the air he was controlling to push the boat quickly toward their ship.

"I'd appreciate you not doing that again," Drenan said as they approached the ship.

"What?" Devin said.

"You know what I'm talking about."

"Honestly, Drenan, I don't."

"Question my actions in front of subjects."

"They're not your subjects."

"Are we not regents, Devin?"

"Chancellor, actually."

"Yes, of course you are, as I will be before long."

"You think so?"

"Sheal will obviously need to be replaced."

"And Thena's going to choose you?" Devin said with a raised eyebrow. "How presumptuous."

"I presume only that Sheal is no longer suited to lead."

"And that Thena, when crowned Empress of Dradonia, will name you Chancellor of the Northern Realm?"

"If you wish to ever bed your precious Karina again, I suggest you show me some respect," Drenan said, his anger flaring.

"Are you threatening me, Drenan? Because I don't respond to fear the way you expect your *subjects* to."

"That's because you're weak."

"You haven't found Thena to be in possession of any sort of an army, Drenan, let alone convinced her to come to your glorious aid yet. And if we do find her, do you think she'll respond to your threats the way you've trained your subjects to? If you're not careful, you may find yourself having to find your own way back across the East Sea."

Drenan couldn't help but feel like he was a boy again, being chastised by his elders. He ignored Devin, however, because they were back at the ship.

He used threads of Energy to retrieve the hooks that fastened to the ends of the dinghy, looped them in place, then started pulling the small boat out of the water. Back on deck, he stood by the railing and watched as Devin made his way up the steps to the quarterdeck. The anchor rose, and the sails moved back into position. He shook his head, disgusted with his brother, and went below deck.

Revald, he thought as he walked through the finely adorned cabin and stepped out onto the balcony, looking back to shore. The inhabitants of the small village, who lived in more luxury than his own subjects, were already indiscernible.

The apprehension he'd been feeling about the abandoned villages and the city of Thena started melting away. He'd always disagreed with the emperor's edict, in large part because he had never explained himself, but he also knew that the emperor didn't *have* to explain himself. He was, after all, the emperor. But such a monumental decision would have been much better received by those chosen by the emperor to rule if they had known why—especially given the effect it would have on the empire. He didn't agree with the decision, but he followed it nonetheless. But Thena—Thena hadn't. Perhaps she abandoned some of her territory—he understood how the other regents in the south had simply abandoned their provinces—but those she ruled over seemed to be better off.

Empress Thena… She'd done more than ignore the infamous edict.

Drenan watched as the village grew smaller. *Sir.* It would seem Thena had made more changes in the east than just ignoring an edict. His instinct was to condemn her as a traitor, but now that the emperor was dead, did it really matter? Surely if the emperor had known what was happening in the east her actions would without question be treason, but now… now he wasn't so sure. At the very least he decided to withhold judgment until they arrived in Revald. Or, as it was, New Thena.

CHAPTER 16

Is that it?" Javen said when the capital of the Southern Realm came into view.

"What did you expect?" Tabora said.

Javen had thought she would be feeling the same disappointment he was, but the look on her face indicated she was confused. His eyes fell from hers, attracted by the thin red shirt clinging to her damp body. They'd purchased some clothing more appropriate for the south's hot and wet air when they passed through Portstown. Their thicker northern clothes were now stuffed into their bulging saddlebags.

He remembered the sense of complete wonder he'd felt when he first sailed into the Onta Bay aboard Devin's ship and saw the gleaming city. He also remembered the exhilaration he'd felt when he rode the Train into Kyinth. The towering buildings in the capital of the empire were unbelievable. And as they moved farther into the south, following along the Kvorgan Sea, the road slowly rising higher above the water, he'd imagined that Hantlo would at least resemble Onta, if not Kyinth, in its beauty. But from a distance, Hantlo resembled a jagged crag towering above the sea.

"It's just not what I expected, is all," he said.

He stared at the distant city as their horses steadily took them closer and suddenly felt nervous about the possibility of seeing Hadie. He hadn't seen her since the morning he'd had his lesson with Drenan—the lesson that had ended in Astora's death. She'd warned him about Drenan, but he didn't listen. So much had happened since that day; neither of them were the same people they were when they'd last seen each other. Then she started haunting his dreams. He'd lost count of how many times he had to watch, unable to save her, as Drenan killed her. But after visiting with Astora's parents, the dreams had stopped.

When they left Lonely Oak, he was at first apprehensive about the prospect of seeing Hadie again—especially since he would be doing so as Yolken's envoy—but when he and Tabora arrived in Matis, the sight of the Blue Mountain rekindled his feelings for her.

Javen convinced Tabora to stay the night there; when they checked in, he saw that the room he and Hadie had shared was available. Tabora hassled him about how much it was, but he insisted—he was an envoy to the Emperor of Dradonia, after all. She finally relented, but chose a room on the second floor for herself. Being back in the same room, seeing the tub and the bed, evoked in him a longing for Hadie. It wasn't the same feeling he'd had for Lannary or Melina, or any of the women he'd bedded since he last saw Hadie. Somehow it was... different.

He remembered changing his clothes and asking Tabora to accompany him for dinner. He had to ask directions several times, but eventually found Zuri's pub. Later, he'd fallen asleep thinking about the night he and Hadie had shared in that very room: the bath, the embarrassment he'd felt when the servant delivered their truffles, their passionate bedding in the very bed he lay in. By the time they'd left the next morning he couldn't stop thinking about her. He rode out of Matis longing to embrace her again. But now that he was riding into Hantlo... his stomach grew increasingly unsettled.

The traffic moving in the opposite direction had increased considerably after they passed Portstown. There was a near constant stream of wagons. In recent years the number of southerners passing through Lonely Oak had been steadily growing—and to the chagrin of many residents, many of them settled there, disrupting Lonely Oak's orderliness by building homes at random around the small town's neat row of buildings. But what really bothered the locals was just the growth. Of course, the inn proprietors, such as Brall and Astora's father, didn't mind because it increased their business—Brall's inn even brought in enough taxes that Dalia had elevated Brall to the status of a Suit.

But the flow of travelers and settlers into Lonely Oak was nothing compared to what he now saw as they drew closer to Hantlo. Wagons and tents were crammed together on the left side of the road, and there were even a few perched precariously along the cliffs to the right.

"Well, we can confirm the reports we've been getting about the state of the south," Tabora said.

Javen surveyed the dirty faces watching them and said, "I didn't realize it was this bad."

Ramshackle buildings soon replaced the city of tents. Their progress slowed considerably because the road was so crammed, but they made their way as best they could, weaving around wagons and through throngs of people. Eventually the dilapidated structures gave way to buildings made of brown stone. They passed a few guards on horseback, wearing gray dragon armor and yelling at obviously weary travelers to keep the road clear.

They eventually made it to the roundabout at the heart of the city. Javen noticed the empty platform in its center. There had been a statue of the emperor on a similar platform in Onta. "I wonder what happened to the statue," he said.

"I think that's obvious, don't you?" Tabora said. She pointed down the road to the east and said, "You can just make it out, but that's the Regent of Hantlo's palace down that way."

Over the tops of a sea of wagons, Javen saw the rising building.

"My guess," Tabora said, turning her horse to the west and urging it into motion, "is that we'll find our queen this way."

Javen's heart thumped in his chest at the sight of the towering building down the road to the west, but he followed Tabora. "How do you think she's going to react?" he asked nervously.

"It's hard to tell," Tabora said. "What do you think? You're the one who knows her."

Javen had certainly had plenty of time to think about their impending meeting. He clearly remembered the first time he'd looked up into her green-and-brown-mixed eyes, but he realized he knew surprisingly little about Hadie. He hadn't really known her all that long—a couple of weeks maybe? He tried to remember how many days it had been from their kidnapping in Lonely Oak until his lesson with Drenan. But so much had happened since then that much of it was a blur. He and Hadie talked a lot in that time; he remembered that her parents were Silks, so they were rich—she was rich, or at least had been—which meant she'd grown up privileged. She talked about it, about going to galas with her parents and such. But she had also been acutely aware of the poverty surrounding her. And in the end, she'd chosen to leave her riches behind in search of a better life. What did that tell him about her? That she was compassionate? Brave?

She was certainly leery of the Regency. She tried her best to talk him out of getting involved with them, but had still supported him when he ignored her advice. What did *that* tell him? She was loyal to those she cared about? But she was also the type of person who had the capacity to murder. He never would have thought she could do something like that. *Ever.* When he'd first heard what had happened from Drakonias he didn't believe it. It was impossible. But it had happened. And it wasn't just anyone she'd murdered. It was the Blessed. Dozens of them. The details of how she did it were sparse, but what kind of mental fortitude did planning something like that require? Javen didn't think he could do it. Just thinking about it—thinking about facing Drenan, who was just one regent—made him sick. But she'd somehow plotted, and successfully executed, taking down the entirety of the southern Regency.

"Honestly," Javen said, finally, "I have no idea what to think."

The one thing that continued to ring true every time he thought about her, even though he hadn't seen her in a long time, was that she somehow continued to captivate him like no one else ever could.

A crowd of finely dressed people stood on the steps of the palace to greet them. Yolken didn't want their arrival in Hantlo to be a secret like his arrival in Kyinth was originally supposed to be, so they'd sent advance notice by condor before they'd even left Kyinth. Yolken wanted Hadie to know an emissary was coming so she could prepare. He wanted her to know from the very beginning that his intent was peaceful. But still, Javen was a little surprised that they were waiting for them. He guessed it made sense—Drakonias had been waiting and prepared for Yolken's arrival in Kyinth.

When Javen and Tabora dismounted from their horses, a woman and two guards separated from the group and descended the steps. The woman gave a small bow and said, "Greetings. My name is Tara, and as the queen mother, it's my pleasure to welcome you to Hantlo." She gestured to the guards and said, "They will see to it that your horses are attended to."

Javen gave the reins to one of the guards. When they started off with the horses, Tabora said, "I am Tabora Alon, advisor of His Blessed Highness, Yolken Danavin Dairion Drake."

Tara bowed again, then looked from Tabora to Javen. Tabora nudged Javen with her elbow.

"Oh, uh… And I'm Javen Danavin Dairion Drake," Javen

said. The name sounded foreign as he spoke it. He was a Thornhill, not a Drake, but Yolken had insisted he use his true name. "Regent of Onta."

"It's a pleasure to meet you," Tara said with a bow. "Come."

Javen's heart started pounding harder than it already was when Tara turned and started back up the stairs. He leaned in close to Tabora and said, "What's a queen mother?"

"My guess would be mother of the queen," Tabora said wryly.

Javen stopped.

"What?" Tabora said.

"She's her *mother?*"

"It would seem. Why?"

Javen shook his head. "Nothing." His pulse felt like it had doubled. He wondered if Tara knew who he was. She had to, unless Hadie never talked about him. But why wouldn't she? "Does she know who Yolken sent?"

"You mean you?"

Javen nodded.

"No. We didn't name the emissaries."

Javen put a hand on his stomach. "I don't know if I can do this."

Tabora took Javen gently by the arm. "Yes… you can."

Javen followed behind, hardly reacting when Tara introduced him and Tabora to the Silks gathered on the steps of the palace. All he could think about was how he had always intentionally avoided meeting the parents of the women he bedded. Astora had been adamant about telling her parents about them the night he'd bedded her in the hayloft—she'd mistakenly thought that there was more between them than there was—but it was the last thing he'd wanted to do and he'd gone out of his way to avoid it. And now, without even having a chance to prepare, he'd met Hadie's mother. All he could think about was whether she knew he'd bedded her daughter. She didn't seem to have reacted strangely—she'd been very polite.

But that didn't stop his mind from spinning.

They were taken to a waiting room off the side of the atrium at the entrance of the palace. There was a table with simple food—fruits and slices of meat—as well as a selection of wine and ale. Javen ignored the food—he was too nervous to eat—but helped himself to more than one glass of the ale. Compared to Yolken's it was mediocre at best, but he drank it nonetheless, hoping to calm his nerves.

Javen's mood soured as what he'd thought was an imminent reunion with Hadie turned out to be hours of waiting. The ale didn't help—especially since Tabora recommended he stop after his second.

"We have to keep our minds clear," Tabora said.

Javen resorted to pacing the room. "I don't know how you can just sit there," he said as he passed Tabora sitting calmly on a couch.

"What would you have me do?"

"I don't know," Javen said. He threw his arms up in a huff and resumed pacing.

CHAPTER 17

The last two months had been a storm the likes of which Hadie knew not how she survived. It rivaled the cyclones that had slowly destroyed the kingdom she had somehow found herself in charge of. She'd seen sketches of what the cyclones supposedly looked like from a condor's perspective: a swirling mass of chaos circling a center area of calm. Draego had seen fit to land her in the center of the cyclone that was the south, only there was no calm. She longed desperately for Javen to be there, to hold her when she needed comforting, but she couldn't very well send for him. And she certainly couldn't *go* to him.

First came the coronation. The whole charade was a blur; she only remembered bits and pieces of it. A dress redder than the Blood River; a crown that immediately started hurting her head; arguing with her mother about what to do with her father—Tara wanted him locked up, but Hadie refused. Then there were the Silks bowing to her. Most of them were no different than any other citizen of the south, except that they were wealthy. A few of them, however, were Blessed. She couldn't understand why they bowed instead of taking power. They certainly had the ability to do so. But they didn't. They'd pledged their loyalties to her—gave her their strength.

As much of a whirlwind that night had been, the memory that stood most clear to her was standing on a balcony overlooking the city the next morning before a sea of people and hearing herself announced as Hadie Morrigan, Queen of the South. She didn't want to be the queen of anything; it wasn't why she'd done what she did. But she would do it for the people. She didn't want the greed of the regents to be replaced by the greed of the Silks.

She'd walked from the balcony back into Dorlan's personal chamber—*her* personal chamber now—to her gathered advisors. There were ten Silks, only one of them Blessed, plus her mother and Sethlan. And Ursella. She wasn't an advisor, but she'd wanted to remain with Hadie as her personal attendant. The others, at her behest, had left Hantlo. Most of them boarded ships and went to Onta; a few had hired passage north.

There, after looking out the large glass window at the Kvorgan Sea for what felt like an eternity, but was probably only a few moments—moments in which she desperately tried to calm her racing heart—she took her initial assessment of her kingdom.

Things were much more dire than she had ever imagined. She'd known about the influx of refugees from provinces farther to the south, had seen them pass through Hantlo even before she left the south herself. Even though she preferred to travel alone, there had been nights she'd welcomed the added safety of camping with a larger group. Most of the people she'd stayed with and talked with over campfires were farmers whose crops had failed and had to choose between leaving their homes or watching their families starve.

Since then, she spent most of her time reading reports. She never imagined ruling largely consisted of reading them.

"Your Highness."

There were reports about everything imaginable.

"Your Highness?"

And then she was expected to make decisions about them as

though she knew what she was doing. She was lucky to have her mother and other advisors to help her parse the vast amounts of information she took in every day.

"Your *Highness?*"

Hadie looked up from the parchment she was reading. Sethlan was standing at the end of the couch. He bowed when she looked up at him.

"Still not used to the title?" Sethlan said.

"Huh?"

"I had to repeat myself three times before you looked up."

"Oh. Sorry, I was trying to make sense of these numbers."

"Are those the grain reports?"

Hadie nodded.

"Not good, is it?"

"If these numbers you've annotated are accurate..."

"They are," Sethlan said.

"Then I have no idea how we're going to feed everybody this winter."

"We'll figure something out," Sethlan said. "But I didn't come here to discuss grain with you, Your Highness."

"What, then?"

"The emissary from the emperor has arrived."

The day had finally arrived. It was inevitable. Hadie had known they were coming. It had been two months since she'd killed Dorlan. After her coronation, the reality of what she had done set in, and she feared Drakonias would send an army to reclaim the south. But then barely a week had passed before word reached her that the emperor was dead and someone named Yolken had taken his place. Javen's brother. Somehow, for reasons she still didn't understand, the brother of the man she loved—a man from a small town she'd never heard of before she found herself staying the night there—had managed to do what no one had been able to accomplish for hundreds of years. And rumor had it that he'd used a dragon. *That,* she couldn't believe. Everybody knew dragons were creatures of fable.

The door to Hadie's chamber opened and her mother bustled in. She gave Ursella a side look before saying, "We need to talk about this emissary."

Hadie set the parchment on the knee-high table in front of the couch, returning it to the pile still demanding her attention, and stood up. "What's there to talk about?"

"About how you, Queen Hadie, are going to respond to this… emissary."

"What? I figured I would just meet with them."

"It's not that simple."

"Ma…"

"If you grant them an audience right away, it'll make you seem weak."

"We've discussed this."

"She's right," Sethlan said.

Hadie scowled at Sethlan.

"You'll seem eager. Which translates into weakness."

"What? Why?"

"Well, it's hard to explain."

"Try." Hadie tried her best to make her voice sound queenly. She glanced out at the afternoon sun reflecting off the Kvorgan Sea, then sank back into the couch.

"This is all so new," Tara said.

"New?" Hadie said.

"There have been numerous rebellions over the years, but none have ever been successful. And now we're in a time where we have a new emperor *and* a queen who successfully broke away from the empire. We need to be sure we handle the first envoy between the two entities properly."

"So what do you suggest I do?"

"Make them wait."

"How long?"

"At least a couple of days," Sethlan said. "Maybe as long as a week."

"A *week*?" Hadie exclaimed. "This is ridiculous."

"Well, you're the queen," Sethlan said. "So the choice is yours."

Tara shot Sethlan a glare. "At least wait until tomorrow."

Hadie looked to Ursella, who shrugged. She looked out the window pensively. Truth was, she was in over her head, and she knew it. She had no idea how to solve the problems overwhelming the south. There just weren't enough resources in Hantlo, let alone the fledgling kingdom, to meet the needs of all the southerners. The year's failed growing season had been devastating. She was eager to learn whether the new emperor—she could hardly believe it was Javen's brother—could offer some assistance.

"I'll wait until morning," Hadie said.

"Yes, Your Highness," Sethlan said with a bow. "I'll see to it that they're comfortable until then."

"Thank you."

Tara turned to Ursella and said, "Can we have a moment?"

Ursella looked at Hadie. When she nodded, Ursella curtseyed and took her leave.

When both Sethlan and Ursella were gone, Tara said, "There's something else."

"What?"

"You're never going to believe who they sent."

"*Who?*"

Tara hesitated.

"Ma..."

"The emperor sent his brother."

"*Javen?*"

Tara nodded.

A rush of emotion flooded into Hadie. Feeling light-headed, she sat heavily on the back of the couch and placed a hand to her heart. She'd lost count of how many times she'd thought of Javen since her coronation, longed to be embraced by him.

"I know what you're thinking, Hadie," Tara said.

"How could you possibly know what I'm thinking?"

"Because I'm a woman. And your mother. And I'm telling you right now that you can't."

"I can't what?"

"Do you really want me to say it?"

Hadie felt her face go red. She shook her head.

"You're the queen. So you need to act like it."

She *was* the queen, so she could do what she wanted. But she knew what her mother meant. It was just her luck that all she'd wanted to do after she killed Dorlan was to go to Javen in Onta and now he'd come to her—but she had to *act* like the queen.

"Get some sleep," Tara said. "You should be well rested tomorrow."

It was too early for her to go to bed. What she needed was wine. No… what she *needed* was to go to Javen, to envelop herself in his embrace. But she forced herself to settle for wine—and a bath.

Once settled in the tub with wine in hand, Hadie's mind swirled with thoughts of Javen and how she was going to feed her people this winter. At this point she had no idea what to do about either. She just hoped she didn't make a fool of herself tomorrow.

CHAPTER 18

Tabora calmly rose to her feet when the door finally opened and a man dressed in a suit entered the waiting room.

It was all Javen could do to stop himself from running out of the room.

The man bowed and said, "Greetings. I am Sethlan, one of Her Highness' advisors. Sorry to keep you waiting."

"That's quite all right," Tabora said. "I'm Tabora, and this is Javen. We're—"

"*Javen?*" Sethlan said with a quick look at Javen. His eyes lit up.

Javen returned Sethlan's look. He thought he recognized him, but he couldn't quite place him. "Do I know you?"

"We've met, yes," Sethlan said.

Javen narrowed his eyes, trying to remember. "Where?"

"I..." Sethlan looked from Javen to Tabora and back, then said, "I was the chancellor's personal servant."

Javen remembered. Sethlan had been there during his lessons with Dorlan—he'd lifted the blinds in the carriage in preparation each morning. But he was confused. "And Hadie... er, the queen... and now you're the queen's advisor?"

"Well, yes. I understand how that might seem a little odd to you, but..." Sethlan looked from Javen to Tabora again, who was looking at Sethlan with narrowed eyes. "Do you know a man by the name of Jorgan?"

Tabora's face lit up. "How do *you* know him?"

"Let's just say I've worked closely with him for a long time."

"*What?*" Javen said. "How?"

Tabora's eyes widened. "You're his contact."

Sethlan smiled.

"You're the spy?" Javen exclaimed. Jax had boasted about his many contacts within the Regency during their talks as they traveled.

"I was, yes."

"Was?" Tabora said.

Sethlan nodded. "My loyalties are elsewhere now."

"With the queen."

"Yes. But just let me say, Jorgan was instrumental in aiding Hadie in her... endeavors."

"Jax did *what?*" Tabora said.

"If it wasn't for him, Hadie would have died a traitor's death."

Javen was taken by surprise. Jax hadn't said anything about that. He wondered why.

"But I'm sure you're tired from your travels," Sethlan said. "I'm here to show you to your quarters."

"You're not taking us to see Hadie?" Javen exclaimed.

"Yes, we'd rather meet with her right away," Tabora said.

"Again, my apologies for keeping you waiting so long, but the queen is presently unavailable."

Disappointment washed through Javen. He felt like it was the eve of a moon festival and his aunt had suddenly declared that the festival was cancelled. He wanted to beg Sethlan to let him go see her, but he resisted.

Sethlan moved toward the door. When neither Javen nor Tabora followed, he gestured toward the door and said, "Please allow me to show you to your quarters."

Javen followed numbly behind Tabora as Sethlan guided them through the palace.

Sethlan opened a door and waved them in. Tabora stepped in first, then Javen followed her into a large room. There were tables and couches, and a large window on the far side. One of the tables contained food and decanters.

"There are bedrooms on either side," Sethlan said. "You'll be kept supplied with food and drink."

Javen surveyed the decanters and found them filled with either wine or water. "Do you have any more ale?"

Sethlan smiled. With a bow, he said, "Yes, Your Majesty."

"Might I inquire as to when the queen will meet with us?" Tabora said.

"She didn't say," Sethlan answered. "I was just instructed to see to your needs. May I interest you in baths?"

Tabora looked disappointed, but she said, "Yes, that would be most welcome."

"I'll see to it. That and ale," Sethlan said with a bow. He spun on his heel and took his leave.

Tabora poured herself a glass of wine and picked a couch to sit on.

Javen went over to the window and looked out, then took a step back, feeling a little disoriented. Far below, almost straight down, was the Kvorgan Sea. He tentatively leaned closer to the glass and peered down. The palace was perched on the very edge of the cliffs, which he could barely see below them. When he looked straight out at the setting sun, it almost felt like he was floating in midair.

A door opened behind him, causing him to turn. He half hoped it was Hadie, unable to wait any longer to greet him, but it was only a pair of servants wearing modest brown dresses. One carried two decanters. Javen met her at the table and poured himself a glass of ale the moment she set the decanters down.

With a bow, the woman said, "We'll prepare your baths."

When the servants entered the rooms on opposite sides of the sitting room, Tabora said, "At least she had sense enough to properly clothe her servants."

"Huh?" Javen said.

"Palace garb used to be so sheer they might as well not have been clothed at all."

"Oh." Remembering his own servant in Onta, Oshie, he said, "You should have seen what they wore in Onta."

"I have," Tabora said with a small shake of her head.

Javen took his ale back over to the window and watched as the sun sank below the horizon. The waiting was eating at Javen's sanity. "Do you think she did it on purpose?" he said over his shoulder.

"It's hard to tell," Tabora said. "It could be political posturing. Draego knows the Regency was fraught with internal wrangling. So it very well could be the case here."

After the sun dipped below the horizon, Javen joined Tabora on the couch.

"She's a new ruler, so she's probably trying to position herself as best she can."

"Yolken's a new ruler, too."

"Yes. But she's at a considerable disadvantage."

"Why?"

"Well, for one, he's Blessed and she's not."

"That didn't seem to have been much of a problem for her before."

"No, it did not." Tabora stood. "I think I'll be retiring after my bath." She gestured to the doors on either side of the room. "Preference?"

Javen shook his head. "I'm sure they're both equally nice."

"See you in the morning," Tabora said. She set her empty glass on the table in front of the couch and headed for a door.

Javen refilled his glass and proceeded into the other room. The servant awaited him by the tub. Remembering how embarrassing it was to have Oshie wash him, especially since she was half naked, he said, "I think I can manage on my own."

"Yes, Your Majesty," the servant said with a bow.

"Ma'am," Javen said just before she exited the room.

"Yes?"

"What's your name?"

"My *name?*"

"Yeah."

"Uh… Karli, Your Majesty," she said with a bow. "Will there be anything else?"

"Actually," Javen began, "I was wondering… does she know I'm here?"

"She?"

"Hadie… I mean… the queen."

"Ah… I'm sorry, Your Majesty, but I don't know."

"That's all right. I just thought I'd ask. Thank you."

Karli bowed and took her exit.

After a welcoming bath, Javen drew the curtains in his room, which had large windows like the sitting room. He retrieved more ale, bringing one of the decanters with him back to his room, and enjoyed the view of the Kvorgan Sea in the dusky light. It had a calming presence to it. He leaned against the back of a couch and enjoyed his ale, trying not to think too much about Hadie. But that proved to be all but impossible. He was anxious to see her and wondered how their reunion might go. He was, after all, there in an official capacity. Their meeting wouldn't be one of one-time lovers reuniting, but of an emissary come to petition a queen. He was afraid it was going to be awkward. He *knew* it was going to be awkward. He just hoped she didn't keep them waiting too long. He was ready to get the whole thing over with.

His anxiousness made him wonder what he actually hoped to get out of this meeting. There was the official part of it, but he didn't want this meeting to *only* be official. Now, more than ever, he realized he wanted to rekindle what they'd started so long ago. His feelings for Kaylan had set like the sun—he could still feel them a little, sort of like the light that still remained, but soon they would fade fully into darkness. And he'd never felt anything more for Lannary or Melina than lustful passion. But what he'd felt with Hadie, he knew was different. He only hoped she felt the same.

CHAPTER 19

Spending the night in the same building as Hadie without seeing her turned out to be harder than Javen imagined it would be. The knowledge that she was close and his anxiety about the impending meeting combined to prevent him from getting much sleep. And when he did sleep, it was filled with stressful dreams. At least they weren't about Drenan killing Hadie or Astora anymore. Even though he was tired, he was glad when morning arrived. Hopefully, it would bring Hadie with it.

Fortunately, they only had to wait the one night. Sethlan was awaiting him when he emerged from his bedchamber. After eating a hasty breakfast and getting dressed, Javen and Tabora followed Sethlan back through the palace.

When Javen yawned, Tabora smacked him on the arm.

"What? I didn't sleep well last night," he protested.

"Just don't yawn in front of the queen," Tabora said. "You don't want to insult her, do you?"

As they walked, Javen found himself wishing he could step out into the sun and absorb some Energy. What seemed like ages ago, Devin had taught him how to use Energy to melt away fatigue, albeit for an entirely different reason. Doing so now would prevent him from yawning in front of Hadie. He certainly didn't want to insult her. But his worries evaporated when they arrived at doors magnificently carved to resemble a city standing on the precipice of craggy cliffs.

Sethlan guided them into the throne room, already packed with a weary and rundown crowd crammed on seats and along the walls. Silks were clustered together at the front. Sethlan led them forward then said, "Wait here."

Javen looked up at the empty throne at the top of the dais. He could still hardly believe that Hadie was a queen, or how she had come to occupy that seat.

After a few minutes, a side door opened and a procession of men and women started in. Hadie followed behind them. Her clothing was befitting royalty and she wore a modest crown on her head. Javen watched, fixated on her, as the procession made their way toward the dais. Halfway between the door and the dais Hadie looked toward him. Their eyes locked, but then she missed a step and quickly looked away. She was every bit as captivating as Javen remembered.

* * *

Hadie took a deep breath, then followed her advisors into the throne room. She was trying her best to remember the postures her mother had taught her—stand straight, look straight, chin up, shoulders back, and on and on—but every time her mother droned on about it she couldn't help but think back to when Ursella had taught her the proper way to entice Sonja's guests. Plus, exuding the demeanor of a queen was all but impossible when Javen consumed her thoughts. "Your subjects should be the ones excited to be in your presence, not the other way around," her mother had said when they'd left her quarters.

But Hadie couldn't help herself. She glanced left and immediately saw Javen standing at the foot of the dais. Her eyes found his as naturally as a bee finding its way home. Why did it have to happen now, and not when she'd seen him in Onta? Everything would have been so much simpler if he'd seen her then. She wouldn't have had to kill anyone. She wouldn't have been made queen. She would have just been with the man she loved, far from all the death and suffering. She missed a step and looked away, feeling her cheeks redden. She stared at the back of her mother's head and focused on not missing another.

Her mind raced. *What was he doing here? He's the Regent of Onta? What happened to Devin? That woman he's with isn't Lannary. Where is she? Is he still bedding her? Why him?* She wanted to run and hide.

Her advisors took their places before their chairs on the dais, which were arranged in an upside-down V, two on each step, with her mother and Sethlan occupying the top two. She walked between them toward the throne at the top of the V. Her mother nodded to her as she passed. Her thoughts throughout the night had ranged from wanting to run into his arms, hug him and kiss him, to wanting to slap him for forgetting her so quickly. As she settled onto her throne, her mind settled on wanting to slap him. Except for Sethlan, her advisors followed her lead, and sat in unison.

How could she possibly engage Javen in any sort of stately discussion when she was thinking about seeing him and Lannary together in a market in Onta? She'd gone there like a fool, thinking he would love her as much as she loved him. But Sonja had been right; he'd already forgotten her. Even so, looking down at him, she also desperately wanted to hug him. Draego's Fire, she wanted to hug him. And kiss him.

In a loud voice, Sethlan declared, "The court of Her Royal Highness, Hadie Morrigan, Queen of the South, is now in session. As her first point of order, she would like to welcome the envoy of the United Realms into her kingdom. You are invited to pay your respects."

Hadie felt her pulse race even faster than it already was. Javen was looking up intently at her, their eyes locked on each other again. He broke their gaze and bowed deeply. The woman beside him bowed as well. She kept her eyes on Javen until he looked back up. When their eyes reconnected, she fought the urge to descend the dais and fall into his arms.

"My name is Tabora Alon," the woman with Javen said, "advisor to His Blessed Highness, Yolken Danavin Dairion Drake, Emperor of the United Realms. It honors His Blessed Highness that you have so hastily fit us into what I imagine is a lengthy list of supplicants awaiting your court, Your Highness."

Hadie glanced over at Tabora and nodded her head curtly. She looked back at Javen and said, "And you are?"

Javen's expression was one of confusion. Of course she knew who he was, but she couldn't reveal to the entire court that she knew him, let alone used to bed him. Wanted to bed him. Draego's Fire, but she wanted to bed him again.

"Uh… Javen, Your Highness," Javen said.

"Javen? That's it?"

"Oh… uh… my name is Javen Danavin Dairion Drake." After a bit of a pause, he hastily added, "Regent of Onta."

"*Really*," Hadie said, trying to feign surprise. "Is not Devin Drake the Regent of Onta?" She regretted asking the moment the words were out. She knew her mother would scold her about how being uninformed was a sign of weakness.

"He's…" Tabora started, "ah… he no longer holds a position within the Regency."

That's interesting, Hadie thought. She figured others had gone down with the emperor, but the intel her fledgling kingdom had been able to garner was frustratingly little. She would have to find out exactly what happened in Kyinth. "Well, welcome to my court, Tabora and Javen. Now that we have the pleasantries behind us, why don't you tell me why you made the effort of traveling all the way to Hantlo."

Truthfully, she was just glad it wasn't an army. Her father had made sure that, even as a lass, she was aware of how the Regency dealt with any attempt at rebellion. Retaliation was always swift, brutal, and complete. She hadn't thought far enough beyond killing Dorlan and the others to consider how the emperor might respond. Fortunately for her, and those who chose to make her queen, Javen's brother had killed Drakonias within days of her killing Dorlan. But she hadn't killed them all. The most notorious of the southern regents had escaped her plot.

"And what of the Regent of Hantlo?" Hadie said.

Javen looked over at Tabora but Tabora kept her eyes on Hadie.

"Both Devin and Drenan are missing, Your Highness," Tabora said.

A pang of fear shot through Hadie. It was all she could do to not adjust her bottom on the throne. Was Drenan coming for her? "*Missing?*" she said, trying her hardest to keep her voice from quaking.

"How much do you know about what happened in Kyinth, Your Highness?"

Hadie's mother turned and looked up at her. They knew little, and she knew what her mother would think, but if this was an opportunity to learn what was happening in the United Realms, she couldn't pass it up, no matter how it might make her look. "Not as much as I would like," she said matter-of-factly.

Tabora spent the next several minutes retelling the events that had transpired the day Yolken had arrived in Kyinth. Gasps rolled through the throne room, especially when Tabora spoke of a dragon crashing through the glass ceiling. There had been talk about meeting this emissary privately, but in the end Hadie had decided that what would be said was for everyone in her kingdom to know. "And when it was all over," Tabora finished, "Devin and Drenan were gone. Their whereabouts were still unknown when we left Kyinth."

"We should bolster the palace guard," Sethlan said.

"Agreed," Tara said.

"If you ask my opinion," Tabora said, "I don't think Drenan is coming here."

"What makes you think that?" Hadie said.

"If he were going to come here, don't you think he would

have already arrived?"

"Even so, we should strengthen the guard," Sethlan said.

Hadie looked to Sethlan and said, "Make it so."

"Yes, Your Highness."

"And what of the new emperor?" Hadie said. "Should I be worried about him as well?"

"No," Tabora said. "His Blessed Highness sent us here to negotiate a treaty."

Hadie looked down thoughtfully for a moment. "He has no intention of trying to reclaim the south?"

"No."

"Why not?"

"For the simple reason that the people of Dradonia have not been free to choose how they want to be ruled for thousands of years. Even before Drakonias stole the throne from Draeko, Dradonia was under Draeko's rule."

"But wasn't that in the interest of peace?" Hadie said. She had spent many late nights talking with Sethlan about what was known of the pre-United Realms world.

"It was. But it was a peace forced upon Dradonia's many kingdoms."

"But it *was* peace," Hadie pressed.

"True. But those kingdoms weren't given a choice. And that is something that the emperor wants to change."

"Meaning what? That he intends to break up the United Realms?"

"I cannot speak to what his full intentions might be. What I am authorized to say is that he will not force the south to return to the United Realms."

"You mean he's *letting* me keep my kingdom?"

"Not at all, Your Highness. He acknowledges your autonomy."

"Hmm," Hadie said. She looked from Tabora to Javen— Draego's Fire, she wanted to be wrapped in his embrace—and back to Tabora. "Then, aside from the formal negotiations such a treaty necessitates, I'm certain we can come to a mutually beneficial agreement."

"Yes, Your Highness," Tabora said with a bow. "I'm certain we will."

Hadie nodded toward Tabora. Then she looked at Javen, locking eyes with him. He smiled, which threatened to melt her into a blathering fool. Instead, she nodded, managing to keep from completely betraying her feelings.

CHAPTER 20

Javen followed a step behind Tabora as Sethlan led them back to their private chambers. Sethlan and Tabora were chatting about the formal process of crafting the treaty. He had been relieved when Tabora had offered to take the lead in court. He wasn't afraid to admit that he was woefully unprepared to negotiate with a ruler. The fact that he was now a ruler himself still made him ill when he thought about it. He wasn't looking forward to the day he had to return to Onta. He'd listened to Tabora drone on for hours as they traveled to Hantlo, but listening to her discuss the many intricacies of tact and processes was not the same as actually standing before a dignitary and being expected to *do* it.

"For now," Sethlan said as they entered the sitting room of their chamber, "enjoy Her Highness' hospitality. We'll contact you shortly to schedule our first meeting."

"Thank you," Tabora said.

Javen yawned. "I think I'm going to take a nap."

"Would you like more ale, Your Majesty?" Sethlan said.

"After my nap, that would be great."

Sethlan smiled. "Yes, Your Majesty. I'll return later and check on you both."

After Sethlan left, Javen went to his room. He took his coat off and hung it in the armoire. He sat on a chair to remove his boots but heard a knock on a second door, one that led directly into the hallway. When he opened it, he was greeted by an unfamiliar woman.

"Your Majesty?" the woman said. She curtseyed and said, "I'm Ursella, Her Highness' personal attendant."

"Oh... nice to meet you," Javen said.

"She's requesting a word with you. Right this way."

Ursella turned to walk down the hallway but Javen said, "Um... she wants to see me?"

"Yes."

"Ah." He stalled for time as his mind darted in multiple directions. "Just... let me get my coat."

"That won't be necessary."

Ursella started down the hall and Javen followed.

"What does she want?" he asked.

"I did not presume to ask her, Your Majesty."

After a few turns he noticed they weren't going back to the throne room, so he asked, "Where are we going?"

"Her private chamber."

"Her *private* chamber?" Javen's pulse was racing. It had been months since he was last with her—almost half a year, in the carriage Dorlan had given him when they traveled from Lonely Oak to Hantlo, the day Dorlan transferred his lessons to Drenan. His anticipation of being with her again grew. He might not know how to negotiate a peace treaty, but he knew that he missed her.

They entered what looked to Javen like a ballroom. He followed Ursella across the largely empty space to steps on the side. She led the way to the door at the top and opened it.

Javen stepped through and found Hadie standing at a huge window overlooking the Kvorgan Sea. He hesitated by the door, but when it shut behind him, Hadie looked over her shoulder. She smiled as she turned to face him.

All the emotions swirling through Javen coalesced into the one that mattered: the love he felt for the regal woman standing before him. He strode confidently across the room, around the long couch standing between them, and embraced her. Hadie wrapped her arms around his neck and squeezed tightly. The scent of her consumed his senses, forcing him to close his eyes and completely surrender to the moment.

"I've missed you so much," Hadie said into his chest.

He'd been so preoccupied with everything that had happened to him over the last several months that, until recently, he hadn't realized he missed her as well. "Me, too," he said.

And then all too quickly it ended. Hadie let go of his neck and pushed back on his shoulders. Javen opened his eyes and let her go.

"What are you doing here?" Hadie said.

"What do you mean?" Javen said, confused. "Ursella said you wanted—"

"In Hantlo. What are you doing in Hantlo?"

"My brother sent us to meet with you."

"But why you? He could have sent anyone."

"He wanted someone who knew you." Javen sensed the concern with which Hadie looked at him. "And... because I wanted to see you. So much has happened since..." Javen's throat caught. *Astora.* "I wanted to help her. I did. But I couldn't. I didn't know how. I watched her bleed to death, Hadie."

"I know," Hadie said. She wiped tears from her eyes and said, "I'm so sorry that happened to you."

"The next thing I knew I was on a ship heading for Onta."

"I know."

"You do?"

Hadie took Javen by the hand and sat on the couch, pulling him down next to her. Through tears and fitful starts and stops, Hadie told Javen what had happened to her that morning.

"Oh, Hadie, I had no idea." His hatred for Drenan flared to life. One more thing he needed to be held accountable for. He leaned toward Hadie, wanting to comfort her, but she leaned back.

"I went after you," she said.

"What? You did? Where?"

"Onta. Not at first, though. I couldn't let him get away with what he did." Hadie wiped more tears from her eyes. "I tried to kill him."

"You did *what*?" Javen exclaimed.

"I almost succeeded. I had him."

"How?"

"I became what he wanted most." Javen looked at her, confused. "I became a whore, Javen. Bedding whores was the only thing he thought about when he wasn't killing innocent people."

"You bedded him? After he tried to—"

"Of course not."

"What happened, then?"

"I don't know. I was there, in his chamber, but then he got called away. And that was it. My opportunity was gone." Javen leaned toward her again, wanting to take her back into his arms, but stopped when she said, "I saw you with her."

He knew exactly who she meant. Panic crept into him, replacing his desire to embrace her. He was afraid to ask because he already knew.

"I realized something while you lay unconscious on our bed back in the caravan. So, after Drenan left Hantlo, I went to Onta to find you." She touched Javen's cheek and smiled briefly. "I wanted to get you away from them." She dropped her hand into her lap. "And then I saw you. They wouldn't let me in the palace to see you. So I wandered the streets looking, hoping. And then I saw you at a market. You were with her." Hadie blinked tears away. "Javen, I…"

Javen watched the tears helplessly, wanting to wipe them from her cheeks, but he didn't. She'd seen him with Lannary. Whatever he'd thought might happen, he now realized it wasn't going to.

"I looked for you too," Javen said half-heartedly. "I asked Devin to find you for me, but he never did. Honestly, I don't even know if he tried."

"Javen, I miss you so much. Not a day has gone by that I haven't thought about you. Everything I've done since Drenan forced me away in Portstown I've done in part because of you. But now that you're here, I need you to know that I'm not the same person."

"Neither..." Javen's voice cracked. "Neither am I."

"I hate what's happened. I didn't want this," Hadie said with a look around the room, "but now that I'm here, I need you to know that I intend to sign that treaty when it's ready."

"That's good."

"And that's it."

And just like that, all the hope that had been building in Javen about what might happen when they were finally reunited was gone.

Javen wiped tears from his cheeks and said, "Yes, Your Highness."

CHAPTER 21

J aven startled awake when he felt someone climb into his bed. He instinctively reached for a dragon bone he'd gotten in the habit of keeping by his bed—he'd never learned to trust Drenan, even when he became part of the Regency—but there wasn't one. Then he remembered: Yolken had banned them, so he hadn't brought any with him to Hantlo.

"Shh," a familiar voice said.

"*Hadie?*"

The thin sheet that covered him in the warm winter night was pulled back. Hadie, who was completely naked, straddled his lap.

"What are you doing here?" he said.

Hadie put a finger over his mouth. "Don't talk. Just kiss me. Like you did that first night."

"I... we did more than k—"

Hadie put her hand over Javen's mouth again. "I said don't talk."

She leaned in and kissed him passionately, but only briefly. It ended quickly, leaving Javen wanting more. She kissed his neck instead. She traced the scar with her lips, then kissed her way down one side of his body and up the other. When she reached his mouth once more, she kissed him again, this time a little longer. But she moved on again. She worked her way down one side of his neck, shoulder, and chest, but stopped. She looked up at him, their eyes locking, then she returned to his mouth for another kiss.

The passion of lovers reunited consumed them. When it subsided, Hadie rolled off Javen and lay next to him. She pulled the sheet up to their waists, then snuggled into the crook of his arm. They were both damp with sweat.

"I thought you said this wasn't going to happen?" Javen said.

"I changed my mind."

"Does that mean you've forgiven me?"

"I don't know. All I know right now is that after seeing you today, I couldn't sleep."

"Well," Javen said, running his fingers through her hair, "I'm not complaining."

"I should go."

"Stay. Please."

"I... can't."

But she didn't move. In fact, Javen thought she might have fallen asleep. He waited, holding her. The smell of her hair took him back to Lonely Oak, to the caravan, to the Blue Mountain. Her rhythmic breathing changed to a quiet snore. He grinned, realizing that he'd actually missed it. He ran his fingers across the soft skin of her shoulder, arm, and back. He wanted more than anything to fall asleep with her, but at the same time he knew she couldn't stay. Or didn't want to stay. So after a while, he shook her gently to wake her, and whispered, "Hey."

"Mmm?"

"You fell asleep."

"Oh. Sorry."

"Don't be."

Hadie rolled out of Javen's arms and sat up on the side of the bed.

Javen mentally berated himself for waking her. He wanted

more than anything for her to stay. He ran his fingers down her spine when she bent over and picked up a thin robe. She slid the robe on, then stood up. "Can I see you again tomorrow?" he asked.

"I don't know," Hadie said. "I shouldn't have come tonight."

"But you did."

Hadie looked at Javen for a moment. He tried reading her eyes, but she looked away.

"I'll see you tomorrow," she said, making Javen hopeful until she added, "at the meeting."

Then she was gone.

Javen looked over at the open balcony doors. The sky was still dark. He closed his eyes. Hadie's visit confused him—she seemed determined that whatever relationship they'd had was in the past. By the time he fell asleep, however, he was content. He didn't know if there was still something between them, but she had come. For now, that was all that mattered.

* * *

A distant knocking coaxed Javen out of sleep, and he groaned. He'd never been a morning riser, but at least the light told him it wasn't *that* early. He rolled to the edge of the bed and retrieved his pants. As he pulled them on, he heard the knocking again. Not bothering with his shirt, he opened the door to the adjoining room, annoyed. The two smiling faces that greeted him immediately dissolved his irritation.

"Morning, lad!" Lyoll said with a healthy slap to Javen's shoulder.

"Who let you guys in?" Javen said.

Ganip gestured over his shoulder.

Javen looked past him and saw Tabora sitting at a table drinking tea.

"When I heard you were here," Lyoll said, "I knew we'd better come at first light or we wouldn't get the chance."

"Tabora and I are supposed to meet with Hadie—I mean, Queen Hadie about treaty negotiations today," Javen said.

"Well, it's a good thing we came by." Lyoll held up a large jug and said, "Now, to business!"

Javen looked at the jug and waved his hands dismissively. "No, no, no, no. Not that."

"Why not? Old friends require proper reunions."

"You'll have me drunk before I've even washed."

"Just one toast, Your *Majesty*," Lyoll said with a wink. He popped the cork out of the jug and looked around the room. "Where's the glasses?"

With a groan, Javen pointed to a table. "Over there."

Lyoll retrieved three small glasses and handed one to Javen and another to Ganip. He filled Javen's first, then Ganip's, then his own. He held his glass up and said, "To old friends."

Ganip held his drink up next to Lyoll's and Javen's, and the three of them clinked their glasses together, then upended them simultaneously. Javen coughed violently and Lyoll patted him on the back, then refilled his glass.

"No, no, no!" Javen protested again. "I'm serious. I don't want to show up to the meeting out of my wits."

"I suppose not," Lyoll said. "How'd you find yourself negotiating with the queen anyhow?"

"How'd you find yourself in the queen's palace? Don't teamsters typically stay with the horses?"

"Fair enough, lad, but last we knew you were in Onta."

"How'd you know that?"

"She didn't tell you?"

"Who? What?"

"Hadie," Lyoll said.

"Oh," Javen said. He didn't want to think about how Hadie had gone all the way to Onta looking for him, only to find him with Lannary. "Yes, she told me." He looked at Lyoll and then Ganip, confused. "She told you?"

"She didn't *tell* us; we were with her."

"You were?"

"Aye, lad. Ships are no place for a lass."

"How'd she do it?" Javen said. "I mean, I heard what happened"—the memory of meeting with Drakonias to discuss the events in Hantlo still made Javen feel sick when he thought about it—"but I don't know how. I mean, it doesn't make sense. How did Hadie manage to kill Dorlan and all those regents? A year ago, I never imagined killing even one regent would have been possible, not even for me. But for someone who can't Synthesize?"

Lyoll gestured toward Ganip with the jug. "Ask him."

Javen looked at Ganip.

"Go ahead," Lyoll said, "tell him."

Ganip's cheeks reddened. He turned his head away but held his glass up for Lyoll to refill.

"Tell me what?" Javen said.

"Ganip here specializes in certain botanical concoctions." Lyoll downed another glass of his homemade whiskey.

"He poisoned them?" Javen said.

"Well, technically, Hadie did the poisoning—her and her whores—but Ganip made the poison."

"*Ganip*? I'd never have... How'd you know how to do that?"

Ganip's face was blood red and he turned away, embarrassed.

"The lad has always had an affinity for tea," Lyoll said. "And one day, after adding a certain flower he'd found while we were up north, he got sick."

"But there's lots of plants people know not to eat," Javen said.

"True. But the lad picked a bunch of them and held onto them for... what was it you said you were doing?" Lyoll said.

Ganip looked over at them, his face still as red as an apple. "Collectin' 'em."

"That's not the word you used. What was it? 'Cue' something."

"Curating," Ganip mumbled.

"Yeah, that's the word."

"Meaning what?" Javen said.

"It's just a fancy way of saying he was making himself a flower collection." Lyoll looked at Ganip askance. "But he wasn't just making a collection to look at, he saves 'em up to make oils with."

"My ma taught me," Ganip said.

"Only she'd never encountered this particular flower, had she?"

Ganip shook his head.

"And that's that."

"Well... not entirely," Ganip said.

"We don't want to bore the lad, now do we?" Lyoll said.

Ganip shook his head.

"So," Lyoll said, turning back to Javen, "you never answered my question."

"What question?"

"How'd you find yourself negotiating for the new emperor?"

"He's my brother," Javen said.

Lyoll gagged on his drink—something Javen did every time he drank the stuff, but he'd never seen Lyoll do it—and thumped his chest several times with a fist. "Well," Lyoll said hoarsely, "I suppose that explains it." He filled himself another glass and took a swig, thumped his chest a few more times, and said, "Well, we don't wanna be keeping you. Just wanted to stop by and say hello before obligations come calling."

"It was really nice to see you," Javen said. "Truth is, I'd much rather be hanging out with you in the stables than up here in the palace."

"You do realize we don't *actually* live in the stables, right?"

"You know what I meant."

"At any rate, we aren't in the stables anymore."

"You're not? What happened?"

Lyoll stood tall, put his feet together and puffed out his chest. "Promoted."

"To what?"

"Head of Her Highness' guard."

"Congratulations," Javen said.

Lyoll stuck out a hand and Javen shook it. "We'll be seeing you, lad."

"Thanks for the drink."

"Any time. Maybe we can have a few more once today's business is seen to."

"Deal."

Javen saw Lyoll and Ganip out, then set about preparing for the day.

CHAPTER 22

Javen sat next to Tabora at the ornately carved table made from black Kvorgan wood. Hadie and several of her advisors sat across from them, and Ursella stood off to the side. Javen had agreed to let Tabora take the lead—he knew absolutely nothing about treaties or negotiating in general. As a former Council member in the Order of the Dragon, Tabora had decades of experience relevant to their current task.

He couldn't concentrate anyway. The only thing he could think about was Hadie's visit last night. He gazed at her sitting across from him—Draego's Fire, she was beautiful—and wondered how she was able to focus. All he wanted was for the day to be over in the hopes that she would come to his room again.

Lyoll and Ganip, as well as several others, stood behind Hadie along the floor-to-ceiling glass window. Several others stood around the room as well. Javen had to stifle a snicker every time he looked at Ganip—compared to the other men, his thin frame looked humorous. And to think *he* was responsible for making it possible for Hadie to become queen!

Javen watched Hadie as she talked with Tabora. He could tell by her poise and intensity that she had matured a lot since their brief time together. She wasn't the happy-go-lucky girl out on an adventure that she'd been when they met in Lonely Oak. She looked stressed. Maybe that was why she had come to see him; she didn't love him anymore but needed something to take her mind off the many burdens that came with ruling.

"I understand your need, Your Highness," Tabora said, "but you aren't really in a place to negotiate. We were sent here to offer you peace."

"And I want peace," Hadie insisted. "But what we need more is supplies. My people are starving."

"What do you have to offer in return?" Tabora said.

Hadie looked from Tabora to Javen, which made him feel self-conscious. Looking into her eyes made him want to talk about last night, not the business at hand. Instead, he shifted his gaze to look out the window at the cloudy sky.

"If you were part of the empire," Tabora continued, "it would be in the emperor's interest to see to the well-being of his people, but you have chosen to secede from the United Realms."

"The emperor can't be that cruel," Hadie said. "He would let us die?"

"Cruelty has nothing to do with it."

"Javen?" Hadie said.

Hearing Hadie address him directly—the first time she had done so thus far in the negotiation—made Javen look back inside.

"What?" he said.

"I know for a fact your brother isn't the type of person who would permit this."

"Permit what?" He should have been paying better attention.

"Us to starve. You've seen the city. You both have. I specifically took you on a tour so you could see our plight."

Their tour of the city had indeed been disheartening, Javen agreed. The streets were packed with refugees from the rest of the Southern Realm who'd had to abandon their homes. It made the number of families fleeing the south that he'd encountered over the years seem trivial. Many of them looked wan, and they gazed with pleading eyes as the carriages slowly made their way through the densely packed streets. It took an escort of guards on horses—including Lyoll and Ganip—to clear a path for them, sometimes forcefully.

"I understand your plight precisely, Your Highness," Tabora said.

"Then why won't you help us?" Hadie's eyes pleaded with Javen.

Javen wanted to help her, to take her side—but if he did, he would be overstepping Tabora's lead, which he'd agreed to give her.

"We were sent here to negotiate a peace treaty," Tabora said.

"Which includes give and take on both sides."

"And you have absolutely nothing to give. It sounds cruel, I know—"

"It *is* cruel."

"—but as I've said, the conditions under which the emperor will extend his benevolence have already been stated."

Javen disagreed. He felt Yolken should help whether Hadie agreed to return the south to the empire or not. Letting people die of starvation was cruel, and he knew Yolken wouldn't agree. He *didn't* agree, in fact—Javen knew his brother was going to help, but as part of their negotiation they were to make every effort to bring the south back into the empire, which included making them think Yolken didn't care.

"Then I have no choice but to go with our contingency," Hadie said.

"And what is that?" Tabora said.

Hadie looked first at Javen, then at her advisors sitting on either side of her—one was Sethlan, who had been working with Jax for years, and the other her mother. Both of them nodded.

Before she could speak, the door to the room opened and a servant entered. "Your Highness," the servant said, then his voice caught as he realized he was interrupting a meeting.

"What is it?" Hadie said in a patient voice.

"I-I'm sorry, Your Highness—"

"That's all right. Just tell me what's so important."

The servant bowed and held out a rolled-up parchment. "An urgent message has arrived from Aerons."

Hadie gestured to Sethlan, who retrieved the message from the servant and brought it to Hadie. Javen watched her face as she opened it and read it. Her eyes betrayed her fear.

"What does it say?" Tara said.

"It was sent nearly a week ago," Hadie said. She lowered the parchment and looked across the table, locking eyes with Javen.

"Yes, but what does it *say*?" Tara said.

"Aerons was..." Tears fell from her eyes, but she didn't wipe them. "A cyclone... the city was... the damage... there's nothing—" Hadie's voice faltered. She handed the parchment to her mother.

Tara read the parchment quickly, then said, "Draego's Fire."

"The cyclone is headed this way," Hadie said. "We need to prepare."

Javen looked past Hadie at the window. The clouds outside looked so ominous he involuntarily stood.

"What?" Hadie said, looking at him.

He pointed at the window.

Hadie looked over her shoulder. "Draego's Fire."

CHAPTER 23

Torrential rain assaulted the glass windows in Javen's room, and the wind threatened entry. He had never experienced a cyclone before and didn't know what to expect. It was worse than the squall he'd experienced in the gap while sailing from Portstown to Hantlo with Devin. And it was certainly worse than the thunderstorms that grew over the Mindons in the summer. Carefully watching the glass, he didn't notice someone enter his room. Arms turned him and enveloped him in a hug.

"What have I done?" Hadie sobbed into his chest.

"What do you mean?" Javen said.

"I can't do what they do…"

"What are you talking about?"

"If I hadn't… they'd be able to…" Hadie trembled uncontrollably. "What have I done?"

Javen pulled her over to the bed and sat her down. He didn't know what she was trying to tell him, but she didn't seem to be in the state of mind to communicate right now. So he just held her as the rain pounded and the wind howled.

She eventually lay down and curled up into a ball on her side. "Hold me," she said.

Javen lay down behind her and wrapped his body around

hers. The wind and rain muted her sobs.

The storm persisted for hours, making it difficult for either of them to sleep.

The sound of shattering glass in the other room jolted them. Javen tentatively went to check but when he cracked the door, the force pushing against it almost threw him to the ground. He shoved the door closed. "I think we need to go somewhere safer."

Hadie nodded, then took him by the hand and led him out into the hallway. Javen checked on Tabora but her room was empty.

"She's probably in the shelter," Hadie said.

Every floor, Javen had learned, had a room that was designed to shelter in during cyclones. The floor where he and Tabora were staying had a banquet hall with heavy panels that slid out of the walls to cover the windows. "We should join her, then," Javen said.

Hadie shook her head. "I need to collect my thoughts."

Hadie pulled Javen through the empty palace and back to her quarters. When she opened the door to the ballroom, Ursella leapt from a couch and ran to her.

"Your Highness!" Ursella said, hugging Hadie. "I was so worried."

"I'm fine," Hadie said.

The doors leading out to the balcony were boarded closed. Except for the sound of wind and rain outside, the large room was eerily calm. She climbed the steps to her private quarters but couldn't open the door.

"What is it?" Javen said.

"Something's pushing on it."

By shoving on the door Javen finally got it to budge, but wind howled around it, carrying with it sheets of rain. He let the wind push the door closed again. "I think the window's broken."

"We should go to the shelter," Ursella said.

"Yes," Javen agreed. Hadie wouldn't listen to him, but

maybe Ursella's suggestion would convince her.

"No," Hadie said. "I'll stay here until the storm passes."

Javen looked around, deciding not to press the issue. He certainly didn't want her to be more angry with him than she already was. "I think we're safe here with those doors boarded up."

Ursella shot him an angry look. Javen tried to nonverbally convey that he'd already tried that but failed. Ursella folded her arms across her chest and looked away with a quick snap of the head.

Hadie sat heavily on the steps.

Javen sat next to her and placed an arm around her.

"What am I going to do?" Hadie said after she regained some composure. "I remember going out with my father and watching the regents clean up the city after a cyclone came through. They were rare back then, but even then, they absolutely destroyed the poorer parts of the city. The peasants were left to rebuild on their own. I'm not like them, Javen. I don't have their gift to clean the city up with."

"Some of the Silks are Blessed," Ursella said.

"I know, but it's not enough."

"We'll be all right."

"No… we won't."

"Come on," Javen said, taking Hadie by the hand. He led her over to a couch and sat on it. "It's more comfortable than those stairs."

But Hadie didn't join him. Instead, she paced the room.

The wind and rain weren't as loud in here, so Javen's fatigue succeeded in coaxing him to lie down. He tried to stay awake, to be there for Hadie, but sleep eventually took him. When he woke, Hadie was curled up beside him.

He noticed that, except for Hadie's gentle snore, the room was quiet. He worked his arm out from under her head and gently climbed over her, trying his best not to wake her. Ursella was asleep on another couch. He went over to the boarded-up doors and listened. Quiet. He undid the locks, opened the doors, and peered out. Rain was still gently falling, but the wind was calm.

He went back to the door to Hadie's quarters and tried it. Something was blocking it, but he pushed slowly, easing the door farther open without making a lot of noise. When he was able to step through the door sideways, he found complete disarray. A couch was shoved up against the door, and the rest of the furniture was strewn around the room. The floor-to-ceiling window was shattered. Glass was everywhere.

"Draego's Fire," he heard Hadie say behind him.

Both Hadie and Ursella stepped into the room. Hadie had a hand over her mouth.

"Sorry, I didn't mean to wake you," Javen said.

Hadie shook her head. "No, I needed to get up." She walked over to the glassless window, her feet crunching with each step, and peered out through the hole.

Ursella stayed by the door.

"Is it over?" Javen said.

"I think so," Hadie said. "This doesn't look like the eye."

Javen didn't know what that meant.

"I shouldn't have let myself fall asleep. I should have been… I don't know. I should have been doing something. Not sleeping."

"Hadie, there was nothing you could've been doing. You certainly couldn't have been outside."

"I need to go see."

"See what?"

"What's left."

Together, the three of them left Hadie's quarters in search of one of her advisors. When they stepped out into the hall, they found Sethlan walking determinedly toward them.

"Are you all right, Your Highness?" Sethlan said.

Hadie shook her head. "I'm fine. Will you ready a carriage? I need to go assess the damage."

"I've already done that, Your Highness."

"You have?"

"As soon as the wind let up."

"And?" When Sethlan didn't immediately offer a response, Hadie said, "*Sethlan...*"

"It's what I think you're already expecting."

"I need to see for myself." She started down the hallway.

Sethlan followed after her, saying, "I advise against it."

Javen and Ursella hurried right alongside them.

"I have to."

"Your Highness, it's not safe. You aren't going to be able to get a carriage anywhere. The streets are—"

"Then I'll go on foot."

Sethlan took Hadie by the arm. "Your Highness, please."

"Let go of me!" Hadie shouted, pulling her hand away.

"I'm sorry. I shouldn't have. But if you want to see, I think the bell tower would be a better place. It's high enough that you can see all you want." Sethlan turned to Javen for support.

"Maybe he's right," Javen said.

Hadie looked crossly at Javen.

"If that's not enough," Sethlan said, "I can put together a guard to escort you. But a cart is out of the question. At least right now."

"Fine," Hadie said.

Hadie allowed Sethlan to lead her, Ursella, and Javen through the palace and up a spiraling staircase. The bell tower provided a view of the city in all directions. Hadie walked the perimeter while the others stood back.

Javen couldn't believe what he saw. Sethlan had been right; the streets below were clogged with overturned carts and wagons and all sorts of debris. It was hard to make out the decrepit structures in the distance through the mist and rain.

When Hadie stopped and stared north, Sethlan approached. "How bad is it?" she said.

"Complete ruin, Your Highness," Sethlan said.

"How many dead?"

"It's too early to know for sure."

"How many would you guess?"

"Given how crowded the city is and the widespread damage—I don't think Hantlo's ever seen a storm this bad."

"How many?"

Sethlan hesitated.

"How many?" Hadie repeated.

"I would guess thousands, Your Highness. If not tens of thousands."

Hadie gasped, her hand going to her mouth. "And it's my fault."

"Dorlan wouldn't have been able to prevent this any more than you could have. And with the city so crowded, the casualties wouldn't have been any better."

Hadie stared pensively into the distance.

"Your Highness, I've already initiated the mobilization of Blessed to begin the cleanup process."

"We can't clean this up," Hadie said.

"It'll take longer, but we'll eventually get it done."

"Tabora and I will help," Javen said. "And we can have Yolken send more help."

"No," Hadie said.

"What then? More help would—"

"That's not what I meant. What we need is not to clean Hantlo up, but to finally leave it."

Ursella gasped.

"You want to… evacuate?" Sethlan said.

"Hantlo is dead, Sethlan. Assemble my advisors."

"Yes, Your Highness," Sethlan said with a bow.

CHAPTER 24

Javen once again sat next to Tabora, across the table from Hadie and her advisors. They were in the main ballroom now since their previous location, her private guest room, was in shambles.

"The south is dead," Hadie said matter-of-factly. The grim look on her face was shared by everyone. "I have no choice but to order an immediate and complete evacuation. Before the storm, Hantlo was already being squeezed of every ounce it had to give. And now... now there's nothing left. My people were already starving... too many have died. This storm shouldn't have happened—their season is past—and yet it did. I won't stay here not knowing when the next one will arrive. No, we must gather what provisions we have left and leave."

"Where do you intend to go?" Tabora said.

"Where we know there's food—and safety from the storms."

"You would invade the empire?"

"If that's what you want to call it."

"What else *would* you call it?"

"We aren't a military force seeking to take land that isn't ours. We're simply a people trying to survive. Now," Hadie said, pushing her chair back and standing, "if you'll excuse us, we have work to do."

"Certainly," Tabora said, standing herself. Javen rose with her. "This certainly wasn't anticipated by the emperor, but if you have any condors, I might be able to send word to Kyinth."

Hadie looked to Sethlan and he shook his head.

"Then it's time we make our departure," Tabora said. "We need to inform the emperor. Your Highness," she said with a bow.

Hadie extended her arm, gesturing toward the door.

Tabora started for it; initially, Javen just watched. He looked back at Hadie and she gestured with her eyes toward the door. He didn't want to leave, but he bowed to her and followed Tabora.

Javen jogged down the hallway to catch up with Tabora, who was walking briskly. "Tabora," he called. She didn't stop. "Why do we have to leave?" he said when he finally caught up with her.

"Because Yolken will want to know he's about to be invaded."

"But she said she isn't invading."

"He still needs to know that a hundred thousand hungry people are making their way into the empire."

"I don't want to," Javen said.

This brought Tabora to a stop. "What?"

"I mean… I want to stay."

She looked at Javen for a moment. "Suit yourself," she eventually said. She started off again, but Javen didn't follow.

He watched her until she turned a corner, then he returned to Hadie's chambers. Hadie looked up at him in surprise when he walked through the door.

"Javen?"

"I'd like to stay, Your Highness. I mean, if that's okay with you?"

Her eyes lit up and he could tell she was fighting back a smile. "Yes, of course. We could use your help."

"Thank you," Javen said with a bow.

CHAPTER 25

The *Soaring Dragon*'s sails furled. Drenan looked past them at the iron ships blocking their way. More were moving into flanking position, and several flying Machines circled overhead as well. Two had been following them day and night for the last three days. And now, with New Thena visible in the distance, their path was impeded.

He considered directing Devin to turn the ship around, but he doubted the *Soaring Dragon* could outrun those iron ships. Plus, they'd never be able to lose the flying Machines. And besides, he wasn't about to leave empty-handed.

Once the blockade was complete, from between two of the larger vessels, which boasted impressively large Cannons, a smaller ship emerged and proceeded toward the *Soaring Dragon*. As it drew near, men wearing shiny silver uniforms became visible standing along the railing. As they drew even closer, Drenan saw that they wore Glasses and were armed with ancient weapons. "They have Guns," he said.

It was Draeko who had first developed them and used them in battle. He'd won several battles before Devin had realized they were just miniature, hand-held Cannons, such as the ones they had on their ships. Guns used bursts of Energy to fire a projectile, just as Cannons did. After that, it was only a matter of time for them to design the Machines necessary to produce Guns in mass. And just as with every other Machine they'd invented during the war, the Gun increased the ease with which they were able to kill each other.

"Thena has been busy, indeed," Devin said. "Do you see the Cannons on those ships? The barrels are huge."

"How are those ships powered, do you think?"

"I have no idea. I've never seen anything like it before."

As the smaller ship drew up alongside the *Soaring Dragon*, Drenan gave up any notion of refusing whatever they might want. There was no possible way for him and Devin to defend themselves against the weapons those men possessed.

Drenan watched helplessly as grapples flew from the iron ship to the *Soaring Dragon* and pulled the two ships together. Several men boarded the *Soaring Dragon* and filed up the stairs to the quarterdeck. Devin and Drenan turned to face them.

"Disperse of any Energy in your Cores and come with us," one of the men said.

Drenan's Core was full, but what was he going to do? The moment Energy left his body, each of them would pull the trigger on their Gun and he'd be dead before he could mount any sort of attack. Instead, he touched the dragon bone inlaid on the wood railing and transferred the Energy from his Core into the bone. At the same time, Devin gripped the helm.

The armed men led Drenan and Devin down the stairs to the gangplank connecting the two ships. They boarded the iron ship and were ushered along a narrow walkway along the side of the ship to an iron door. Inside, the walkway echoed loudly with their steps. Bulbs illuminated their way. They were led down a metal staircase and into a small room. Blackness enveloped them when the metal door clanged shut. The sound of a turning lock meant there would be no escape.

"Seems a bit drastic," Devin said.

Drenan felt for the wall, then slid his back down the cold

metal to the ground. "She's paranoid."

They sat in the dark and, except for a steady drone, silence.

The darkness didn't last long. The lock turned, and the door opened. A silhouetted person appeared in the doorway. A male voice said, "Who are you?"

The Gun the man carried was clearly outlined, so Drenan didn't move. "Drenan Drake," he said.

The man's head shifted. "And you?"

"Devin Drake," Devin said.

"Your purpose?"

"To speak with Thena," Drenan said.

The man stepped back and the door slammed closed.

The darkness lasted longer this time. Drenan grew hungry as well as thirsty. Did he sleep? He couldn't tell. The darkness didn't change whether his eyes were open or closed. They were completely cut off from any source of light—the cell couldn't have been more perfect to hold a Synthesizer.

When the door finally opened, the sudden light hurt. Drenan clenched his eyes shut and shielded them further with his arm. A hand grabbed him by the arm and pulled him to his feet. His weakness reminded him of his father dragging him farther into the mountains after beating him near to death.

He grasped at the light in the hallway, hoping to draw it in and strengthen himself, but it wasn't sunlight, only the artificial light of those cursed Bulbs. From the iron hallway, they emerged back out onto the deck, but the ship was in a dark building, its boxy structure illuminated by dim lights. Drenan required help crossing the narrow gap between the ship to the dock—how long were they in there?—then they made their way through a door and immediately down a set of stairs.

They walked for what seemed like an eternity.

"I hope you're taking us to Thena," Drenan said. The way they were being treated was ridiculous.

The guard, who was ushering them along holding his Gun in a low ready position—Drenan hadn't used one since

Drakonias' war, but he still remembered the tactics—ignored him at first, but after several echoing steps said, "Why would the empress see the likes of you?"

"Do you even know who we are?"

"Nobody that merits the empress' attention."

"We have urgent business we need to discuss with her," Drenan said.

The guards finally stopped, and one of them opened another metal door. The guard leading Drenan gestured toward the opening with his Gun. Drenan reluctantly obeyed and stepped into another small room. Devin followed him in.

Thena obviously considered them a threat, otherwise she wouldn't be treating them as she was: starving them of sustenance as well as shielding them from sunlight. But he couldn't let them shut him away without planting some seed that Thena needed to meet with them.

"Tell her Drakonias is dead!" he shouted as the door swung shut.

The door clanged and the turning of the lock echoed in the small chamber.

"She's threatened by our presence," Devin said.

"Why would she be?" Drenan wondered aloud.

"She's been autonomous for a long time. Would you give up power once you had it?"

He knew Devin was right, but hated admitting it, so he didn't say anything. Instead, he sat down against the wall, drew his knees up to his chest, wrapped his arms around his legs, and waited.

* * *

Drenan recoiled in pain when the door opened and a piercing light shone in.

"What happened?" a female voice said.

Drenan squinted at the silhouette standing in the doorway. He lifted his head off the hard ground and tried pushing himself to a sitting position, but he was too weak. They'd been denied any sort of sustenance except for the smallest amount of water. His lips felt dry and his throat parched, but he managed to croak, "Danavin."

He doubted the name held the same level of revulsion for her as it did for him—Thena had no spouse or children that Danavin would murder—but the name had plagued the empire long before contact with the east had been lost. And he knew for a fact that Danavin had caused a fair amount of discord in the east.

Thena stood in the door without moving. Drenan laid his head back down on the ground while he waited, keeping his eyes on his aunt. His comment to the guard had been enough, just as he'd hoped.

A warmth entered Drenan and melted away his fatigue.

"Come with me," Thena said.

Feeling refreshed, Drenan rose to his feet.

He and Devin followed Thena, who strolled briskly down the dark hallway ahead of them. They entered a Lift and rode it up in silence. Drenan wanted to start right into explaining why— and how—they were there, but knew it wasn't the time or place.

The doors of the Lift opened and Thena strode out. The brighter light revealed that she hadn't aged a day since the last time Drenan had seen her. That was no surprise to him—it had been nearly seventy years since they'd lost contact with the east, so for her to even be alive meant Drakonias had indeed taught her Regeneration. He felt perturbed that he had never learned it himself, but pushed the feeling back. He didn't want that to interfere with what he needed to accomplish. There would be plenty of time to coerce Thena into teaching him. Then there would be no reason to feign allegiance to anyone anymore.

Drenan shielded his eyes when they exited the building, then stopped walking. The bright light stung, but he couldn't help but look around. A man in a trim black suit stood next to an open door at the back of a long black Auto. The Auto was sleek and shiny, unlike any he'd ever seen before—its black, reflective windows were particularly intriguing. Behind it, a continuous stream of Autos of various sizes passed by on the road.

Drenan realized he had fallen behind Devin and Thena, so he hurried to catch up. He arrived just in time to hear Devin say, "Your Auto is almost as beautiful as you are, Thena."

"I call it a Limo," Thena said. "And how's Karina?"

"As luscious as the day we met," Devin said. "You're looking rather luscious yourself. She'd be envious if she knew I was with you. Perhaps when we're finished with all this, Rongin'll write your own edition of *Lovers*. Several have asked for one, you know."

Thena had often been the subject of discussion in Regency circles—she was as desirous as Karina, but had never married. Drenan would be lying if he said he'd never thought of her in less-than-becoming ways. But then, like Devin and Karina, he'd never subscribed to the puritanical preaching of the Dragon Priests.

Thena climbed into the Limo first, followed by Devin. That brief exchange between Thena and Devin worried Drenan. He didn't want Devin wringing control of their plans from him, so he hurried to enter the Limo as well.

Incandescent light illuminated the inside and both sides were lined with leather couches. Devin was settling opposite Thena. As Drenan settled himself, Devin opened a bottle of wine and poured Thena a glass. He poured another and handed it to Drenan. Drenan gladly took a drink. It had been since before they left Kyinth that he'd drank anything. Looking at Thena sitting across from him, he realized it had been equally as long since he'd bedded anyone.

The door shut as Devin poured himself a glass of wine, leaving the Limo dimly lit by the interior lighting. When the Limo rolled smoothly into motion, Thena said, "Now, tell me what happened."

Drenan started talking immediately, wanting to make it clear to Thena that he was in charge. Devin was the older brother, but *he* wanted to control the forthcoming events. His entire life he'd been forced to follow, and he was tired of it. Moving forward, he intended to lead. He would have to impress upon Thena that he would follow her back to Kyinth—he needed her army, as well as to learn Regeneration—but then he would follow no longer.

As the Limo wound through the city Drenan conveyed everything that had happened—and not just over the last few months with Danavin and his get. He began with what had happened since contact had been lost with the east. Devin, to his satisfaction, contented himself with drinking wine. He refilled his glass more than once as they rode along. As he talked, Drenan looked through the dark windows at the city outside. The towering buildings reminded him of Kyinth, but what drew his curiosity was the sheer number of Autos that packed the streets. The streets were also lined with light poles, which he knew at a glance were powered by Energy. There would be time enough to ask her about it all when he was finished, so for now he kept talking lest Devin interrupt.

When the Limo arrived at the palace, conversation stopped as they were led through the opulent estate to Thena's personal quarters. Food was laid out on tables, and the smell reminded Drenan of how hungry he was. He attempted to exercise some modicum of decorum as he ate but his ravenous hunger made it impossible. At least he wasn't the only one: Devin was also having a hard time eating with proper manners.

When they finished, Thena led them out to her balcony overlooking the Revald Bay. The air was warm, but the onshore breeze made it pleasant. They reclined in comfortable chairs with wine in hand.

"Where were we?" Thena said.

Drenan resumed where he'd left off and they talked into the night and Energy-powered lights illuminated the balcony. It was late—Devin had fallen asleep from drinking too much wine—when Drenan finally got to the events that resulted in Drakonias' death. "We had no choice but to flee."

"What of the others?" Thena asked. "What became of them?"

"As we made our way to Tieger, we began hearing rumors that Sheal and most of the regents in the north were on their way to Kyinth to pledge allegiance to Danavin's get."

"But that was just rumor. Perhaps he didn't."

"I'm certain he did."

"How can you be sure?"

"Because we passed him in Aliza."

Thena sipped her wine. "So why are you here? What do you want from me?"

"To give you what is now rightfully yours," Drenan said. "With Drakonias dead, the empire is yours."

"Hmm…"

Drenan sat and watched as she held her glass to her lip, obviously in thought.

"The East Sea *is* navigable; Devin and I proved that by coming here. Come with us and claim the Dragon Throne."

"I've lived here so long I hardly remember the rest of the empire," Thena said. She took another sip of wine and said, "This is my empire now. I've been empress here for seventy years. I have no need for anything else."

Agitation crept up in Drenan. How could she *not* want absolute power? But more than that, he couldn't permit Danavin to continue roaming the empire, nor allow his get to rule. "Then lend me your army and navy, and I will claim Kyinth for myself. You rule here, and I'll rule there."

"What about him?" Thena said with a look toward Devin. He was slouched in his chair, chin on his chest, fast asleep.

"Look at him," Drenan said. "He cares more for wine then he does ruling. Besides, he's perfectly content in Onta." He didn't know if that was true, but Thena didn't need to think otherwise.

Thena sipped her wine and said, "I'll think on it."

"Please," Drenan said, not wanting the moment to be lost. Thena was practically handing him his plans on a platter; he didn't want to let it go.

"It's late, Drenan. I said I'll think on it." She rose to her feet and said, "I'll have a servant show you to your quarters."

Drenan pushed back on his agitation and said, "Good." He was *so* close, he didn't want to annoy or anger her. He just hoped Devin didn't mess it up. "I could use a good bedding anyway."

"Still the same Drenan, I see."

"Do any of us ever really change?"

With a thoughtful look, Thena said, "No, I suppose not." She finished her wine and said, "I'll have someone sent to your room."

"The best, I trust."

"But of course."

CHAPTER 26

Drenan woke to a pressure on his neck. When he struggled to move, the force kept his mouth closed so he couldn't cry out.

"Shh," Thena's voice said. "Don't wake the whores."

The pressure holding him pinned to the bed was released. He looked to his left and right and found the whores still sleeping next to him.

"Come with me," Thena said.

Drenan sat up and realized he was naked and uncovered. The covers had been stripped from the bed when the whores arrived. They got in the way most of the time. Thena turned toward the servants' door, unconcerned by his nakedness.

There wasn't a robe readily available and she didn't seem to be inclined to wait while he dressed, so he followed her as he was. She was waiting for him when he stepped into the servants' hallway.

"What is it?" he said, annoyed that she'd woken him so early. He couldn't have been asleep for more than an hour. The light reminded him of his fading inebriation, and he dug the heels of his hands into his temples.

"Here," Thena said, holding out a small dragon bone.

Drenan took the bone and used the Energy contained within to soothe his headache. He had never been particularly good at healing ailments, but he'd long ago learned how to get rid of headaches caused by drinking too much. "So," he said, as his headache melted away.

"I came here to tell you what I plan to declare today. I want you to know in advance what I've decided."

He had an idea, since she had come to his room at an unseemly hour and discreetly woken him. "What's that?"

"To go along with your plan."

"You will?"

"I have no interest in leaving the East. It's been my home for far too long."

"What about Devin? If you aren't interested in the throne, then it rightfully goes to him."

"But he can't secure it without my army, correct?"

"Correct."

"So he'll do as I say."

"Some will consider it an act of treason."

"Against whom? My brother is dead. There's no one to commit treason against. Besides, I long ago gave up worrying about offending my brother. If he'd been willing to cross the East Sea as you have, he would have killed me for disobeying his edict and proclaiming myself empress. Devin doesn't have to be pleased with my decision; he just has to agree to follow it."

"What if he doesn't?"

"Then kill him. Either way, with Drakonias dead, he'll die anyway."

"So you'll teach me Regeneration?"

"Here," Thena said, handing Drenan a thick roll of parchment. "I'll give you command of my army and navy tomorrow. Now, go get some rest. And I trust you know what'll happen if that falls into the wrong hands?"

He nodded. Thena turned to go, but he grabbed her arm. "Why?"

"I have my reasons."

"What?" Drenan didn't normally care about the motivations of others; in the end, all he cared about was getting what he wanted. But he was genuinely curious about why she'd decided to help. When he had talked to her earlier, he'd gotten the impression that she no longer had any interest whatsoever in anything across the East Sea.

"For centuries, I put up with our father trying to wed me off. And when he was gone my brother did the same. His insistence irked me so much that I began to rue my decision to help him overthrow our father. Of course, I never acted on that—I would have been crazy to. But that doesn't mean there weren't times I wanted to."

"Meaning what?"

"I never loved anyone—I don't know why—but I came close. Once. And I had my heart broken."

How Drenan knew he couldn't have said, but he did know, instantly. "Danavin..." That man managed to ruin the life of everyone he came into contact with. "Thank you."

"Just make sure you succeed."

"I will."

"Tomorrow I'll take you and Devin for a naval inspection. At the conclusion I'll offer you my terms. For your brother's sake, try to act surprised."

"I will," Drenan repeated.

He stood naked in the servants' hallway as Thena walked away. When she turned a corner and left his sight, he returned to his bed. With newfound vigor, he woke the whores.

CHAPTER 27

Drenan met the morning with anticipation. He left the whores, who were asleep once more, and found his way to a room with a private bath. A waiting servant ushered him toward a tiled tub set into the floor. He'd bathed upon first arriving at his quarters—he hadn't had a proper bath since he'd left Kyinth—but still felt as though he were covered in his own excrement after being held prisoner in the bowels of New Thena.

He sat in the middle of the tub and watched as the servant disrobed and stepped into the tub with him. She wore a skin-tight suit, covering her breasts and nether area. If he were back in his own palace, he would instruct her to disrobe completely, but he wasn't, so he didn't.

The servant scrubbed him clean, then toweled him dry. She guided him into the next room, which was lined on both sides with clothing. A suit had already been set aside from those hanging along the walls, a dark gray coat and pants with a light gray shirt. Not a color a regent would wear, let alone a future emperor.

He permitted the servant to dress him nonetheless, then met Devin in the hallway. He was wearing similar clothing.

"If you please," another servant, this one dressed in a trim black suit, said, "I'll show you to Her Highness'."

"Pleasant evening?" Devin said when they started down the hallway.

"Yes. Yours? You enjoy your whores?"

"I sent them away."

"Why in Draego's Fire would you do that?"

"Can we just go see about getting our army?"

"Because of Karina?"

Devin gave Drenan a quick glance.

"I don't understand."

"What? What is it you don't understand, Drenan?"

"When have you ever denied the opportunity to bed a woman? You're *Lovers*, aren't you?"

"This is different," Devin said.

"How?"

"*We* are *Lovers*. Without her it's just whores."

Drenan snorted. "I'll never understand why you insist on being such a prude. She certainly isn't."

The servant led them through Thena's personal quarters and out onto the balcony where they'd met yesterday. The servant poured each of them a glass of wine then they met Thena by the railing. The Revald River was visible, emptying into the bay in the distance. And as majestic as the scenery was, the forested mountains surrounding the bay, it was the bay itself that drew Drenan's attention.

Grey ships packed the water. They varied in shape and size, but every single one of them was bigger than any ship he'd ever seen in Dradonia. Four of them were flat on top except for a small structure on one side. The flat surfaces of those ships were laden with the flying Machines that had been following Drenan and Devin as they'd made their way toward New Thena.

"The Eastern Fleet," Thena said. "Every one of them more capable than the finest the *empire* has to offer."

"If you had such a fleet, why did you never cross the sea?"

Drenan said.

"Because I had everything I needed here. I'm not interested in the Dragon Throne, but I will loan you my army and navy."

The area between the palace and the water's edge was packed with row upon row of uniformed soldiers. Even from this height, the Guns held at their shoulders were discernible.

"The throne is yours, Thena," Devin said.

"I don't want it," Thena said. "And with Drakonias on the throne I had little worry of being attacked. But with an unknown entity—"

"Not an *unknown* entity..." Drenan said.

"Yes. Well. I would rather not have to worry every day about whether a threat was coming or not. I'd rather have a known entity on the throne in Kyinth."

"But not you?" Devin said.

"No."

"But we came here so you could claim it." Devin shot a quick look toward Drenan, who tried to act surprised.

"And I thank you. But as I said, I don't want it. I'm satisfied with being Empress of the East."

"Surely you don't intend to give the throne to Nera?" Devin said. "She *is* the next in line, according to the line of succession."

"The emperor is dead," Thena said. "As are his ways."

"Then who?"

Thena stopped and turned to directly face Devin. "I'll give you my navy and army on one condition: I will remain Empress of the East and Drenan will become Emperor of the West. Two halves ruled separately, but a part of the whole."

A gasp escaped Devin's mouth.

"I..." Drenan began, trying his best to sound shocked. "Why me?"

"Because it's my army, so I get to establish the terms."

"If you aren't going to follow the line of succession," Devin said, "then it should be me."

"I've already decided," Thena said.

"No," Devin said. "I agreed to come here to make you Empress of Dradonia. Not to split the empire into two. And Drenan," he said, looking at Drenan with a furrowed brow, "he is not fit to be emperor of anything."

"Careful, *brother*," Drenan said.

"Then go home in that rickety vessel of yours," Thena said. "Pledge your allegiance to the *Dragon King*, live out your remaining days in whatever role he sees fit to bestow upon you, and bed your precious Karina while you still can. Because, Devin, you will either take my offer or you will die just like everyone else. I alone have the army required to retake Kyinth, but more importantly, I alone possess Regeneration. If you don't want to die, you'll do as I say."

"And what is that?" Devin said through clenched teeth. "What is my role in this… plan?"

"You will help Drenan capture Kyinth—"

"And retake the south," Drenan interjected.

"And retake the south," Thena repeated. "Then, you will return to Onta."

CHAPTER 28

It took a couple of days to finalize preparations, but as the sun rose to greet the warm winter morning, Drenan stood aside in the control deck of one of the four flat-topped ships transporting flying Machines—what Thena referred to as Carriers—and watched as the fleet sailed from New Thena. In total, the fleet consisted of fifty ships: ten Carriers transporting Aeroplanes as well as other equipment, twenty transporting war Machines, ten transporting soldiers, and ten ships designed to protect the fleet.

Drenan was glad to be largely rid of Devin. While the fleet made its way across the waters of the Eastern Realm—or as Thena referred to it now, the East—each of them occupied themselves by becoming familiarized with the equipment at their disposal. The fleet sailed together for now, but after passing the cyclones, the plan was to split the force in two: Devin would march on Kyinth, and Drenan would start by reclaiming the south. They coordinated through small Aeroplanes, about the size of condors, that flew back and forth between Devin's and Drenan's Carriers. Initially Drenan watched with fascination as dozens of the miniature Machines flitted from ship to ship, carrying orders and communications where they needed to go, but he soon became accustomed to their presence.

In the evenings, when Drenan retired to his quarters, he studied the instructions Thena gave him on Regeneration. The steps for reversing the natural aging process turned out to be rather intricate, and it was not something he would master quickly. She recommended he practice on animals before attempting it on a human—he would inevitably not get it right initially, and the results of improperly manipulating someone at the cellular level was disastrous. The very concept of 'cells' was something that was going to require much study.

The fleet encountered and weathered the first storm without much issue, but it was only an outlying storm wandering by itself. Two days later the fleet met the full cyclones. The ships spread out and the flying communication Machines stopped. Overall, Drenan was impressed with how well the large ships handled the swells and the wind, but two ships drifted too close together. They ended up colliding, and one of them—a soldier transport—suffered a catastrophic hull breach. It happened at night, which severely limited the ability of Drenan or any of the other Synthesizers to intervene. More than half of the soldiers on the ship were lost.

Then they were back in the West—Drenan's empire. Devin boarded Drenan's ship for one last meeting to finalize plans before the fleet split in two. As Drenan watched Devin's half of the fleet diverge in course from his own, he worried Devin might take the throne for himself when he got to Kyinth. But then he chuckled at the thought of watching Devin grow old and die. If Devin was foolish enough to betray his and Thena's wishes, he would never restore Devin's youth. And Karina had long grown accustomed to youth and beauty, so he didn't think she would permit Devin to take the throne.

As the two fleets pulled farther apart—Devin's bearing northwest and Drenan's bearing southwest—Drenan turned his attention toward Hantlo. He wanted to personally dispose of Danavin's get occupying his throne, but his hatred of the woman who called herself the Queen of the South currently burned fiercer. He couldn't have cared less about Dorlan—what little respect he'd had for him had evaporated when he decided to start teaching Danavin's get to Synthesize—and except for his two sons, Loid and Rik, most of the southern regents had kowtowed to Dorlan, so he didn't respect them either. But now Loid and Rik were dead. So, before he ascended to his throne, he was going to open Hadie's throat the same way he'd done to that lass Dorlan had taken from Lonely Oak.

CHAPTER 29

Yolken set the parchment he was reading down on the desk and leaned back in the worn leather chair. His eyes hurt from spending the morning reading. Again. He'd been the emperor of what was left of the United Realms for a month and a half, and he felt as though he'd spent most of that time sitting at this desk—Drakonias' desk. He rubbed his hands across the smooth wooden arms of the chair and wondered how many times Drakonias had sat back in frustration, like he had just done.

His days had become routine. He woke with the first light of the sun and, after enjoying time being married to Kaylan, he rose from their bed and went out on the east balcony. He knew from Sahri that Drakonias used to rise before the sun every morning and stand out on the east balcony, just as he'd started doing.

Solarian, as Deth called the sun, was dying, knocked out of balance by Drakonias' war. And he was supposed to somehow restore that balance. But he didn't know *how* he was supposed to do that, and he didn't know how long he had to figure it out. The Order's assessments of the astronomer's report seemed to indicate that he didn't have long—a few years at best. His sense of urgency was why he spent so much time reading through Drakonias' writings.

What did he think when he stood out here? Perhaps he'd had the weight of Dradonia on his shoulders, just like Yolken did now. It gave Yolken a near-constant ache in his stomach, and he'd hardly had an appetite the last month. According to Deth, the Great Dragon had chosen him to restore balance, but aside from replacing the Energy taken from the sun—which was impossible—he had no idea what he was supposed to do.

He recharged his bones each morning, even though he was hardly Synthesizing anymore. Mostly he used Energy to operate the Lift so Sahri could come and go.

It didn't take long for Enif to figure out Yolken's routine. The first time he'd appeared in the Lift with Sahri when the door opened was also the last. Yolken forbade him from doing that again. Unless specifically invited, Yolken limited interactions with his advisors to his daily council, for which he allotted three hours in the morning and, if need be, again in the afternoon.

Mornings were special to him. He enjoyed his time with Kaylan while they ate breakfast, even though most of the time he just picked at his food. Kaylan urged him to eat more, but every bite was forced. That didn't stop him from reveling in her presence, though.

He had about an hour to prepare each morning in his office before council. Sahri brought with her, on a silver cart, an agenda for the day, as well as pertinent parchments he needed to review so he had an idea what they would be discussing. Kaylan knew how stressful adjusting to ruling had been, so she largely left him alone. However, she didn't leave their quarters until he did. She enjoyed riding the Lift with him—a final moment together before they went about their day's responsibilities.

He held court in the throne room once a week, but today hadn't been one of those days, so after council ended, he'd returned to his quarters where Sahri waited with his midday meal. He'd felt bad knowing that she had to use the pulley system to access his quarters when he wasn't there. It wasn't nearly as efficient, requiring a couple of additional servants to pull the large wooden box up and down. Enif declared that its age made it unsafe, but Yolken ensured it was inspected and repaired as necessary before it was used.

He looked at the stack of parchments he'd been reading—the report from Vashon, the astronomer Drakonias had commissioned to study the sun—and ran his hands through his hair, entwining his fingers behind his head. He'd been studying the report for almost two weeks, but the details were hard to understand. The Order had been studying it ever since his father had obtained a copy of it, over a century ago. The conclusion remained undisputed—the sun was dying—but there was still no definitive time frame on how long that would take. Over time, they'd refined their estimates and were able to accurately predict when the sun would consume the planet Detron. Further refinement had resulted in the eventual trip Jax made to Lonely Oak—which just so happened to coincide with Dorlan's stay.

Things would have been so different if Issa hadn't fallen the next day. Jax had planned to take both Yolken and Javen to see Deanna on the island of Kvorga. Everything that had happened from that day until now would have been different. Selena would still be alive. Probably Deborah too. But he wasn't studying the report to determine how much time they had left. He was looking for a way to stop it from happening altogether.

Needing a break, Yolken turned his attention to the stack of parchment Nera had given him from the Synod. There was a record of every individual the Black Sodality had assassinated or attempted to assassinate. He didn't have the time to read them all, so after he'd disbanded the Sodality, he'd asked her to bring him the reports on his father. When he wasn't trying to understand the astronomer's report, he read through—with amazement—the reports Nera had written of the many failed attempts to assassinate his father. As hard as it was, he even read the final one—the one when the Sodality had finally succeeded.

He thought about picking up the report from an attempt in Turnig, because what happened there didn't make sense. Or at least he hadn't made sense of it yet. He had also been surprised to read a particular name in that report: Relan. That was another thing he added to the list of lies Jax had told him—or misrepresented, at best. When Jax told him about the night his father died, Yolken had been surprised to find out old Relan knew his father. He'd asked Jax if Relan was in the Order, and Jax had said no—but Relan *was* with his father in Turnig during a rebellion.

Reading through those reports was just for his own gratification, however, and he had actual work he needed to get done. So instead, he picked up a letter from Sheal.

Sheal was back in Tieger, after arriving ragged and weary in Kyinth with several regents from the Northern Realm to pledge his loyalty to Yolken. While in Kyinth, Yolken had informed him of the ban on dragon bones and armor, and Sheal sent word back to Tieger ordering the full implementation of the edict. Sheal was now reporting that the process was largely complete and that he would personally accompany the wagon train transporting the bones and armor to Kyinth.

Much to Yolken's surprise, the Regency used dragon bones for almost everything. His personal exposure to them had been the Harachin sword and the few bones Jax and Deborah possessed—such as the string of bones Jax had sewn into his coat—but the Regency had them everywhere. There were what he considered the more traditional bones—swords, daggers, small figurines—but he'd learned there were also dragon bones inlaid in all sorts of things, such as furniture, so regents had access to Energy almost everywhere. Even Drakonias had dragon bone inlaid in his desk so he wouldn't be without a source of Energy when in his office. Yolken had a carpenter remove the bone and repair the desk. Regents across the empire would have to do the same. He didn't expect it to happen overnight; he knew the process would take weeks, if not months.

To hear that Sheal would have all the dragon bones in Tieger collected within a month was phenomenal news.

Yolken turned to the second page of the letter and stopped halfway down. A man by the name of Erigin was dead and the emperor's flagship, the *Soaring Dragon*, was missing. Erigin, Sheal wrote, had been the captain of the *Soaring Dragon*. Drakonias had kept him alive even though he hadn't used the ship since before contact was lost with the east. Reports indicated that two men had boarded the ship, prepared her for sail, and took her to sea. Alone. Yolken knew immediately, without Sheal even having to speculate, who those two men were: Devin and Drenan.

Where are they going? They couldn't possibly be going to the east, could they? Nobody had crossed the East Sea in almost seventy years because the cyclones had become so powerful that most who attempted it didn't survive. Could they be going to the south? Drenan didn't think he was going to take the south back, did he? He still hadn't heard from the regents in the Olivara, Harachin, Orla, or Reega provinces. Maybe he was going there to rally help. If they could get a few regents on their side, it would make it easier to reclaim the south. If that was the case, or even within the realm of possibility, he had to warn Javen, Jax, and Tabora.

Yolken's thoughts were interrupted when Energy left him to operate the Lift. It didn't take any effort for him to stay connected to the Lift, so during the day, when he was in his quarters, he kept a thin connection in case Sahri needed to use it. Was it time for his and Kaylan's evening meal already? He looked at the light out the window and knew it couldn't be. The door to the Lift opened a moment later and Kaylan stepped out. His heart leaped at the sight of her—she grew more beautiful every day—but the thought quickly turned to worry. His being the emperor meant she was empress. And the empire had not had an empress since long before Yolken was born. The city, he learned, had been abuzz about the prospect of Drakonias marrying his lover, Angania. Now she was living in self-imposed isolation in one of the palace's many suites—Yolken couldn't bring himself to evict her after Drakonias' death. The buzz surrounding Angania had quickly transferred to Kaylan. Being empress had kept her busier than she wanted to be. It was more than either of them had ever wanted with their lives. They regularly pined for simpler times, longing to be back in Lonely Oak running their tavern. Seeing her after they'd finished breakfast had become so rare that her appearance now was cause for concern.

As she crossed the room, circumnavigating the semicircular couch and spiraling staircase that led up to their sleeping quarters the Lift clanged back into motion. He stood as she approached and, stepping around his desk, opened the glass door for her. He looked past her at the Lift, then focused on her and said, "Hi." She came in and embraced him in a hug. "Everything okay?"

"Mm-hmm," Kaylan said. "Why? Is everything okay with you?"

"Yeah," he said, confused. "It's just... you've been so busy. I wasn't expecting you."

"Well," Kaylan said, stepping back, "there's something I wanted to tell you."

Yolken looked down at Kaylan, curious. The Lift started back up, making him look up.

"After our ride down in the Lift I wasn't feeling well. I felt... nauseous, like I wanted to throw up. Actually, I *did* throw up."

Yolken took Kaylan back into his arms and said, "I'm sorry, honey." But he was distracted by the Lift and wondered who could be using it this time. He was going to be very annoyed if it was Enif. He looked down at Kaylan and said, "Do you think it was something we ate? I've felt fine."

The Lift stopped and the door opened.

"I didn't know, but it scared me, so I went to see the nurse. She took a quick look at me and sent me straight to the—"

Jax stepped out of the Lift.

"What in Draego's Fire—" Yolken said.

"What?"

"What is *he* doing here?"

Kaylan looked over her shoulder. "Jax?"

As Jax approached, Yolken grew angry. "What in Draego's Fire are you doing here?" he said when Jax stopped at the door.

"Nice to see you too, Your Highness," Jax said with a bow.

"Why aren't you with Javen? You should be in the south by now."

Jax looked up and to the side in thought. He nodded and said, "That sounds about right. Maybe the lad's meeting with the queen as we speak."

"*You* should be there with him, Jax. What are you doing here?"

"Something more important. But first I think you should sit."

"Sit? I have a mind to throw you off the balcony."

Jax furrowed his brow. "Why so violent?"

"Maybe I'm exaggerating—the dungeon is probably more appropriate."

"Please," Jax said, gesturing toward Yolken's chair, "sit."

Yolken stared at Jax, but Jax returned his stare. Begrudgingly, he walked back around his desk and sat. Kaylan sat in one of the chairs on the other side of the desk, and Jax sat on the arm of another.

"You better have a good reason for not being in Hantlo, Jax," Yolken said. "Negotiating peace with Hadie is really important to me."

"I wouldn't be here unless it was of the utmost importance."

"Out with it then."

"Remember when I told you about the Machines used during Drakonias' war?"

"Yeah?"

"You're going to need them."

"What? Why?"

"A war's coming."

"What are you talking about?"

"I don't have all the details, only that you need to use the Machines to defend the capital or everyone you love will die."

"Jax, you aren't making any sense. There are only a few regents who haven't pledged their allegiance yet."

"Yolken, I wouldn't have returned if it wasn't important."

"All right," Yolken said, thinking. He believed Jax; he wouldn't have disobeyed and left Javen for no reason. "How did you hear about this… war?"

"I…" Jax started. "Well, how I heard about it doesn't matter. That I know it's coming is what's important."

"So you're refusing to tell me?"

Jax nodded.

"But you want me to prepare for a war using Machines."

Jax nodded again.

"Machines that are powered by dragon bones."

"I know how this sounds, Yolken. But if you don't, it'll be the end of Dradonia. At least as we know it."

"Jax, you know very well I can't do that. Not two months ago I publicly banned the use of dragon bones and now you want me to use Machines to defend Kyinth? Machines, Jax! Most people don't even know they exist!"

"It's crazy, I know."

"Yes. It's crazy. Even if for some reason I agreed to this, I have no idea where the Machines are. I haven't found anything in any of Drakonias' writings."

"They're under the city."

"What? How do you know that?"

Jax stood and clasped his hands behind his back.

"Let me guess, you can't tell me?"

Jax shook his head. "I swore not to say."

"You also swore to me, Jax."

"I am not betraying my oath to you, Yolken. I'm trying to protect you. You and all you hope to accomplish."

"Yolken," Kaylan said.

Yolken shook his head. "This isn't crazy. It's madness."

"Please, Your Highness," Jax said.

"No, Jax. And don't think you can sway me by getting all formal on me. I won't break the promise I made Deth."

"Yolken!" Kaylan shouted over them.

Yolken stopped and looked from Jax to Kaylan. It was only now that he realized he'd been ignoring her from the moment Jax barged in. "I'm sorry, Kaylan. Jax, could you give us a moment?" Yolken looked at Jax, but Jax didn't move. Yolken furrowed his brow and looked back at Kaylan. "What was it you were going to say?"

Yolken watched her as she looked from him to Jax and back, disappointment on her face. "This isn't how I wanted this to go," she said.

"How you wanted what to go?"

"The midwife says that—"

"*Midwife?*"

Kaylan nodded. "The nurse sent me to see the midwife."

Yolken noticed her eyes were glistening. He stood from his chair. "Kaylan?"

Kaylan stood, her hands clasped before her. "I came because I wanted to tell you that I'm with child."

Yolken's throat caught. *With child?* He thought back to this morning when he woke next to her and was once again driven by her beauty to bed her, as they'd done almost every day since they became man and wife. She didn't seem different... or look different. His eyes drifted down to her stomach, where her hands fidgeted.

Kaylan's fidgeting stopped as her hands felt her stomach. "I'm only just." She walked around the desk and he took her into his arms. She buried her head in his chest and hugged him just as tightly as he hugged her.

"I'll... give you two a moment," Jax said.

Yolken looked over Kaylan's head at Jax. The anger he'd felt only moments ago toward Jax for leaving Javen and returning to Kyinth was gone.

CHAPTER 30

Yolken embraced Kaylan, wavering from pure joy to absolute fear. Kaylan was with child, which meant he was going to be a father. What did he know about being a father? Except for Jax's wandering presence—though he'd been Jorgan then—he'd grown up without a father. And now he was going to *be* one? Kaylan was with child... and the baby growing in her belly was his...

Yolken fell to his knees and pressed his cheek against Kaylan's stomach, wrapping his arms around her waist. He immediately felt the need to protect the child, to ensure no harm ever came to it. Here, at the top of the palace, the unborn child was as safe as it possibly could be. But the thought of running flashed through his mind. Where? To the Mindons. He could hide away from the world with Kaylan. But if he did, what kind of world would his child grow up in? Would there even *be* a world for it to grow up in?

"So?" Kaylan said.

Yolken kissed Kaylan's stomach and stood back up. He kissed Kaylan and hugged her again. He squeezed her tight, then stepped back. "You're sure?" he said, even though he had no reason to doubt her.

Kaylan nodded.

"I can't believe it," he said.

"Neither could I."

"I wanted to wait."

"Well, what did you expect?"

"I..." he began, but stopped when he felt his cheeks redden.

"You don't have to be embarrassed." Kaylan stepped closer to him and pulled his head down for a kiss. "We're married."

"I know. It's just—"

"No 'just', Yolken."

"I don't know what to do."

"Nobody does at first. Besides, I'm only just with child. We have plenty of time to figure things out."

"That's not what I meant. I—"

"I know exactly what you meant, Yolken. And it doesn't matter. I'm here. You're here. We're having a baby. And I'm not in the least bit sorry."

"I... neither am I. But aren't you scared?"

"I'm terrified. I have been since the day my mammy dragged me away from my home and up into the Mindons. But we can't be afraid to live our lives. We'll never be safe. Even if we can somehow leave this all behind and go home."

"That's all I've ever wanted..."

Kaylan slipped her arms around Yolken again. "I know. But this is our home now—at least for now."

"For now," Yolken conceded. He had no intention of spending the rest of his life here. When he finished whatever it was he needed to do, he *was* going back to Lonely Oak. He would build their home—not here, but in the maple grove outside of Lonely Oak.

Kaylan stepped back. "We can celebrate this evening. It seems you and Jax have things to discuss."

Yolken felt annoyed that he couldn't spend the rest of the day with Kaylan. He looked past her to see if he could see Jax, but didn't. He kissed Kaylan and said, "I'll see you this evening."

He placed his hand on Kaylan's stomach again, smiled at her, then pushed the glass door open.

He stepped out into the atrium toward the Lift. After a few steps, he saw Jax sitting on the couch situated inside the spiraling staircase. He was leaning back with his legs crossed, stretched out in front of him, and his arms resting out to his sides on the back cushion.

"About time," Jax said.

"You interrupted what would probably have been the most special moment in our lives."

"More special than the day you married?"

"I don't have time for this, Jax."

Jax sat up on the couch and said, "You're right." He gestured toward the couch a quarter of the way around the circle and said, "Sit."

"I'll stand, thank you."

"Look, lad. I know—"

"I'm not a lad anymore, Jax."

"I know, I know."

"Then don't talk down to me like I'm that boy from Lonely Oak whose hair you tousled when you came to visit."

"I'm sorry, Yolken," Jax said, standing. "Truly, I am."

"Then you understand why I can't allow the use of Machines."

"Because you promised Deth."

"Precisely."

"But Yolken…"

"Jax, you weren't in the cave with me."

"No. I wasn't."

"So you don't understand like I do."

"I don't *understand?* Please…" Jax plopped back down onto the couch. "…explain, Your Highness."

Yolken pursed his lips. "If you're not careful, I'll adjourn this meeting. In fact, I have a mind to send you back down and make you wait until council like everyone else."

"Are you *sure* you want me down there? The moment they see me they're going to want to know why I'm back, and I can't promise you I'll lie. You know how Enif opposed this particular ban."

"Jax! Dragons aren't just creatures of fable anymore!"

"I never said they were. At least not since you *were* a lad and listened so intently to my stories."

"What I mean is, they're... well... Deth is a living, breathing creature. To continue using dragon bones... it wouldn't be any different than if you killed me and used my bones."

"Yolken..."

"What? I can store Energy in my bones now. Would you find it acceptable to use my bones as weapons?"

"Of course not."

"Then why a dragon's bones?"

"We're not talking about killing Deth and using his bones."

"Just the bones of his species. Maybe even his mate."

"But if we don't it'll—"

"—be the end of Dradonia," Yolken said. "You already said that. What you didn't say was why. Or how you know this."

"I can't."

"Why not?"

"Because I promised."

"Well, if you want me to even consider going back on my promise, you'll have to go back on yours."

"Fine," Jax said, sitting forward on the edge of the couch. He rested his elbows on his knees and his chin on his clasped fists.

Yolken waited. He looked down at Jax, who appeared deep in thought.

"Relan told me," Jax finally said.

"*Relan?*" He wasn't expecting that. He loved old Relan, appreciated his loyalty to the tavern, but old Relan was a drunk.

Jax settled back on the couch again. "How much do you know about Relan, Yolken?"

Tired of standing and looking down at Jax, Yolken finally decided to sit. "More than I used to."

"What do you mean?"

"I read Nera's report about a certain rebellion in Turnig." Jax gave him a quick look. "You lied... again."

"No, I didn't. Relan was *not* a part of the Order. But as you now know, he was a longtime friend of your father."

Yolken gave a small snort through his nose and sat back on the couch as well. All this time, he'd thought he knew him... But really, now that he thought about it, he didn't know anything about Relan. He was just someone who was always there. "What was he doing in Lonely Oak? I thought the whole point of my father going to Lonely Oak was to leave his old life behind."

"It was. It was a coincidence they met there. Relan was passing through and stopped at the tavern for a meal. When he saw who was tending the bar, he never left."

"I guess that explains why he was always at the tavern," Yolken said. Suddenly curious about this new aspect of his father's past—he loved learning about his parents—he asked, "How did they know each other?"

"They met during a rebellion in Turnig. Well," Jax said, "actually, Relan convinced your father to help start it."

That was curious. It was a side Nera's report didn't cover. "And?"

"And it's a long story, but that's not the point right now. The point is that I promised Relan I wouldn't say who my source was, but now I have."

"I don't understand why. What's the big secret?"

"I am a purveyor of information, Yolken. And purveyors such as myself and those who confide in me have a certain understanding. An agreement, if you will."

"You lost me."

"Possessing certain information, let alone disseminating it, can get someone killed. So sources have strict rules of confidentiality with people like me."

Yolken was confused. "Why would I kill Relan?"

"Old habits are hard to let go of, I suppose," Jax said. "But all this is beside the point. The point is that there's a war coming, and you need to prepare."

"How does Relan know this?"

"Does it matter?"

"Yes, it matters. I'm not going to just undo one of the most important decisions I've made since I came here."

"Don't tell Kaylan that..."

"You know what I mean." Yolken stood. "I've got some more reading to do before dinner."

Jax stood as well. "Please, just consider it."

"There's nothing to consider."

"At least promise me this: After dinner, come with me to see them."

"What?"

"The Machines. Don't tell me you aren't at least curious to see them. I know I am."

Yolken hesitated a moment, but then said, "I'll think about it." He walked back toward his office but stopped after a few steps and turned back toward Jax. "And in the meantime, stay out of sight. I don't want to have to answer more questions from Enif."

CHAPTER 31

Yolken stood at the top of the stairs leading from the front entrance of the palace down to the street. He hadn't realized it until now—he'd been so incredibly busy he hadn't had time to think about it—but this was the first time he'd been outside the palace since he had arrived in Kyinth two months ago.

He looked at the Grand Station, which was on the opposite side of the street from the palace. Just like all the other buildings in the city, the Grand Station's carved-stone architecture amazed the boy in him who'd grown up in Lonely Oak, where Brall's three-story inn was the tallest building. The sun had already set, but he could still easily make out the building's details. The top tapered in a series of arches to a single arch in the middle, which contained an enormous clock. It indicated half past six—his second council meeting of the day had gone long, and he'd cut his dinner with Kaylan short.

Of all the people he'd interacted with and all the things he'd learned since becoming the emperor, it had been Javen who told him about the Grand Station. It was one of the early galas he held in his personal quarters—he had personally run the Lift to transport his many guests up and down. He didn't want to hold the galas, but his advisors convinced him of how important it was to establish relationships with the regents. On one particularly warm evening, he'd been out on the balcony talking with Javen when he'd started talking about the building. He was even more surprised to learn that Javen had traveled from Onta to Kyinth in a Train. A part of him regretted his decision to ban the use of dragon bones; traveling the empire in a matter of days instead of months would have been much more efficient.

Jax had told Yolken to meet him in the Grand Station after dinner. He still didn't know why he'd agreed to go. He already knew he wasn't going to allow the use of weapons of war powered by dragon bones again. But, as Jax said, he *was* curious to see them. He hadn't even known such things existed until after he'd healed Issa.

He started down the palace steps alone—his advisors would be furious if they knew he was leaving the palace unguarded— and wondered why Jax wanted to meet in the Grand Station. At the bottom he crossed the street, weaving around wagons and other passersby, and walked through the center of five tall archways into a large, domed foyer. He looked around but didn't see Jax, so he proceeded across the chamber toward a dark passage on the far side. His boots echoed on the tiled floor with each step he took. Jax emerged from the dark recess, carrying two lanterns.

"Ah, there you are," Jax said. He handed one of the lanterns to Yolken. "Was beginning to wonder if you'd decided not to come."

"The meeting went long."

"You're in charge, aren't you? Can't you put an end to it whenever you want?"

"You'd think," Yolken said. "As it was, I had to eat hastily, and Kaylan's annoyed that we couldn't celebrate."

"My apologies, lad... er... Your Highness." Jax spun and headed back into the dark. "I'll try to get you back as quickly as possible."

Yolken clenched his jaw and followed.

Jax started down one of two odd-looking sets of stairs. His boots clanged suspiciously. Yolken stopped at the rusted metal grate at the top of the stairs and knelt down to inspect them. They were grooved and made of metal.

"I'm told they used to move," Jax said. "One went up, and the other down."

A Machine, Yolken thought. After Drakonias' war, war Machines had given way to Machines that were used for good. Machines such as the Train that had brought Javen to Kyinth, or the Lift in the palace. There were countless others that Drakonias had banned back in 295 once he realized what they had done—and were continuing to do—to the sun. He often wondered what Dradonia had looked like before that infamous edict. He only had the few stories Jax and Deborah had told.

"Come on," Jax said, "or I'll never get you back to your empress."

Yolken stood and followed Jax down the metal staircase, which descended down a tunnel. It was unbelievably long, taking them well below ground. Darkness quickly enveloped them. They traveled in their bubble of light, but at the bottom they entered an enormous cavern that swallowed it up. With the Energy stored in his bones, he created a large flame high above his head, which revealed row after row of small buildings lined up along thin metal rails. The fire's light flickered over ceiling tiles high above. The rails ran parallel to each other, about six feet apart, from one end of the cavern to the other, and disappeared into smaller tunnels. There were five sets of these rails that Yolken counted. To his eye, the long rectangular things resembled carriages with large metal wheels, and four of them sat on the closest set of the odd rails.

Jax led Yolken around a waist-high fence and said, "That's the Train that brought Javen to Kyinth. It belonged to Reago. It was treason for him to use it, but after your little interaction with Devin in Onta, he knew it was time to confront Drakonias."

Jax hopped off the landing at the edge of the rails and crossed over to the other side, stepping over the two metal rails. "Train rails used to crisscross the empire, but most of them were removed."

Yolken followed, letting his fire die. He didn't want to waste Energy unnecessarily. He climbed up onto the landing on the other side near the next small building. There was another set of metal stairs rising up into the ceiling. Jax started hopping over the rows of fencing rather than walking around them.

"They did a pretty thorough job," Jax said. "I didn't know about them until I happened across the rails up in the Ontalis. It's one of the only lines left."

As interesting as that was, what Yolken wanted to know was where they were going. He expressed as much when Jax climbed down onto the next set of rails.

Jax gestured to the far side of the cavern. "Over there."

Yolken followed Jax across the next three sets of rails and ended up on a ledge along the far wall. The tiles on the wall shimmered in their lanterns' light.

Jax walked along the ledge and stopped in front of a door. It stood out from the rest of the wall because of its conspicuous lack of shimmering tiles. Jax reached into a pocket and produced a key.

"Where'd you get that?" Yolken said. Jax looked at Yolken out of the corner of his eye as he fit the key into the lock on the door. "Let me guess; can't say?"

"Reago brought it with him from Onta." Jax turned the key, then pushed the door open.

"That doesn't answer my question."

"You're right." Jax went through the door, holding the lantern out before him.

Yolken followed him into a tunnel. It had rough-cut walls and was only about ten feet high. There was another set of tracks with what looked like a sort of miniature Train sitting on them.

"This," Jax said, gesturing to the foremost carriage, "is the

Engine cart."

The Engine cart was a small open-topped carriage with a padded bench and a set of levers. It was connected to several empty carts that looked sort of like the wagons farmers used to carry their goods into town, but made of metal instead of wood. Jax unhooked the Engine cart from the others.

"You're kidding, right?" Yolken said, taken aback.

"I suppose we could walk," Jax said. "I don't know exactly how far down it is, but it can't be any worse than when you went to visit Deth. But don't you think this would be way more fun?"

"Fun?" Yolken said, incredulous. "How could you possibly even know how to operate this thing?"

"I read the instructions," Jax said.

"*Instructions?*"

Noticing that the seat was covered in thick layer of dust, Jax swept his hand across it a few times. "Sit."

Yolken wanted to ride, but he also knew Transports— whether Trains, Autos, or… this—ran on Energy.

Seeing Yolken's hesitation, Jax said, "I know what you're thinking. This thing runs on dragon bones. Which is true. However, what if *you* powered it?"

"You mean like the Lift?"

"Exactly." Jax moved to the front of the cart and pointed. "Look here." Between the levers protruded a cylindrical dragon bone. Jax reached in and pulled the bone out. He turned it over and pointed at the hole on the bottom of the bone. "See this? This sits down on a metal prong. If you directed Energy onto that prong, *you* could power the cart. That's what the dragon bone does—stores Energy and feeds it into the cart."

Yolken smiled. "Fine."

Jax climbed in. He slid over to the far side, where the levers were, and hung his lantern on a hook sticking up in the corner. Then he patted the space next to him and said, "Your Highness."

Yolken sat next to Jax. Sitting shoulder to shoulder, it was indeed tight.

"Since the cache is *under* the city, I imagine it's downhill most of the way. So it'll probably only need a little Energy to get it rolling."

Yolken transferred Energy into his Core and, with a thin thread of Energy, reached into the slot where the dragon bone had been. He found the metal probe Jax had mentioned and pushed Energy into it. "All right," he said.

Jax pulled back on the left lever. A loud, metallic clang echoed from outside the cart.

"What in Draego's Fire was *that?*" Yolken said.

"The brakes letting loose." Jax pushed forward on the other lever and the cart lurched forward, throwing them both back into the seat. "Sorry. Too much."

Yolken raised his lantern with one hand and held onto the front of the cart with the other as the cart accelerated. Jax pulled back on the right lever when the cart reached about the same pace as a trotting horse, and Yolken felt the flow of Energy from his Core to the cart stop. The cart glided down the tunnel for a while, then started slowing. Jax eased forward on the lever, moving it only a little this time. Yolken felt the flow of Energy resume, smaller this time, and the cart slowly accelerated.

The tunnel they moved through went from having a ceiling that was ten feet high to one that was low enough Yolken thought he could reach up and touch it. The grade of the tunnel also dipped sharply. Jax pulled back on the right lever, cutting off the Energy draw from Yolken, as the cart accelerated on its own. The rails tilted sharply to the right, making Yolken slide to the side.

"Slow down!" Yolken shouted over the sound of the metal wheels grinding on the rails.

Jax pulled back on the left lever. The screeching of metal on metal echoed in the small tunnel.

The cart continued its spiraling descent, and Jax kept the speed at a rate they both felt comfortable with. Yolken wondered how far below the ground they were. After several minutes the track straightened and leveled out.

A light appeared ahead and grew steadily as the cart coasted. Yolken felt Energy draw from his Core again as Jax eased forward on the right lever. The light took the shape of an arch—an exit to the tunnel. They passed through it out into an enormous cavern illuminated by dozens of lights atop tall poles. Its size reminded Yolken of the cavern where he met Deth. The moment of awe he felt faded when they passed the first of the lights and he saw that it wasn't a typical lantern. Somehow, it was light, but not a flame like their lanterns, contained within what looked like a glass ball. There were dozens of them scattered evenly for as far as he could see. And below them sat row upon row of perfectly arranged Machines.

Yolken stared, fixated, as they moved farther into the cavern. It was a scene unlike anything he had ever seen before. The Machines looked to be made of metal, like the Train, but with fully enclosed sides and tops. They were boxy in structure, with sharp, abrupt edges. They were also longer than they were wide and tall. Instead of wheels like carriages they had a series of six small wheels, similar to the Train, that were encased in a continuous looped track of some sort. A long, thin tube protruded from the front of each Machine. The only window he could see on them was a small one just above the tube.

"What in Draego's Fire..." Yolken said. He tapped Jax on the arm and said, "Do you see that?"

Yolken pointed down one of the rows. There were people—he counted six—working around one of the Machines.

"Did you know there were people down here?" Yolken said.
"No, I did not."
"What are they doing?"
"I have no idea."

As they continued, the large rectangular Machines gave way to smaller, boxier Machines. They had the same wheel system and protruding tubes as the larger Machines, only smaller. After several rows of those, they gave way to even smaller, open-topped Machines. In place of the protruding tubes was a sort of crow's nest, to which a small round metal device, about a pace long, sat affixed to a mount.

"This is unbelievable," Yolken said. The sheer number of these Machines, lying hidden beneath Kyinth, was mind-boggling. He wondered what they did.

The track curved right, bringing a long building into view. The building looked to be only one floor, but there was a tower at the far end. The track ended adjacent to the building, where there was a landing. A solitary man stood hunched over on the landing, his hands clasped in front of him. As they approached the building, Jax pushed forward on the right lever and pulled back on the left, slowing the cart. Yolken watched the man as the cart came to a stop. He had gray hair and pasty white skin. The man's squinted eyes suddenly widened. He bowed, then reached down and opened the door to the cart.

After Yolken climbed out, the man's eyes narrowed again and he said, "Who are you?"

"My name is Yolken."

"Yol...?" The man had a confused look on his face.

"I am the Emperor of the United Realms."

He didn't look any less confused.

"Drakonias is dead," Yolken said. "And I took his place."

"Yes, Your Blessed Highness." The man bowed again. "It is not my place to ask, only to obey."

Hoping to ease some of his own confusion, Yolken said, "What are you doing down here?"

"We are the Caretakers."

"Caretakers?"

"Yes, Your Highness. We are here to serve."

"Serve how?"

"We ensure the Machines are ready."

"Ready for what?"

"I... it is not my place to ask, Your Highness. Only to ensure that they are ready."

"But what does that mean?"

The man looked up at Yolken, still confused. "To ensure that—"

"Okay, okay," Yolken said. "I get it." He looked past the man at the tower and saw that there was a large bell at the top. "And do you have a name?"

"One," the man said.

"One?"

"Yes, Your Highness. There are five hundred Caretakers."

"I didn't ask how many of you there were, I asked what your name was."

"My name is One."

"You go by numbers?"

"Yes."

Yolken glanced over at Jax, who shrugged his shoulders. "Why?" Yolken said, turning back to the man.

"I do not know, Your Highness. It is the name the emperor... er... yes... that we were given."

"Drakonias named you?"

"Yes."

"He named you One?"

"Yes."

"And the others?"

"Each of us is given a number when selected."

"Selected?" Talking with this man—One—was not clearing things up.

"We are selected to serve."

"By whom?" Yolken said.

"I was selected by the Regent of Aliza, Your Highness," the man said with a bow.

"Dane? Is that where you're from? Aliza?"

"Yes. I lived in Aliza before I was selected."

"And your job is to keep the Machines ready?"

"Yes, Your Highness."

"And how long have you been... serving?"

"Three hundred ninety-two years."

Yolken let out a gasp. "Three hundred years!"

"Three hundred *ninety-two*, Your Highness."

"Draego's Fire," Jax said. "You're older than me."

One turned to look at Jax.

"He Regenerates you," Jax said.

"We are blessed with immortality when chosen to serve."

"And you live down here?"

"Yes," One said. "Er, I'm sorry, but his Highness always came alone." One bowed and said, "My apologies if I have not shown you proper respect. Who are you?"

"My advisor," Yolken said.

"Ah. Yes, Your Highness."

"So you've lived here for three hundred years?"

"Three hundred and ninety-two, Your Highness."

"What about the others?"

"I am number one."

"Meaning?"

"I have been here the longest—although Two through Twelve all arrived with me. Thirteen through Nineteen"—One paused, thinking—"I believe it was a few weeks later. It's hard to remember for sure. Twenty through Thirty arrived—"

"That's enough," Yolken said, holding up a hand. He looked at the long, single-story building and said, "Is this where you live?"

"Everything we need is here. Food, water, supplies."

"Monstrous," Jax said. "You're prisoners."

"No," One said. "We are the Caretakers."

"You can't leave. He couldn't permit it. Else his secret would get out. He brought you here to maintain the Machines and sentenced you to an eternity of... I couldn't think of a more horrible way to live."

"I agree," Yolken said. "This has to end. If I'd known about this before, I'd have ended it immediately."

"The Machines must be ready," One said.

"Uh, Yolken," Jax said. He grabbed Yolken by the arm and tried to pull him away from One.

Yolken resisted. "What?"

"A word?"

Yolken looked at One but then followed Jax.

Jax stopped a few paces from One and said, "I know what you're thinking, but you can't just bring five hundred men up to the city. What are you going to tell people? Word will get out about what's down here."

"I'm really starting to regret agreeing to come down here with you," Yolken said. He looked back at One. "But I can't just leave them down here."

"It's not as though they'd know the difference."

"But I'd know. And I can't imagine how much Energy they use down here—or where it's coming from. And someone is keeping them supplied! This is barbaric!"

"So what do you propose?"

Yolken shook his head in disgust. "I don't know." He looked from Jax to One, then out at the Machines. "Do you know what any of these actually do?"

"No. I've tried looking for information about them but Drakonias left no evidence behind."

"Hmm," Yolken said. He walked back to where One patiently waited with his hands clasped before him and said, "So you and the others were tasked by Drakonias to care for these Machines."

"Yes, Your Highness," One said.

"Do you know how they work?"

One's eyes widened briefly. "Er... yes, Your Highness."

By his reaction, Yolken figured One thought that was a stupid question. If they'd been tending to the Machines for as long as they had, of course they would know how they worked. "Can we go look at one?" he said.

"Er... yes, Your Highness. After all, they belong to you."

Yolken hadn't considered that. He still wasn't used to the

idea that he was the emperor—he didn't need to ask permission. "Show me," he said. After a pause, before One had the opportunity to react, he added, "Please."

"Any particular one you'd like to see?"

"Let's start here," Yolken said, gesturing toward the nearest Machine.

They stopped in front of one of the smaller Machines, one with the crow's nest with the metal device mounted on it.

"This is an Auto," One said. "And that," he said, pointing to the round metal device, "is called a Gun."

"What does it do?" Yolken said.

"It fires Bullets very rapidly."

"What's a Bullet?"

One opened a latched box built into the side of the Auto and pulled out a smaller box. He set it on the ground, opened it, and pulled out a round piece of metal with a pointed end. He held it out toward Yolken.

Yolken took it from One and looked it over.

"The Gun propels these out very rapidly, and at very high speed."

Yolken tried to imagine what kind of damage this... *Bullet...* would cause when it hit something.

They went from Machine to Machine, One explaining in dizzying detail how each operated and what they were used for. Yolken was overwhelmed by the amount of chaos these Machines could cause, especially the large rectangular ones with the long round tubes. One had called them Tanks. The Bullets propelled from Tanks were actually called Shells, and they were enormous. Yolken couldn't fathom the amount of damage one single Shell from a Tank might inflict.

When they returned to the cart, Yolken was completely bewildered. "Thank you," he said.

"We live to serve," One said.

"Thank you," Yolken said again, not knowing what else to say in the moment. He had agreed to come down here and look at the Machines with Jax, not fully knowing what to expect. He certainly hadn't expected to find hundreds of slaves that only Drakonias knew about. Now the question was: What was he going to do about them?

Yolken and Jax climbed back into the cart.

"Your Highness?" One said.

"Yes?" Yolken said.

"When I heard you coming, I thought you were bringing supplies."

"Supplies?"

One nodded. "We are running low, Your Highness. Food, water, recharged Cells."

"Drakonias brought the supplies..."

"Yes, Your Highness."

Yolken nodded. "Do you have a list?"

"Just a moment," One said. He turned and shuffled toward the building.

Yolken sighed. The discovery of these poor Caretakers was another problem he didn't have a solution to. He certainly couldn't allow them to starve, and he couldn't keep them down here in the dark either.

A few moments later One returned and handed Yolken a rolled-up parchment. He accepted it from him, then reached into the port with Energy and connected himself with the metal probe. Jax pulled back on the left lever, releasing the brake, and pushed forward with the right lever, and the cart lurched into motion again. The track continued past the building, then looped back around on itself in a big circle. One shifted a large lever as they came around the loop and Yolken heard the rails clang. The cart rejoined the rails, only now going in the opposite direction.

Yolken considered the Machines as they slid by: instruments of war. He wondered how many people had died as a direct result of them. Moreover, each of them contained a dragon bone. Reports indicated they were making real headway in the effort to collect dragon bones from around the empire. He felt like he'd taken several steps backward—there had to be thousands of bones hidden in these Machines, not even counting the bones the Caretakers used to power their lights and whatever other Machines they might use down here.

He relit their lanterns when the cart left the cavern and went back into the tunnel. The ascent, powered by the Energy stored in Yolken's bones, took much longer than the descent, and the conundrum of what to do about the Caretakers weighed on him the entire time. They needed supplies, which included charged dragon bones, or they would starve. And if their Energy supply gave out before their food, they'd starve in complete blackness. Would they try to escape up through the Grand Station? Or worse, would they emerge from the depths of Kyinth using the Machines?

As they climbed back up the metal stairs leading from the Grand Station to the surface, Jax said, "I hope you realize now the importance of using the Machines."

"My answer is no," Yolken said.

"How can you still say that?"

"Because you've given me no reason to use them. I'll consider the threat you've mentioned, but I'm not authorizing you to bring those Machines up to the surface until I verify your claims." He *did*, however, need to decide what to do about the Caretakers.

"So you don't believe me?"

"Well, it's not the first time you've lied to me." As much as he hated it, he added, "See to it they get the supplies they need. I need to figure out what to do with them and I can't very well let them starve in the meantime." Remembering what it had been like to be in complete darkness in Deth's cave, he added, "Or be stuck down there with no light."

"Yes, Your Highness."

They walked out of the foyer and back onto the street. Jax bowed and started walking down the street.

"Where are you going?" Yolken called.

"I can't very well go back into the palace with you, now can I?"

Yolken conceded that Jax was right. He was supposed to be with Javen in the south. "Jax," he said.

"Yes, Your Highness?"

"Why did you really come back?"

"I told you, Your Highness."

"You honestly think there's a war coming in which we'll need Machines?"

"I wouldn't have come back if I didn't. Now if you'll permit me, Your Highness, I'd best be going."

Yolken nodded. Jax turned and walked away. He watched Jax for a moment, thinking about what Jax said, then headed back across the street to the palace. *If there was such a threat,* he wondered, *why wouldn't Jax just tell me?* It would certainly make his decision that much easier to make.

Maybe Deth would have some insight. But as he climbed the steps, he couldn't help but think about how stupid he was going to sound going to Deth, to whom he'd promised to end the use of dragon bones and armor, and discussing the possibility of using them again. Should he tell Deth about the Caretakers? Until he figured out what to do with them, he would have to keep them supplied with dragon bones—or, as One had referred to them, Cells.

Being emperor was much harder than he ever imagined. How did Drakonias do it?

CHAPTER 32

Enif and several other advisors bombarded Yolken the moment he walked back into the palace. They were furious.

"I haven't been outside since the day I got here," Yolken said in his defense.

"You should have at least taken some guards with you," Enif protested.

"I'm quite capable of protecting myself."

"Even Drakonias wasn't that conceited!"

"Leave me alone," Yolken said. He wasn't in the mood for Enif's antics. He strode away, glad Enif had sense enough not to follow him. If he'd tried, Yolken would have ensured he couldn't.

He strode down the Hall of Relics toward the throne room. The displays that had once held the armor and weapons of those who had fought against Drakonias were now empty. A guard pulled open the door to the throne room as Yolken approached, and bowed to him as he passed. Another guard opened the inner door and bowed as well.

There was loud banging overhead where masons were working diligently to repair the hole in the ceiling Deth had caused. He'd forgotten that Deth wasn't in the throne room anymore. He turned around, exited through the double set of doors, and went down the hall to the Lift. A guard opened the door for him and bowed. All the bowing was unnecessary, he'd long ago determined, but he had yet to convince the guards to quit.

Yolken fed Energy into the Lift and rode it up to his quarters. Kaylan greeted him with an exuberant kiss. "I need to talk to Deth real quick," he said when their kiss ended. She frowned up at him, but he said, "We can celebrate in *just* a moment."

"Hurry," Kaylan said. The look in her eye betrayed what she was planning, and it wasn't a glass of wine.

Yolken went outside to the balcony and walked all the way around the palace, hoping to find Deth. The dragon wasn't around as much as he used to be when he was in the throne room, but he usually chose the balcony when he was. Unfortunately, he wasn't there. Yolken sighed and went back inside.

Kaylan wasn't on the bottom floor anymore, so he climbed the spiraling staircase to their bedchamber and found her in the bath. She smiled when she saw him.

"That was quick," she said.

"He wasn't there."

"Join me?"

The water in the tub was covered in a thick layer of bubbles, but he could just see the tops of Kaylan's breasts. He began disrobing as quickly as he could. "I can't believe we're going to have a baby," he said while he worked at unbuttoning his shirt.

Kaylan slid her hands down into the bubbly water. "Me neither."

"How do you feel?"

"Right now, fine. But the midwife told me mornings might not be too pleasant for a while."

"I'm sorry."

"Don't be. It's part of the process," Kaylan said. "So?"

"What?"

"Where'd you and Jax go?"

Yolken removed his pants and climbed into the tub. "To look at the Machines." He told her all about the Engine cart that had taken them deep under the city, and the enormous cavern filled with Machines.

"And?"

"They're incredible. The Caretakers say that, when powered, they—"

"Caretakers?"

Yolken shook his head, still in disbelief. "It's unbelievable," he said. Kaylan looked at him with deep interest. He loved that she cared so much about the most mundane things that consumed so much of his time. He wanted to spend less time ruling and more time researching. "There are five hundred people living down there—they have been for centuries—with the sole purpose of caring for the Machines in case Drakonias ever needed to use them again."

"Wow. Who would have ever guessed?"

"Nobody. Which was the point, I think."

"What did you decide?"

"Nothing, yet. If anything, going down there has complicated matters."

"How?"

"Because now I need to decide what to do with the Caretakers. I can't leave them down there. And they need to be resupplied with food, water... and dragon bones."

"Oh."

"Apparently Drakonias kept them supplied himself. And he's been gone for over two months."

Kaylan leaned forward. "Yolken..."

He couldn't help but notice her breasts were now visible, though still partially covered in suds. "I know what you're going to say. I'm only human, but I took this responsibility as my own. And there's no way I can leave those people down there.

Draego's Fire—they looked like ghosts."

"So bring them up. Sounds simple enough."

"And say what? Nobody besides me and Jax—and old Relan, apparently—knows about the cavern. What am I supposed to tell Enif and the others when five hundred ghosts suddenly appear in Kyinth? And where would they live?"

"Here," Kaylan said. "At least until you find them permanent homes. And who cares what Enif says? The man's incorrigible. I wish you'd send him away."

"I wish I could."

Kaylan slid back into the water. "What about the Machines?"

"They're powered by Energy, which means every single one of them uses a dragon bone. And Jax is lying to me, I know it. Which I hate."

"Tell him."

"I do. But he denies it. Even after all this time, for some reason, he still keeps things from me."

"Are you sure?"

"Think about it. He was supposed to be in Hantlo with Javen. Instead, he's back here telling me there's a war coming and that if we want to win, we have to use Machines. And I'm supposed to believe he got this information from old Relan?"

"You're right."

"How could Relan possibly know this?"

"Doesn't Jax pride himself on his ability to gather information?"

"Yes."

"Maybe Relan is one of his sources."

"*Relan?* I love old Relan—he's supported the tavern for as long as I can remember—but he's a drunk. Besides, if there was a threat that serious out there, wouldn't you think I'd know about it?"

"I suppose."

"I know Jax is good at gathering information—he did it for the Order for Draego knows how long—but the Regency can't be oblivious."

"I'm sorry you're so frustrated," Kaylan said. She reached a hand forward in the water and found one of Yolken's.

"It's not your fault."

"I know. But I can still be sorry. Turn around and let me scrub your back for you."

Yolken turned around, trying not to slosh water out of the brim-full tub.

Kaylan found a sponge on a table next to the tub and started scrubbing. "What do the others think?"

A laugh escaped Yolken's lips.

"What?" Kaylan said, stopping her scrubbing.

"Enif was angry that I'd left the palace without him or a guard. He'd be furious if he knew Jax was back. At the very least he'd use Jax's disobedience as leverage. He tries to gain some control at every opportunity."

Kaylan resumed her scrubbing. "Well, you need to do something."

"I know."

"Talk to Jax."

"I'm sorry."

"For what?"

"We're supposed to be celebrating."

"You don't have to be sorry, Yolken. Lift your arms."

Yolken held his arms up in the air.

"You don't have to carry these burdens by yourself."

"I know."

"I'm your wife, which means your burdens are my burdens. And we *are* celebrating."

Yolken turned his head to the side and said, "Thanks."

Kaylan kissed him on the cheek and said, "I love you."

"I love you, too."

"The least he could have done was brought some of my ale with him."

Kaylan laughed. "The nerve."

When Kaylan was done scrubbing him, Yolken leaned back and rested his head on her shoulder. She wrapped her arms around him and rested them on his chest. He closed his eyes and tried to think about the fact that they were going to be having a baby, but the astronomer's notes kept creeping into his head. He knew they didn't have much time before things started getting really bad in Dradonia. He feared that what was happening in the south and the East Sea was just the beginning of Dradonia's death throes. Defending Kyinth from Jax's coming war might be futile: What was the point of winning a war if everyone was going to die anyway?

"Yolken?"

"Mmm?"

"We're supposed to be celebrating..."

"We are."

"Then why have you been in a tub with your wife all this time and have yet to touch her?"

Yolken sat up, feeling embarrassed. She was right. He'd been unable to keep his hands off her since the day they'd married. He pushed his worries off until tomorrow and turned to look at Kaylan. Her beauty consumed him. "How would you like to celebrate?"

"How about you take me to bed?"

* * *

Jax ducked into the Emperor's Heel. The tavern was dimly lit and the air was thick with smoke. The patrons, Jax knew, were all here doing the same thing he was. There were dozens of such taverns in Kyinth, where the Suits, Reds, Silks, and at one time the Pearls met to scheme and connive. It had been years since he'd been here. In fact, thinking back on it, the last time he was here was when Sethlan had news regarding the whereabouts of the Harachin sword. He counted the years in his head. *Sixteen*, he concluded.

He nodded to Teven, the owner of the Emperor's Heel, as he walked to the rear of the tavern. Teven returned the nod and went back to absentmindedly wiping a mug.

Jax sat across from Deanna at a table in the back. Before he even had the chance to pull his chair in close to the table, a barmaid set a mug of ale down before him.

"So?" Deanna said.

Jax took a deep swig of his ale. He looked at the porcelain cup sitting on the table in front of Deanna and said, "Tea? Really?"

"Did he agree?"

"Not exactly," Jax said before taking another swig.

"Meaning what?"

"He agreed to go with me, but ended up saying he'd think about it."

"Do we have time for that?"

Jax smiled and took another swig of ale.

"Jax," Deanna said through clenched teeth. "You were supposed to convince him. That's why you went down there. We don't have time for him to think if I'm going to train an army how to use them."

"You won't have to," Jax said. "Or at least it's going to be much easier than we thought."

"Meaning?"

"That we already have an army." Jax smiled again and upended his mug. He turned in his seat and signaled to the barmaid for another.

CHAPTER 33

Yolken woke when the first hints of dawn began illuminating his and Kaylan's bedchamber. He nuzzled her awake, then bedded her, just as he'd done since they married. When their passion subsided, he slipped his robe on and went out onto the balcony. He clasped his hands behind his back and settled into pensive thought. When the sun crept over the horizon he began recharging his bones.

Drakonias, he now knew, had spent his mornings doing this very thing. He stared at the farms filling the landscape east of the city, thinking about the empty fields beyond and wondering what Drenan and Devin were up to. He thought about sending Jax and a contingency of Synthesizers to investigate, but the members of the Order weren't strong enough to challenge them, and of the regents who had pledged themselves to him, there was no one he trusted enough to send. Whatever they were doing didn't matter anyway, not if he couldn't figure out how to restore balance to the sun.

A shadow momentarily blocked the sun, making Yolken look up. He watched Deth soar in the sky, his wings held firmly out to his side. When he dipped in the sky, he beat his wings, lifting him higher. His path didn't veer in either direction: He was heading straight for the palace, growing in size. When he was almost upon Yolken, he lifted his head and body and began moving his wings in a different fashion, like a bird preparing to land. The great beast's wings beat hastily, buffeting Yolken with gusts of wind. Deth held his enormous rear claws out and gracefully landed on the stone railing of the balcony. He perched there, not moving except to gently fold his wings along his sides.

Yolken watched as Deth sat as motionless as a gargoyle. "What?" he eventually said.

"You must restore balance," Deth said.

"You've said that," Yolken said wryly. "And I'm trying as hard as I can to figure out how I'm supposed to do that."

"Replace what was taken."

"I know… but I can't. Despite the changes I've experienced, I still can't create Energy."

"Ignite the flame."

Yolken was really starting to get annoyed. Deth was starting to remind him of when he was a lad and his aunt Selena used to nag him about something, repeating herself over and over until he did what he was supposed to do. "But we're short an assembly of dragons, remember," he said sarcastically.

Deth exhaled a plume of smoke and climbed off the railing. His claws scratched at the marble as he lay down on the balcony, wrapping his tail around his body like a cat.

Next to Deth, Yolken watched the sun rise. He considered talking to the dragon about the Machines and Caretakers, but decided against it. He wasn't going to use the Machines, and he wouldn't let the Caretakers die. He couldn't believe he was going to disobey his own edict, even if it was only until he came up with a more permanent solution. When the sun was fully in the sky, he went back inside.

The servant's bell rang so Yolken energized the Lift and went to rouse Kaylan, who had a habit of falling back to sleep after they'd bedded. He walked into their bedchamber just in time to see her slip her arms into her robe. Seeing her naked breasts made him want to crawl back into bed with her and not leave for the rest of the day, but he knew that wasn't possible.

"Sahri's on her way up," he said.

Together they walked to the dining area, a room on the northern side of their suite which afforded them a spectacular view of the mountains. They sat just as Sahri entered, pushing a cart. She set a covered silver platter down in front of Kaylan and removed the lid. A blast of steam shot up.

Kaylan gagged and covered her mouth. She shook her head and signaled for Sahri to take the food away.

"Dawn ills?" Sahri said.

Kaylan nodded.

"Some tea, perhaps?"

"Yes, please."

Sahri poured Kaylan a cup, then served Yolken.

When he finished eating, he chatted with Kaylan for a few minutes, then excused himself. He'd barely settled into the chair in his office when the servant's bell rang. Enif was the first name to enter his head. At first, he'd tried incessantly to meet with Yolken one-on-one, but when Yolken consistently refused he'd stopped trying. The others respected his wishes to be left alone until council. Jax, perhaps?

Sahri appeared at the door and said, "Shall I see who it is?"

"Yes, thank you," he said. Using Energy, he reached across the palace to the Lift on the far side and powered the pulley system.

Sahri returned a few minutes later and said, "Nera Drake requests an audience, Your Highness."

Yolken furrowed his brow. "*Nera?*" She'd been the head of the Synod before he disbanded it. She'd been directly responsible for the murder of his parents and countless other members of the Order. He had yet to assign her a new position and was still assessing how much he trusted her.

What could she want? From what he understood, she had barely left her personal quarters because she held no position in the Regency, so the fact that she had come to the palace to speak with him made him genuinely curious what it could be about.

"Should I send her up?"

"Yes," he said.

Sahri returned to the Lift, and he felt Energy leave his Core as it went down. There was a pause, then Energy once again flowed, indicating the Lift was on its way back up. When the door opened, Yolken stood.

Nera emerged first, followed by Sahri. Sahri returned to the dining room while Nera proceeded toward Yolken's office.

Yolken watched as the former head of the Synod approached. He'd warily accepted her allegiance when the other regents pledged their loyalties to him.

At the door to his office Nera bowed and said, "Your Highness."

"Yes?"

"Do you have a moment?"

"I do."

"Thank you. I was wondering if you've ever heard of Mount Mazam?"

Remembering his lessons with Selena about the Great Dragon, he knew it was supposedly Draego's home on Dradonia, located in the mountains northeast of Kyinth—the direction from which Deth looked to have come that very morning, in fact. "I have," he said, his curiosity suddenly piqued.

"Did you know that about halfway up its slope is a cave that's home to a community of devout worshipers?"

"I did not," Yolken said. "Why?"

"Because I know you're searching for answers."

Yolken looked at Nera thoughtfully.

"I think you might find them there."

"What makes you think that?"

"Because I visited there once. There's no one in the entire empire more pious than those who live in that cave. If anyone has answers, for whatever your questions are, they will."

He still didn't fully trust her. "What about the high priest here in Kyinth? Wouldn't he have the answers?"

"Maybe," Nera said. "But then again, maybe not. But there was something different about the people in the cave. I can't explain it. But I thought you should at least know."

"Thank you, Nera."

She bowed and turned to leave.

Yolken looked over at the stack of parchment from Nera's office. "Nera…"

"Yes, Your Highness?"

Yolken lifted the top several sheets and held them out toward her. "Can you tell me what happened here?"

Nera took the sheets and looked them over. "What's there to say? Danav—uh… your father got away."

"That's the thing. I know the Black Sodality made several attempts on his life, and I've been reading through these reports."

"Your father was very hard to catch."

"What happened in each instance made sense. But this one"—Yolken pointed at the sheets Nera held—"doesn't. It looks to me like the Sodality had him. What happened?"

Nera hesitated.

"Nera?"

"I…" Nera looked down at the stack and then back at Yolken.

Yolken waited, giving Nera time.

"I… let him go," she eventually said.

Yolken fell heavily into his chair. He looked up at Nera, stunned. "You did? Why?"

"Does it matter? We eventually… succeeded."

"I just can't believe you would. Did Drakonias know?"

Nera shook her head. "But Drenan did. I mean, he didn't at first, but somehow he found out."

"Drenan?"

"I-I'm so sorry, Your Highness. It was my fault." Nera fell

to her knees and covered her face with her hands.

Yolken stood. "Nera?"

"I did it to protect myself."

"Let my father go?"

"No. Javen."

"*Javen?*"

"Somehow Drenan knew I let your father go. He knew why. And he threatened to tell Drakonias if I didn't kill Javen."

"It was an assassin who tried to kill Javen."

Nera nodded. "Please, Your Highness"—she held her hands out toward Yolken—"I beg you for mercy."

"I'm not going to hurt you, Nera." Yolken stepped around his desk and held a hand out to her. She took it and he pulled her to her feet. "I just want to know what happened." He gestured toward one of the chairs and said, "Sit."

Nera sat and took a moment to compose herself. When she had a little more control over herself, she said, "At the time we didn't know where your father was. But then there was an attempt on Darek's life." He was the Regent of Turnig, Yolken knew. "The news I received about what happened left me confused."

"What do you mean? How?"

"The details didn't line up with what Darek reported. From what I could tell from the actual report, your father had him— Darek should have been dead. But according to Darek himself, he'd foiled your father's plan and escaped. So, naturally, I was interested in finding out what had actually happened. Darek, obviously, wasn't any help, even when I pointed out the inconsistencies in his report. He insisted that he'd been able to overpower Danavin, but that wasn't what happened. Turns out, your father wasn't there to kill Darek."

"So what was he doing there?"

"He was helping a man named Relan."

Yolken's eyes widened. "*Relan?* He was *helping* Relan?" He'd read the report and knew Relan had been there, but the report hadn't said why.

"You know him?" Nera looked surprised.

"Yeah. He's this drunk from Lonely Oak. We called him old Relan. He came to my tavern every day. It was only recently that I learned he knew my father, but it wasn't until I read this report that I knew he was involved with the Order."

"He wasn't, though. He had nothing to do with the Order."

So Jax wasn't *lying*, Yolken thought. "Then what was he doing there?"

"Because he'd *asked* the Order to help him. Specifically, your father."

"What?"

"I needed to find out what happened in Turnig and I knew Darek wouldn't be forthcoming," Nera said. "And I certainly couldn't talk with your father... so I went to Relan."

"*You* know Relan?" This time it was Yolken's turn to be surprised.

"I tracked him down."

"And?"

"He told me what really happened."

Yolken shifted in his seat.

"Relan had no interest in the Order. At least not until Darek murdered his wife."

Yolken's eyes widened again—for more reasons than one. He'd had no idea Relan had been married. In all his drunken blathering over the years, he'd never once mentioned a wife.

"And for no reason except that she didn't show proper subservience when he passed by in the street," Nera continued. "Up until then, Relan revered the Blessed. But that changed when he watched Darek use his gift to throw Relan's wife across the street. Naturally, he wanted justice for her. Who wouldn't? And your father agreed to help him.

"Your father had Darek in his grasp, giving Relan the chance to look him in the eyes, to do whatever he pleased to him. Relan had the chance to kill a regent—something no one had ever done, no matter how unjust they might have thought they were—but he didn't do it. And..." Nera said, looking down into her hands, "I guess... after talking with him... I grew sympathetic toward him. I stayed in contact with him and..." Nera looked up at Yolken with tears in her eyes. "I fell in love with him."

Yolken choked on his saliva, making him cough. He thumped himself on the chest and said hoarsely, "*What?*"

"Later, when the Sodality went in to kill your father, Relan was with him."

Yolken cleared his throat. "So you let them go."

Nera nodded.

Yolken sat back, beside himself.

"Somehow Drenan found out. But he never said anything to me about it until he came to Kyinth with Reago and Devin."

"And Javen."

"And Javen. He waited for the perfect chance to use what happened that day against me." Nera slid off the chair and onto her knees. "Please, Your Highness. I beg you to forgive me."

Yolken nodded and stood. "Please, get up."

Nera stood. "Thank you. I... I should go."

Yolken nodded again.

"This certainly wasn't what I planned to discuss when I came here."

"Sorry—it's just, I've been reading these reports you sent over and had questions."

"There's no need to apologize, Your Highness. Please consider what I told you earlier, about Mazam."

"I will. Thank you."

Nera bowed and left.

Yolken watched her as she made her way back to the Lift. Energy left him as it carried her down. He put the thought of Relan out of his mind—as incredible what Nera had just revealed to him was—and thought about what she'd said about Mazam. That, in turn, made him think about the conversation he'd had with Deth just that morning. Was it a coincidence? What if it wasn't?

Yolken made his way back out to the balcony, hoping Deth was still there. Thankfully, he was, curled up with his head on his tail. "Deth?"

Deth lifted his head.

"Have you ever heard of Mount Mazam?"

Deth dipped his head in a nod.

"Is it Dimra's home?"

Deth nodded again. "Though that is not our name for the mountain."

"Do you think I might find out how to restore balance there?"

Deth's deep breath rumbled. Tendrils of smoke escaped his nostrils each time he exhaled. "I don't know."

"I'm told there's a cave there where Draego's worshipers live."

"Humans have been soiling Dimra's home for millennia."

"Have you ever been there?"

"The Assembly gathered at the top of Mazam. But I've never been inside. Our homes are sacred."

"Should I go there?"

Deth's breath rumbled again.

"I know, your homes are sacred, but you let me in *your* home."

Dimras snorted, sending a small burst of flames out of his nose. Yolken shielded his face with an arm.

"I'm trying to do what you've told me to," he said after the wave of heat passed, "and I'm not having any luck. I'm not any closer to an answer than I was when I first met you."

Deth's reptilian eyes pierced Yolken to his very core. The dragon's presence—one of power that could at any moment end his life, yet always exuding peace and calmness—continuously evoked in him awe and admiration. He wanted to do what Deth was telling him, to perhaps earn from Deth some of that same admiration. But thus far he'd been a bungling fool, twice now putting himself in situations requiring Deth's rescue. And now he was betraying the promise he'd only recently made, while at the same time begging permission to defile what Deth considered sacred.

Deth's breath rumbled like distant thunder rolling through a powerful storm—the kind that groaned just before releasing its torrential rain and hail. Deth's reptilian eyes finally blinked. Then he said, "Go."

CHAPTER 34

Yolken stepped into the opening in the semicircular red couch and looked at those gathered: Jax, Deanna, Enif, and Kaylan. Enif dabbed his bald head with a towel.

"Sahri told me this is where Drakonias held meetings he didn't want others to overhear," Yolken began, "and I figured if we were fifty stories above the next set of ears, our conversation wouldn't be overheard."

"So what secret thing are we here to discuss?" Enif said. With a side glance at Jax, he added, "And I would really like to know what he's doing back."

Yolken ignored Enif's comment and looked over at Kaylan, who was sitting at the end of the couch to his right. He'd already discussed his plans with her beforehand, wanting to ensure she approved of what he intended to do before he did it. She nodded at him, so he turned his attention back to the group. "I called you here because my work is not done. I didn't come here to overthrow Drakonias, but to undo the great evil wrought upon Dradonia during his war. And as impossible as it still seems, I am the Blessed of the Dragon—the *only* Blessed of the Dragon. And it's my responsibility to restore balance to the sun."

"But how?" Jax said. "The task Deth has laid upon you is

impossible."

"I know," Yolken acknowledged. "But somehow, I must replace the Energy that was taken."

"You're just repeating what Deth keeps telling you."

"And we've already concluded that what he's telling you to do is impossible," Enif added.

Yolken agreed. And he felt completely helpless to do what he knew he needed to. "But it needs to be done."

"He can't even tell you how."

"I've spent my every waking hour—except when I'm with you in council—poring over Drakonias' notes and reports. None of it has helped me. But now I might know who can." Everyone's eyes stared at him, transfixed, waiting. They were going to think he was crazy. "Nera told me about—"

"*Nera?*" Enif said.

"Yes. She said—"

"You would listen to anything she says?" Yolken took a deep breath as Enif continued his interruption. "*She* was the head of the Synod! She's directly responsible for the deaths of hundreds of members of the Order."

"She pledged her loyalty to me," Yolken said calmly.

"She ordered your father's assassination!"

"She has information that might be relevant to our problem—my problem," Yolken said. He wasn't here to argue with Enif, who continued to try and assert whatever authority he thought he still had. "And I've decided to listen to her. Unless you have a better suggestion?" Yolken paused, giving Enif—and the others, if they wished—the opportunity to speak.

"What does she suggest?" Deanna said. Ever since their confrontation with Drakonias and her near death, she had been quiet and reserved, hardly speaking during council meetings.

"She told me about a cave in Mount Mazam where a group of worshippers live—"

"Zealots!" Enif exclaimed.

"—who, given their extreme piety, might know what I'm

supposed to do."

"What could they know that we don't?" Enif said incredulously.

"I don't know," Yolken said. "But what Nera didn't realize when she told me this was that the cave was the Dragon King's home—the *original* Dragon King, Dimras."

"So you're suggesting we send a delegation there to investigate?" Jax said.

"No," Yolken said. He looked back at his wife, then back at Jax. "I'm going there myself."

Enif jumped to his feet and shouted, "Out of the question!"

"I'm not asking permission," Yolken said tersely.

"We have yet to understand the threat lurking practically on our doorstep and you're leaving? Abandoning us? For *what*? The possibility of learning—"

Using Energy stored in his bones, Yolken gathered air and pushed Enif back into his seat. "I'm tired of your impertinence, Enif." He looked down into the man's fear-filled eyes and said, "Leave."

Enif stared up at Yolken. "Your Highness?"

"I said leave, Enif!"

Enif hesitated long enough for Yolken to grab him by his shirt with a thread of Energy and lift him back to his feet.

"Your Highness, I'm sorry," Enif said.

"Leave," Yolken said tersely.

Enif stared at him, intently enough to make Yolken become uncomfortable. He stood his ground, though, and waited until Enif walked past him through the opening in the couch. Yolken watched Enif until he left the room and the tall door clicked shut behind him. He waited until he felt Energy leave him to operate the Lift, then turned back to the rest of those present.

"He sort of had a point," Jax said.

"Which was what?" Yolken said.

"Drenan and Devin are still out there, and there have been a number of defectors from the city. Who knows what they might be plotting and what sort of support they might be gathering? That and the war..."

Yolken rolled his eyes. Jax still refused to talk about *what* war was coming. "This is more important."

"You're right," Deanna said.

Jax clenched his jaw. He let out a sigh, then said, "Who's going with you?"

"Nobody," Yolken said.

"*Nobody?*"

A silence hung over the group.

"How long do you think you'll be gone?" Jax finally said.

"I don't know," Yolken said.

"Dragon caverns are massive," Deanna said. "It took me months to navigate the caverns on Kvorga."

"Which is why you're all here," Yolken said. "Kaylan is empress and you are my advisors, which means that you are her advisors. While I'm gone, I want to ensure that she has your full support."

"This should go without saying," Deanna said.

"Good."

"Yolken," Jax said, "if you are going to do this..."

"I am."

"I'm not going to try to stop you. But I insist that you take someone with you."

"Jax, I know you made a promise to my father, but I don't need you to—"

"You're beyond needing my protection, I know. As far as I'm concerned, I fulfilled my oath to your father. But it would be wise to take someone with you."

"I hope you're not thinking it would be you, because I need you here."

"No. Not me," Jax said.

"Then who?"

"Me," Deanna said.

CHAPTER 35

Yolken stood behind Kaylan with his arms wrapped around her. He smelled her hair while he looked at the distant mountains.

Kaylan turned around and enveloped herself in Yolken's hug. "I don't like that you're leaving," she said into his chest.

"I don't either, but—"

"You're human," Kaylan said, looking up at him. "How in Draego's Fire are you supposed to do what Deth is telling you to?"

"Honestly, I don't know."

"Maybe there really is someone in that cave who can help you," Kaylan said. She buried her head in Yolken's chest. He looked at the tall buildings, none of which reached quite as high as they were. He found it rather ironic—here he was in the capital of the empire, the epicenter of all of Dradonia, and he barely marveled at the towering buildings that until recently he'd only seen in paintings. Back when he was deciding what painting he wanted to buy for the tavern, he'd actually thought about one that showed the Kyinth skyline—there were some amazing ones—but ended up deciding on an image he thought he had a chance of actually seeing one day. And he *did* get to see the

Mindon Falls—if from a rather peculiar angle.

"Kaylan?"

"Mmm?"

"I want you to know that I love you."

Kaylan looked up at him. "I love you, too."

"More than everything. All I ever wanted was to live my life with you. I'm constantly imagining kissing you and the kids goodbye as I leave for the tavern and how happy you all are when I come home. And that night of the festival, I thought for the first time that it might actually happen."

"Thanks to me," Kaylan said coyly.

She was right. Jax had convinced Selena to let him go out to the festival that night, but he probably would have spent the evening wanting to ask Kaylan to dance but deliberately avoiding her.

"I'm glad you came to find me," he said.

Kaylan poked him and said, "I was tired of waiting."

Yolken felt his face redden. "If I could undo everything so we could have our lives in Lonely Oak back, I would."

"But poor Issa…"

Yolken clenched his jaw. He didn't for a moment regret saving Issa, but he hated pretty much everything that had happened since then. "Except for Issa," he said. "I would save her a thousand times over."

"Then we're stuck with the rest, too."

"I suppose so."

Kaylan looked up at Yolken again and said, "Promise me you'll be careful."

"You know I will."

"Say it."

"I'll be careful."

With her eyes locked on his, she said, "And promise me you'll come back as quickly as you can."

Yolken hesitated, not breaking eye contact. He didn't know what was at Mazam, or how long it would take him to find it.

Deanna was right about the size of Deth's cavern. The Dragon King's cavern could be as big or bigger. It could take them months to search the entire thing.

"Promise me," Kaylan said.

"I promise." Yolken said it, but he didn't know if it was the truth. He hoped it was. He'd already lied to Deth and he didn't want to lie to Kaylan as well.

CHAPTER 36

Yolken walked out of the palace hand in hand with Kaylan. Jax was on the other side of him, and Deanna trailed behind, along with the rest of his advisors.

"You know," Jax said, "when this is all over, there's going to be stories about the emperor who saved Dradonia."

"I'm not really looking to be in any stories," Yolken said.

"Most people who ended up in them weren't."

"Promise me you won't make a story out of this." He grew up loving Kaylan's uncle's stories, but he certainly didn't want to *be* one.

"Are you asking me, or ordering me?"

Yolken shook his head and turned to hug Kaylan. "I love you," he whispered into her hair.

"I love you, too," Kaylan said. She held him tight and wouldn't let him go.

"I'm coming back, you know."

"I know. I just don't like the thought of being apart again."

"Neither do I. But if I figure out what I'm supposed to do, it'll be worth it."

"Then we can go home and build our house in the maple grove."

"That's what I want," Yolken said. He couldn't promise it, but if he was able to somehow restore balance to the sun, he would love more than anything else to give the throne to someone else and go back to Lonely Oak with Kaylan.

Kaylan finally ended the hug and stepped back. Jax stuck his hand out and Yolken shook it.

"Don't tarry," Jax said.

"I won't," Yolken said. He hugged and kissed Kaylan again and said, "Don't let Enif push you around."

"I won't," she said.

"And you," Yolken said to Jax, "don't do anything stupid while I'm gone."

"Do you really think that little of me?" Jax said.

"I'll be back as soon as I can. Hopefully before you've had enough time to turn the empire on end."

"He'll only do what's prudent—won't you, Jax?" Deanna said.

"I am but here to serve," Jax said with a bow.

Yolken kissed Kaylan on the top of the head, then walked down the steps to the waiting horses. The saddlebags of one were stuffed with hard foods ideal for traveling. The bags of the second contained dragon bones. They were going to be descending into the depths of Mount Mazam, the largest mountain in all of Dradonia, and even though he could store Energy in his bones Yolken knew it wouldn't be nearly enough for them to descend into the belly of the mountain and return. It had been with great hesitation that he'd asked Deth's permission to use them. Thankfully Deth didn't object. His task was already impossible as it was; he didn't need to add navigating underground caverns in complete darkness.

Yolken climbed onto his horse and looked back up the long set of stairs to his wife. She stood with her hands clasped into fists at her side. A sense of finality washed over him, but he pushed it away, knowing their parting was only temporary.

Yolken urged his horse into motion. He and Deanna

followed the street as it circled around the palace. It had taken him several days of standing out on the balcony atop the palace to realize that the street encircling the palace was mimicked in Onta with a statue of Drakonias in the center. He imagined Hantlo, Tieger, and Thena had the same feature.

They left the circular street on the East Road and followed it through the city to the enormous gates. They passed through them, then followed an arching bridge across the North River, which also reminded him of Onta.

After crossing the East Bridge, they traveled through the outer city, and then for three days east through sprawling farmland. Towering snow-capped mountains loomed in the distant north. They were largely paralleling the mountains as they made their way to a pass through the front range.

They made good time riding through the relatively flat terrain. Yolken wanted to minimize the time he spent away from Kyinth, so he suggested they use Synthesis to boost the horses' stamina, as they had done after fleeing Onta. However, Deanna pointed out that the body needed time to recover after sustained use of Synthesis. She also reminded him that Croff had specialized grooms to care for the horses when they arrived. He knew they would need the horses for their return trip, so he understood Deanna's wisdom.

The mountain pass should—at this time of year, the first month of winter— have been impenetrable. But with unseasonably warm temperatures and hardly any precipitation, the crossing was uneventful. The temperatures only dropped below freezing at night, but by day Yolken warmed enough to take his cloak off. It took them only four days to make the crossing.

A beautiful valley peppered with lakes greeted them as they exited the front range. Fortunately, the flooding of the North River hadn't reached this far. They rode through birch, aspen, and spruce trees, and passed herds of caribou. After another day of travel, they stopped in a village. They told the villagers that they were going to worship the Great Dragon, and the villagers warned them that temperatures in the next pass were dangerously cold. They happily sold Yolken and Deanna coats made from wolf pelts and blankets for their horses. Passage of this range took them four days as well. The temperatures plummeted at night, so Yolken and Deanna took turns using Synthesis to keep the horses warm.

Yolken wasn't ready for the scene that greeted him when they exited the second pass. As impressive as the view had been when they'd exited the first pass—the valley below, the second range in the distance—it was nothing compared to the mountain that greeted them now.

Mount Mazam towered over the surrounding mountains like the oak tree in Lonely Oak stood high above the children playing under it. The paintings he'd seen of it did it no justice. Its base was wide, but lacked the vegetation that spread across the valley. A few glaciers clung to crevices starting about a third of the way up, and covered it fully by its midpoint.

Another day of riding through league after league of tundra brought them to a village at the base of the mountain. There they traded their horses for mules, which could more securely navigate the winding paths that would take them to the cave entrance. They left the village behind the next morning, the villagers promising to care for their horses while they were gone, and started up the mountain.

The climb up the icy slopes was slow. The trail wound its way through crags and along steep ledges, and Yolken was thankful for the mules' sure-footedness. Their hooves were shod with tiny spikes to give them traction on the ice. As the sun was setting, the mules followed another crag which, after a few turns, widened and ended at an opening in the rock.

Yolken dismounted and surveyed the crack. To him it looked rather large, but he imagined that if a dragon attempted to pass through it, it would be a tight fit.

He led the mule by the reins through the opening and into

the cave. The passage was several paces deep, and the cold air grew warmer with every step. The path turned and widened, then gave way to a cavern. There were two fires just inside, one on either side of the opening. It took a moment for Yolken's eyes to adjust after they walked between them. When they did, they were standing in a small village. Several people were staring at him and Deanna.

"Who are you?" one of them called.

"I am the Emperor of the United Realms," Yolken said.

A woman clad in a plain brown robe scurried up to them and peered at Yolken with narrowed eyes. "You are not Drakonias."

Yolken looked at the woman, her skin pale and her hair white, and noticed the dragons embroidered on her robe. "No, I am not."

"Then who are you?"

"My name is Yolken." He didn't like the sound of his true name and had decided he wasn't going to use it. He was the emperor, after all.

The woman's eyes widened for the briefest of moments. "Come with me," she said. "We've been expecting you."

CHAPTER 37

It took forever for the ships under Devin's command to pass through the stone breakers outside Tieger. When they'd left Tieger in the *Soaring Dragon*, the passage had looked wide enough for two ships to pass through abreast each other. But it wasn't wide enough for two of the enormous iron ships to safely pass together, so they had to make the passage one at a time. And with every ship that entered the calm waters inside the breakers, Devin knew his presence—or at least the navy's presence—was being made known. There was no keeping it a secret. By now Sheal had to have an idea of what was happening. But the beautiful part was that there was nothing anyone could do about it—not even a powerful Synthesizer like Sheal.

As Devin stood on the deck of a Carrier, Aeroplanes lined up behind him ready to take flight at his command. He surveyed the city with pent-up frustration. He needed Karina. The palace, which stood proudly on the top of a hill on the north side of the city, was but the first obstacle between him and her lustful embrace.

"Shall we begin?" asked the commander of the fleet, standing next to Devin.

Devin looked from the city to the enormous barrels on the

Gunships lined up next to the Carrier, and back. The memory of assaulting this very city during Drakonias' war was vivid. Only instead of being defenseless, as it was now, Tieger had hidden behind fortifications, protected from sea assault by a battery of Cannons. His aunt Bathsheth had been in charge of the city's defense. He'd assaulted the city with the best ships in Drakonias' navy but had been unable to win it for his father. The defeat had humiliated him.

But what would humiliate him even more was having to kneel before Drenan and acknowledge him as emperor. He didn't know what Thena had been thinking—but it didn't matter now. She was stuck in the East without her navy, which meant she had no control over what happened in the West. She probably didn't even care.

"Yes," he said.

At the commander's signal, the transport ships carrying Tanks began a slow advance, followed by the loudest booms Devin had ever heard. His hands went instinctively to his ears. The booms were followed by explosions up and down the palace walls. A second volley echoed shortly thereafter. And then a third.

Smoke rose into the air. Dockworkers fled the docks. Gangplanks were jammed with sailors attempting to flee. Several jumped onto docks from dangerous heights; some even jumped into the water. He didn't know how that was going to help them. He wasn't interested in killing them anyway. He didn't even want to attack the city, but if he was going to take the West, Sheal needed to die. Nera as well. Then, since Thena wasn't interested in the throne, the only legitimate claim would be his. And when Drenan arrived, thinking he would be claiming the throne for himself, he would get what had been coming to him for a long time—assuming Danavin didn't get to him first, of course. Then Devin would return to the East, and if Thena wouldn't teach him Regeneration, he would turn her own navy on her.

Once the Tanks were unloaded and rumbling through the

city, the ships transporting the soldiers moved forward. Then the Aeroplanes took flight. They didn't attack—he wasn't planning to destroy the city—but their presence flying overhead would be ominous.

Through his Glasses, Devin saw different areas where there was Synthesizing. But there were also accompanying blasts from a Tank, and the rapid reverberation from Guns mounted on the backs of Autos. As it was, the resistance was small and quickly tapered off.

Once the city was subdued, Devin disembarked from the Carrier and rode in the comfort of an Auto through Tieger to the palace. Sheal was waiting for him, on his knees, outside. Two soldiers pointed Guns at him to keep him from doing anything stupid—such as Synthesizing.

"Devin?" Sheal said as Devin exited the Auto. "*What* are you doing?"

"Why, Uncle, I'm liberating Dradonia."

"Don't do this, Devin. I've been to see Yolken."

"Swear fealty to him, you mean."

"He's trying to save Dradonia."

"*Save* Dradonia? From whom? Drakonias?"

Sheal looked around at everyone surrounding him, then back to Devin. "Can we speak privately? I... I have a letter from Reago..."

"*Reago?* He died as the traitor that he was." Reago had said he'd sent a letter to Sheal, Dorlan, and Thena as well. But he'd also sent a letter to Drakonias, which he'd read himself. The letter had been laced with accusations and impossibilities. His father had denied it, said Reago was delusional. And Devin believed his father. He'd spent enough time with Reago in Onta to know his uncle had let his guilt over the war cloud his mind to the point he could no longer decipher between truth and fiction.

"He wasn't a traitor. He knew... but I was skeptical. I-I should have met him in Kyinth when he gave me the chance, but…"

"I've heard enough from you."

"Yolken confirmed everything Reago said."

"You betrayed Drakonias."

"Drakonias is dead. And as far as I'm concerned, he got what he deserved."

"You are a traitor," Devin said. He stared his uncle in the eyes.

Sheal's gaze didn't waver. "So you're going to execute me like Drakonias executed Drashon—his own son?" Sheal made no attempt to move. He just sat back on his haunches.

"If you believe that, you've become as delusional as Reago."

"Danavin's son is the Blessed of the Dragon, Devin."

"We're *all* Blessed of the Dragon," Devin shot back.

"No, we're not. We were never meant to have the gift."

He was done with this. Devin shook his head. "You're pitiful," he said. He turned his back on his uncle and strode toward his Auto.

"You're making a mistake!" Sheal called. "Reago was right!"

Devin lifted up an arm and clenched his hand into a fist.

"The sun really is—"

The blast of a Gun cut Sheal's words short.

CHAPTER 38

To Javen's surprise, plans for the evacuation were already in place. Once Hadie firmly decided that was what she was going to do, it was just a matter of putting the plan into motion. It didn't happen overnight—in fact it took two weeks. Javen's days were busy with tasks Hadie gave him in the morning meeting wherein they all coordinated the day's activities. Each night, Hadie visited him and they bedded each other until they fell asleep. She was always gone when he woke in the morning, and he had the same instructions not to discuss what happened between them with anyone.

That was easy enough, for the most part, since he didn't know anyone. Only on the days he was assigned to work with Lyoll and Ganip was it hard, especially since they relentlessly tried to pry information from him.

But the night before the evacuation was to begin, Hadie didn't come.

The morning found Javen decently rested—probably better than he would have been if he'd been with Hadie. He met her in her quarters as he'd been doing since preparations began. The others were already present.

"Today…" Hadie began, then stopped to wipe a tear from

her eye. "My mother told me that as queen, I'm not supposed to show my emotions. But how can I not? I'm abandoning my home. *We're* abandoning our home. But it's necessary. We have no choice. Truth is, this was inevitable. That storm ended any good we were trying to accomplish. And it's time to leave it behind. It pains me to admit it, but it's the right thing to do. I don't want to leave, but we don't linger over our dead once we bury them, hoping they'll somehow come back to life." She wiped another tear. "The south is dead. Our dead have been buried. And now it's time to leave them behind. I won't stay and watch one more person get buried because I couldn't protect them.

"What's the point of rulers? What is it that Drakonias gave the United Realms? What was it that Dorlan gave the south?" She looked around the room and said, "Hope. To many of us, they represented hope." Hadie paused and wiped tears from her eyes. "I can't give the people of the south anything. There's nothing I can do to stop what's happening here. I can't bring the south back to life. But what I *can* do is give my people hope. Our future is not with the dead, but with the living. Now"—she paused and took a deep breath—"let us go."

Lyoll and Ganip, wearing swords on their hips, led the somber procession out of Hadie's chambers and through the palace to the front.

There were two main components to the evacuation: the caravan by land, and supplies by sea.

Javen came to an abrupt halt when they exited the palace and emerged on the front landing. It was winter, but the air was warm—warmer than it should have been. Carriages were lined up at the bottom of the sweeping granite steps. One of Hadie's advisors—Kuri, he thought his name was—bumped into him, making him lurch forward. He was a Silk from the… Harwa Province? He'd met and worked with so many people over the last two weeks he was having trouble keeping them all straight in his head.

"No sword?" Kuri said.

Javen looked down and for the first time noticed the sword on Kuri's hip. "Are you kidding? I don't know how to use one of those things."

"I suppose you wouldn't need to."

"We're not riding in those, are we?" Javen asked.

"Those of us lucky enough."

He really didn't want to ride in those carriages. They reminded him of his trip from Lonely Oak to Portstown. The sight of Drenan's old carriage almost made him throw up. "What do you mean, lucky enough?"

"Many of the regents' old carriages have been set aside for those unable to walk."

Javen hadn't been involved in that part of the preparation, so providing for the invalid wasn't even something he'd thought of.

"There were a number of other wagons—from the garrison, for instance—but there simply weren't enough, so they had to use regents' carriages as well."

"At least they're being put to good use." Javen surveyed the carriages as they descended the steps. The foremost was Dorlan's—he recognized it easily. It was the biggest, and besides, he'd spent several mornings in it for his failed Synthesis lessons. "Who gets a carriage, then?"

"Well, the queen, obviously; her mother, Sethlan, and a few others."

"You?"

"No. But you lucked out," Kuri said.

"I did?" He hoped it wasn't Drenan's carriage. He would refuse if it was. He couldn't stay in the carriage where he had watched Astora be murdered.

At the bottom of the steps, teamsters ushered them to saddled horses waiting at the very front of the line. Javen was ushered to a horse behind Hadie's. He climbed into the saddle, confused, and saw Sethlan sitting on the horse next to him.

"What's Hadie doing?" he said. "Why isn't she in her carriage?"

"She wants to ride out of the city in full view of her people. To impress upon them that she's leading them to safety."

"Makes sense," Javen agreed.

Hadie urged her horse into motion. She sat high in her saddle, crown on her head, wearing regal riding attire. Her pants were black with gold trim running down the outside of her legs and her shirt was purple silk, also trimmed in gold.

As the horses' hooves clopped on the stone roadway, the teamsters urged the horses pulling the carriages into motion as well. The procession moved toward the roundabout in the center of the city, where the statue of Drakonias once stood. The roadway was lined with citizens of the south, all prepared as well as they could be for their forthcoming journey. At the roundabout, they turned north. The crowds continued to pack the street. Intermixed with the people were hundreds of wagons, each one loaded with the belongings of those who had lived their entire lives in Hantlo—or those who'd fled to Hantlo from elsewhere in the realm. Now they were all fleeing. To where, no one really knew. Javen didn't. And neither did Hadie. But as she rode out of Hantlo, they followed.

A long snake—thousands of wagons and a hundred times more people—slowly slithered out of Hantlo, with Hadie as the head. She rode first through what was left of the ramshackle buildings where Hantlo's poorest had lived. Seeing it up close for the first time made Javen realize how complete the devastation had been. Then they passed through the countless camps sprawled along the road and out into the empty fields. Many of them were busy at work disassembling their tents and loading carts and wagons.

Hadie continued to ride at the head of the procession for several leagues, then retired to her carriage. Her mother and advisors were already assembled, having long ago sought refuge from the sun. Javen waited with the others while Hadie went farther back into the carriage to her room. She returned a few minutes later with a clean shirt.

"Well, that went as well as could be expected," Tara said.

"Considering we left behind most of our possessions," said Kirin, one of Hadie's advisors. If Javen remembered correctly, he was a Silk, second only to Hadie's parents in wealth.

"You're welcome to go back and join Phenor in his obstinance if you want."

"I was just saying..."

"We all left our homes behind," Hadie said. "What choice did we have?"

"I'm sorry, Your Highness, I'm just frustrated."

"We all are. Nobody *wanted* to leave. But we've been leaving our homes for years. We're just the last to have to do it." Ursella handed her a glass of water. She took a sip, then said, "Are the messengers in place?"

"Yes, Your Highness," Sethlan said.

"Good. I want updates three times a day."

"Yes, Your Highness."

"Have we heard back from any of the emissaries we sent ahead?"

"Not yet, Your Highness," Sethlan said. "I'd be surprised if we heard anything before Portstown."

Hadie shook her head. "I know we're doing the right thing; I just wish I knew where we were going."

"Javen," Tara said, "you're from the north. Why haven't you said where you think we should go?"

"I... Because I have no idea. A year ago, I'd never been farther from Lonely Oak, my hometown, than a couple of surrounding towns."

"You have no suggestions?"

"I mean, there's not a lot out there. Except for grass, the valley's pretty barren."

"Which is why I suggest that, when we get to Portstown, we make for Reega," Sethlan said. "Orla is not far from there, and we can make our way up the coast to Harachin, settling people along the way."

"I wish I already knew where my people were going," Hadie said.

"Yolken will let you stay," Javen said.

"How can you be sure?" Tara said.

"Because he's my brother. He's not cruel like… like Drenan or any of the others."

"He's right," Sethlan said. "My master… er, Jorgan spoke highly of Yolken."

"He might not be cruel, but that doesn't mean he'll let us stay," Hadie said.

"Perhaps we shouldn't have given up on negotiations so fast," Kirin said.

"I didn't give up," Hadie said tersely. "I've sent emissaries ahead. Hopefully Portstown will have condors so we can communicate with the emperor."

"We'll do our best," Sethlan said.

"I know," Hadie said. "That'll be all for now. I want to rest." Everyone stood.

"We'll meet again this evening when we make camp," Hadie said.

"Yes, Your Highness," Javen said with everyone else. He bowed toward Hadie and left with the others.

CHAPTER 39

Stepping up into the carriage made Javen sick to the stomach. It was the same carriage Dorlan had given him in Matis when the Regency had first taken him prisoner. It turned out that Dorlan had been instructed by Drakonias to make him a regent as a blow to the morale of the Order of the Dragon. It had infuriated Drenan—which, after the way Drenan treated him, brought Javen a modicum of satisfaction. Javen hadn't appreciated being used like that, but in the end, he preferred it to being murdered. The Regency was bad, he realized now, but he did, in a way, owe his life to Drakonias.

The motion of the carriage as they lumbered north was soothing enough to make Javen realize how tired he was. He went into the private chamber at the back end and took off his sweaty clothes, everything except his small pants. He looked for some water to wash his face with, but all he found were the two ewers of drinking water. Water in the wash basin was filled morning and night but would slosh out during the day, while the ewers had small openings and were affixed to the table. A quarter-twist of one of the ewers released it from the table, and he used it to wet a small towel. Javen wiped himself, enjoying the cool water. Feeling relatively clean and increasingly drowsy, he lay down on the bed, eschewing any covers, and promptly fell asleep.

He woke to a gentle shake and a voice whispering his name.

"We've stopped for the night."

Javen looked up and saw Karli, the woman who had attended to him in Hadie's palace. She wore modest silk clothes. He'd expected her to be in the carriage when he entered earlier—to save space and free up the servants' carriages for those unable to walk or ride on their own horses or wagons, Hadie decided that servants would stay with those they were serving—but she hadn't been. "Where were you earlier?"

"Busy getting ready for tonight," Karli said. "You're expected in Her Highness' carriage soon."

Javen saw that the wash basin was now full, so he went over and washed himself again. The breeze through the open windows was nice but it had done nothing for the heat. He was soaked in sweat. He looked back at his bed and saw that it was wet where he'd been lying.

"Don't worry about that," Karli said. "I'll change it for you."

"Thanks," Javen said. He got dressed and left the room, saying, "I'll see you tonight."

"Yes, Your Majesty. Enjoy your meal."

When Javen stepped outside, he found the carriages arranged in a large circle just like they'd been when he and Hadie had traveled with Dorlan as his prisoners. Dorlan was dead, but the teamsters who had run his caravan also ran this one, so it made sense that their methodology remained the same. It was an efficient setup that also provided safety.

He started across the camp, remembering his morning visits with Dorlan, but didn't see Hadie's carriage. After stopping and looking around, he realized that his carriage was parked right next to hers. He started back and was greeted at the door by a servant. There were several who attended the queen and although he recognized this man, he didn't know his name.

Inside, he joined the other advisors who were sitting on the couches lining both sides of the entry room. They were drinking wine and chatting amongst themselves. Javen found an empty space—next to Sethlan, thankfully, and not Hadie's mother—but the moment he sat, the door to the next room opened and another servant said, "Dinner is served."

Javen stood right back up along with the others, and got in line as they filed through the door. Dinnerware adorned the long, narrow table in the center of the room. Javen recognized the black wood of the table as Kvorgan spruce. It was rare—not because the tree was rare, but because the island's reputation prevented most people from going there—and only the finest furniture was made from it. Two servants waited along a sideboard built into the wall, made from the same wood. The silver dinnerware and platters contrasted sharply with the dark wood.

Everyone chose a place, pulled their cushioned chairs—also made from Kvorgan spruce—out from under the table, and sat. They resumed chatting amongst themselves while they waited for Hadie to emerge from her room at the back end of the carriage.

Javen listened to the conversations, which ranged from supply chains to alliances forming amongst the Silks. Their influence had already been diminished as their lands were lost and they'd gathered in Hantlo. The evacuation made them scramble to remain relevant. Javen focused on Hadie's mother when she and a few others began discussing Hadie's father, who had refused to come with them. As the caravan made its way out of the city, known associates of Phenor had been seen attempting to convince people to stay. There had even been a few reports of forced coercion. Another report said Phenor had declared himself to be the rightful ruler and named himself King of the South. That had yet to be substantiated, but Hadie had instructed the rear guard to prevent any further attempts to harass those who had decided to evacuate.

Hadie entered a few minutes later with Ursella at her side.

They all stood when her door opened, and sat after she settled into her place at the end of the table. Ursella took up position in the corner. The servants began serving food from the sideboard and Sethlan initiated a review of the day's progress. As far as Javen could tell, with the exception of Phenor's minions, the evacuation had gone according to plan. Progress was going to be slow—even slower than Javen remembered the caravan traveling when he'd first begun his journey south. But with supply wagons positioned throughout the miles-long convoy and more waiting ahead as they made their way north, the people of the south wouldn't starve.

"I feel selfish, sitting here eating a feast in comparison to what everyone else is getting," Hadie said.

"You are the queen," Tara said. "The evacuation didn't just dissolve all custom."

"I know," Hadie said. The opulence in which she had grown up and lived, when she could clearly see that most others in Hantlo weren't so lucky, had been part of the reason she'd decided to leave. "That doesn't change how I feel."

"Right now, we just need to survive," Tara said. "Things will be better for us all when we arrive—wherever that might be."

"I know we discussed this earlier, but has there been any news from the north?"

"Not yet, Your Highness," Sethlan said.

"Be patient," Tara said. "The journey is going to be long. I'm sure we'll hear from them soon."

Javen knew how excruciatingly slowly these caravans moved. He tried not to compare it to his journey from Onta to Kyinth. It still amazed him how fast the Train was. To make matters worse, he was stuck here listening to bureaucratic discussions. He never would have thought he'd feel this way, but right now all he wanted was to be sitting around a fire, drinking whiskey with Lyoll and Ganip.

Javen ate his meal and fought back a yawn while the conversation continued after the meal was over and the table cleared. He sipped his wine, not really in the mood to imbibe, and breathed a sigh of relief when Hadie dismissed them for the evening. The caravan would break camp early, so he went straight to his carriage. Karli was curled up on her side, asleep on the couch. *Poor lass,* he thought. With everything it had taken to get the caravan ready over the last few days she, along with the rest of the servants, had to be exhausted. *He* was exhausted.

He quietly went back to his room and found that Karli had changed the sheets on his bed. He stripped his sweaty clothes, washed up at the wash basin again, and climbed into bed.

Hadie woke him later with a kiss.

When their bedding ended, he said, "Is that why my carriage is next to yours?"

"Sethlan thinks it's a good idea to have a Synthesizer close," Hadie said, her head on his chest. "I suppose I could have picked from any of the Blessed at my disposal, though."

Javen lifted his head and looked down at her. Her grin was rather sly. He relaxed his head and ran his fingers through her hair. "So I'm just your protector?"

"No," Hadie said.

"What then?"

"More than that."

"What?"

She kissed his damp skin and said, "I don't know." They lay in silence for a minute, Javen lightly running his fingers over her shoulder and back, before Hadie said, "It's complicated."

"It doesn't need to be," Javen said. "The world's falling apart around us and I don't know what's going to happen. But I do know that there's nowhere else in all of Dradonia I'd rather be than here with you."

"I can't help but think about Lannary," Hadie said.

"Draego's Fire, Hadie," Javen said. He clenched his jaw when she rolled away from him and covered herself with the sheet.

After a moment Hadie sat up on the bed and said, "I need

to get back."

"Don't be angry, please."

Hadie kept herself covered with the sheet as best she could while she dressed.

Javen lay propped up on his elbow and watched as she awkwardly put her clothes back on. "I thought you were gone," he said. "Karina tempted me relentlessly. I told them I only wanted to be with you. I sent for you, remember."

Hadie stood up.

Javen sat up. "It was a mistake. Everything that's happened since I met you has been a mistake. Everything except you. I'm sorry."

A small smile crept onto Hadie's face but disappeared just as quickly. "I'll see you tomorrow."

When she was gone, he flopped back onto the bed and found the driest spot. He ended up lying curled up on his side with his back against the wall, and fell asleep.

She didn't come to his carriage the next night. Or the night after that.

CHAPTER 40

From the flat back of an Auto, Drenan watched as Tanks emerged from the bowels of transport ships and rolled down the long ramps onto land. The enormous iron ships still amazed him. Farther down the beach, soldiers were also disembarking from their ships. They were each equipped with a long-barreled Gun, which hung by a shoulder strap across their stomachs. They left their transport ships and set to making camp. The bay in the crook of the peninsula turned out to be an ideal place to make landfall, protected from the swells as it was. The inhabitants of the surrounding villages, he imagined, had to be consumed with both awe and fear at the sight of the ships, emerging Tanks and Autos, and the flying Aeroplanes that heralded his arrival.

The process to unload the soldiers, Autos, and Tanks took several hours. All the while, Aeroplanes flew in formation overhead. Drenan oversaw the entire process with intense satisfaction. His army was just now making landfall, but he could already taste his complete subjugation of the West. His crossing of the peninsula to Hantlo would be swift. The fall of the Queen of the South would be quicker.

By day's end, the process of disembarking was complete.

And by morning, Tanks and Autos of various sizes and utility were rumbling down the road from the village where they'd landed toward Hantlo. Aeroplanes flew in formation overhead. It was only about seventy leagues to Hantlo, which meant they would arrive before sundown.

He was not expecting the devastation that greeted him upon his arrival. The outlying slums were completely destroyed. Debris from once-decrepit buildings cluttered the road, slowing his triumphant liberation of the capital of the Southern Realm. A cyclone had obviously passed through Hantlo, which shouldn't have happened, given that it was now winter. And it certainly shouldn't be as hot as it was.

Eerily absent from the rubble was any sign of gawking faces. The arrival of an army of Machines should have brought the masses to the streets in curiosity, wonder, and fear. The city should have been crowded, but as the soldiers worked clearing the road, Drenan didn't see a single onlooker. When he had last been here, it *was* crowded. Most of the provinces in the Southern Realm were abandoned, and many of those citizens were crowded into Hantlo, spilling out into the slums and beyond— slums that were now destroyed. There should have been people everywhere, but they were well into the city before they started seeing gawkers.

When they arrived at his palace, Drenan waited outside while soldiers searched it, giving it little thought. He was no longer the Regent of Hantlo, and the palace meant nothing to him now. Drakonias had never deigned to visit him there whenever he'd been in Hantlo—he'd always stayed in Dorlan's palace—so he wouldn't deign to enter his former palace either.

He watched with interest as the cadre of soldiers exited the palace and approached his Auto.

"Your Highness," the captain said with a bow when he arrived. "The palace is largely unoccupied."

Drenan nodded. "Proceed to Dorlan's palace, then." When the captain didn't immediately respond, he said, "Was there something else?"

"Yes, Your Highness."

"Out with it, then."

"According to some of the palace occupiers, the south has been evacuated."

"*Evacuated?*" Of course the south had been evacuated. That was the only explanation to why the city was largely empty.

"Yes, Your Highness."

"Did they happen to say where?"

"North, Your Highness."

"Well, if the *Queen* thinks she can avoid what's coming to her by fleeing, she's wrong."

"There's more, Your Highness."

"Yes?"

"It would seem the Queen has been replaced."

Drenan jumped down off the back of the Auto and stepped close to the captain. "Replaced? By whom?"

"A man by the name of Phenor Mor—"

"*Phenor?*"

"—rigan has named himself King of the South."

"And were you able to ascertain as to the location of this… *king?*"

"He is in his palace, Your Highness."

Well, it was easy to deduce where *that* was. If Phenor wasn't in Drenan's palace, he had to be in Dorlan's. Of course he would be. Why would a king settle for the lesser of the two? He knew he wouldn't.

"Then let us go pay our respects to the King of the South, shall we?"

Drenan used Energy to boost his jump up onto the flat back of the Auto. Within moments, they were rolling through the empty streets toward Dorlan's old palace. He could destroy it if he wanted to by simply ordering his army of Tanks and Aeroplanes to assault it, but he didn't see the point. Once he assumed his throne in Kyinth, he would need to install his own vassal to help govern what was left of the south.

He glanced at the empty space at the center of the roundabout, where the statue of Drakonias should be. He would rather have torn it down himself, but it didn't matter who tore it down—Drakonias was dead either way. All the statues throughout the empire would need to be replaced.

When Drenan's Auto arrived at Dorlan's palace, he jumped down and unceremoniously proceeded up the palace steps. No one was expecting him, so no one greeted him. He made his way through the palace uninhibited, soldiers in his trail.

He was fortunate enough to have arrived when Phenor, the King of the South, was holding court. The throne room was largely empty, as there didn't seem to be that many people left in the south. But Phenor sat upon his throne nonetheless. And he seemed surprised to see Drenan enter with soldiers.

Drenan proceeded forward, ignoring the petitioner seeking what Phenor probably lacked the resources to provide, and stopped at the base of the dais. Phenor stared down at him, his eyes betraying sheer terror.

"Y-your M-majesty," Phenor stammered.

"How pathetic," Drenan said, looking up at him. Phenor had always been a coward. He hadn't even had the nerve to stop his own daughter from executing the single biggest embarrassment to the Regency since its inception.

Phenor stood and said, "I-I can explain…"

Drenan held out a hand. The soldier nearest to him unslung his Gun and handed it to Drenan.

There was nothing *to* explain. Phenor's cowardice had cost the lives of Drenan's last remaining sons.

He lifted the Gun unceremoniously and pulled the trigger. The trigger connected the dragon bone stored in the Gun with the barrel. The transfer of Energy launched the Bullet from the barrel with a deafening blast.

Phenor fell backwards and plopped back onto the throne.

Drenan handed the Gun back to the soldier and strode

briskly from the throne room, leaving Phenor's few subjects stunned.

"Where to now?" his captain said when Drenan emerged from the palace.

"North."

CHAPTER 41

Swaying in his saddle, Javen mentally berated himself for being short with Hadie. Despite his efforts, she had yet to return to his carriage. He worried that he'd permanently ruined things with her. She was all he thought about, day and night.

An explosion buffeted the air.

Javen instinctively fell forward on his saddle before looking over his shoulder to see what had happened. A column of smoke was rising into the air toward the back of the caravan. An enormous flying object hurtled toward them, nearly making Javen fall out of the saddle. The object—some sort of flying Machine, by the look of it—flew over their heads. It pulled up steeply and went straight up into the air, then curved until it was upside down and flying toward the back of the convoy.

"What in Draego's Fire is that?" he exclaimed. He turned to Lyoll, but his friend just looked up, stunned. Javen pulled on the reins, turning his horse so he could more easily track the Machine. It continued south. Beyond the column of smoke, Javen saw a cloud of dust rising off the road.

"Go to Hadie," Lyoll said, drawing his sword. His normally calm voice quaked. Javen had never known Lyoll to show any sign of fear, but there was terror in his voice. "Lad! Now!" Lyoll turned his horse several times, looking off to the left and the right, then shouted, "Ganip!" He urged his horse into motion and galloped toward the rising smoke with Ganip following in close pursuit. The relatively straight column of travelers was splintering as people fled in all directions.

Javen turned Kena—he'd named the beast after his family's horse—back toward the front of the convoy and urged her into motion. He held tight to the reins and drew Energy into his Core as Kena galloped. More explosions sounded around him. He turned his head to see more columns of smoke rising off to the sides of the convoy. Several Machines flew over his head, repeating the pattern of the first one.

They're boxing us in.

He looked frantically for Hadie as he approached the line of carriages at the front of the convoy. She had been riding when he'd left her a couple of hours ago to go do inspections with Lyoll. He found her horse, but she wasn't on it. Sethlan and several guards were on their own mounts outside Hadie's carriage.

"Where's the queen?" he shouted.

"Inside!"

"No!" That wasn't good. He felt his temperature rising. "We need to get her out of here!" He slid off of Kena and hurried to the carriage door. "Ready her horse!"

The guard stepped aside, and Javen threw the door open. Heat transferred from his Core to the handle, causing it to smoke. She wasn't in the first room. "Hadie!" he shouted as he moved deeper into the carriage. He heard more explosions outside. She wasn't in the meal room either, and the door to her room was closed. "Hadie!" he shouted again.

Her door opened and Javen saw her. His heart leapt.

"Javen?" she said in an unsteady voice.

"What's going on?" Ursella said.

He hurried to Hadie and hugged her tightly.

"I don't know." He took her by the hand and said, "But we

need to get you out of here."

He led her back through the carriage, and Ursella followed. He started drawing in Energy the moment they were back outside. Thankfully, Sethlan sat on his horse nearby, holding the reins of Hadie's.

Javen ushered Hadie toward her mount. He waited as she climbed up; over the horse's back he saw another one of those flying Machines approaching. It was flying directly toward them. A burst of fire erupted from the tip of one of its wings and a long, cylindrical object shot toward them. Javen smacked the horse on the haunch, sending it running, then reached toward the approaching object with a tendril of Energy. The tendril thinned as it stretched from him, but he used it to nudge the object, deflecting it. He turned, shielding himself as the projectile crashed into Hadie's carriage and exploded. Wood and fire burst in all directions. A piece hit him in the back and threw him to the ground. He lay curled up, waiting for the debris to settle, then sat up with a groan.

His side screamed in pain. He deadened it with Energy and braced his ribs as best he could with his hand as he stood. He checked on Ursella, who was lying on the ground next to him. Finding her unharmed, he staggered over to Kena and climbed into the saddle. He frantically looked for Hadie, and saw her galloping off to the northwest with Sethlan. As he urged Kena into motion he saw the flying Machine that had just flown over them veer sharply to the left—toward Hadie.

Javen forced Kena into a gallop, sending some strength into her muscles. Her speed increased, but it wasn't enough. The Machine was pursuing them. It had several more of those cylindrical projectiles attached to its wings and it would need only moments to overtake them. He had to stop it from firing on Hadie again.

Javen pushed even more Energy into Kena; as he urged her to move even faster, he wondered for the first time who was attacking them. Hadie's father had stayed behind, but there was no way it could have been him. The south didn't have Machines. Nobody except regents even knew they existed. Lyoll's reaction was proof of that.

As Kena raced, Javen pulled as much Energy into his Core as he could—more than he'd ever attempted before. His lessons with Devin over the months had caused him to grow in strength, stretching his Core, until his strength rivaled Devin's, but now he pushed himself further. It hurt. It physically hurt. But the Machine was closing in on Hadie.

The Machine swerved toward her.

Javen threw his fist forward, punching at the Machine. He knew he didn't have to physically do that, but he could never stop himself from outwardly acting out what he was doing with Energy. A much thicker tendril of Energy shot from him in a burst, draining his Core. But he'd pushed too hard and lost connection with the stream. Unable to see his stream without Glasses or further manipulate it, he hoped he'd aimed accurately.

He waited for a second, then another, refilling his Core all the while. Then the Machine flipped sharply to the side. It tumbled in midair several times before veering away from Hadie, then flew high up into the air and back toward the rear of the convoy.

Javen caught up to Hadie. He stopped feeding Energy into Kena, and she slowed to pace Hadie and Sethlan on their horses. Together they continued to run for several minutes before Hadie pulled her horse to a stop. Javen reined Kena in and trotted back to Hadie. She was looking back toward the convoy and the Machines circling overhead. From here, he could see the cloud of dust approaching the rear of the convoy.

"What's happening?" Hadie said. She looked over at Javen as though he'd have an answer.

"I don't know," he said, "but we need to keep moving."

"I'm not running away."

"I don't know what those things are, but they're killing people."

"Which is exactly why I can't leave."

"Hadie—".

"No. I'm going back."

They were too far away to see Hadie's carriage—or what was left of it—but the smoke rising in the air was visible.

"Whoever that is tried to kill you," Javen said.

"Then we need to find out who it is and make them stop." Hadie urged her horse back into motion.

They rode much more slowly back toward the convoy. They slowed even more as what Javen knew were Machines rolled up along the sides of the convoy, herding people back toward the road. Each Machine had a large flat surface on the back, on which several men stood. They were holding some sort of long black devices across their stomachs with both hands.

"What are those things?" Hadie said.

"Machines," Javen answered.

"I've never seen anything like it before."

"No one has."

Hadie looked over at Javen.

"Devin told me about them. And I rode on one from Onta to Kyinth."

Hadie looked at Sethlan and said, "Do you have any idea who it could be?"

Sethlan shook his head.

Javen watched as a man and woman at a wagon the Machines had not yet reached picked up their three children—the woman carried one, the man two—and ran as quickly as they could away from the convoy. Burdened as they were, they weren't moving fast. They ran right in front of the foremost Machine. One of the men standing on the back of it lifted the cylindrical device he held and pointed it at the fleeing family. The end of the device flashed. The fleeing man fell, followed by a loud blast. The woman screamed. Setting her child down, she helped the other two to their feet. She took the two smaller ones by the hands and pulled them away from their father. The cylindrical device flashed again and she fell. A second blast reverberated.

Hadie screamed.

When she urged her horse forward, Javen reached for her reins to stop her, but he missed. He and Kena raced after her. She was riding straight toward the fallen mother and father. Several of the armed men on the Machines pointed their weapons at Hadie, Javen, and Sethlan as they neared.

Hadie slid off her horse and ran the final distance to the children, who were crying over their parents. She wrapped them in her arms and looked up at the Machines. "You monsters!" she yelled.

A door to one of the Machines opened and a man wearing Glasses stepped out. He strode confidently toward them. "Monsters?"

Javen's heart sank and he tasted bile.

"*Drenan*," Hadie sneered.

Javen opened himself to the sun's Energy and let it flow into his Core.

Drenan continued walking toward them. "You remember what happened last time you attacked me, *get?*"

Javen stood his ground. He wanted to double over and vomit, but he forced himself to think about what Drenan had done to Astora... to Hadie... to Selena... to his parents. "Yes. But this time, I know what I'm doing."

"And no one's here to protect you," Drenan said. He stopped a few paces away.

Javen squeezed his hands into fists. "I don't need protecting."

"If even a thread of Energy leaves your body, Draego's Fire will rain down on you *and* your whore."

"She's *not* a whore," Javen sneered. He stopped drawing Energy into his Core, but held onto what he already had. He immediately started to sweat.

"I'm told it was whores who killed Dorlan," Drenan said.

"Including your sons," Javen said.

Drenan's hands formed fists of his own.

"What do you want?" Hadie said.

"Your head," Drenan said. He shifted his gaze from Hadie to Javen and back. With a sick smile, he added, "His, too."

Javen looked over at Hadie. There was no way he was going to let that happen. But he looked past Drenan at the Machines continuing to gather around the convoy, then up at the flying Machines that circled overhead. He might be able to defeat Drenan one-on-one, but there was no way he could take on an entire army of Machines.

"True, you may have killed Loid and Rik," Drenan said, "but you see, today I get my retribution. For them, for Therese, and for Cara."

Javen opened himself to the sun again.

"It's quite simple, Your *Highness*," Drenan said, "either you both surrender to me, right here, right now, or every one of your *subjects* will die in your stead. And then you'll die anyway. Now, *get*, do the prudent thing and disperse of your Energy, or I'll kill your queen first." Drenan took a step toward Javen. "And just like that whore I killed before, you'll be powerless to do anything but watch."

Javen fell to his knees. He pitched forward, overcome by the urge to vomit. As he dispelled the Energy from his Core into the ground, causing the dry grass to smoke, he simultaneously expelled his morning meal.

Drenan's feet approached, and Javen craned his neck back.

"You're as pitiful now as you were then," Drenan said. He shifted his gaze over to Hadie and said, "Kneel, Your *Highness*."

Hadie didn't move.

"I said *kneel*."

Javen looked over at Hadie. She boldly defied Drenan. Regal authority oozed from her pores. But just like what had happened to his aunt all those months ago, Hadie's knees buckled against her will. She looked over at Javen, pain evident in her eyes. In that instant he realized how much he loved her, even if she didn't love him. He couldn't let her die—wouldn't let her die. He had to protect her. Her and her people. He didn't trust Drenan to spare anyone.

"Now," Drenan said, "I understand you poisoned Dorlan, yes?" When Hadie didn't respond, he yelled, "Answer me!"

Hadie fought to control her emotions but cried out. She sobbed heavily but managed to get out, "Y-yes."

"How?"

"I... how... how what?" Hadie said through sobs.

"You don't think attempts have been made to poison us before?" Drenan said. "Who made your poison?"

"He... why does it matter?"

"Because he's obviously quite talented. I'd like to know how he did it. Call him here, or your mother dies."

Javen heard a shuffle off to the side and saw two men, those cylindrical weapons hanging by straps on their chests, escorting Tara toward them.

"What in Draego's Fire are you doing, Drenan?" Tara said with an air of authority to her voice.

Drenan didn't say anything, but Javen watched as she fell forcibly to her knees, making her cry out.

"Tell me his name."

"Why does it matter?" Hadie said. "It's done. In the past."

Tara gagged. Her hands went to her throat.

"Tell me his name!" Drenan yelled.

"P-please, don't hurt her," Hadie said. "His name is G-Ganip."

"*Ganip?*" Drenan said. Tara fell onto her side, gasping deeply. "That gangly teamster? Bring him here."

Several of the armed men jogged off behind Drenan, between the Machines.

Javen's mind whirled while they waited. He had to do something. The ground was still hot from where he had dispersed his Energy. He looked over at Hadie. She was sitting back on her feet, hands on her knees, staring straight ahead. Their situation was truly hopeless, and she knew it. He knew it. *Where did they come from?*

The armed men returned with both Ganip and Lyoll. Their clothes were torn, their faces bloodied. Ganip's right arm hung limp at his side. One of the guards had Lyoll's sword and threw it to the ground.

"*Queen* Hadie, here," Drenan said, "tells me you're responsible for making the poison she used to assume her throne."

Ganip trembled, clutching his limp arm with his other hand, and looked at his feet.

"*Answer me,*" Drenan growled.

Ganip didn't respond at first, but then Lyoll, who had one eye swollen shut and a large gash down the side of his face, said, "It's all right, lad."

Ganip nodded. "Y-yes, your Maj… yes."

"Pardon?" Drenan said. "Your what?"

"We've given you all the respect you deserve," Lyoll said.

An invisible force caused Lyoll's head to snap sharply to the side. He stood frozen for a moment, then defiantly wiped blood from the corner of his mouth. He looked at his bloody hand, then turned his head back to look Drenan in the eyes.

"On your knees," Drenan said.

"I kneel only for my queen."

Lyoll fell to the ground with a sickening crunch. Javen fought back more vomit when he saw that the man's legs were bent at impossible angles. Lyoll pushed himself up, groaning, until he was sitting on his backside.

"You've… never deserved respect," Lyoll said through his pain.

I have to stop him, Javen thought.

"And you think she's a true ruler?" Drenan said. "Look at her. She's not Blessed. She's powerless to do anything but grovel."

"*You're* not Blessed," Javen said to himself.

"Please, Drenan," Hadie said, "you don't have to do this."

"But that's where you're wrong," Drenan said. "Unlike Dorlan did with Danavin's *get* here—"

"Who?" Hadie said.

"—I will not permit treason to go unpunished." He held his hand out to his side, and one of the armed men handed over his weapon. Drenan pointed the long cylindrical Machine toward Ganip. Then he pulled something on the handle, and the thing made a deafening sound. Javen's hands went reflexively to his ears.

Ganip fell forward.

"Lad!" Lyoll yelled, though Javen could barely hear him over the ringing in his ears.

Lyoll fell forward and pulled himself toward Ganip. He rolled the thin man over and revealed the bloody mess of his chest.

"You monster!" Hadie yelled. She tried scrambling to her feet, but quickly fell to the ground on her stomach. She visibly struggled to move but couldn't lift herself off the dried grass.

Javen wanted to lunge at Drenan, but he didn't dare. If he attacked Drenan, people would die. And if he didn't, Hadie would die.

But then Hadie lifted off the ground. She didn't push herself up—her whole body lifted. As she rose, she drifted closer to Drenan until her face was inches away from his.

"Do you remember what I told you when I saw you last?" Drenan said.

"Burn in Draego's Fire," Hadie sneered. She spat in his face, then cried out when Drenan back-handed her.

That's it, Javen thought. *He will* not *hurt her.*

He loved her.

Javen couldn't draw the sun's Energy in, he knew—Drenan would know the moment any of the sun's rays bent in his direction. Instead, he dug his nails into the ground. He could still feel the warmth he'd dispelled only minutes ago. Synthesis was nothing more than drawing the sun's Energy into your Core and manipulating it, and the warmth he felt in the ground was still the sun's Energy. It just wasn't coming directly from the sun. Did that matter? He'd never thought about drawing Energy from anything other than the sun, but did that mean he couldn't?

He couldn't absorb the Energy because it wasn't flowing toward him. The sun's rays were like a torrential rain pouring down. With his eyes closed he felt its warmth on his head, neck, and arms. But he had to ignore it. Drawing in enough of the sun's rays to do anything of consequence would alert Drenan.

"It's not me who's going to burn," Drenan said.

Javen thought of the ground as if it were a dragon bone. He started small, pulling the Energy he felt in the dirt back through his fingers and into his Core. When a small pool had developed, he reached into the ground with that Energy and pulled in more. What had at first been a small trickle quickly became a raging river.

"It's you," Drenan continued. "Danavin's get, too."

Javen tried not to move as he filled his Core, but when Drenan said his father's name he took the opportunity to look up at Drenan while at the same time digging his toes into the ground. He continued drawing in Energy, reaching farther and farther into the ground, and flexed his leg muscles. He sent excess Energy, Energy that would no longer fit into his Core, into his legs and torso. Lastly, he sent Energy to his shoulders and neck, strengthening them.

"Devin will take care of his brother, and then, when I become emperor—"

Javen launched himself toward Drenan.

"—I will finally kill his—"

Javen rammed Drenan in the stomach with his shoulder. His momentum sent them both flying up into the air, over the Machines lined up behind them. They landed on the ground with a grunt, Javen on top of Drenan.

They lay there, dazed, then Javen felt a push against him, and he flew into the air—but he didn't fall. He hung, suspended.

Below, Drenan pushed himself to his feet. He looked up at Javen and said, "You're a fool. And now you're going to watch your whore die, just like that girl. What was her name? Doesn't matter. She was a whore, too."

Drenan started walking back toward Hadie while Javen drifted overhead. He struggled against the invisible force holding him, but he felt like a struggling child held in its father's arms. He was powerless to break free. Instead, he did the only other thing he could do: He reached out to the sun and drew its Energy in. It was stupid, he knew, but he didn't have a choice.

A force punched him in the stomach. He gasped for air and tried to curl up into a ball, but Drenan held him rigid. Pain radiated through his body.

Drenan threaded his way through the lined-up Machines. The men standing on the backs of them looked up at Javen as he floated overhead.

"Let him go," someone said.

The force holding Javen suspended evaporated and he fell to the ground with a grunt.

"*Danavin*," Drenan sneered.

Javen looked up. Norin, the Train operator, knelt next to Lyoll. He stood, holding a long, black sword in his hand. Yellow ribbons woven throughout the sword shimmered in the sun. Norin offered his free hand to Lyoll and helped Lyoll to his feet.

"And here I thought your son was a fool," Drenan said.

Javen studied Norin.

"He's no fool," Norin said. "And neither am I."

Drenan gestured with wide-spread arms. "Look around you, Danavin." He still held the odd weapon that had killed Ganip in his right hand. "What other explanation could there be for why you'd show up here?"

That's impossible, Javen thought. *He's dead.*

Danavin looked around at the Machines and armed men

surrounding them. Every one of them had their cylindrical weapons pointed at him. "True, your army could kill me and my son quite readily, but you and I both know that won't happen."

"You know this how?"

"Revenge, Drenan. It's what drives you. Hatred and revenge. You hate what happened to Therese, even though that was an accident—unlike what you did to *my* wife."

Javen stared at Danavin—his father—dumbfounded. *He's alive? How?*

"She got what she deserved."

"Neither of them deserved what happened to them," Danavin said. "But Cara—"

"Do *not* speak of her."

"—deserved what she got."

Drenan lifted the cylindrical weapon, but Danavin launched into the air. Javen watched as his father flew off to the north while Drenan screamed and threw the weapon to the ground. Javen flinched as Drenan ran past him at a blurring speed.

CHAPTER 42

Y ou've been expecting me?" Yolken said. "How is that possible?"

"He said you would come," the old woman said.

"He who?"

"Him."

Him?

The woman scurried away. "Don't worry about your mules."

Yolken stared after her until Deanna placed her arm on his shoulder and said, "Come."

By the time Yolken shook off his confusion, dozens of individuals, all wearing the same type of robes as the woman, had emerged from the simple wooden huts. As he and Deanna approached, every one of them fell prostrate on the ground. Yolken heard whispers of 'Blessed,' making him feel more self-conscious than he ever had—even more than when Kaylan had asked him if he wanted to dance.

The woman opened the thatched door to one of the huts and gestured for them to enter. Yolken ducked through the door and stepped into the circular room, which was furnished with a simple wooden table, a lamp, and a cot.

"It is too late to start," the woman said. "Eat, rest, and

tomorrow you may begin. I will return shortly with food and water." The woman bowed and said, "I am Tana. If there's anything else you require, please, let me know." Then Tana looked at Deanna and said, "This way. You, we weren't expecting."

Tana and Deanna left. When the door shut behind them, Yolken stood in the hut, alone and completely confused. *They were expecting me? Too late to start? Start what?* He looked around the empty hut and, not knowing what else to do, sat on the cot. Shortly, a new person—a man this time—entered with Yolken's satchel. He bowed and set it by the door.

When the man turned to leave, Yolken said, "Hey, what did Tana mean when she said you were expecting me?"

"That we knew you would come, Blessed."

The man left before Yolken could formulate his next question.

A short time later, Tana returned with a platter bearing a bowl of soup, a hunk of bread, a porcelain ewer, and a cup. She set the platter on the table and said, "Please, eat."

She bowed and left, leaving Yolken alone with his now growling stomach. The smell of the bread made him realize how hungry he was.

He ate the food quickly then sat back on the cot. He should go to sleep—he needed to rest—but there was no way he could settle with his mind racing as it was. He got back up and stepped out of the hut. He stood by the door and watched the village go about its business. People in brown robes were standing around fires, carrying pails from here to there, chopping wood, and performing a myriad of other tasks. There was a fenced enclosure on the far side of the cavern, built along the wall. The mules were inside, and a man was forking hay over the barrier. It intrigued him that these people lived *in* a mountain. Another thing he noticed after watching for a few minutes was the conspicuous absence of children.

He started walking, moving deeper into the cavern.

Whenever he passed anyone, they acknowledged him with a bow and a whispered, "Blessed." Several minutes later he reached the end of the huts. The cavern continued farther back, so he kept walking.

Deanna was standing up ahead with her arms folded across her chest. She was gazing at the rock wall, and as he approached her, he saw that it was covered in paintings. The first one was of a dragon breathing fire. The dragon's body was clearly detailed, but it also included sharp points of white scattered throughout. He stopped and looked at it, confused at first, but when he ignored the multiple colors of the dragon and focused only on the points, he realized it was the Great Dragon constellation. As the fire proceeded from the dragon's mouth, it split into a hundred different lines which all ended at a painting of a sun.

Deanna wasn't looking at this painting, though, but at one farther down. Yolken walked toward her, looking at the paintings as he went. The next one was of a yellow dragon—the Dragon King, Dimras, as he'd learned from Deth—and the one after that was of Dimras and a red dragon. Deanna was standing in front of a painting of eight dragons: yellow, red, blue, violet, orange, green, white, and black.

"It's the Assembly," Yolken said.

"Deth told you about the Assembly?" Deanna said.

"Yes."

"I just can't understand how, after so many years, we knew so little about the dragons."

He still didn't know much about them. Only the little he'd learned from Jax and Deth.

Yolken looked at the next few pictures. The dragons were paired off: blue and violet, orange and green, white and black. The blue and violet ones stood above oval shapes: eggs. He looked to the next image, of the orange and green dragons, and saw brown baby hatchlings newly emerged from their eggs. *The blue and violet dragons' eggs didn't hatch.* Next came the white and black again, with their gray hatchlings. *Deth's ancestors were black and white.*

"Blessed," Tana said, drawing Yolken's attention away from the paintings. "The next few days will be wearisome. Please, come and rest."

The days of traveling *were* catching up to Yolken. He conceded that Tana was right and started back toward the huts. "You coming?" he said to Deanna.

"Soon," she said.

Yolken nodded and followed Tana back to his hut.

"I'll wake you in the morning," Tana said.

"Thank you," Yolken said. He went into the hut, blew out the lamp, and lay down on the cot. It didn't take long for sleep to wash over him.

* * *

Yolken woke to someone gently shaking him.

"It is time," Tana said.

Yolken sat up on the cot. A tray with bread and cheese sat on the table.

"Eat, then come."

Tana left.

Yolken wasn't hungry, but he wrapped the bread and cheese up in the cloth folded on the tray and put it in his satchel containing the dragon bones.

"That was fast," Tana said.

"I wasn't hungry," he said. "Besides, I'm ready to get going."

They met Deanna by the paintings, then Tana led them deeper into the cavern, past the paintings. An enormous dragon carved into the rock met them at the end of the cavern. Yolken looked up at it in awe. The sculpture was an incredibly accurate version of a creature the inhabitants of this cave had probably never actually seen. It made him wonder about the paintings as well. Who painted them? And how did they know so much about the dragons?

Tana gestured toward a crack in the wall beyond the dragon's tail. "There you will find the answers you seek."

Yolken looked from the carving to the woman. *How could she possibly know why I came here?* "What answers?"

"He said you would come seeking an answer, and that we were to show you the way."

"Who?"

"The answer you seek is there." Tana again gestured toward the stretched-out tail of the dragon.

Yolken ignored her gestures and said, "But someone told you I would be coming?"

"Long ago, yes."

"Who?"

"Him. We have for centuries been waiting."

Nera hadn't said anything about that when she'd told him about this place. *Did she know?*

"Yolken," Deanna said, "at this point, does it really matter?"

"But who could've possibly known that I would be coming here?"

"I don't know. Even if we did, it wouldn't matter. Instead, let's go do what we came here to do."

Yolken acquiesced with a nod. Deanna started toward the crack and he looked at the sculpture again before following her.

They needed light. Yolken reached into the satchel for a dragon bone. He was immediately annoyed that he'd had to come without the Harachin sword. Somehow it had gone missing. At the time he'd been beside himself with anger. Jax assured him that it had just been misplaced during caching— thousands of bones had been gathered. He pulled out a small dagger, the very first bone he'd used the night he fled Lonely Oak. They'd brought as many as they could fit into the satchel and, except for the dagger, chose the most powerful bones they had. He had brought the dagger for sentimental reasons, but the rest of the satchel was filled with more powerful bones, including Deanna's Aliza sword and Lio Drake's broken Mattath sword. There were seven more swords somewhere. He wished he'd had time to scour the palace for them. Made from Dimras' bones, they were the strongest bones available.

Yolken and Deanna proceeded down a winding natural corridor. The corridor turned and swerved. They came across dead ends and proceeded through cracks into new passages. He had known it was going to take them a while to arrive at wherever it was they were going, but as they burned through bone after bone, he began to worry.

They walked for hours. Days? Yolken didn't know. He did know they stopped several times to rest, and twice he fell asleep. During one of their rests Yolken said, "We're more than halfway through the bones."

"Then we need to lower the light even more," Deanna said. "Conserve the Energy."

But when they set off again, they found there was a limit to how dimly they could light the passages but still see enough to move safely and without slowing down considerably.

"I'm worried we're not going to have enough Energy to find our way out of here," Yolken said. "I don't know how you did it."

"I had years, remember," Deanna said. "I memorized the passages as I went."

They didn't have that luxury, Yolken thought. Were they getting themselves hopelessly lost?

They had emptied all the bones and were halfway through the Aliza sword when the passage ended and they stepped out into the open. He increased the size of the flame, and the gnawing fear that they wouldn't have the Energy they needed to get back out was tamped down.

They were in a cavern similar to the one where he'd met Deth. It was a single vast chamber with numerous stalactites and stalagmites, as well as several pillars where the stalactites and stalagmites had grown together.

Yolken stepped farther into the cavern and thought, *Who was he? And why did he think the answer would be here? Did he leave something here for me to find?* He scanned his surroundings, hoping that was exactly what had happened and that he would find something obvious. But even after they walked around the entire cavern, they didn't find anything. They continued their search, looking in every nook and crevice. He even used Synthesis to jump up to ledges they wouldn't otherwise have been able to reach.

After searching every possible spot and not finding anything, Yolken sat heavily on a ledge high above the cavern floor, dejected. Deanna eased herself down into a sitting position next to him. "It has to be here," Yolken said.

"I don't think we're searching right," Deanna said.

"What do you mean?"

"We've been looking for something that a human left."

She was right, which gave Yolken an idea.

Yolken dimmed the fire that had been steadily consuming the remaining Energy in the Aliza Sword and let it go out completely. The darkest of darknesses enveloped them. He lost all reference to where he was, reminding him of Deth's home. If he stood up and stepped forward more than a few steps, he would step out into nothingness without even knowing it.

Yolken blinked, changing his eyes. With his new lenses in place, the blackness turned to various shades of gray. There was no light here, and yet he could still see. His head was tilted down, his body exploding into view—his arms and hands bright oranges and yellows, his clothes darker, with some orange and yellow, but predominately greens and blues.

He looked up, keeping his bright hands and arms out of his line of sight, and let his vision adjust. The cavern slowly came back into view. It was dim but had a purple and blue glow about it. For some reason, the pillars stood out, glowing almost as brightly as his hands and arms. *That's odd,* he thought. Was there some source of Energy in the pillars causing them to glow?

Yolken stood and Deanna said, "What is it?"

"The pillars are glowing."

"I don't see anything."

Yolken lit the chamber up again with fire from the Aliza

sword and said, "Come on." They climbed off the ledge and went to the closest pillar. The glow wasn't the glow of Energy, or heat, he realized, but surprisingly, what looked like some sort of flowing script.

"I think it might be writing," he said.

"I still don't see anything."

It didn't make sense to Yolken. If it was writing, he'd never seen anything like it before. He thought about it for a moment, then traced the beginning of the script in a thin line of Energy. He heated the line until it glowed, making a few lines appear.

"Draego's Fire," Deanna said.

"You see it?"

"More importantly, I understand it."

"You do?"

"Deth taught me. All those years he spent teaching me their language. It was one of the conditions he set for my continued presence. He made me practice writing it until I had it perfectly. But I never once actually saw anything written in their language. They don't have books. At least I didn't think they did."

"The pillars are covered in it," Yolken said. "I think we may have just found their books."

"But how can you see it? I don't see anything."

Yolken hadn't told anyone but Kaylan about his eyes. He didn't know why, but now there was no reason not to. "I can see Energy," he said.

Deanna looked at him, stunned. "You mean like Glasses?"

Yolken nodded.

"Unbelievable."

"But you *can* read this?"

"Yes. The portion you illuminated says, 'Ever the Ribbon of Time drifts in the Ether. Draego floats above; not in, but not out.'"

"Ribbon of Time?" Yolken said.

"I think this might be their history."

"Well, then, let's read it."

CHAPTER 43

Jax paced his room. He had hardly touched his morning meal, which now sat cold on the table. It was all he could do to stop himself from immediately going to Kaylan with his plans—or rather, Orwyn's plans. Even after taking Yolken down to the cache of Machines that Drakonias had hidden under the city, Yolken had refused to heed his warning about the impending war. But Yolken was gone, and Jax fully intended to prepare Kyinth. He didn't want to do it without Kaylan's permission, though. It was imperative that he succeed with her where he had failed with Yolken.

The time had come to make his way to the council chamber, where Kaylan was going to hold her first council with Yolken's advisors. Everyone else was already assembled when he arrived, including Kaylan, which made him feel a bit foolish.

"I'm sorry, Your Highness," Jax said with a bow.

Kaylan shook her head and said, "I only just arrived myself."

Jax took his place at Kaylan's right, and sat with everyone else after she did. He watched her as she looked around the table at the others. Each of them had their eyes fixed on her.

"They're waiting for you," Jax whispered to Kaylan.

"Huh?"

"To start."

"Oh." Kaylan's cheeks flushed, but then she said, "Um, shall we begin?"

"There are many important matters on the agenda this morning, Your Highness," Enif said at once.

"Actually," Jax interjected, "I believe I have the most pressing issue that needs to be addressed."

"What could be more important than—"

"War."

"*War?*" Enif said. He sounded incredulous.

"Is coming," Jax said. "And we need to begin preparations. Immediately."

"If there's a war coming, why wait until the emperor is gone to say something?"

"I *did* say something. He just didn't believe me."

"Then why would I?" Kaylan said.

"Yolken… His Highness didn't believe me when I told him there was a war coming because he wanted to know how I knew, and I couldn't tell him."

"Why not?"

"Because I was instructed not to."

"By whom?" Enif said.

"His father."

Several of the advisors gasped.

"His… *what?*"

"Why would you say that?" Aleena Harrin said.

"He's dead," Jerle Sage added.

"Yes," several others agreed.

"No. He's very much alive," Jax said.

The stunned faces staring at him all said they didn't believe him.

"How?"

"Where?"

"If he's alive, why isn't he here?"

"More importantly, why have you kept this from us?" Enif

said.

"His Highness couldn't know," Jax said.

"Why not?"

"I'm not exactly sure. And as I wasn't able to offer him any evidence, Yolken refused to listen to me."

"But—he's alive?" Enif said.

"Very much so."

"How long have you known?" Kaylan said.

"Since Javen, Tabora, and I stopped in Lonely Oak." Jax shook his head with a smirk. "I'm so stupid. All this time I thought he was dead. I *saw* his body."

"What does this mean?" Enif said.

Jax shifted so he could look directly at Kaylan. "Your Highness, Yolken didn't believe me, but I'm telling you: War *is* coming. And we must prepare."

"War with whom?" Kaylan said.

"And how are we supposed to prepare?" Enif said.

"I don't know who. Only that Orwyn told me, and I believe him," Jax said. "But how... I know exactly how."

Jax let a silence descend over the advisors. He waited until Enif said, "Go on..."

With a grin, Jax said, "Drakonias has a cache of war Machines not far from here."

"*Machines?*" Kaylan said.

"Where?" Enif said.

"Below us. Deep below the city."

"So what are you asking?" Kaylan said.

"There are weapons below us which, if utilized, will guarantee our victory. I'm asking for permission to ready those weapons and bring them to the surface. If there really is a war coming, we need to be ready."

"I agree," Enif said.

"As do I," others chimed in.

"What of the fallout?" Dannl Kand said.

"What do you mean?" Kaylan asked.

"We've known about such devices because of our association with the Order, but Drakonias worked very hard to erase the past. The general populace has never seen such things and—"

"Neither have any of you," Jax interjected.

"True, but we know what they are. I'm worried bringing Machines to the surface could cause hysteria. *Will* cause hysteria…"

"People deserve to know the truth," Jax said.

"Agreed," Enif said.

Kaylan sat pensively for a moment, but then finally said, "I agree too."

"Your Highness…" Dannl said.

"And if there is war coming—"

"There is," Jax said.

"—then we need to be prepared. I won't allow the empire to be taken from Yolken while he's gone," Kaylan said.

"So I have your permission to ready the Machines?"

Kaylan stared thoughtfully, but not for quite as long this time. "Yes."

* * *

Jax pushed forward on one of two levers, making the cart accelerate along the level track. They exited the tunnel into the large cavern where Drakonias'—Yolken's—Machines lay hidden from Dradonia.

"Draego's Fire," Enif said.

"That was His Highness' exact reaction," Jax said.

"This is unbelievable."

"Isn't it?"

They passed by the rows of Machines and the mysterious lights affixed at the tops of tall poles. The track curved and the Caretakers' home came into view. One was waiting for them when the cart came to a stop at the end of the track.

"You've returned, eh… pardon, but I have forgotten your name," One said.

"Jax."

"Jax, yes." One surveyed the cart and said, "Where are our supplies?"

"I don't have them."

One's face turned grim. "Then how may we be of service?"

"There's a war coming."

"Yes," One said.

"Wait. You knew?"

"No. But we are ready. We are always ready."

"Good, because we need you to teach us to use these things."

"We are ready," One said. "Moving the Machines to the surface will require time, Your... Jax."

"Then let us be about it," Jax said.

One bowed toward Jax, then shuffled off to the building. Jax and Enif followed him into a room at the base of the tower. With both hands, One pulled on a rope that dangled from the ceiling. A bell rang.

CHAPTER 44

Orwyn flew high into the air. He'd worked for years to master the skill, until flying came as naturally to him as it did to dragons. He'd only ever known one—Deth—but flying with Deth was one of his favorite things to do.

He flew north, away from the innocent refugees. The queen had finally done what had needed to be done for at least twenty years—something Dorlan never had the courage to do. His people suffered, and he did nothing. And now that they were finally on a path out of suffering, he wasn't going to allow any more of them to die because of Drenan's feud with him.

Orwyn landed several leagues away from the refugees. He held the Harachin sword at his side. It pulsed with Energy. *He* pulsed with Energy.

Drenan came into sight and burst into flame—or at least from Orwyn's vantage it looked like he did. The approaching fireball looked as though it was consuming Drenan. For someone as adept at manipulating the air as Orwyn was, protecting himself took little effort. The approaching flames bent up and over him, dispersing in the air. The flow of fire continued, however.

Orwyn readied himself by siphoning off some of the air he

was controlling to divert the river of fire, and stripped it of carbon. He sent the carbon down the surface of the sword, infusing it with heat. The carbon hardened, turning the relatively fragile bone into the hardest, sharpest of weapons. The key to Synthesis, he had taught Jax long ago, was knowledge. Other than the lack of Energy, Synthesis' only real limitation was the knowledge the Synthesizer possessed. Which was why he had ensured Selena taught his sons well.

Orwyn held the Harachin sword at low ready, gripping the hilt with both hands. He took up a defensive stance and waited.

The silhouette of a man appeared in the flames before they finally parted and Drenan fully appeared. The fire continued out and around them, setting the dry grass ablaze. Drenan swung at Orwyn with what looked like a six-inch dragon-bone dagger. Orwyn stepped to the side and instinctively parried. The Harachin sword sang out as it made contact with an invisible force more than two feet past the tip of the dagger.

Drenan skidded to a stop and turned to face Orwyn.

Flames grew all around them.

* * *

Javen watched as his father grew distant and small in the sky. With him and Drenan gone, a relative calm washed over the convoy. The soldiers with the mysterious weapons stood with their weapons still pointed, but none of them moved. Hadie was back on her feet and Lyoll was once again hovering over Ganip.

Javen eyed the soldiers. Many of them wore Glasses, but they didn't seem too concerned with him, so he moved toward Hadie. He embraced her in a quick hug, thankful to the Great Dragon that Drenan hadn't harmed her, then they joined Lyoll.

Lyoll was sobbing. He had a hand on Ganip's forehead. "There was nothing he could do," Lyoll said.

Hadie placed her hand on Lyoll's back.

"He healed my legs like it was no big deal," Lyoll said, "but Ganip was already gone. Said there was nothing he could do."

Hadie looked at Javen and said, "Your father's alive?"

Javen shook his head. He could hardly believe it. *How?* "I don't know. I mean, I know him—at least I've seen him before—but I had no idea."

"There are others," Lyoll said.

"Others?" Javen said.

"Dead. He's a monster. Those... those things killed dozens. We have to do something."

Lyoll stood.

Javen looked around him. Beyond the soldiers surrounding them, southerners huddled together in groups surrounded by more soldiers. Smoke also rose from several different sources. He took a step, but several soldiers pointed their weapons directly at him.

"Don't move," one of them said.

"I suppose we wait," Javen said. He looked over his shoulder in the direction his father had flown.

His father was alive. He was standing here surrounded by soldiers armed with impossible weapons. He should have been completely terrified. But oddly, he felt calm, even happy.

His father was alive.

* * *

Drenan was no longer directing fire at Orwyn, so Orwyn abandoned the river of air he controlled. Instead, he siphoned water from the air and made it rain around them. The flames grew, but the rain kept a protective circle around him and his foe.

Drenan's clothes quickly became soaked and clung to his muscled body. "The usurper used to tell stories about—"

"Your grandfather, you mean," Orwyn said.

"—how knights used to duel with clunky broadswords to settle disputes. They would even fight over a woman's honor. Imagine that."

"Isn't that what we've been doing all these years? Fighting over women's honor?"

"You killed my wife."

"And you killed mine. And you know Therese's death was an accident."

"Don't speak her name."

"So that's what you want to do? Fight because we killed each other's wives?"

Drenan stared icily at Orwyn. The fact that they were standing in the middle of a rainstorm on a perfectly clear day added some levity to the situation. The growing fire, however, worried Orwyn. Drenan didn't seem to be fueling it anymore, but the fire spread quickly through the dry grass. They were a few leagues from the refugees, but given the conditions, the fire could quickly spread toward them.

Drenan lunged toward Orwyn, saying through gritted teeth, "And Cara!"

"*Cara* was a regent," Orwyn said, deflecting Drenan's thrust. "Which means she was a soldier. And sometimes soldiers die." They stood facing each other again, Orwyn holding the Harachin sword at low ready and Drenan holding his dagger at his side, blade pointing toward the ground. "Besides, wasn't she there to kill me?"

Drenan stepped in again. He alternated thrusts with swings, each of which Orwyn easily parried. Drenan stepped in close, almost getting inside of the swing of Orwyn's sword, but Orwyn pushed him away with a blast of air.

"Was I supposed to just *let* her?" he said when Drenan was a safe distance away.

"How did you do it, anyway?" Drenan swung out with the dagger and Orwyn's chest erupted in pain.

Orwyn jumped back and looked down. His wet shirt was sliced open and blood was flowing from a gash. The pain was sharp, but the wound was already closing. He barely had to think about healing anymore. He'd done it so much over the years it was almost like breathing. But if the cut had been a little higher, opening his throat, there would be nothing he could have done.

"How long *is* that thing?" Orwyn said wryly.

"Apparently not long enough." Drenan swung the dagger from side to side before him and the sun reflected off the transparent extension of his blade. "You didn't answer my question."

"I was busy healing myself, thank you very much."

"Well?"

"How'd I do what?"

"I saw your corpse."

"Corpse?"

Drenan's eyes narrowed. "Draego's Fire."

"I always figured you to be one who'd pay more attention to detail."

Drenan shook his head. "Don't think you're going to escape this time, Danavin."

"I hadn't planned on it." Orwyn slashed the air in front of him with the Harachin sword, then took a defensive position. "Shall we?"

Drenan feigned an attack but then jumped back, landing a dozen paces away. He swept his hands out around him and fire streamed from his fingers.

Orwyn watched in horror as the fire spread, moving unnaturally fast. Not toward him but back the way they'd come—toward the convoy. He reached out with Energy and felt the air Drenan was using to fan the flames. Time was running out, he knew. If he didn't stop Drenan now, the fire would reach the convoy.

He ran toward him.

Drenan stood ready, holding his dagger with both hands. Orwyn caught a few glints of the sun off the invisible extension, but didn't know exactly how far the diamond-hard blade extended past the visible tip of the dagger. It didn't matter, though—he didn't intend to get that close to Drenan.

When Orwyn was within a few paces, Drenan swung his dagger, but Orwyn jumped. He flew well clear of Drenan—behind him, where the grass was afire. Orwyn gathered water from the air and doused the flames as he landed. Then he turned and waited in a circle of blackened grass.

Within seconds a shape appeared in the flames. Drenan emerged swinging his blade, but Orwyn was ready. He countered, then went on the offense. The Harachin sword swung rapidly while he advanced, forcing Drenan back toward the wall of fire. The fire cleared around them as Orwyn drove him back.

It was evident to him that neither of them was going to better the other so long as they both had access to Energy, so he changed tactics. He feigned a stumble, which made Drenan switch from defense to offense. But when Drenan stepped closer, Orwyn threw the Harachin sword at him, pushing it with Energy. Drenan ducked it as it flew toward his head, and Orwyn took the opportunity to launch himself into the air. As he climbed, he pulled his sword back. He pivoted in the air when he was about twenty feet up and looked back toward the convoy. Flames shot up toward him but swirled away harmlessly.

The grass fire was still racing toward the convoy. He could see that they were boxed in by the army of Machines, so when the fire reached them, they would have nowhere to flee. Drenan's army would be safe inside their metal Machines while the southerners' wagons and carts burned.

Even if he killed Drenan right now, it wouldn't stop the fire.

"Get back down here, you coward!" Drenan shouted from below. It always pleased Orwyn that Drenan wasn't powerful enough to fly.

Orwyn looked down at his long-time foe, who was back in the circle of sodden grass. He wanted to confront him, get retribution for him killing Elen, but had no choice—he had to stop the fire. Vengeance would have to wait.

Orwyn flew toward the convoy. The fire was spreading incredibly fast. The unusually dry and mild winter had left the grass ripe for burning. He knew Javen had been practicing with Synthesis, but he didn't know for sure whether he had the ability to stop the flames, and he didn't want to take the chance. Too many lives were at stake for him to not act.

He looked over his shoulder instinctively, but knew he had time—it would take Drenan longer to return to the convoy since he couldn't fly.

Orwyn caught up to the front of the fire less than a hundred paces from the convoy. He landed adroitly, facing the fire with his back to the convoy. His Core was still full to the brim—since his altercation with Drenan had begun, a steady flow of Energy had been flowing into his Core for him to manipulate. He directed the river of power from his hands, concentrating it before him. The air erupted in fire. He simultaneously directed the air from behind him forward. The fire set the grass ablaze.

Pain erupted in Orwyn's back and exploded out his chest. He heard a loud boom behind him and stumbled forward. Blood splattered the ground in front of him. Distantly, from behind himself, he heard Javen yell, "Father!"

The wound closed quickly, his muscles, tendons, vessels, and lung all healed in the process.

Orwyn continued to work, back-burning the grass to stop the fire. He'd thought about soaking the grass with water but doubted he could create a line long enough. If there was no fuel for the fire to burn, though, it would stop. Unless Drenan redirected some of his own Energy to keep it going, of course. Orwyn hoped he would; that could possibly give him edge enough to stop Drenan.

Another Bullet took Orwyn in the side before he heard the boom from behind. He was all too familiar with Guns—he'd personally used them during Drakonias' war. They were one of the most efficient methods of killing people his family had ever invented. He healed himself without thinking.

His fire had spread far enough to both sides, so he ended the flow of Energy from his hands.

He fell to a knee when a Bullet took him in the leg. The concussion of the Guns started in rapid succession, so he forced

Energy into his good leg and jumped into the air. He gathered the air around himself as he simultaneously healed his leg.

He surveyed the fire-line he'd made. Bullets whizzed by as he looked down, but none of them found their target. Satisfied his line would stop the natural progression of the fire, he turned his attention back to Drenan.

Orwyn found him running toward the convoy, about half a mile from the fire line. Then Drenan stopped; he had probably seen Orwyn's manipulation of the sun's Energy through the Glasses he wore and knew he was overhead.

Orwyn flew just past Drenan and landed in the fire. He created an eddy around himself to keep the flames away. The grass below his feet crackled and glowed orange.

Drenan appeared through the flames and attacked. But Orwyn went on the offense. Except for the Energy required to keep the flames at bay, he directed every bit of what was in his Core into his muscles. His movements became a blur as his body pulsed with Energy. Dragons had been the most powerful species on Dradonia before the Drakes butchered them. Now, as the Harachin sword whizzed through the air, barely visible to his eyes, he felt as powerful as a dragon.

Orwyn drove Drenan back. Drenan could barely keep the Harachin sword at bay, and Orwyn didn't let up. He continued to push Drenan.

Then Drenan stumbled on the burned branch of a sage bush, and for the first time the Harachin sword found its mark. A line of blood appeared on the upper portion of Drenan's right arm.

Drenan abandoned his two-handed grip on the dagger, shifting it to just his left hand.

Drenan's wound didn't slow him, but it made him unable to get an edge on Orwyn. So Orwyn continued to press him, driving him back.

"You're slipping," he said.

"It doesn't matter," Drenan snarled. Even with the aid of

Synthesis, his breath was labored. "Your get is as good as dead anyway."

Orwyn knew that what Drenan said wasn't true. Yolken's fate, he had learned from Deth centuries ago, had already been decided.

"Don't believe me?" Drenan said. "Devin is on his way to Kyinth right now to put an end to his foolish claim to the throne."

"Well, then, I guess it's a good thing he doesn't really care about the throne."

Orwyn didn't let up on his assault; he knew Drenan was just trying to distract him.

"What's this about, then?" Drenan said.

"Restoring balance," Orwyn said. The look that briefly crossed Drenan's face told Orwyn that the other man really didn't know what was happening. Drakonias had done a superb job of keeping the truth from the Regency. "Haven't you wondered what's been happening to the weather?" Orwyn slowed to give Drenan time to consider what he said, but he only turned it into an opportunity to strike back. So Orwyn resumed his attack, putting Drenan back on the defense. "Your stupid war," he said.

"What about it?"

"You killed the sun."

"That's impossible."

"Your realm imploded on itself, Drenan. And yet you still deny the truth."

"The emperor—"

"Lied to you. All of you. Only Reago knew the truth and you branded him a traitor."

"You're the traitor, Danavin. Or at least the son of one, which is the same thing."

"And what exactly are you doing, Drenan? This army—what is it?"

"I'm cauterizing loose ends."

"What loose ends?"

"You. Your get is *not* the rightful emperor."

"Who, then? Thena? Is that where you got this army?"

"She doesn't want it."

"Then who?"

Despite Drenan's difficulty repelling Orwyn's assault, a smile blossomed on his face.

"*You?*" Orwyn stifled a laugh.

"You think that's funny?"

"None of you deserve to rule."

"Still with your blasphemy." Drenan attempted to turn the course of their duel but Orwyn easily rebuffed him.

"The truth is before you, Drenan, but you still deny it."

Orwyn pressed Drenan. He didn't want to kill him—he believed all the regents deserved the chance to right their wrongs, just as Reago had done—but Drenan, he knew, was so driven by hate that he wouldn't stop until he felt he had achieved his retribution.

"I'm sorry," Orwyn said, making one last effort. "For Therese; for Cara."

"Ahhh!" Drenan screamed.

"It was never my intention for them to die."

"But I fully intended to kill *your* wife," Drenan sneered.

Through his exertion, Orwyn sighed. He knew there was only one way this was going to end, and it wasn't by convincing Drenan to let go of the past.

Orwyn restricted the Energy required to keep the fire at bay to the absolute minimum, and transferred the extra to his muscles. His speed increased ever so slightly, but it was enough to push Drenan past his capabilities. The Harachin sword began connecting with its mark, opening new wounds on Drenan. With each landed blow, Drenan slowed, allowing the Harachin sword to connect with increased frequency. Wounds soon covered Drenan, but his Energy-fueled body wouldn't quit. Still, Orwyn knew he wasn't far from landing a life-ending blow.

Orwyn pressed Drenan.

Drenan bled from an increasing number of wounds.

Orwyn's assault pushed Drenan out of the flames and into the fire-line Orwyn had burned. Machines were visible in his peripheral vision. He continued to assault Drenan, but he stumbled when his stomach exploded in pain. He heard the blast of a Gun, then fell to his knees when another Bullet took him in the chest. Another blast. Orwyn slammed the Harachin sword point-first into the ground to brace himself, and diverted all his available Energy to healing himself. But Bullets continued to strike him. His ears rang from the cacophony of the Guns firing.

Orwyn did his best, but for every wound he healed, two more Bullets struck him. Thankfully, none had yet taken him in the head or heart. Neither of those he would survive.

A large shadow moved over Orwyn, cutting him off from direct access to the sun. He looked up to find a Machine hovering overhead.

Bullets continued to strike him, so he drew Energy from the Harachin sword. But he was falling behind, growing weaker.

Drenan stood over him, not confidently or in smug satisfaction, as he was in significant pain himself. But his eyes communicated to Orwyn that he had won—and Orwyn knew it. Drenan he could best—had all but bested—but he was no match for the Machines. They'd been designed to kill Synthesizers. He regretted driving Drenan toward the convoy. Why had he done that? A stupid decision.

Orwyn's grip on the Harachin sword slipped. One hand fell to the scorched grass, burning his knuckles but the pain was nothing compared to what he felt elsewhere.

The volley of Bullets stopped, giving him a respite; time in which he could heal himself. Drenan's doing, he wondered? But why?

Drenan stepped close, into the shadow, and peeled Orwyn's hand from the sword's hilt. Then he pulled the point of the sword from the ground and took a step back, back into the sun.

"Don't worry," Drenan said.

Orwyn looked up at him. *Ah. He wants to do it himself.* The yellow ribbons in the black blade glinted in the sun.

"Your get will follow swiftly."

In the midst of fire and pain, Drenan's gaze was cold. Killing Orwyn would not satisfy Drenan, Orwyn knew. Neither would killing Yolken or Javen. Drenan was a man who, given the chance, would rule with ruthless abandon.

"You don't have to do this," Orwyn said. His mouth tasted of iron. Without the continuous supply of Energy, he had grown weak.

"But I'm going to." Drenan lifted the Harachin sword.

Movement behind Drenan caught Orwyn's eye, but he dared not avert his gaze. The movement was fast; too fast.

The diamond edge glinted in the sun as Drenan took a step.

"And I'm going to enj—"

A blade sprouted from his chest.

Drenan looked down at it as he fell to his knees, blood oozing from his mouth and nose. The Harachin sword slipped from his fingers.

Orwyn looked past Drenan and saw Javen.

Drenan fell forward.

Orwyn smiled at his son, but then his strength gave out and he fell.

He closed his eyes, knowing his sons would prevail.

Darkness closed in, but before it enveloped him completely, he saw Javen kneel beside him. Javen was yelling, but Orwyn couldn't hear him.

Satisfied, Orwyn closed his eyes and turned his attention to Elen. She'd died for a cause she knew little about. He'd never wanted to hurt her—only to protect her, to make her happy. He had avoided love for most of his life because death followed him everywhere, and he didn't want to risk the life of someone he loved. But at the same time, he knew it was inevitable. Deth had told him as much all those many years ago when he had ventured to Kvorga in search of Deanna's help.

For a long time, he'd avoided the love Deth promised him would come, but eventually it caught up to him. He had Selena to blame for that—she'd introduced him to Elen. And now, he could finally return to it after it had been stolen from him not that long ago. He was ready. He anticipated it.

But then a warmth entered his hand. Energy flowed from the warmth to his Core. Centuries of instinct kicked in and his body began to heal.

Orwyn's pain abated, then it was gone. He felt pressure on his forehead, though. Something warm fell on his cheek, then slid down the side of his face. It itched. Or did it tickle? He opened his eyes, but couldn't focus on the face hovering above him—it was too close. The itch, tickle, became too much, so he reached up to wipe at it. The pressure on his forehead lifted and he saw Javen's tear-filled eyes.

Javen looked down at him in surprise, then buried his head on Orwyn's chest.

CHAPTER 45

Yolken emerged from under the dragon statue, back into the entrance chamber, terrified. As he shifted his eyes back to normal in the increased light, Deanna's final words still echoed in his mind: *Draego's Fire. He's abandoned us.* At least he knew what he needed to do. But he didn't know what terrified him more.

Draego's Blessing flowed continuously from the Ether to Solarian, the sun. This connection sustained Synthesis—and thereby, all life on Dradonia. But when Deth had given Synthesis to Marcin, the man who would become Draeko, that connection was severed.

Yolken remembered from his lessons with Jax that plants passively used Energy from the sun, but humans used Energy actively, and ever since the connection between the Ether and the sun had been severed, humans had been using Energy the Ether wasn't replacing. As human usage of Energy steadily increased, they had unwittingly further destabilized the sun. Drakonias' war pushed the sun over the edge and sent it spiraling out of balance. And Dimras knew this.

He also knew how to fix it—how to restore the balance lost.

Yolken and Deanna were halfway down the row of paintings when Tana came scurrying up. With wild gesticulation and gasping breaths, she said, "Your-your Highness. You-you've returned." She grabbed Yolken by the arm and attempted to pull him forward. "Y-you n-need to come."

Yolken gave into her pull and said, "What is it?"

"Come. Come!"

Yolken and Deanna followed Tana as she made her way past the huts and toward the front of the cave.

"He's returned," Tana said over her shoulder.

"Who?" Of everything he and Deanna had learned in Dimras and Devrith's cave, they hadn't learned who *he* was.

"The dragon," Tana said at the same moment Deth came into view.

Yolken looked at Deth curiously. *Him.* "What are you doing here?"

In a booming voice, Deth said, "I've come for Deanna."

"*Me?*" Deanna said.

Yolken looked from Deth to Deanna.

"Your work here is complete," Deth said.

Deanna looked at Yolken, confusion on her face. "Did you plan this?"

Yolken shook his head.

Deanna looked at Deth. "What about you?"

"The Dragon King does not need you to complete his task," Deth said.

"He's right," Yolken said. "Go."

"Are you sure?"

"No. But I know what I need to do now. Your help's been invaluable."

"I'm here to serve," Deanna said.

"I'm serious," Yolken said. "Without you I wouldn't have known what was written on those pillars."

"It has been an honor working with you, Your High…" Deanna stopped herself. She smiled and wiped a tear from her eye. "It has been an honor, Yolken."

"This isn't goodbye." He felt his own eyes begin to water.

"Isn't it?"

"No. I fully intend to return."

"I'm sorry, I just—"

"Why wouldn't I?"

"I don't know."

"Kaylan is with child." Yolken's tears fell. "We have plans."

"Plans?"

"When this is done, I'm taking her home, to Lonely Oak."

"What about the empire? Who'll rule?"

"I don't know. But I want to go home. I want to build the house in the maple grove that my father always wanted to build. I often went to that grove, to where they were buried. It was so pleasant; the sound of the rushing water…"

"It sounds amazing," Deanna said through sniffles. "I truly hope you get what you wish."

Yolken wiped his eyes and said, "You should rule."

"*What?*"

"You're next in line, after Drakonias."

"Yolken, I—"

"And your rule would be legitimate. You fought alongside your father."

Deanna looked at him intently. "Let's discuss this when you return, shall we?"

"Deal."

Yolken and Deanna turned toward Deth.

"Climb onto my neck," Deth said.

Yolken noticed that the dragon had a horse's harness around his neck. There wasn't a bit in his mouth, but it was something for Deanna to hold onto.

"I'll see you back in Kyinth," Deanna said.

Yolken started to reply, but she moved in and hugged him instead. "Do what you came here to do," she said.

Yolken nodded.

Deth rested his head on the ground, making it easy for Deanna to climb up. She settled as best she could before Deth pushed himself up onto his feet. Without any fanfare, Deth lumbered toward the exit. Yolken had been right—Deth barely fit through the opening.

He followed them out. Deth crouched on the landing at the exit. He craned his neck to look back at Yolken. He dipped his head, then turned back. His muscles tensed and he launched into the air.

Yolken stood on the ledge and watched Deth and Deanna grow smaller in the sky. He was amazed that Deanna was *riding* on a dragon. Who would have ever imagined such a thing? He felt jealous, and wished it was him. He wondered what it was like. What could Deanna possibly be experiencing? She was flying on a dragon!

"Come," Tana said from behind him. "You need to rest. But first, you must eat."

The importance of what Yolken knew he must do slammed the curiosity and jealousy out of him. He didn't want to rest— he didn't know how he could—but he bid Deth and Deanna farewell in his mind and followed Tana back into the cave.

It was at this point that he noticed he and Tana were the only people there. "Where is everyone?" he said.

"Gone." Tana continued toward the hut he'd slept in when he first arrived.

"Where'd they go?"

"It was time."

"So you're the only one here?"

"It was my duty to await your return."

Tana ushered Yolken into the hut; food was waiting for him. "I will return and wake you when the appointed hour has arrived."

Yolken ate, then lay down on the cot and stared at the ceiling. His mind swirled. He finally knew what he needed to do. He closed his eyes, knowing it was almost over. Soon he could put everything behind him and return home with Kaylan. He imagined standing with his arm around her on the front porch of their home, watching their daughter play under the maples. Before he could even wonder how he knew the child growing in Kaylan's stomach was a girl, he fell asleep.

CHAPTER 46

Kaylan tried to ignore the cramping in her stomach as she peered down at the two armies gathered far below. They were lined up in long rows. From this distance, the two forces appeared similar. There was one noticeable distinction, however: The other army had flying Machines and Jax's army did not. She was no longer convinced by Jax's assertion of guaranteed victory. Even so, the sight of Machines was unbelievable. She'd lived her whole life not knowing about their existence. Even after her journey in the Train with Javen, their existence still marveled her.

"Come, Your Highness," Sahri said from behind her. "We need to get you to safety."

Yolken's advisors were getting themselves worked up because she had thus far refused to go underground with them. She didn't like the idea of going into hiding when innocent people would be dying to protect Kyinth. They seemed more concerned about what might happen to themselves if something were to befall her than they were about protecting the city. Now that Jax and the army were gone, they were only thinking of themselves. She couldn't bring herself to go into hiding while all those brave individuals who had been training without ceasing for the last two weeks were out there risking their lives.

"I'm not going," Kaylan said, without looking away from the two armies. She pressed her hands to her stomach.

"Will you at least come inside?"

Thus far the armies had not attacked each other, so she wasn't in any immediate danger.

"No."

After she'd given Jax permission to prepare for the as yet unforeseen war, barely a week had gone by when a condor arrived with a message that Tieger had been attacked. Sheal and all the regents who had pledged their loyalty to Yolken stood no chance against Devin and his army, especially since they had no dragon bones or armor to protect themselves. Enif immediately attributed blame to Yolken for his decision to ban dragon artifacts, but the Machines Jax brought up from beneath the city proved that even without the ban in place, it wouldn't have made a difference. In fact, it probably would have increased the already unacceptably high number of reported casualties, because Sheal and the regents might have been emboldened to fight back more than they did. As it was, Devin had ruthlessly murdered them when they tried to surrender. She'd also received reports that provincial regents had abandoned their posts. She couldn't blame them. Those who didn't met the same fate as Sheal.

The flying Machines soared in the sky, but nothing else seemed to be happening.

They'd decided that Devin must have come from the East. It was the only explanation. Drakonias' Machines had all been cached below Kyinth, Jax confirmed with the mysterious man called One, so they were able to rule out the possibility that Devin had accessed a cache somewhere else. But the fact that the East had Machines left them with many unanswered questions.

First of all, how in Draego's Fire did Devin cross the East Sea? No one had successfully crossed in the last seventy years, Kaylan understood.

If Thena had Machines, she must have disobeyed Drakonias' edict banning dragon bones. Machines, Jax had explained, were powered by Energy, which was stored in dragon bones. And if she had ignored that edict, what else had she been up to all this time?

Was she still loyal to Kyinth?

Did *she* give Devin this army?

And where in Dradonia was Drenan?

They'd sent word out to all the coastal cities in the Northern Realm to be on alert, but they hadn't heard back from any of them.

Kaylan watched intently as one of Jax's Machines—a Tank—separated from the army and moved forward. It stopped about halfway between the two forces. A Machine from Devin's army separated itself from the rest and moved forward as well.

Devin was going to give them the opportunity to surrender, she imagined. She hoped. But what he did to Sheal worried her. Based on the time she'd spent with Javen under Devin's care, she'd thought he was more civil than the other regents. He seemed mostly interested in Karina and wine. But now he was acting more like Drenan, who was ever as ruthless as their father had been. Drakonias had killed his father at the end of the war.

* * *

Jax looked through the small opening at the front of his Tank. The long metal barrel projected forward into his line of sight. In training, he'd learned this tube was capable of launching what One called a Shell at high velocity. The damage Shells did was something he would previously have thought unimaginable. And he was in command of thousands of them, plus even more Machines of other sizes and capabilities.

Visible beyond the barrel was another army. An army commanded by Devin.

The two armies sat opposite each other for moments that stretched on. Jax waited to see if Devin would approach before he moved his Tank forward. He was under instruction from

Kaylan to give Devin the opportunity to surrender. If there was to be war today, it would be only because Devin refused to consider the peaceful offer Jax was going to present.

Devin gave no indication that he was going to initiate the parlay, so Jax pushed forward on the lever rising between his legs from the metal floor. The Tank lurched forward. No matter how gracefully he tried to operate it, there was simply no grace built into it. The thing was a weapon of war, heavy and clunky, more representative of one of the Regency's travel carriages than their nimbler personal carriages.

As Jax pulled away from the secure surroundings of his army—he could still hardly believe he was in command of a force he'd only heard fragmented tales about—a lump of fear rose in his throat. He knew what the Machines he commanded were capable of, and had to assume the Machines he was approaching had, at the very least, the same capabilities. In fact, it was more likely the power of Devin's Machines far exceeded his; Thena had had the better part of seventy years to improve on the technology while Drakonias' Machines sat idle far below Kyinth.

Jax breathed a sigh of relief when he saw a single Tank separate from the opposing army and move in his direction. He stopped halfway between the two forces, as best as he could tell, and waited for the other Tank to meet him.

A few minutes later—Tanks weren't the swiftest of things—the other vehicle arrived.

Jax sat, staring through the porthole, and waited. He couldn't help but think he was walking straight into Draego's Fire. There was, after all, a Cannon barrel pointed straight at him. All it would take was for Devin—assuming it was him in the other Tank—to wait until he opened his hatch and climbed out, then fire on him. It was a parlay, so theoretically that shouldn't happen—but the Regency had never been known to engage in parlays. They only responded to opposition with complete ruthlessness. Draego knew he'd experienced it more times than he could remember. He thought briefly of Selena, trying not to picture her lying dead in Orwyn's tavern, and took a deep breath. She was but one example of how they treated rebels. If war was to be avoided, it would be up to him.

Jax spun a lever counterclockwise several times to unlatch the overhead hatch. He pushed it open and stuck his head out. The warmth of the sun felt good on his head, instilling in him some confidence. Synthesis waited with neutrality. It would respond to his demands with unbiased obedience. Devin was stronger—his bloodline being much purer than his own—but Jax would not go down without a fight. Devin wouldn't dare attack him with Synthesis—he hoped—because doing so would certainly initiate the fighting. And if Devin were outside, unprotected by his Tank, his death would come just as quickly as Jax's.

Jax climbed fully out of the Tank, hopped down onto its tracks, then from there to the ground. He walked out in front of it, toward the Tank waiting in front of him. He couldn't help but stare at the Cannon as though at any moment death would explode out of it. But the Cannon didn't fire. The other Tank's hatch swung up instead, and Devin's head emerged. He soon stood mere paces from Jax with his hands clasped behind his back.

"I see you found the cache," Devin said after they had stared at each other for a few moments.

"It would appear we did," Jax replied. "Sorry to ruin your plan."

"You've done no such thing."

"Surely you didn't expect us to be waiting for you."

"It was a possibility."

"Then you know we stand ready to defend ourselves."

Devin looked past Jax, presumably surveying the army behind him, then said, "A formidable defense, to be sure. But all you'll achieve is the complete destruction of Kyinth. You wouldn't want to ruin your young emperor's beautiful capital, now would you?" Devin looked from left to right and said, "Where is he, anyway?"

"His location is none of your concern."

"Isn't it?"

"All you've ever been interested in is your own selfish ambition."

"Now, Jax, there's no need to be rude. This is a parlay; civility is expected."

Jax snorted. "You've never been civil. If it matters, His Highness is dealing with more pressing issues."

"Well, that's a shame," Devin said.

"Is it?"

"I was hoping he'd be able to pass on some tragic news to that brother of his."

Jax wondered what Devin was getting at. "I'd be more than obliged to pass the news on myself."

"It's a shame, really." Devin paused. Jax figured he was waiting for him to show some curiosity, and he was indeed curious, but he simply waited patiently for Devin to continue. "He had such potential. Drakonias made him a regent, you know. Then his brother had to go and ruin it all. Where'd you find that dragon anyway? Could have sworn we killed them all."

"What news, Devin? We don't have all day."

"Don't we? Did you have somewhere else to be?"

"As I said, I'd gladly pass any news you might have on to His Highness, and he can do with it what he wishes."

"If you would, then, let His… the lad know we've avenged Dorlan's death."

Javen…

"Meaning what, exactly?" Jax knew what he meant—but Devin thought Javen was here, when in truth he was with Hadie.

"That, using the other half of our army, Drenan has seen to the quick end of that whore's little kingdom. His… *Highness* should be pleased, I'd imagine, as we've returned the south back to the empire. Though I suppose it won't be his for much longer."

Draego's Fire. Javen. Hadie. And if this was only half *the army…*

"Now, if you'd be a good little errand boy and deliver that message for me. Oh, and there's no rush, really. I'm more than willing to pull my army back until Drenan arrives with the other half. You could attack, I suppose, but you'd more than likely weaken yourselves such that when Drenan arrives you'll be even easier to subdue." Devin looked over his shoulder. "Have you seen the flying Machines? I must admit, when we first arrived in the East, I was quite taken aback myself."

Jax stood firm even though he was shaking inside. Bile rose in his throat. Devin could be bluffing, but if Drenan really did have an army of his own, there would be no way they could prevail.

"Be off now," Devin said with a flick of his wrist.

Jax swallowed the bile and said, "You haven't heard my offer yet."

"*Your* offer?" Devin said with a laugh.

Jax ignored him and said, "If you surrender—"

"Surrender?" Devin said, still laughing.

"—and pledge your allegiance to Yolken, the true Blessed of the Dragon and chosen ruler of Dradonia—"

"Really, now, this is too much."

"—His Highness will allow you to return to your post as chancellor."

"Oh, will he? He'll *allow* me to return."

"If you kneel before him and swear yourself to him," Jax said. He hoped his voice sounded assertive; he sounded like a bumbling fool in his own mind. "I imagine it's more than Thena is offering you."

"And what do you think that is?"

"You were wondering where His Highness is, but where's Thena? Look at yourself, Devin—you're no more an errand boy than I am. If Yolken gives her the throne, what becomes of you?"

"Thena isn't interested in Kyinth."

Jax laughed. "You're to be emperor?"

"Drenan is."

"*Drenan?* He isn't fit to rule, and you know it," Jax said, incredulously. "What, then? You get to retain your chancellorship? You'd be better off disposing of Drenan and taking the throne yourself."

The look that flashed across Devin's face betrayed the truth to Jax: That was exactly what he intended.

"Anything else?" Devin said.

"That's it," Jax said.

Devin abruptly turned and walked back toward his Tank.

Devin was right, Jax knew. There really was nothing he could do. Even if he attacked Devin and somehow defeated him, his own army would sustain substantial losses. What remained would be no match for whatever Drenan might be bringing. And if he waited for Drenan to arrive, their combined forces would surely defeat his.

But then, Devin could be bluffing. Maybe there wasn't a second army. Maybe Javen and Hadie were still safe—hopefully on their way north with the citizens of the south, but safe.

Jax watched as Devin walked away and considered how he was going to convey to Kaylan what he and Devin had discussed. While Devin climbed back into his Tank, spun it around, and made his way back to his army, Jax's gaze shifted to the flying Machines.

They truly were amazing—something he had never imagined could be possible. They flew around in formation like a flock of geese, approaching his army, then turning back. Or at least they had been turning back—the current formation hadn't done so yet. It was advancing. Then, to his horror, projectiles launched from their wings toward his army.

"Draego's Fire!" Jax yelled. Devin had never intended to wait for reinforcements. What was the point of the parlay? At this point it didn't matter. He was alone and extremely exposed. He turned to run back to his Tank but stopped when he saw a shape falling straight down between the formation.

No, not just a shape.

A dragon.

* * *

The rush Deanna felt left her momentarily breathless. She looked down to her side at the shrinking mountain.

Deth climbed rapidly into the sky and said, "I didn't want to alarm him, but I came because you're needed."

Deanna didn't say anything—she already knew. She'd known since Danavin had come to visit her all those many centuries ago. How Deth knew, she didn't understand. It didn't matter. What mattered was that he knew, and that Yolken had ended up exactly where he needed to be. Now to ensure Drenan didn't destroy what Yolken was trying to preserve.

"Draw Energy into your Core," Deth said. "It's going to get very cold. Breathing will also be difficult."

Keeping herself warm was the easy part. As Deth climbed high in the sky, Deanna felt the air rapidly cool. She adjusted the amount of Energy she let seep into her body as necessary to maintain a comfortable body temperature. She didn't know what to do about the increasing difficulty she was having breathing, though. "Can't you go down?"

"Will take longer to return," Deth said. "Force the air in when you breathe."

Deanna thought about it for a moment, then understood what he meant. She gathered air from around her and guided it into her lungs. Once she figured that out, all it took was an adjustment of how much air she guided in as the dragon climbed higher, just like adjusting the Energy she needed to keep warm.

The ground was far below and sometimes obscured by clouds. The whole experience both terrified and amazed Deanna. They soared over snowcapped mountains whose beauty was absolutely majestic, but they soon gave way to the sprawling farmland she and Yolken had recently passed through.

Before she knew it, the North River was visible, then Kyinth itself. Two armies of Machines gathered on the east side of the North River: one back against the swift-flowing water and the other farther east. Deanna looked down in amazement at what looked like Machines flying over the Eastern army. The Machines darted toward the army by the city—Yolken's army—but turned around before they covered half the distance between them.

"Are you ready, Daughter of the Betrayer?"

"I am."

"I have never used my Gift for harm."

"You fly, Deth. I'll fight."

They circled. Waited. The scene reminded her of the final tense moments between her father and Drakonias. It had been no secret what Drakonias wanted, what he was planning. Her father had been urged to take preemptive action against Drakonias, but he'd refused. If there was going to be war, he would not be the initiator. And neither would she.

But then it happened.

The pattern of the flying Machines changed.

They advanced.

They attacked.

And just as she'd come to her father's defense so many years ago, to defend what he'd stood for, she would defend what Yolken stood for.

"Hang on," Deth said. He tucked his wings and dove toward the invading army.

The sudden shift in direction and speed almost ripped Deanna off Deth's back. She reacted quickly, sending Energy into her arms and hands to increase the strength of her grip on the rope, and narrowly prevented herself being blown off by the wind. She held on, her body tucked tightly against Deth's scales, and tensely watched the army rapidly approach. Her heart rate increased—she feared they were going to crash straight into the flying Machines.

Deth twisted and they zipped between two Machines. Deanna reached out with several tendrils of Energy and grabbed as many as she could. The tendrils stretched as Deth dove until they were safely below the Machines, then she pulled on them.

The rearward pull nearly yanked Deanna from Deth's neck, and jolted the dragon enough to slow his descent. A few of the tendrils broke loose, but the Machines she clung to were pulled together and crashed into each other. Deth beat his wings and Deanna's tendrils drew taut. Deanna clung to them as Deth clawed his way downward, the now-smoking Machines trailing behind them like sails.

Deanna braced for what looked like a nosedive into the fast-approaching Tanks below. She knew Deth wasn't going to get them killed, but the sensation was unavoidable.

When impact seemed imminent, Deth's wings opened. He craned his neck back, abruptly changing their direction, which pressed Deanna down onto his neck. The pressure increased greatly. She let go of the trailing flying Machines and focused solely on not blacking out. She struggled to breathe and her vision closed in at the sides. It continued narrowing as the pressure rose until it went completely black. Then she heard an explosion behind them and the pressure was lessened, allowing her vision to return. They were climbing steeply, Deth's wings beating powerfully. Deanna looked over her shoulder and saw billowing smoke where the flying Machines had crashed into the unsuspecting Tanks.

The remaining flying Machines turned and veered toward Deth. Their element of surprise was gone. Now the real work would begin.

* * *

Jax watched Deth dive through the formation of flying Machines. When he emerged below the formation several of the Machines veered sharply inward, crashing into each other. They trailed behind Deth, who continued to dive toward Devin's army. It almost looked as though Deth was pulling the Machines behind him. Deth veered at the last moment—but the flying Machines trailing behind him didn't. Instead, they crashed into the Tanks and other Machines on the ground, causing a large explosion. "Draego's Fire!" he yelled again.

He turned and ran toward his own Tank, drawing Energy into his Core. When he had enough, he pushed Energy into his legs and launched himself into the air. He landed roughly on the top of his Tank, wrapping his arm around the barrel of his Cannon to prevent his momentum from carrying him off again. He jumped into the porthole and pulled the lid closed just as a Shell exploded nearby.

Jax clambered into the operator's seat and yanked back on both levers. The Tank lurched rearward, its tracks spitting dirt forward into the air as he accelerated.

He reached for another control and pulled the trigger. His Tank boomed as a Shell launched out of the barrel.

"Draego's Fire!" he cursed again.

* * *

Kaylan watched the two Tanks sitting between the two armies in the middle of the empty field, about a league wide. Jax was taking a huge risk to deliver her message to Devin, but he understood, as she did, that if things actually resulted in fighting, hundreds of thousands would likely die—most of them Yolken's subjects. Jax would defend the city if need be, but only if Devin attacked first. Their primary objective was what they all knew Yolken wanted: peace.

She watched, hand pressed on her stomach, through a telescope set up on the edge of the balcony. It wasn't one of the automated Telescopes Jax had told her about, powered by an Energy-infused dragon bone, but an older, mechanical one.

The sickness was just nerves, her midwife, Kariss, had told her. It would take time for her to grow into this new role she found herself in. Less than a year ago she was just a baker's daughter, hoping daily that the man she loved would finally declare his love for her. Now she stood atop the tallest building in the empire, forced to make decisions that could possibly affect the lives of everyone on Dradonia. Until she acclimated to her new role, Kariss assured her, her sickness would likely continue—exacerbated by the fact that she was also with child.

Fear rose in Kaylan's throat when she saw Jax emerge from his Tank. He was exposed, she knew, putting himself at risk for the empire. She worried that, despite his talent for convincing people to agree with him, the parlay would fail. Thousands were going to die if it did. And for what?

At least the city was prepared. After news had arrived that the invading army was moving from Tieger toward Kyinth, Kaylan ordered the city evacuated. Everyone not directly involved in the defense of the city had been sent underground, to the caverns where the Machines were stored. Word was sent out to the surrounding areas of the safety provided within the city. It had been no easy task, but the evacuation and supplying of the cavern was successful. Even her advisors were hiding like cowards—not in the caverns below the city, but in the depths of the palace. Yolken would hear of their behavior when he returned, she vowed. The only ones not hiding were herself, Sahri, and a few other servants. She hadn't wanted them to stay on her behalf, but they'd refused to leave her alone.

She breathed a small sigh of relief when Devin emerged from his own Tank. Flying Machines circled overhead of Devin's army as Jax stood alone in the field with Devin. Occasionally they flew out over the field toward the parlay, but then turned back.

Devin returned to his Tank, signaling to Kaylan that the parlay had ended. She closed her eyes and prayed Jax had been successful.

Jax didn't immediately return to his Tank, which worried Kaylan. She stepped back from the telescope to survey the entire battlefield. *What is he doing?* He should be returning to report to her. Her eyes drifted up from the field to the flying Machines. She watched as they swerved and turned in the air, flying seemingly random patterns. Then the pattern suddenly changed. The Machines didn't swerve. They continued forward.

Kaylan watched in horror as fire erupted from below their wings and projectiles launched forward. They exploded into the

Tanks behind Jax, sending debris flying everywhere.

"Jax!" she screamed.

Something dove between the Machines, causing several of them to crash into each other.

"Deth!" Kaylan exclaimed.

Deth dove toward the ground with the flying Machines trailing behind him in a big clump. He swerved over Devin's forces, and the flying Machines crashed to the ground among the army. The explosion was devastating.

Booms soon began to echo from the field below, followed by more explosions.

"Jax!" Kaylan yelled again when she realized Jax still wasn't back to the safety of his Tank. She peered through the telescope just in time to see Jax slip through the porthole of his Tank. It began to move backwards, back toward their army. "Blessed Dragon," she said.

Kaylan turned from the battle, deciding to move indoors. The palace would be a target, she knew, so she decided to give into Sahri's plea at last.

"Thank you, Your Highness," Sahri said with a sigh of relief. "Let's get you somewhere safe."

Kaylan nodded. She pulled the doors leading out to the balcony closed, then followed Sahri toward the stairs. She didn't want to hide like the rest of the advisors, but she needed to be with them to make decisions as needed. She hated that they were essentially forcing her into hiding as well.

She was halfway across the room when she screamed and doubled over in pain.

"Your Highness!" Sahri cried.

CHAPTER 47

Yolken woke to a gentle shake on the shoulder.

"It's time," Tana said.

Yolken sat up groggily, then followed her out of the hut. "Thank you," he said.

"Thank *you*, Blessed," Tana said with a bow.

"For what?"

"We have devoted our lives to the Great Dragon. For generations we have studied the history Drakonias would have us believe. We do not have the full truth—only you possess that—but we have enough to know that your task is not small. And for what you must do, I—we; not just us here, but all of Dradonia—thank you."

Feeling awkward and not knowing what else to say, Yolken said, "You're welcome."

He walked toward the exit, rubbing his eyes, and stepped out into the light. He stopped at the edge of the landing. There was a trail leading down to his right. He needed to go up, to the top of Mazam, but there was no path. *"I wouldn't be surprised if one day you're able to fly like a bird,"* he remembered Jax telling him. He looked out over the valley far below and gathered air around himself. His grogginess instantly abated. Unlike when he stood on the cliffs next to the roaring Mindon Falls, crippled in fear, he confidently jumped.

Yolken pushed downward with the air at his command. His body jerked up and away from the mountainside. As he moved, he channeled the air immediately above him around his body and used it to push down. He soared higher into the air, in complete exhilaration.

He circled Mazam as he climbed toward the peak. He wanted to keep flying, to never stop—it was an absolutely incredible feeling. However, when he crested the top, he looked for a good place to set down. He couldn't let his incredible feat distract him. He wanted solid rock under his feet, knowing that what he was about to attempt would generate considerable heat. He didn't want to worry about melting snow and ice while he worked.

Six pillars sticking up out of the ice caught his attention. He hovered over them, looking down curiously. Having read the entire history of the dragons in the cavern below, he knew this was where the Assembly had gathered. He drew more Energy into his Core—the amount required to harness enough air to fly didn't take his full capacity—and melted the ice with fire. It was surprisingly thick, and took some effort, but he eventually revealed the circular area in the middle of the pillars where dragons had brought their hatchlings to ignite their flames. Once the area was free of ice, he descended slowly and gracefully alit on the rock.

Yolken took a moment to look around. Standing atop Mount Mazam, the highest peak in all of Dradonia, located at the extreme northern boundary of the Northern Realm, he was literally standing on top of the world. But more amazing than that were the six pillars, each three or four paces high and big enough for a dragon to sit upon. How impressive it must have been to be a hatchling looking up at all the colors of dragons— yellow, red, blue, violet, orange, green, white, black. He blinked, shifting his eyes to a dragon's, and saw the pillars were covered in their flowing script.

The moment of wonder passed as his task weighed down on him, so Yolken changed his eyes back. He couldn't read what the pillars said anyway. Yolken took a deep breath and turned his attention to the sun. It hung low in the sky to the south and west. Dimras had stood on this very spot after Draego created him and drew Energy from the sun into himself, igniting his fire. And now, Yolken needed to do the same. Only he possessed nowhere near the strength of a dragon, let alone that of Dimras, the Dragon King.

Could he really ignite the fire within himself?

Yolken closed his eyes and felt the faint heat of the sun on his face. It was not as strong or warm as it was farther south, but with his eyes closed, he could feel it on his skin despite the frigid air. He felt the warmth and knew that the sun was dying. The selfish ambitions of Draeko's descendants had knocked it out of balance. Deth was confident that Yolken could restore that balance, but he himself doubted. With his eyes closed, he blinked, switching his vision back to that of the dragons.

He opened his eyes and considered the Energy streaming all around. He took a deep, slow breath, and drew Energy into his Core.

* * *

Sahri ran to Kaylan's side and fell to her knees. "Your Highness, what's the matter?"

"I... think it's..." Then Kaylan cried out in pain, unable to speak.

"Is it the baby?"

"I... don't... know."

"Can you stand?"

Kaylan took Sahri's arm, but when she tried to move, the cramping pain in her stomach stabbed even harder. Kaylan shook her head.

"Wait here. I'm going for help, all right?"

Kaylan nodded again.

"I'll be right back."

Sahri jumped to her feet and ran toward the stairs.

She didn't know how long she lay there on the ground, but the next thing Kaylan knew she was in her bed with people hovering over her. Her vision was blurry, so she didn't know who they all were.

"She's bleeding out."

She recognized the midwife's voice.

"No!" Kaylan said.

"You can't control it, dear."

She knew exactly what that meant. "No," she said, her voice resembling a growl, "I'm… not…"

* * *

Despite the frigid temperature, Yolken began to sweat.

Dragons breathed fire. They created Energy. They weren't leeches like humans. If he was going to replace the Energy Synthesizers had taken from the sun over the last millennia, he needed to ignite the fire within himself so that he, too, created Energy. He needed to breathe fire, just as the dragons did—not the kind of fire he made to illuminate his way in the dark, but a fire of pure Energy.

Deth had spoken of the Assembly breathing Energy into each hatchling that was born and igniting their flame. But Yolken didn't have an Assembly. Sitting atop Mount Mazam, he had only himself. However, he was not without the Energy required to accomplish the task of the Assembly. Like Dimras, he had the sun.

Yolken felt like he was standing way too close to a bonfire. Unable to step away from the heat, he took off his shirt. He stretched out his arms, and even though he was already full of Energy, he opened himself fully to the power of the sun. He drew it in. Streams of Energy bent toward him from all directions. His Core was full, but he forced it in. The Energy's heat overflowed into his body. But it wasn't enough. If he was going to ignite the flame within himself, he needed more.

With a resolute mind, Yolken increased the flow of Energy he permitted into his Core. Sweat poured freely from his every pore. Ignoring his body's attempt to counter the heat building within him, Yolken didn't stop. With coercion, his Core stretched, flexed, and yielded to his demands. It grew. Energy no longer overflowed into his body, and the heat abated.

As Yolken continued drawing more Energy in, his Core continued to grow. But nothing seemed to be changing. He still couldn't create Energy. After giving it a little thought, he shifted tactics. He increased the rate at which he absorbed Energy, staying ahead of the rate of his Core's expansion. He began to concentrate the Energy he held within it. As he felt the pressure in his Core increase, so did its heat. It once again began to spill out of his Core and into his body.

Yolken worked for what seemed like an eternity. Each time his Core reached its limit he forced it to grow more. Then he noticed something, and stopped pulling Energy in.

The sun was visibly growing.

CHAPTER 48

J ax fired as fast as the mechanism reloaded itself. One had warned against firing at such a rate because the barrel would overheat, but until he was back with the rest of the army he didn't care. Trouble was, there was a line of Tanks moving toward him and there was no way he could know which one—or ones—were firing at him. He wasn't taking the time to aim anyway.

A Shell exploded close, showering his Tank in dirt and momentarily blocking his view. But he didn't need to see to know he was in serious trouble. All that mattered was that he continued making his way back toward his army.

Another Shell exploded nearby, this time so close the Tank was buffeted violently and lurched. Jax's hearing went with a loud ringing. When he regained his senses, he saw that the Tank was turning clockwise.

"*Draego's Fire,*" Jax said. That last Shell must have damaged the track on the left side of the Tank.

He centered the right lever, and the Tank stopped. He moved the left lever forward and backward, but it had no effect on the Tank's movement. He pushed forward on the right lever, making the Tank turn back toward the approaching army. When it came into view, he resumed firing his own Shells, now taking the time to pick out targets, while at the same time thinking about how he was going to escape. He couldn't very well climb out of his Tank and run. At least while he was inside, he was relatively protected.

Shells began landing around him again, each one a little closer. It wouldn't take long for whomever was aiming at him to zero in. Could the Tank survive a direct hit? If so, how many?

The Shells continued to explode around him, but he had yet to sustain a direct hit. *They have to be better than this,* he thought. Then something hit the top of the Tank.

The round latch began to turn.

Jax grabbed his handheld weapon—One had called it a Gun—from its sheath mounted on the wall, and pointed it at the porthole.

* * *

Deanna clung to Deth as he climbed back into the air. Several of the flying Machines broke away from their formations to follow them.

Deth exhibited an adroitness Deanna had never before seen in a dragon. He swerved, dove, climbed, and rolled with a skill that defied her memories. Hardly a day went by that she didn't close her eyes and see a dragon being plucked from the sky as giant spears impaled them. Spears that she herself had launched, from enormous crossbow-like catapults.

Deth flew and together they pulled flying Machines from the sky. When one of the Machines got close enough, Deanna grabbed it with Energy and pulled on it. Most of the time her efforts just made the Machine veer off course, but sometimes she managed to cause a Machine to crash into another one. When that happened, both Machines went spiraling to the ground. A few of them managed to recover control before crashing, but most of them didn't.

The flying Machines adapted to Deanna's efforts and began keeping their distance. The Machines fired their weapons at them, but Deth ensured they were never in front of them long enough for an accurate shot, and before long, the Machines began ignoring them altogether.

Deth circled over Yolken's army while Deanna thought about how they might be of use. After making a couple of circles, Deanna noticed a solitary Tank moving toward their army. It was under heavy attack from several Tanks on the opposing army's side. It took a hit that nearly disabled it. She didn't know who was in it, but it continued to take fire, which meant that whoever it was, they were in trouble. And if that Tank was returning to their army, perhaps she and Deth had arrived just at the end of a parlay. And if *that* was true, then whoever was in it was important.

"We need to help!" Deanna said.

Deth tucked his wings and dove toward the disabled Tank. He was actually aiming for a spot behind it, Deanna noticed. Deth opened his wings and pulled out of his dive well behind the Tank. Deanna could only hold on as his wings beat furiously. Deth's movement slowed rapidly. A Shell whizzed by Deth and Deanna, then another. Deth landed firmly on top of the disabled Tank.

"Hurry," he said. "I can't deflect them all."

At that moment, Deanna realized that the enemy Tanks were only missing them because Deth was using Energy to deflect the projectiles, just as she had used Energy to make the flying Machines crash into each other. She slid off Deth's neck in awe. She couldn't even *see* the projectiles flying past them—Deth was not only able to see them, but adroit enough to push them away as well.

She spun the round handle on the hatch, remembering the Tanks from Drakonias' war, and lifted it up. She was surprised to find Jax pointing a Gun at her. Thankfully he didn't fire.

"Let's go," she said, offering him her hand.

Jax took her hand and she pulled him out.

Deanna climbed back onto Deth's neck, then helped Jax up

behind her. Without delay, Deth launched himself into the air, climbing almost straight up before his body angled back toward the army guarding Kyinth.

"What are you doing here?" Jax said, using Synthesis to boost his voice so she could hear him over the rushing air.

"Rescuing you," Deanna said.

It only took a moment for Deth to arrive back at the army. He landed behind all the Tanks, with much more grace than he had landed on Jax's. Deanna and Jax slid off his back.

"I meant here in Kyinth," Jax said.

"I don't know," Deanna said. "Deth was waiting for me when Yolken and I returned from Dimras' lair."

"Did he find what he needed?"

"I think so. You should have seen it. The columns in the cavern were covered in ancient dragon script only Yolken could see."

An explosion rocked nearby Tanks, sending dirt and debris into the air, then showering down around them.

"Maybe this isn't the best time to be having this conversation," Jax said.

"No, you're right," Deanna said. "What's the plan?"

"I'd hoped it wouldn't come to actual fighting," Jax said. "And Devin didn't sound as though he was interested in attacking either. But then he did."

She watched Jax intently as he surveyed the scene.

"Yolken wouldn't want this," Jax said.

Deanna wondered if she'd ever met anyone more loyal. The man had literally dedicated his life to keeping a promise. It was a loyalty unlike anything she'd ever known. Her loyalty to her father had never wavered, especially when Drakonias tore the family apart, but that was her family. What did Jax owe Yolken? Or the Order? As far as she knew, he had nothing to gain from his devotion. Yolken would have ended up where he was with or without Jax. So what drove him?

Deanna suddenly realized she was looking at Jax with intense admiration. Something she'd never felt for a man before.

"Even if we can somehow stop Devin," Jax said, "Drenan's not far behind with his *own* army."

"*Drenan?*" Deanna said.

Jax continued to study the battlefield. Their Tanks had their cannons pointed up, firing Shells toward the flying Machines. It looked to Deanna as though the Machines were slowly starting to advance again.

"They're not going to stop," Deanna said. "They've had too much power for far too long to give it up now."

"We have to try," Jax insisted, "or they'll destroy the city."

"No," Deth said.

Deanna and Jax both looked at the dragon. Steam emitted from his nostrils. His breath rumbled like rolling thunder. His piercing eyes locked on Deanna, striking a fear in her she hadn't felt since she first encountered Deth deep below the mountains of Kvorga.

"We avoided human conflict and we died," Deth said. "No longer. Today"—the rumble in Deth grew—"we fight."

The change in Deth left Deanna stunned.

"Climb back on," Deth said.

"Both of us?" Jax said.

Deth nodded.

They climbed back onto Deth's neck. Jax sat close behind Deanna, his body pressed against her back.

"If we're going to do this, you'll need to hold on," Deanna said.

"To what?" Jax said.

"Me."

Jax's arms slid around her stomach. She tried not to think about the fact that a man had not had his arms wrapped around her in a very long time.

Deth pushed himself back to his feet. He let out a roar that shook Deanna to her Core. He crouched, then launched himself back into the air. Jax's grip tightened, forcing a grunt out of her.

She tightened her stomach muscles, pushing Energy into them. With the forces they would experience, she knew Jax would have to hold tightly to prevent getting thrown off.

Deth climbed quickly, circling over their Tanks. When he was the same height as the flying Machines, he flew toward them. His scales warmed to the touch then fire erupted from his mouth. The heat on Deanna's face quickly grew unbearable. She turned her head to the side and pressed her face to Deth's neck. She felt Jax lay his head on her back. She looked up when the heat abated and saw flying Machines crashing to the ground in fiery explosions.

Below them, Yolken's army of Tanks advanced. Deth advanced as well. A formation of flying Machines turned toward them, and cylindrical projectiles launched from beneath their wings. The projectiles whizzed by them, careening off in random directions. Deth's scales warmed again. But instead of attacking the approaching Machines, he dove beneath them.

Deanna turned her head to the side and shouted, "Grab a Machine with Energy!"

As Deth flew straight toward Devin's Tanks, she reached out and grabbed two Machines and heard them crash into each other.

Several Tanks turned their Cannons up but Deth was beyond their range of mobility. He swooped down on them and breathed Draego's Fire. Deanna again ducked her head and held on with all her might as Deth's upward pull pressed her down. Jax's chin dug painfully into her back.

Deanna looked down when the pressure decreased and saw that the Cannons of several Tanks were partially melted. She realized just how lucky her family was that dragons never retaliated. Their fire was absolutely devastating. They would have been no match for the wrath of dragons.

"I got one!" Jax shouted with elation.

"Excellent!" Deanna cheered.

But a deep rumbling from Deth cut their celebration short.

"What is it?" Deanna shouted. But she knew exactly what it was the moment the words left her mouth.

She looked at the sun.

It was changing.

Growing.

"Draego's Fire."

CHAPTER 49

Kaylan screamed.

"Why is this happening?" Sahri said.

"I don't know," said Kariss, the midwife. "It happens sometimes."

"Why aren't you doing anything?" Sahri said. Her voice frantic.

"Because there's not anything I *can* do."

"So she's just—"

"Quiet," Kariss said through clenched teeth.

The damp rag was pulled away from Kaylan's forehead and the blurry images of Kariss and Sahri receded. She turned her head and saw them standing off to the side. Kariss was gesturing and saying something, but Kaylan couldn't hear her. She knew what she was saying, though. She wouldn't have pulled Sahri away to tell her privately if it weren't so.

She was bleeding out... dying.

All this time she had worried about whether Yolken would return to her, but it was going to be her who wasn't there when he returned. Her and their child.

An overwhelming sense of sadness dulled her pain. Yolken was out there somewhere trying to save Dradonia, and she was here dying. Yolken didn't deserve that. He was the most loving and selfless person she had ever known. Even before he'd healed Issa, he always considered others before himself. He wasn't perfect—he and Javen certainly had their issues—but he didn't deserve this. It wasn't fair.

The light outside began to change.

Kaylan looked over. "What's happening?" she croaked.

Kariss stepped back to the bed and blotted Kaylan's forehead. "I don't know, lass."

Yolken must be doing something. She didn't fully understand what it was he was supposed to do—even he hadn't known when he'd left—but she knew it had something to do with restoring balance to the sun.

A wave of pain washed through Kaylan's abdomen and she cried out. Kariss reached down and took her hand, and Kaylan squeezed it.

"There's got to be a way to stop the bleeding," Sahri said.

"If there was, don't you think I'd have done it already?" Kariss said.

"Draego's Fire, you have to do *something*! She's the empress!"

"I know who she is, child. And if I had the power to stop what's happening, I would. Now, change the towels."

When the pain subsided, Kaylan looked down to where Sahri was removing towels from between her legs. They were crimson red, soaked in her blood.

"Don't look," Kariss said. "Eyes on me."

Why shouldn't she look? Not looking wouldn't stop the bleeding.

Light hit Kaylan's face, and she shied away from it. She shielded her eyes with an arm and turned her head toward the balcony doors. Many an evening she and Yolken had stood out there and watched the sunset, so she knew the sun was getting low in the sky.

The sun looked different. It was much larger, redder. Its soft light felt warm on her face. Almost as if it were soothing away her pain. That happened, she'd read, just before someone died. Their suffering, their pain, ended as their bodies began to shut down. She'd never witnessed such a phenomenon herself, but she'd heard others talk of their loved ones entering a state of calm right before death took them. Sahri and Kariss must have known, because they both came close, one on each side, hugging her arms.

The warmth spread through her body. Her time had come, she knew, but instead of being afraid, all she felt was calm. She worried for Yolken—he'd loved her his whole life, she knew—but she also knew he would be okay. He had been chosen by Draego to lead Dradonia, so she knew everything would work out for him exactly as it was supposed to. Life might not seem fair right now, but that was just her selfish nature talking.

The warmth grew.

"What's happening?" she said.

"We're right here," Kariss said.

"That's not what I—"

"We're here, Kaylan," Sahri said.

Kaylan felt something strange. Her pain was gone, but she didn't feel like she was dying. She felt... stronger. Like she was alive.

The sun's warmth pooled like a lake inside of her. She'd never felt that before. She loved lying in the grass and feeling the sun's warmth on her skin, but this was different. The sun wasn't just warming her skin, it was warming her insides.

Kaylan touched the lake. She felt... power.

She was dying.

But it didn't have to be so.

Suddenly she knew what was happening.

She was Synthesizing.

Well, not yet. But she recognized the sensation. Yolken had talked about what it felt like to Synthesize. He said it felt powerful. And she could feel that power pooling, waiting.

CHAPTER 50

The sun grew fast, changing in color from yellow to red. Yolken became suddenly frightened.

His Core had grown to an unimaginable size and he was absorbing vast amounts of Energy at an incredible rate. But in only moments, he'd accelerated the evil it had taken the Drake family a millennium and a war to accomplish.

The sun was now visibly racing toward its death.

But he hadn't absorbed enough Energy yet, because he still couldn't create it.

He needed more.

Reluctantly, necessarily, Yolken resumed his work and pushed against the limits of his ability.

The sun doubled in size. Then it doubled a second time. Yolken faltered. He had reached his limit—he couldn't draw any more Energy in. Standing atop Mount Mazam, he trembled, oblivious to the temperature around him. His Core would accept no more. He stared at the expanding sun. It was now destabilized to the point that its death was imminent.

He had within him enough Energy that, were he to release it all, he would set all Dradonia on fire. But it still wasn't enough. In that moment of desperation, he questioned Deth's wisdom.

He questioned what was written on the pillars in Dimras' home. He questioned whether the flame would ever ignite. Why had it worked for Dimras but not for him?

Yolken watched the sun slowly grow and knew he had to press himself further.

He drew more in and screamed. Smoke rose up around him, and he looked down. His leggings and boots were burning. In an instant, they were gone. Then his feet began to melt the stone upon which he stood. Ice around the edges of the stone circle also began to melt. Water flowed toward him and boiled, evaporating before it reached him.

"Draego's Fire!" he yelled, directing his frustration toward Deth. "Why isn't it igniting?"

Yolken fell to his knees, his hands and legs melting into the rock. If there was pain, he was oblivious to it. He looked up at the sun, which was now more than quadruple the size it had been when he began his work. Clinging desperately to the hope that he had not doomed Dradonia, he again drew more Energy from the dying star.

With a blast of light and heat, Yolken drew into himself the last of the sun's Energy. He flinched, pulling an arm out of the molten rock to shield even his dragon eyes from the brightness.

Darkness enveloped him.

CHAPTER 51

Kaylan didn't want to die. She'd dreamed of having a family with Yolken her whole life. Yolken wanted nothing more than to build a home in the maple grove for her and their family. She didn't know what his future with the empire was, but she wanted him to at least have the opportunity to decide.

Kaylan reached into the lake—her Core, she knew. She took hold of the Energy and directed it to her womb. She felt a heartbeat. It was small, weak. She closed her eyes and breathed a sigh of relief. Their baby was still alive.

Using the sun's Energy as if it were eyes, she searched her womb and found the cause of the bleeding. Kaylan didn't fully understand what she was doing. Based on what she had learned from her conversations with Yolken, a person needed knowledge about what they were trying to use Synthesis to do. Synthesis was just the agent that allowed you to do what you already knew how to. But she didn't have to understand this. She just needed to do it.

With minute precision, Kaylan healed herself.

"What's happening?" Sahri said.

Kaylan looked up at her and smiled.

The sky went dark.

Kaylan lost her connection with the sun. She burned quickly through what Energy remained in her Core. The strength Synthesis had given her vanished. Then the darkness that surrounded them closed in on her and she lost consciousness.

CHAPTER 52

Yolken hesitantly looked up. All that remained of the once enormous red sun was a tiny white light.

Had he failed? The sun had no more Energy to give. He was bursting with it, yet it wasn't enough. But then he remembered that dragon bones all around Dradonia stored Energy. In darkness, Yolken closed his eyes and reached out. Tendrils of Energy raced out faster than his mind could conceive. They moved on their own, seeking, finding. When they connected with an Energy source, Yolken instinctively drew it in, forcing it into his Core. He found sources slowly at first, but then in rapid succession. There was a huge concentration of them near Kyinth. He stole them at lightning speed. He found Energy stored all over Dradonia, even on the other side of the world. He stole it all.

And then it was over.

He couldn't find any more.

He had taken from the sun everything it had. He'd taken from every dragon bone. Still, he couldn't create Energy.

He had failed.

There was nothing more to be done. The death of Dradonia was imminent. He looked down at the rock below him as he slowly melted farther into it. Waves of water and mud were flowing away from the mountain with tumultuous force. He considered letting go of all the Energy he held, bringing an immediate end to life and preserving those he loved from having to experience whatever was about to happen. But then he stopped. He thought about when Jax had first taught him to make fire.

For the first time, he knew what he needed to do.

* * *

The sky went dark. Not completely dark, but like the last vestiges of twilight, just as stars were becoming visible in the sky.

"Draego's Fire," Jax said from behind her.

Deanna stared at the sun—what was left of it—as Deth circled. It was a tiny white light. Barely brighter than the night's brightest stars.

"I feel him," Deth said. "He's searching."

Moments later, the flying Machines fell from the sky and the booming of the Tanks stopped. The flying Machines crashed to the ground then an eerie silence descended over the battlefield.

Deanna looked back at what was left of the sun. She tried to draw Energy into her Core, but all she felt was sheer terror. For the first time in her life she was powerless. Sure, she had felt powerless when Deth made her leave behind the dragon bones that day she'd met him, but at least then she had been able to return to the warmth of the sun. That was gone now. But it didn't matter. How long could life possibly go on without the sun?

Hours?

Minutes?

Seconds?

"I hope he finds what he's looking for," Deanna said. Without the ability to warm herself with Energy, she started to feel the cold.

"Me too," Jax said.

"He is the Blessed of the Dragon," Deth said.

Yolken threw aside all doubt about the task he faced. He'd been going about it wrong. Up until now, he had forced his Core to expand. It had grown to an immeasurable size, holding all the Energy that there was to have. But he needed his Core to do more than *hold* Energy. He needed it to *create* Energy.

With no more Energy available from the sun to draw in, he pushed inward on his Core. It resisted at first, but then, slowly, it began to contract. And as it contracted, he felt the pressure within it increase. With the rising pressure came more heat. His breathing slowed. Or at least it felt like it had slowed.

It was going to work, he knew.

Yolken closed his eyes. As time seemed to slow, he thought of Kaylan. He pushed in on his Core with every vestige of his being. As his Core shrank, the pressure increased exponentially. He hoped she was okay—would be okay. The heat grew unbearable. The molten rock that still held his weight melted and he sank completely into the fiery liquid.

The air exploded into fire.

His body burned.

The flames moved as if half frozen, slower than they should have been.

But he continued.

I'm sorry, Kaylan.

Yolken's Core shrank to the size it had been when he'd first begun to condition it in the Mindon Mountains all those months ago. But rather than holding the small amount of Energy he could hold then, it contained all the sun's Energy. It burned with a fire that liquefied the top of the mountain. Lava flowed down all sides, quickly shrinking its overall height.

Yolken pushed his Core smaller and smaller until it could fit inside a grain of sand, not letting any of the Energy escape in the process.

Everything slowed as the pressure in him increased.

Then it happened.

Time stopped.

Yolken *became* Energy.

His body was gone, but he was not. He rose above the fiery mountain and looked—past a snout emitting steam—at the tiny white light in the sky. The sun had no more Energy to give, but Energy flowed around him. But instead of flowing toward him, it flowed out of him.

He craned his long neck and examined the world below him, frozen in place, and knew he was going to save it. He looked back at the remains of the sun and smiled, baring razor-sharp teeth.

"Solarian," he said, speaking the name of the star, in a thunderous voice.

He felt for it, connected to it.

He'd made it so many eons ago. He closed his eyes and reveled in the Energy within him. It was without limit. *He* was without limit.

He opened his reptilian eyes and looked back at the tiny white ball—all that remained of Dradonia's life source, destroyed by greed and a never-ending thirst for power. That struggle was over now. From now on, it would be different. "Solarian," he said, "All will be well."

He opened his mouth and roared, intending to be heard around the world. He released the spring contained within him and poured forth Energy. A torrential flood flowed from him through his reestablished connection to Solarian. He refilled Solarian without worry of running out. He *was* Energy. He had no limit. He'd made billions of stars, both big and small, each one unique. He filled Solarian, knowing its exact need for balance.

Solarian grew. It changed from white to red, and finally to yellow. He reset Synthesis to its original purpose, then closed his mouth, cutting off the flow of Energy.

Solarian shined brightly in the sky.

Balance restored, his work finished, he paused. He wasn't

ready to return to the Ether. There was no rush. He had time. He *was* time.

Yolken's essence surveyed the world. He knew each inhabitant, human or not. He felt a presence long thought gone from the world. He searched for it and found it deep below the mountains known as Draego's Spine. His heart warmed. Satisfied, he turned his attention to Dradonia's history stretched out before him. It wasn't the history the Regency had propagated, not what he'd been taught, but history as it truly was. There was so much he didn't know, so much the world still didn't know. He zeroed in on specific events that were of particular interest: Marcin receiving the gift of Synthesis; Dimras' death; his father meeting his mother; Jax and Selena in love; his parents' deaths. His eyes widened when he saw what had actually happened that night. He cried for his mother.

Dradonia needed to know what had happened—not just in his tavern, but all of it. Everything. He couldn't do it, though, not personally. His role in Dradonia was now different. No longer the simple brewer, or even the emperor, he was Energy. However, he knew the perfect person to convey his message. He wouldn't be pleased, but he would do it. He would need time, however, so he Regenerated him.

He turned his attention to Javen. He loved his brother. Despite their many differences, he always had. He had probably been too hard on him, expected too much of him. He regretted that he wouldn't have the chance to tell him in person. He hoped Javen knew how proud of him he was. He smiled as he watched Javen hug their father. He was jealous for the time Javen would get to spend with him.

Then he turned his attention to the reason he had done everything he ever did: Kaylan. He saw every time she had looked at him as they grew together: hopeful, disappointed, and finally relieved, ecstatic, happy. He cried as he watched Kaylan realize what had happened to him and the many times she cried after. All he had ever wanted was to spend his life making her happy, build her a home, and raise a family. He wanted to be for his children what he had grown up without. But that wasn't going to happen. He wished he hadn't wasted so much of their lives, and hoped she wouldn't hold it against him. Their time together as husband and wife had been so short, but he didn't regret a moment of it—and she didn't either. His tears turned to those of joy when he saw their daughter. She would miss him like he had missed his father, but together... together they would be happy.

When the last vestiges of Yolken had finished joining with Draego, Draego looked ahead. He couldn't look far—the farther he looked the blurrier the future became—but he saw enough to know he didn't like it. Something was missing. Balance. Not the balance of the sun, but something else. Then he saw Deth, soaring so high that no eye below could behold him. He was going home, to solitude. Dragons were not meant to be alone. They were meant for companionship.

Draego lifted, not upward but outward. Out, so that he was no longer in the realm he had created, but above it, apart from it. Before him, the ribbon of time waited to be written, but it stretched back to the beginning. He floated back and reentered the realm at the point just before Deth's mate had been gored in the sky. The moment was frozen before him. Having control over time, he kept it still. Deth's mate was frantic, wings frozen mid-beat. She was hastily trying to escape the danger, but she would fail. Frozen just inches from her body, approaching from below and behind, where she couldn't see, was a giant metal spear. Smoke still wafted from the catapult hundreds of paces away that had launched it.

Draego considered the female dragon frozen before him. He couldn't remove her from this situation; such an action would cause his whole ribbon to unravel. However, her survival was essential. The survival of the human species depended on her. And the future was not just for humans. It was also for dragons. Together, not separate. It wouldn't happen immediately, but the future was clear enough that he saw there would be a day when humans and dragons would live together, in harmony. It wouldn't be perfect—nothing ever was—but it would be good.

Draego considered simply giving Deth a replica, but he knew that that wouldn't work. She needed her essence, and he couldn't create someone's essence. The bond Deth had with his mate was with the essence of who she was. This was crucial. It couldn't be manufactured; it could only be formed through experience. Their relationship must be genuine.

But he was Draego. He was in control. So he fashioned before himself an exact replica of Deth's mate, and, with time frozen, swapped the replica with the original.

Draego once again lifted himself out of the realm and re-entered it just moments before Deth returned to his home in the mountains of Kvorga. In the cavern where the man once called Yolken had met Deth, Draego deposited Deth's mate to await his arrival. He waited as well. He felt Dethoicrinth's emotion when he entered the cavern on Kvorga and saw his mate. Draego watched for only a moment, then left. But before he did, he Blessed them.

AFTER

Ten months later

The leaves of the oak tree standing over the buildings of Lonely Oak were a cornucopia of yellows, reds, and oranges. Even with balance restored to the sun, the summer had been hot—hotter than Jax preferred. He was thankful for the arrival of autumn. It had certainly made his journey more pleasant. It was more scenic as well, with all the changing colors.

He mumbled to himself about the task being impossible as he rode through town—unnoticed, as it should be. He was, after all, just another passerby on a horse. He didn't wear anything that would indicate he was on an errand for the Empress of Dradonia. He had a mind to turn around, never to run an errand for her again, each time his *task* entered his head.

He'd been here countless times to check in on two lads who were destined to live lives larger than the small town in which they'd been reared. It had been just his luck that the person the Council had chosen to raise them was the one person he'd been trying to avoid. It was almost like they were rubbing it in his nose that he and Selena had gone against the Order's rule. They'd come to their senses, so he didn't see why the Council saw fit to punish him.

Smoke was rising gently from the brick chimney at the top of the Thornhill tavern. Jax rode across the wooden bridge that spanned the happily bubbling Little Mindon and slid off his horse in front of the tavern. He wrapped the reins around the hitching post and just stood there for a moment, looking at the building. So much had occurred in this stupid little two-story structure—both good and bad. Lives saved and lives lost. Jax shook his head, having promised himself he wouldn't allow himself to get nostalgic—or sentimental—and went inside.

It smelled ever as good as he remembered it. But he knew whoever was cooking wouldn't be the woman he had once loved.

"Jax?" He barely heard the voice over the boisterous din that greeted him.

Jax smiled when he saw Relan behind the bar.

Relan grabbed a mug and filled it with ale. He set the mug on the bar in front of Jax and said, "What brings ya here?"

Jax scooped up the ale and took a long drink. "Why, I came to see you, of course."

Relan gave a raucous guffaw. "I am a man of vast repute."

"You look really good, Relan."

"As do you. I hardly recognized you."

Jax felt younger than he had in ages. Deanna said he looked no older than thirty, which was about twenty years younger than he'd aged since the last time Orwyn had Regenerated him. He didn't quite know how to respond to Relan, so he settled on, "I don't look half as good as you, old Relan."

"Now I know you're lying," Relan said. He took Jax's mug and added, "And if you're not careful, I might not fill this for you again."

"Now, now, Relan. No reason to go getting drastic on me. Else I might need to speak with the owner of this shabby hole in the road."

"Here," Relan said, shoving the mug back across the bar, making some of the ale slosh out. "Take this and get out. He's out back anyhow."

"Thanks, Relan," Jax said.

Jax took the mug but didn't move right away. He took a moment to watch the bustle. It was midday and the tavern was busy. More than one lass came in and out of the kitchen carrying plates of food or taking dirty ones away. It looked as though Orwyn had done what Selena and Javen had repeatedly pestered Yolken to do—he'd hired help. Of course, he couldn't run the tavern alone.

Jax finally made his way through the kitchen to the back of the tavern, ale in hand. The large doors to the brewhouse were wide open. He stopped at the entrance when he saw Orwyn busy working. He leaned against the door jamb and sipped on his ale.

"Are you going to just stand there or were you planning on helping?" Orwyn said over his shoulder.

"I'm enjoying my ale, thank you very much," Jax said.

"You always were useless." Orwyn turned to look at Jax, raising an eyebrow.

"Useless? You know how much trouble those lads of yours caused me?"

"Come now, Jax, it wasn't that bad."

Jax took a couple of steps into the shed and said, "*That bad?* Only one thing ever caused me more trouble than Yolken and Javen, and that was that cursed mule that hauled supplies up to that cabin you made me build. But now that I think about it, maybe the mule was second only to you."

"Well, it's all behind us now," Orwyn said. "Hand me that bucket, will ya?"

Jax walked over to the bucket Orwyn pointed to, which was filled to the brim with green cone-shaped flowers. He handed it up to Orwyn, who stuck his face close to the flowers and inhaled deeply.

"Mmm," Orwyn said. "Fresh off the vine. I almost forgot how much I loved this part of brewing." He dumped the entire bucket into the kettle.

"It's too bad you have to use actual fire to heat those things," Jax said.

"It's better this way," Orwyn said. He climbed down from the stairs. "Requires concentration and attention to detail. Especially that one," he said, gesturing to the middle of the three-tiered kettle. "If you let it get too hot or too cold, the ale won't turn out right."

"You don't miss it? Synthesis?"

"We were never intended to have it in the first place."

Jax held out a hand to shake as Orwyn approached but Orwyn stepped in and embraced him in a hug instead.

"Well, I miss it," Jax said. "I feel so… ordinary."

"You'll never be ordinary, Jax."

"But we are. It doesn't bother you that you're going to age like everyone else now?"

"I've lived a long time," Orwyn said. "And I deserve to follow the natural cycle just as everyone else, including you."

"Yeah, well, I hate that it feels like an itch in my head when I'm out in the sun."

"An itch? That's weird."

"You don't feel it?"

"No. I feel perfectly… what was the word you used?"

"Ordinary."

"Yeah, I feel pretty ordinary."

"It's like the sun is trying to tell me something. I have all these memories—or, what seems like memories—but they come and go."

"Huh…"

"*Huh?* That's all you've got to say?"

"Er…"

Jax scratched the top of his head, then took a drink of ale.

"I'm guessing this isn't a social visit?" Orwyn said.

Jax shook his head.

"Then why don't you tell me what brings the empress' most revered advisor to my humble tavern."

"I bring news of the royal birth." Jax took a drink of his ale.

"I heard the proclamation," Orwyn said. "And you didn't think to bring me a mug?"

"Well, Kaylan wanted you to be the first to know your granddaughter's name."

"And?"

"Elen Deborah Thornhill."

"A good name," Orwyn said.

Jax suspected he saw tears form in Orwyn's eyes. "She calls her Elie."

As many times as Jax had seen Orwyn force himself to be strong over the many decades they'd known each other, Orwyn didn't feign strength now. He unabashedly wiped his eyes with the sleeve of his shirt.

"And how is she?" Orwyn said.

"Healthy and strong."

"I meant Kaylan."

"She's struggling. But Elie forces her to be strong." Jax took another drink, then said, "She doesn't want to be empress."

"I don't blame her. I wouldn't wish that on anyone."

"Which is why you need to come to Kyinth and rule. At least until Elie's of age."

"Absolutely not," Orwyn said. "Besides, I have no interest in ruling. I'm nearly finished building my home. And if you mention it again, I'll ban you from the tavern."

Jax held his hands up in the air, making sure not to spill his ale. "Not another word."

"What did she decide to do with Devin?"

"He begged her to send him back to Onta with Karina."

"I'm guessing she didn't agree to that?"

"No, she did not. She's not even letting Karina down to the dungeon to see him."

"Serves him right. What of Thena? Has she heard from her yet?"

A fleeting memory entered Jax's head.

"Jax?"

"What?"

"You're staring at me like…"

"Like what?"

"…like you don't know who I am or something."

Jax narrowed his eyes. "Did you and Thena—"

"I'll take that as a no," Orwyn said. "Have you heard from Javen?"

Jax shook his head, the fleeting memory gone. "No."

"Well, I'm sure we won't for a while yet."

"Who would have thought that lad would ever settle down."

"The only settling he's doing is helping Hadie resettle the south, which'll probably take them the rest of their lives."

"I don't know why they went back."

"The same reason I'm here and not in Kyinth," Orwyn said. "It's home."

"Well, technically Lonely Oak is his—"

"*She's* his home now. And her home is the south. Speaking of homes—"

"She's fine."

"What? How do you know what I was going to ask?"

"You think I don't know you? Deanna's fine, that's all I'm going to say." Jax took a drink of ale. Orwyn laughed and slapped him on the shoulder, causing Jax to choke.

"Fair enough," Orwyn said.

Jax continued to cough and thumped himself on the chest, trying to clear his lungs.

"That's got to boil for a while yet, so let's go see about getting me an ale, since you can't seem to think about anyone but yourself."

"Now"—Jax thumped himself on the chest again—"*that's* not true. And you know it!"

"You're right. How about I make it up to you by refilling that mug of yours?"

"How is that 'making it up to me'? That was going to happen

anyway."

Orwyn and Jax walked out of the brewhouse. Jax felt the warmth of the sun hit him and he stopped, lagging behind Orwyn, and closed his eyes. He tilted his head up to the sun and felt it on his face. He tried to pull the warmth into his Core, but nothing happened. He breathed the crisp autumn air in, and finally arrived at a conclusion: Orwyn was right. It was better that humans didn't have that kind of power anymore. That didn't mean he wasn't going to miss it, though.

"Are you coming?" Orwyn said.

Jax opened his eyes, smiled at his friend, and said, "Have I ever told you about the time Yolken fell off the Mindon Falls? I had to drag him out of the river by his heel. He was furious." Jax laughed and said, "Now *that's* a story for the ages."

"You've always been quite the storyteller," Orwyn agreed.

"And now I'm going to be a legend. I mean, who else can claim that they once pulled the Blessed of the Dragon out of a river by his heel? Not even you can make such a claim."

Orwyn sighed. "You're incorrigible, you know that?"

"Most legends are. It's what makes them legends." Jax laughed again and followed after his friend. His mug was empty, and he was ready for a refill.

THE END
of
THE BLESSED OF THE DRAGON

DRAKE FAMILY TREE

Previous Era (PE): the era prior to the establishment of the Dragon Throne became known as the Previous Era

Dragon King Era (DKE): the Dragon King Era commenced when Draeko established the Dragon Throne.

United Era (UE): the United Era commenced when Drakonias sat upon the Dragon Throne and proclaimed himself emperor of Dradonia.

Note: Provided below is the first and second generations of the Blessed of the Dragon. A complete genealogy of those loyal to the emperor is maintained at the palace in Kyinth.

(L) indicates those that pledged their loyalty to Drakonias during Drakonias' war.

GENERATION 1

Draeko Dairion Drake (m) (b. unknown d. 1150 DKE)
    Married to:
        Aliza Varias (f) (b 61 PE d. 1148 DKE)
    Children:
        Drakonias Draeko Arvarin Drake (m) (b. 42 PE d.)
        Deanna Aliza Drake (f) (b. 41 PE d. 1150 DKE)
        Eagan Draeko Calavin Drake (m) (b. 39 PE d. 1150 DKE)
        Reago Draeko Yarin Drake (m) (b. 37 PE d.) (L)
        Anshar Draeko Olivar Drake (m) (b. 35 PE d. 1150 DKE)
        Drae Draeko Harachin Drake (m) (b. 34 PE d. 44 UE)
        Reega Aliza Drake (f) (b. 31 PE d. 1150 DKE)
        Orlan Draeko Dairion Drake (m) (b. 29 PE d. 289 UE) (L)
        Thena Aliza Drake (f) (b. 835 DKE d.) (L)
        Nera Aliza Drake (f) (b. 837 DKE d.) (L)
        Lio Draeko Mattath Drake (m) (b. 980 DKE d. 30 UE)
        Atter Draeko Eber Drake (m) (b. 983 DKE d. 1138 DKE) (L)
        Mattha Aliza Drake (f) (b. 984 DKE d. 1150 DKE)
        Sheal Draeko Kena Drake (m) (b. 986 DKE d.) (L)
        Akim Draeko Nash Drake (m) (b. 992 DKE d. 33 UE) (L)
        Bathsheth Aliza Drake (f) (b. 995 DKE d. 80 UE)
        Esli Draeko Elish Drake (m) (b. 1001 DKE d. 19 UE)

GENERATION 2

Drakonias Draeko Arvarin Drake (m) (b. 42 PE d.)
Married to:
Mariana Hargen (b. 20 PE d. 1120 DKE)
Children:
Drashon Drakonias Irigwin Drake (m) (b 14 DKE d. 295 UE)
Dorlan Drakonias Irigwin Drake (m) (b 150 DKE d.)
Devin Drakonias Metra Drake (m) (b. 820 DKE d.)
Drenan Drakonias Loid Drake (m) (b. 954 DKE d.)
Darsi Mariana Drake (f) (b. 960 DKE d. 1142 DKE)
Donlin Drakonias Ronn Drake (m) (b. 980 DKE d. 1128 DKE)
Dalia Mariana Drake (f) (b. 982 DKE d.)
Married to:
Ceena Realag (b. 1101 DKE d. 40 UE)
Children:
Darek Drakonias Proogan Drake (m)(b. 1 UE d.)
Dreanna Ceena Drake (f)(b. 3 UE d.)
Dunlor Drakonias Metra Drake (m) (b. 3 UE d.)

ABOUT THE AUTHOR

Patrik grew up in the southwest and presently lives in Idaho. Earlier in life he almost exclusively read fantasy novels but has since broadened his horizon and enjoys many genres, both fiction and nonfiction. He has wanted to write a book for a long time but never really had any ideas. Then, one random day, when he least expected it, he had an inkling and started writing. In his spare time, he enjoys hanging out with his family and entertaining his exuberant dog Pearl (or the Black Pearl when she is naughty, and yes, she is black). He also enjoys a good beer. He occasionally brews it as well, but he's not nearly as good as Yolken.

CPSIA information can be obtained
at www.ICGtesting.com
Printed in the USA
LVHW030458011220
673036LV00008B/1623